Frances C. Hoey, Henry W. Bates, Aimé Humbert

Japan and the Japanese Illustrated

Frances C. Hoey, Henry W. Bates, Aimé Humbert

Japan and the Japanese Illustrated

ISBN/EAN: 9783337170165

Printed in Europe, USA, Canada, Australia, Japan

Cover: Foto ©Andreas Hilbeck / pixelio.de

More available books at **www.hansebooks.com**

BY

AIMÉ HUMBERT,

LATE ENVOY EXTRAORDINARY AND MINISTER PLENIPOTENTIARY TO THE SWISS CONFEDERATION.

TRANSLATED BY MRS. CASHEL HOEY

AND

EDITED BY H. W. BATES,

ASSISTANT SECRETARY TO THE ROYAL GEOGRAPHICAL SOCIETY.

A DOMESTIC SCENE.

London:

RICHARD BENTLEY & SON,

Publishers in Ordinary to Her Majesty.

1874.

PREFACE.

THE richly-illustrated work on Japan, of which a translation is now offered to the English-reading world, has acquired high estimation on the continent of Europe, for the evident fidelity with which it portrays the scenery of this interesting country, and the varied life of its singular people. Its author, M. Aimé Humbert, obtained his copious material during a residence of two years in the country, in 1863-1864, as Minister Plenipotentiary of the Swiss Republic; availing himself of the privilege of travelling outside the barriers of the foreign settlement at Yokohama, a privilege at that time exclusively accorded to diplomatists of the Treaty Powers, to obtain subjects for his pen and pencil in quarters inaccessible to the ordinary inquirer. How genially he appreciated all he saw, and how pleasantly he communicates the knowledge he acquired, will be understood by all readers of the following pages.

M. Humbert relates, in the Introduction to the original French Edition, that he was accompanied in all his peregrinations by a faithful *attaché*; to whom, without mentioning him by name, he wishes to be attributed a portion of the credit of his work. Together, he says, they studied the country and the people, visiting the neighbouring towns, and rambling at all seasons over the pleasant country around the Bay of Yeddo. Armed with their sketching implements and a note-book, they jotted down their observations; sometimes seated at the foot of an ancient cedar; sometimes squatted on the threshold of a rustic tavern; or again, more slyly, intrenched in the back shop of some friendly tradesman, who good-naturedly aided them in their inquiries. A large number of photographs were taken, under M. Humbert's own eye; and he speaks of the treasures, in the way of engravings, Indian-ink sketches, and coloured pictures, all valuable illustrations of the hidden scenes of Japanese political life and history, which he obtained by frequent visits to the print-shops of Yeddo. A judicious selection from the copious store of material thus obtained formed the pictorial part of his work.

The original French work has passed through two editions: the second, from which the present translation has been made, adds a summary of events in Japan down to the year 1868 to the original narrative. During this interval the great Revolution, which has so profoundly modified the political condition and social life in Japan, took place. A continuation of the narrative, bringing the record down to the summer of 1873, is furnished by the editor of the English Edition.

Such a work must naturally be of deep interest to the people of Great Britain and the United States of America, whose commercial relations with Japan outweigh those of all other nations put together; and the interest will not be lessened by the reflection that the strange life—art, manners, and costumes—so graphically portrayed, is undergoing a rapid change, and will soon be a thing of the past.

COMEDIANS TO THE KISAKI.

CONTENTS.

BOOK I.—BENTEN.

CHAPTER I.

THE INLAND SEA.

CHAPTER II.

OUR NEIGHBOURS.

CHAPTER III.

THE COUNTRY AND THE PEOPLE.

CHAPTER IV.

DOMESTIC LIFE.

BOOK II.—KIOTO.

CHAPTER I.

THE ORIGIN OF THE JAPANESE PEOPLE.

CHAPTER II.

THE GENESIS OF JAPAN.

CHAPTER III.

THE EARLY SOVEREIGNS OF JAPAN.

CHAPTER IV.

ART AND FASHION IN KIOTO.

CHAPTER V.

THE DECADENCE OF THE MIKADOS.

BOOK III.—KAMAKOURA.

CHAPTER I.

THE RESIDENCES OF THE SIOGOUNS.

CHAPTER II.

THE TEMPLES OF KAMAKOURA.

CHAPTER III.

BUDDHISM IN JAPAN.

CHAPTER IV.

TAÏKOSAMA AND THE TOKAÏDO.

BOOK IV.—YEDDO.

CHAPTER I.

THE GREAT CITY.

CONTENTS.

CHAPTER VII.

DOMESTIC SOLEMNITIES.

CHAPTER VIII.

SOCIAL INSTITUTIONS IN YEDDO.

CHAPTER IX.

SIN-YOSIWARA.

CHAPTER X.

RELIGIOUS FESTIVALS.

CHAPTER XI.

THE SIBAÏA, OR NATIONAL DRAMA OF JAPAN.

CHAPTER XII.

INAKA.

CHAPTER XIII.

THE NEW ORDER OF THINGS IN JAPAN.

CHAPTER XIV.

CONCLUSION.

LIST OF ILLUSTRATIONS.

JAPAN AND THE JAPANESE.

BOOK I

BENTEN

CHAPTER I.

THE INLAND SEA.

EXTENT AND WEALTH OF THE EMPIRE OF JAPAN.—SCENERY AND FEATURES OF THE INLAND SEA.

The Empire of Japan extends over more than twenty-six degrees of latitude (from 24° 16′ to 50° north latitude). It comprises 3,850 islands, or islets, representing a superficies of 7,521 square miles, of fifteen to the degree.

This little insular world, whose population is supposed to amount to between thirty-two and thirty-four millions, is divided into six chief groups, or archipelagoes. The largest is Japan, properly so called, comprehending 3,511 islands, with a superficies of 5,306 square miles. Then come Yeso, the great Kouriles, Krafto, the Bonin group, and the Fiow Kiow Archipelago.

The Inland Sea of Japan is bounded by the southern coasts of Niphon, and the northern coasts of Kiousiou, and Sikoff. It is, however, more like a canal than a real

mediterranean sea, being a communication established, at the height of the thirty-fourth
degree of north latitude, between the Chinese Sea, or, more strictly, of the Strait of
Corea, on the western coast of Japan, and the great ocean which washes the southern
and eastern shores of the same archipelago. The whole of the Japanese Mediterranean
is sometimes known as the Sea of Souwo.

Each of the provinces by which it is surrounded contains one or several "lordships,"
belonging to feudal princes, who enjoy considerable independence, and generally derive
large revenues from their estates. Among others, the family of the princes of Kison may
be mentioned, as drawing from their patrimonial domains an annual revenue equivalent to
the sum of £352,000; the Prince of Aki, whose revenue is £279,400; the Prince of Nagato,
whose fortune amounts to £236,160; and the Prince of Bidzen, who draws £198,400.

The Japanese Mediterranean, like the European sea so called, is divided into several
basins. They are five in number, and are named from the most important of the provinces
which overlook them, so that the Inland Sea bears five different names throughout its
longitudinal course from west to east.

In the midst of the natural wealth which surrounds them, the large, industrious,
and intelligent population of the country parts of Japan have for their entire possessions
only a humble shed, a few working implements, some pieces of cotton cloth, a few
mats, a cloak of straw, a little store of tea, oil, rice, and salt: for furniture, nothing
but two or three cooking utensils; in a word, only the strict necessaries of existence.
All the remaining product of their labour belongs to the owners of the soil, the
feudal lords.

The absence of a middle class gives a miserable aspect to the Japanese villages.
Liberal civilization would have covered the borders of the Inland Sea with pretty hamlets
and elegant villas. The uniformity of the rustic dwellings is broken by temples, but
they are to be distinguished at a distance only by the vast dimensions of their roofs,
and by the imposing effect of the ancient trees which are almost always to be found
in their vicinity. Buddhist pagodas, which are lofty towers with pointed roofs, adorned
with galleries on each floor, are much less common in Japan than in China.

On entering the basin of Hiogo, we came in sight of a town of some importance,
on the coast of Sikoff; it is called Imabari. A vast sandy beach, which is rarely to
be found in Japan, stretched back to a kind of suburb, in which we could discern a
busy concourse of people, apparently carrying on market business. Above the strand

were fertile plains, whose undulating lines were lost in the mist at the foot of a chain of mountains bathed in sunshine. The principal peaks of this chain—Kori-yama, Yafatzowsen, and Siro Yama—are from 1,000 to 1,600 yards in height.

Fortifications, or rather mounds of earth, behind which shone several banners, protected the batteries posted in front of the port. Some soldiers, standing in a

ISLANDERS OF THE INLAND SEA.

group on the shore, followed our corvette with their eyes. There was nothing remarkable in the aspect of the town, except the sacred places, adorned by gigantic trees.

Some time afterwards we passed, within rifle-range, a large Japanese steamer, which our pilot, whom we consulted, and who judged from the colours of the flag, informed us was the property of the Prince of Tosa. His estates are situated in the southern portion of the island of Sikoff, and they bring him in a very large annual revenue.

Most probably he was returning from a conference of the feudal party held in the city of Kioto, at the court of the Hereditary Emperor of Japan; and had embarked at Hiogo, in order to regain his own province by the Bonngo canal. What were his sentiments on beholding a strange corvette cleaving the waters of the Inland Sea? Does he flatter himself that he can repel the civilization of the West by the arms which it places at his disposal? Does he know whither steam will lead him?

Counting up all the war-steamers which, to our knowledge, have been furnished to Japan by Europe and America, we make the number fourteen. The first, the yacht *Solenburg*, was given to the Taïkonn by the King of the Netherlands; another, the yacht *Emperor*, by the Queen of England; the others have been sold by the Governments or the traders of the West, either to the Taïkonn, or to certain of the principal daïmios, such as Mito, Nagato, Satsouma, and Tosa.

A little before sunset we saw, on the coast of Sikoff, a feudal castle, remarkable for its picturesque site upon the summit and the sides of a wooded hill, at whose feet a rustic hamlet seemed to shelter itself under the protection of the ancient lordly towers. It is the Castle of Marougama, the residence of Prince Kiogokow Sanoke, whose revenues are valued at £40,000. The castles of the daïmios are generally at a distance from the towns and villages. They are composed, in most instances, of a vast quadrangular enclosure, within thick and lofty crenellated walls, surrounded by a moat, and flanked at the corners, or surmounted at intervals throughout their extent, by small square towers with slightly sloping roofs. In the interior are the park, the gardens, and the actual residence of the daïmio, comprising a main dwelling, and numerous dependencies. Sometimes a solitary tower, of a shape similar to the other buildings, rises in the middle of the feudal domain, and rears itself three or four stories higher than the external wall. As in the case of the Chinese pagodas, each story is surrounded by a roof, which, however, but seldom supports a gallery. All the masonry is rough, and joined by cement; the woodwork is painted red and black, and picked out with copper ornaments, which are sometimes polished, but sometimes laden with verdigris. The tiles of the roof are slate-colour. In general, richness of detail is less aimed at than the general effect resulting from the grandeur and harmony of the proportions of the buildings. In this respect, some of the seignorial residences of Japan deserve to figure among the remarkable architectural monuments of the peoples of Eastern Asia.

We anchored in a bay of the island of Souyousima, at the southern point of the province of Bitsiou, and at the entrance of the basin of Arima. We were surrounded by mountains, at whose feet twinkled many lights shining in from houses. The stillness was unbroken, save by the distant barking of dogs. Next morning, April 24, very early, we were ploughing the peaceful waters of the Arimanado. This basin is completely closed on the east by a single island, which divides it from the Idsou-minada by a length of thirty miles. It is in the form of a triangle, whose apex, turned towards the north, faces the province of Arima, on the island of Niphon. This is the beautiful island of Awadsi, which was the dwelling-place of the gods, and the cradle of the national mythology of the Japanese. The lowlands at its southern extremity are covered with a luxuriant vegetation, and the soil rises gently into cultivated or wooded hills until they touch the boundaries of a chain of mountains from 300 to 700 yards in height. Awadsi belongs to the Prince of Awa, whose annual revenue amounts to .£160,000. It is separated from the island of Sikoff on the west, by the passage of Naruto, and the island of Niphon on the east, by the Strait of Linschoten.

The greater number of the steamers which cross the Japanese Mediterranean

WINTER DRESS OF THE FISHERMEN AND PEASANTS.

from west to east, pass from the basin of Arima into that of Idsoumi, where they generally touch at the important commercial town of Hiogo; and from thence they enter the great ocean by the Strait of Linschoten. That passage of Naruto which leads directly from the basin of Arima into the great ocean is shorter than the former; it is, however, much less frequented, because it is considered a dangerous channel for high-decked vessels.

We saw the coasts drawing nearer and nearer to us, as we descended, towards the south-west corner of this triangular piece of land. At the same time a promontory of the island of Sikoff rose above the horizon on our right, and seemed to stretch continuously onward in the direction of Awadsi. Very soon we found ourselves in a passage from whence we could distinctly see the beautiful vegetation of the coast of Sikoff and the coast of Awadsi. At length we saw the gates of the Strait: on

JAPANESE BIRDS.

the left, rocks surmounted by pines, forming the front of the island of Awadsi; on the right, a solitary rock, or islet, also bearing a few pines, forming the front of the island of Sikoff. Between them the sea, like a bar of breakers, though the weather was calm: afar, the undulating ocean, without a speck of foam; the tossing of the waves in the passage being solely the result of the violence of the current. All around us, on the waves and at the foot of the rocks, were thousands of sea-birds, screaming, fluttering, and diving for the prey which the sea, stirred to its depths by the current, was perpetually tossing up to them. Several fishing-boats were out, not on the canal—that would have been impossible—but behind the rocks, in the creeks of the little solitary islet and of Sikoff.

Below Awadsi, the united waters of the two straits of Naruto and Linschoten form the canal of Kino, which washes the shores of the province of Awa, on Sikoff, and of the province of Kisou, on Niphon. We sailed for some time yet in sight of the latter; then the land disappeared from our eyes, and we soon perceived, by the vide-rolling motion of the waves, that we were on the outer sea, in the immense domain of the great ocean.

I occupied myself, during the whole evening, in recalling the recollections of my journey; and I could find nothing out of Switzerland to compare with the effect of the beautiful Japanese scenery. Since then, several Japanese, travelling in Switzerland, have told me that no other country awakened so vividly the remembrance of their own. Still more frequently I transported myself in fancy to one or other of the archipelagoes of the Souwonada, earnestly desiring the advent of that hour when the breath of liberty will give them, in the Far East, the importance which formerly belonged, in Europe, to the Archipelago of our Mediterranean.

They cannot be blended into a general impression. Nothing is less uniform than the scenery of the shores of the Inland Sea. It is a series of pictures which vary infinitely, according to the greater or less proximity of the coasts, or to the aspect of the islands on the horizon. There are grand marine scenes, where the lines of the sea blend with sandy beaches sleeping under the golden rays of the sun; while in the distance, the misty mountains form a dim background. There are little landscapes, very clear, trim, and modest: a village at the back of a peaceful bay, surrounded by green fields, over which towers a forest of pines; just as one may see by a lake in the Jura on a fine morning in June.

Sometimes, when the basins contracted, and the islands in front seemed to shut us in, I remembered the Rhine above Boppart. The Japanese scenery is, however, more calm and bright than the romantic landscapes to which I allude. The abrupt slopes, the great masses of shade, the shifting lines, are replaced by horizontal levels; by a beach, a port, and terraces; in the distance are rounded islands, sloping hills, conical mountains. These pictures have their charms: the imagination, no less than the eye, rests in the contemplation of them; but it would seek in vain that melancholy attraction which, according to the notions of European taste, seems inseparable from the enjoyment.

c

Laying aside the question of the picturesque, which is not the essential element of our relations with the Far East, I hope that, sooner or later, a chain of Western colonies will be formed at Japan, peacefully developing the natural and commercial resources of that admirable country, along a line marked by Yokohama, Hiogo, Simonosaki, and Nagasaki. It might have a regular service of steamers. The trading steamers of America, as well as those of China, might maintain the relations of the two worlds with the King of the Archipelagoes of the Great Ocean. Europeans, weary of the tropical climate or the burthen of business in China, might seek pure and strengthening air, and pass some weeks of repose on the shores of the Japanese Mediterranean. How many families settled in China, how many wives and children of Europeans, would be delighted to profit, during the trying summer months, by this refuge, as beautiful and salubrious as Italy, and yet near their actual home!

But while imagination, forestalling the march of time and the triumphs of civilization, evokes the charms of a European society from the bosom of the isles of the Souwonada, I must acknowledge that I privately congratulated myself on having seen the Japanese Mediterranean in its primitive condition, while one may still "discover" something, and has to ask the pilots the names of the islands, the mountains, and the villages, and to cast anchor for the night in some creek called "fair port" by the natives.

On the night of April 24, after having doubled the southern point of the great island of Niphon, *i.e.* the promontory of Idsoumo, situated at the southern extremity of the principality of Kisou, we sailed, during the whole day on the 25th, with the current which the Japanese call Kouro-Siwo, which runs from south-west to north-east, at the rate of from thirty-five to forty miles a day. It is a current of hot water, whose maximum temperature is 30° Centigrade.

The weather was fine, and the sea a shining emerald-green. I passed many hours on the poop, in stillness and vague contemplation. For the first time I enjoyed the pleasure of sailing. The silence which reigned on board added to the majestic effect of the ship, laden up to the summit of her masts with her triple wings of white. It was as though the fires had been extinguished, and the noise of the engines hushed, that we might present ourselves more respectfully at the gates of the residence of the Taïkouns. But when night fell, the fires were lighted again, in case of accident; for the land-winds frequently cause much trouble to the ships in the Gulf of Yeddo. On the 26th, at daybreak, we came within sight of six small mountainous islands, which looked like signals set up at the entrance of this vast arm of the sea.

The sun rose, and presented, amid the salt sea mists of the horizon, that image of a scarlet globe which forms the national arms of Japan. His earliest rays lighted up Cape Idsou, on the mainland of Niphon, whilst in the east we beheld the smoke of the two craters of the island of Ohosima. At the head of a bay in the promontory of Idsou is situated the town of Simoda, the first, but the least important of the commercial places to which we come when sailing up the Gulf of Yeddo. The Americans obtained an authorization to found an establishment there in 1854. Some time afterwards the harbour of Simoda was destroyed by an earthquake, and no mention was made of that place in the treaties of 1858.

A number of fishing-boats are to be seen on the coast, and several three-masted vessels are going to the mainland of Niphon and the surrounding islands. The scene is full of life, and sparkling with brilliant and harmonious colour; the wide sky is a splendid azure; the pale green sea has no longer the sombre hues of the great deeps, but shines with the limpid brightness which characterises it upon the rocky coasts of Japan. The isles are decked in the brilliant foliage of the spring; the harsh brown of the rocks is streaked with shades of ochre; and the white sails of the native barques, the snow-crests of Myakésima, and the smoke from the craters of Ohosima, complete the beautiful marine scene.

Having reached the "Bay of the Mississippi," we made out, for the first time, the summit of Fousi-yama, the "Matchless Mountain," an extinct volcano 12,450 feet above the level of the sea. It is fifty nautical miles from the coast, on the west of the bay, and except for the chain of the Akoni hills at its base, completely isolated. The effect of this immense solitary pyramid, covered with eternal snow, surpasses description. It lends inexpressible solemnity to the scenery of the Bay of Yeddo, already more sombre than that of the gulf, by reason of the closer proximity of the shores, the somewhat sandy hue of the sea-water, and the immense quantity of cedars, pines, and other dark-foliaged trees which crown the crests of all the hills along the coast.

At length we double Point Treaty, a picturesque promontory where the convention between Commodore Perry and the Commissioners of the Taïkoun was signed: and all of a sudden, behind this promontory, we see the quays and the city of Yokohama stretching along a marshy beach, bounded on the south and west by a ring of wooded hills. A score of ships of war, and merchant vessels, **English, Dutch,** **French,** and American, are lying out in the roads, almost opposite the "foreign quarter," which may easily be recognized by its white houses and its consular flags. Native junks are lying at anchor at some distance from the jetties of the port and the store-houses of the Custom House. We pass by these slowly, and steam at half speed in front of the Japanese city, in which all the houses, except a certain number of shops, are built of wood, and seem to have only one storey above the ground floor.

When we had come opposite to the Benten quarter, situated at the extremity of the beach of Yokohama, and at the mouth of a wide river, our corvette anchored, near the Dutch Legation, which was at that time the only European residence in that part of Yokohama.

A STREET IN BENTEN-TORI, AT YOKOHAMA.

CHAPTER II.

OUR NEIGHBOURS.

BENTEN.—THE PEOPLE.—THE TEMPLE.—THE TEA-HOUSES.—OUR LADY VISITORS.

THAT portion of the Japanese city of Yokohama which is called Benten derives its name from a sea-goddess, who is worshipped in an island situated to the north-west of our residence. Before the arrival of the Europeans, this sacred place was surrounded only by a small town, in which dwelt fishermen and agriculturists, separated by a swamp from the not less modest little town of Yokohama. Now, quays, streets, modern buildings, have invaded the entire space which extends from the promontory of the "Treaty" to the river, from which we are divided only by a range of Japanese barracks and a guard-house.

Among the streets which extend to the sea-beach from Benten, there is one shaded by a plantation of firs; and on passing through the municipal barrier which the police keep open during the day and shut at night, the stranger finds himself in front of a long avenue of fir-trees, headed by a sacred gate called a Tori. It is composed of two pillars slightly inclined towards each other; so that they would meet at last at an acute angle, if at a certain elevation their pyramidal development were not checked; and joined by two horizontal transverse beams, of which the uppermost is the thicker, and is curved upwards at both ends. The tori invariably announces the vicinity of a temple, a chapel, or a sacred place of some sort. A grotto, a

THE PORTER'S LODGE AT THE DUTCH RESIDENCY.

waterfall, a gigantic tree, a fantastic rock, all things which we prosaically call natural curiosities, a Japanese regards with pious veneration or with superstitious fear, according to whether he be more or less governed by the Buddhist demonology; and the bonzes of the country never fail to give tangible form to this popular tendency, by erecting a tori close to each remarkable place.

The pine-trees in the Benten avenue are lofty, slender, and for the most part bent by the continuous action of the sea-breezes. At regular distances long poles are nailed upon them crosswise, on which, on festival days, the bonzes hang inscriptions, wreaths, and swinging banners.

The avenue ends in a second tori, which, with due regard to perspective, is not so lofty as the first. On approaching it, one is surprised to find that the avenue

AVENUE OF THE TEMPLE AT BENTEN.

makes a sudden bend and prolongs itself on the right. Here all is mystery; a waste ground, covered with rank grasses, bushes, and slender pines with aërial foliage; on the left, the calm transparent water of a little gulf formed by an arm of the river; in front is a wooden bridge, built in a style of severe elegance, wide, and excessively curved; behind this bridge is a third tori, thrown out against the thick foliage of a grove of fine trees. The whole forms a strange picture, with something in it that excites a secret apprehension. This bridge, whose pillars are decorated with ornaments in copper, finally admits us to the sacred place. The third tori, bearing on its summit an inscription in gold letters on a black ground, is entirely built of fine granite of remarkable whiteness; and the tombs, which are tastefully disposed on the left side of the avenue, are constructed of the same material. The temple, almost entirely hidden by the branches of the cedars and pines which surround it, faces us; but the mysterious gloom hardly permits us to discern the flight of steps on which the people kneel who come to worship before the altar of the goddess. Should the temple be empty, one of the bonzes in attendance may be summoned by shaking a long strip of woollen stuff that hangs beside the entrance, with a bunch of pebbles attached to it. The bonze comes out of his retreat immediately, and proceeds, according to the requirements of the visitor, to give him advice, to distribute tapers or amulets, to undertake to recite prayers, in fact to perform any of the ceremonies of their worship;—of course for the consideration of a fee.

As a Japanese, before he presents himself at the sanctuary, must wash and dry his hands and face, in a small chapel, at some distance from the temple, on the right, is a basin containing the holy water intended for ablutions, and napkins of silk crape suspended on a roller, like the hand-towels in a sacristy. One of two chapels close by contains the big drum which serves the purpose of a bell for the temple, the other the *ex-voto* offerings of the faithful. The bonzes who serve the temple of Benten do not appear to live in opulence. Their attire is generally dirty and neglected; and the expression of their faces is stupid, sullen, and malevolent towards strangers, who are glad to keep at a respectful distance from these holy persons.

I had only one opportunity of seeing them officiate; it was on the occasion of a procession on their local festival day. On ordinary days, it appears that they merely give audiences; and I have rarely seen men resort to their ministrations. Their habitual clients are peasant women, fishermen, and casual pilgrims. But I have frequently heard, at sunset, the beating of the tambourines, which, except at great solemnities, form the whole orchestra of the temple of Benten. The bonzes perform interminable music on this monstrous instrument, always in the same rhythm; four equal loud notes, followed by four equal deep notes, and so on, for hours together, probably the length of time required for driving away the evil influences. Nothing can exceed the melancholy impression produced by this deep-sounding noise, when, in the silence of the night, it blends with the sighing of the great cedar-trees and the booming of the sea. It oppresses one like a nightmare. But indeed it may be said that the religion which finds expression in such customs weighs on the mind of the people like a dream, full of uneasiness and vague terror. Far from being natural religion, paganism is the enemy of human nature, the religion of denaturalized man ; and thence it is that, seen in action, it fills one with an indescribable pain, an instinctive repulsion which seems to me to come from that especial characteristic, rather than to be the effect of our Christian education.

The obligatory accompaniment of the Japanese temples are tea-houses, or restaurants, at which tea is principally supplied, but where saki, a fermented and highly intoxicating drink, may be had. The eatables are fruits, fish, rice, or wheaten cakes ; and everyone smokes. The pipes are metal ; the tobacco is very finely cut, and free from all narcotic admixture : opium-smoking is unknown in Japan. These establishments, where women are the attendants, and where external propriety is strictly observed, are, for the most part, places of ill fame. This is especially the case in respect to those which are situated in the vicinity of the toris at Benten, a circumstance which probably dates from a period at which the little island dedicated to the patroness of the sea still attracted a considerable number of pilgrims. At present the altar of the goddess is singularly neglected ; but there is a great military station in the neighbourhood, with which the rule of the Taïkoun,— that of the sword,—has endowed the city of Yokohama. It occupies the entire space between the island of Benten and our dwelling.

The quarter of the "Yakounines" is composed of the residences of Government officers employed in the Customs, of the harbour police and that of other public places, of the Military Instruction, of the guard of the Japanese city, and the superintendents of the "free quarter."

The Yakounines have no outward and visible sign of their functions except a large pointed hat of lacquered pasteboard, and two swords passed through the girdle on the left side : one of these is large and two-handled ; the other, a kind of blade intended for single combat, is small. These are the only warlike points in the equipment of these functionaries. They number several hundreds, they are almost all married, each has his separate lodging, and all seem to be placed on a footing of equality in this respect. It is not uninteresting to study the means which the Government of the

Taïkoun has adopted for organizing this army of functionaries into a kind of camp, while retaining their domestic surroundings. This has been effected to a certain extent by the application of the cellular system to family life.

Let the reader picture to himself a collection of wooden buildings, forming a long square, a lofty wooden wall towards the street; low doors at regular intervals, each giving access to a court, which contains a small garden, a water cistern, a kitchen,

INHABITANTS OF THE YAKOUNINE QUARTER.

and other offices. Across the yard, on the ground floor, lies a spacious cell, which may be subdivided into two or three rooms by means of sliding partitions; the court and the cell comprise the lodging of a Yakounine family. Each of the long blocks of which the streets in this quarter are composed encloses at least a dozen of these dwellings, six ranged side by side, and then six back to back with the others. The cells are all roofed with green tiles, and no roof is more lofty than another. The

Yakounine quarter is a triumph of straight lines and uniformity. The streets are generally empty, because the men pass the greater part of the day at the Custom House or the guard-houses; and during the absence of its head, every family keeps itself within its narrow enclosure. Even the door, which is so low that one must stoop to pass through, is generally shut during this time of seclusion. This custom is however, in one way, analogous to the precaution with which Turkish jealousy surrounds women. It arises from the position which Japanese habits assign to the fathers of families. In each, his wife beholds her lord and master. In his presence she attends to her domestic duties with perfect ease and simplicity, caring nothing for the presence of a stranger. In his absence she observes an extreme reserve, which we might be tempted to attribute to modesty, but which is more truthfully explained by the dependence and intimidation imposed on her by marriage.

By degrees neighbourly relations were established between our residence and the Yakounine quarter. In Japan, as elsewhere, small presents encourage friendship. We sent some white sugar and some Java coffee to certain families where we learned there were sick persons, or women in childbed, and these small offerings were gratefully received.

A STABLE-MAN.

One day, when I was alone in the house, between four and five o'clock in the afternoon, the Mowban came to announce the arrival of a feminine deputation from the Yakounine quarter, and to ask me whether he should send them away. These ladies had been authorised by their husbands to make their acknowledgments in person, but they had profited by the opportunity to express their wish to examine our European furniture. I told the porter that I would gladly undertake to do the honours of the house to them. Presently I heard the clicking of a number of wooden shoes on the gravel walk in the garden, and, looking towards the foot of the verandah staircase in front of the saloon, I saw a group of smiling faces, among which I distinguished four married women, two young girls, and several children of all ages. The former were remarkable for the plainness of their dress: no ornament in the hair, no light stuffs or bright colours in their garments, no paint on their faces, but their teeth painted as black as ebony, as is becoming to all married women, according to Japanese ideas. The young girls, on the contrary, show off the natural whiteness of their teeth by a layer of carmine on their lips, put rouge on their cheeks, braid their thick hair with strips of scarlet crape, and wear wide girdles of many colours. The children's dress is simply a plain garment and a striped sash; they never wear any head-dress, and their heads are shaven, except a few locks, some hanging loose, others tied together and arranged as a chignon.

After the customary salutations, the orators of the deputation—for three or four always spoke simultaneously—said many pretty things to me in Japanese, to which I replied in French, while I made signs to the company to enter the drawing-room. It was quite clear that they had understood me; I could not mistake the expression of thanks; and yet, instead of ascending the staircase, they seemed to be asking me for an explanation of some sort. At length my fair friends perceived my embarrassment, and, by adding gestures to language, asked me, "Ought we to take off our shoes in the garden, or will it suffice if we take them off in the verandah?" I pronounced in favour of the latter alternative, and my guests immediately ascended the stairs, removed their shoes and placed them in a line upon the floor, and then gleefully trod the carpets of the drawing-room—the children with bare feet, the grown-up persons in socks made of cotton-cloth, divided into two unequal compartments, one for the great toe, and the other for the rest of the foot.

Their first impression was innocent admiration, to which general laughter succeeded when they all found themselves reflected at full length and on all sides, in the long mirrors which came down to the floor. While the younger members of the party indulged themselves in unwearied contemplation of a scene at once so novel and so attractive, the matrons asked me the meaning of the pictures which adorned the room. I explained that they represented the Taïkoun of Holland and his wife, and also several great daimios, or princes of the reigning family. They bowed respectfully, but one of them, whose curiosity was not satisfied, said, timidly, that she supposed they had also taken the portrait of his Dutch Majesty's groom? I took care not to undeceive her, because she would not have understood that it could be correct to represent a prince standing beside his saddle-horse and holding it by the bridle. Others, having

OUR LADY VISITORS.

attentively examined the velvet sofas and arm-chairs, told me how a dispute had arisen between them respecting the use of those articles of furniture. They agreed as to the easy chairs; it was, no doubt, intended that they should be sat upon, but the sofas? Surely one ought to squat on them with crossed legs, especially when eating at the table in front of them. They sincerely pitied the gentlemen and ladies of the

West, condemned to make such inconvenient use of these articles, and actually to sit with their legs hanging down.

My room, being open and on the same level, was speedily invaded, and almost everything in it was a subject of astonishment to my visitors, who were none the less daughters of Eve because they were born in Japan. They were particularly delighted with a set of uniform buttons bearing the Swiss federal cross, according to the military rule of my country. I had to give them some of these buttons, though I could not imagine to what use they could possibly apply them, since all Japanese garments, for the use of both sexes, are simply fastened by silken strings. The gift of a few articles of Parisian perfumery was highly appreciated, but I praised Eau de Cologne quite unsuccessfully. Cambric handkerchiefs are unknown in Japan. I showed them some specimens, very prettily embroidered by the clever needlewomen of Appenzell; but they explained to me that, though the *élégantes* of Yeddo might perhaps use them as cuffs for their wide and flowing *robes de chambre*, not the lowest woman of the people would hold in her hand or carry in her pocket a piece of stuff in which she had blown her nose. There is, therefore, no chance at present that the little squares of paper, made from vegetable substances, which they carry in a fold of the dress, in the breast, or in a pocket in the sleeve, and which are thrown away as each is successively used, will be supplanted by our barbarous method. Eau de Cologne, however, might be used with advantage, to counteract the briny flavour of the well-water which is drunk at Benten.

Another point on which my visitors seemed to regard the superiority of Japanese civilization as incontestable, is their method of writing. The Japanese uses a brush, a stick of Chinese ink, and a roll of paper made from mulberry leaves. He carries those things about with him everywhere: the roll of paper is placed in his breast; the brush and the inkstand hang in a case from his girdle, together with his pipe and his tobacco-bag.

In order to regain my advantage, I exhibited a case containing an assortment of sewing cotton, needles, and pins, and begged the lady yakounines to use them. They unanimously acknowledged the imperfection of the working materials of their country, where the sewing-machine is unknown. Needlework does not occupy in Japan any place like that which it takes in our middle-class households; it is never produced during the long gossipping visits which the Japanese women interchange.

As in Europe men have recourse to the cigar, so in Japan they season their conversation with pipes.

The visit ended by my giving the children some prints representing Swiss landscapes and costumes, and showing their elders a photographic album containing likenesses of all the members of my family, which they examined with more than interest, with really touching emotion. It is within the domain of the natural affections that the unity, the identity of the human race, in every clime and among every people, makes itself most sensibly felt. What signifies diversity of idiom in the presence of that universal language which translates itself by the expression of the eye, by a tear upon the eyelid, by sweet and touching intonations of the voice, like Mendelssohn's "Songs without Words"? The traveller is, in the sight of all primitive peoples, a being who deserves the deepest pity, for he is separated from all that constitutes the charm of life—the family, the paternal roof, the country of his ancestors. Religious admiration would be mingled with the compassion he inspires if he had left his country to accomplish a pious pilgrimage in a distant land, but that a man should cross the seas merely in the interest of terrestrial objects is a thing incomprehensible to the Japanese. They might admit the notion of my being a political exile, the victim of the severity of my Government; but when they learn that I am neither a pilgrim nor proscribed, astonishment mingled with a kind of fright is added to their artless sympathy.

Truly, I am very far from Europe, in a world quite foreign to its civilization, and it was time that the West should come to these insular people, to teach them modes of thought and perception less incompatible with the genius of "business."

THE POPULATION OF THE BEACH

CHAPTER III.

THE COUNTRY AND THE PEOPLE.

THE POPULATION OF THE BEACH.—HUMBLE HOSPITALITY.—SCENERY. SPRING-TIDE.
CULTIVATION.—INDUSTRY.—INVENTIVENESS.

ALL the good people who compose the population of the beach accost me in the friendliest manner. The children bring me beautiful glistening shells, and the women do their best to make me understand the culinary properties of the hideous little marine monsters which they pile up in their baskets. This spontaneous kindliness and cordiality is a characteristic common to all the lower classes of Japanese society. More than once when I have been going on foot about the suburbs of Nagasaki or Yokohama, the country people have invited me to step inside their little enclosures. Then they would show me their flowers, and cut the best among them to make up a bouquet for me. It was always in vain that I offered them money ; they never accepted it, and were not satisfied until I had crossed their threshold and partaken of tea and rice-cakes with them. Spring is the most tempting season for exploring the coasts of the Bay of Yeddo. From the heights on its borders, the inland scene, stretching away to the foot of Fousi-yama, presents an uninterrupted succession of wooded hills and cultivated valleys, diversified by rivers or gulfs, which at a

RICE CULTIVATION.

distance look like lakes. The villages on their banks are half hidden in rich foliage ; and large farms, approached by shady roads, may be traced out at various points of the landscape.

The precocity of the vegetation in the rice-grounds and on the cultivated hills, the quantity of evergreen trees on every side, deprives the springtide in Japan of that fresh and budding aspect which is one of its chief beauties elsewhere. And yet, where can there be found a more luxuriant spring vegetation, more rich in beautiful details ? All along the hedges, in the orchards, and about the villages, tufts of flowers and foliage of dazzling hue stand out against the dark tints of a background of pines, firs, cedars, cypress, laurels, green oak, and bamboos. Here, we find the great white

E

flowers of the wild mulberry; there, camellias growing in the open country, as tall
as our apple-trees; everywhere, cherry-trees, plum-trees, peach-trees, generally laden
with double flowers, some quite white, others bright red, and sometimes white and
red on the same branches; for many of the Japanese do not care at all for the fruit
of these trees, but cultivate and graft them merely for the sake of the double flowers,
and to vary or combine the species. The bamboo, much employed in the capacity
of a support to these trees, frequently lends his elegant foliage to the branches of
young fruit-trees which have no other adornment than their bunches of flowers. But
I love the bamboo most when it grows in solitary groups, like a tuft of gigantic
reeds. There is nothing more picturesque in the whole landscape than these tall green

RICE-FIELDS.

polished stems, with their golden streaks and their tufted tops, and all around the
chiefs the young slender offshoots with their feathered heads, and a multitude of
long leaves streaming in the wind like thousands of fluttering pennons. The bamboo
groves are favourite subjects of study with the Japanese painters, whether they limit
themselves to reproduce the graceful lines and harmonious effects, or enliven the
picture by adding some of the live creatures which seek their verdant shelter—the
little birds, the butterflies, and, in lonely places, the weasel, the ferret, the black
squirrel, and the red-faced brown monkey.

All the waysides are bordered with violets, but they are scentless. The country
produces a very small number of odoriferous plants, and it is remarkable that the lark,

the nightingale, and other singing-birds are very rare. Perhaps the lack of perfume and of song, in the midst of all the wealth of a luxuriant vegetation, helps to diminish the effect upon the imagination which it seems to me Japanese scenery ought to produce. It is certain that in contemplating it one does not experience that sense of dreamy exaltation and tenderness which is produced by the sight of a European landscape in the spring-time, when nature is waking up. Without going into the question of the extent to which our sensibility is fed by the remembrances of childhood, and the traditional ideas which find no application in the world of the Far East, I think the cooling of our enthusiasm may be accounted for by the fact that, in Japan, nature is over-cultivated.

HARVEST SCENE.

With the exception of the forests and other plantations of trees, which the Government maintain with praiseworthy care, the entire soil is invaded by cultivation to an extent which almost defies description. Early in April the fields outside the woods are covered with buck-wheat in full flower. In four, or five weeks' time, on the lower ground, they will be reaping the barley and wheat sown in November. In Japan they sow corn as we plant potatoes in Europe, *i.e.* in regular, perfectly straight rows, and between each of these there is an interval of free space in which are already sprouting a peculiar species of beans, which will spring up when the field shall have been reaped. That green surface which might be taken for sprouting corn is a field of millet, which was sown in March and will be ripe in September.

E 2

Millet is eaten by the natives in as large quantities as wheat; they grind it into flour, and make cakes or porridge of it.

On an adjacent plain there is a labourer tilling the ground by means of a small plough drawn by one horse. In the fertile soil he will sow the seed of the cotton-tree, and in September or October each seed will have produced a plant two or three feet high, laden with twenty capsules arrived at maturity. Several white birds of

A RICE-MILL.

the stork or heron family seem to be working in concert with the agriculturist; they follow him about gravely, and, by plunging their long beaks into the half-opened furrow, they destroy the larva which the plough has just turned up.

In the depth of the valley are rice-grounds, which were laid under water about a month ago, by the opening of the sluice-gates of the irrigation canals. While in this state, the soil is broken up by the plough, and trodden by the feet of the buffaloes and the labourers; the latter treading up to their calves in the clay, and breaking the stubborn clumps with pickaxes. When the earth has been mashed into a kind of liquid paste, men and women go step by step along the dykes of the enclosure, and throw in handfuls of seed upon the square spaces destined to form the nursery ground. Then these are turned over with a kind of rake, in order to distribute and bury the seed. Now the water has subsided, the nursery ground puts forth its thick, close crop, and the cultivators tear it up, roots and stems together, to transplant them carefully in the large squares of soft earth which have not yet been utilised, in tufts arranged in a chequered pattern at regular intervals. There the rice

A FURTHER STAGE OF RICE CULTIVATION.

will grow and ripen, to be cut in the month of October. Until then it has to dread the pretty little red and white breasted birds which fall like hail on the grain-laden stems, shake the ripe fruit to the ground, and set to their work of pillage with shrill notes of joy, dancing on their little feet after a fashion full of charm for the impartial observer, but which inspires the proprietor with far different feelings. The persecuted rice-growers resort to all kinds of scarecrows, which they set up at the most seriously menaced points, but without much apparent effect upon the morals of the thriving birds. In one place, a complete network of cords of plaited straw, garnished with swinging appendages of the same material, is fixed on poles, and extended above the rice-field, forming a perfectly efficacious method of prevention, provided that it is kept in incessant motion. This is the task of a boy, who, when there is not sufficient wind to shake the net, pulls the cord attached to it, like a bell-rope, and thus keeps it going. The child sits in a lofty seat, perched on four bamboos, under a little roof formed of reeds.

Several kinds of rice are grown in Japan. That of the plains is the most highly esteemed : that of the hills does not require to be so long submerged as the former, but I have seen it subjected, in the spring, to processes of irrigation which have cost much labour : in the formation of reservoirs on the upper level of the hill, and the establishment of numerous canals, discharging themselves upon all the terraces prepared for rice culture. Each terrace thus converted into a rice-ground will bear, next autumn, wheat or millet. The Japanese may perhaps clear some mountain-land now and then, but they will never leave land capable of being tilled, fallow.

The tea-plant is not cultivated in our district. It is occasionally met with under certain favourable circumstances, but the real tea-districts are several days' journey north and west of the bay. We are much nearer to the silk-growing districts, and there would be nothing to prevent the development of this industry in our immediate vicinity, if there were sufficient space for the cultivation of the mulberry-tree. It strikes me, in short, that the population by whom I am surrounded, and the inhabitants of the southern coasts of Niphon generally, leave to the natives of the interior the production of the most valuable articles of commerce, such as silk, tea, and even cotton, which is not very abundant on our coasts ; while they devote themselves, some to fishing and water-carriage, and others to agriculture in its strict sense—the production of cereals and leguminous and oleaginous plants ; also to horticulture, and the growth of flax, straw, reeds, and bamboos.

Among the peasant population of the fertile valleys which border the Bay of Yeddo, one frequently meets men of a more vigorous race, whose aspect, though kindly, seems to denote a certain independence of character or of manner of life. These are the " mountain people," or the inhabitants of the chain of the Akoni, at the foot of Fousi-yama. The business which brings them down to the plains is very various in its nature : for some, it is dealing in wood for ships and building ; for others, it is dealing in firewood. Some are carrying baggage on pack-horses from the provinces in the interior to such or such a port in the bay ; others are employed in hauling the canal-boats, and among them recruits are made for a select tribe of hunters, as well as for a portion of the Taïkoun's troops of the line ; *i.e.* the infantry companies, among whom European arms of precision have been introduced.

AN AERIAL BRIDGE.

Unfortunately, the country inhabited by these passing guests is almost entirely inaccessible to strangers. If certain native statements are to be believed, bridges, aqueducts, and dams of most marvellous construction exist there, which baffle the

imagination when one thinks of the imperfection of the instruments with which they
have been made.   The resources which the Japanese possess in raw material are
not accorded to our climates.   The bamboo, for instance, furnishes a natural conduit
for hydraulic purposes, whose excellence yields to no product of modern industry.   It
is employed in the formation of suspension-bridges in the place of wire.   In the
mountains of Kiousiou there is a bridge, flung from one rock to another across a
deep abyss, by means of a hanging staircase formed of huge pieces of bamboo laid in
line, and fitted over one another longitudinally.   The Japanese traverse great rivers on

JAPANESE BIRDS.

bridges made of casks, and managed by straw ropes.   They cross terrific ravines by
bridges of rope, and even by means of a single rope, along which slips a kind of
aërial ferry-boat.

In a country like theirs, where the Government maintains only one public
highway—the great military road called the Toïkado—the inhabitants, reduced to
their own resources, strive to establish the communications which they require at
the least possible cost.   Hence the infinite variety of their contrivances for transport
by land and by water.   A curious specimen of the latter is the means devised to
enable the women who are engaged in rice cultivation to cross the submerged lands.
Four tubs, fastened together between the angles of two crossed planks, are packed

with as many persons and as large a quantity of provisions as this singular equipage can accommodate, and two of the passengers propel it with poles. The same talent for utilizing the simplest means of action, the most primitive instruments, the most elementary processes, is equally to be traced in the arts and handicrafts of Japan. But there is a very important part of their social life which either escapes us or which it is very difficult for us to study. We can only see the people at work in the fields and in some of the village sheds. The docks, the workshops, and the factories in the industrial cities, the artistic conceptions, and the most original productions of their autonomic civilization, are carefully hidden from us by the police restrictions of a jealous Government. Nevertheless, little by little the light is coming, and a day will soon dawn when, in this respect also, Japan shall be opened to the investigations of Science.

A DORMITORY IN A JAPANESE INN.

CHAPTER IV.

DOMESTIC LIFE.

JAPANESE HOUSES.—PERSONAL APPEARANCE OF MEN AND WOMEN.—THEIR HOUSEHOLD
LIVES, CUSTOMS, FURNITURE.—EDUCATION, LANGUAGE, SCHOOLS.

THE country may be reached from Benten without passing through the Japanese city.
Beyond the precincts of the holy place, a wide pathway supported on piles forms a road
alongside the river. From this road, which leads to a suburb occupied by poor artisans,
and terminated by a military guard-house and a Customs' station, we look down upon

the low streets and the marsh of Yokohama. A handsome wooden bridge, built on piles sufficiently high to permit the passage of sailing-boats, crosses the river, and joins the footpath on the left bank.

By following this footpath to the north-east, we reach the high road of Kanagawa; and by taking the south-east direction, we come to the country roads leading to the Bay of the Mississippi.

The country is covered on every side with cultivated land, and the habitations are exceedingly numerous. The isolated houses near the road, and those which border on the village streets, are generally open, and may, so to speak, be seen through. The inhabitants, in order to establish currents of air, slide the screens which form their walls into the grooves on the right and left, so that the interiors of their houses are freely exhibited to the sight of the passers-by.

Under such conditions it is not difficult to form a correct idea of household life, and to observe the distinctive characters of the national type, as well as the domestic manners of the native population.

The conventional separation between classes in Japanese society does not rest upon essential difference of race, or of modes of life.

From the height of the hill on which the residence of the Governors of Kanagawa is situated I have more than once had occasion to examine and observe, on one side, some buildings set apart for the dwellings of the Yakounines, and on the other groups of houses or cottages belonging to artisans and cultivators. In the courtyards, formed by divisions made of planks which separate the military caste from the others, I remarked exactly the same habits, the same modes of life, which I saw publicly in action in the courtyards of the plebeians. My later observation of the houses of the high Government functionaries only confirms me in the belief that we may reduce the chief types and the domestic manners of the whole population of the centre of the Empire —that is to say, of the three great islands of Kiousiou, Sikoff, and Niphon—to certain general features.

The Japanese are of middling height, very inferior to the men of the Germanic race, but not without some resemblance to the inhabitants of the south-west of the Iberian peninsula.

There is more difference in height between the men and the women of Japan than in those of Europe. According to the observations of Dr. Mohnike, formerly

physician to the Dutch Factory of Decima, the average height of the men is five feet
one inch, or five feet two inches (French measurement), and that of the women from
four feet one inch to four feet three inches.

The Japanese, without being precisely disproportioned, have generally large heads,
rather sunk in the shoulders, wide chests, long bodies, narrow hips, short and thin

A GOVERNOR'S PROCESSION.

legs, small feet, and slight and remarkably beautiful hands. Their retreating foreheads
and large and prominent cheek-bones make their faces represent the geometrical figure
of the trapeze rather than that of the oval. The cavities of the eyes being very
shallow, and the cartilage of the nose rather flattened, the eyes in almost every case
are more on the surface than those of the European, and sometimes very narrow.
But, nevertheless, the general effect is not that of the Chinese or Mongol type. The

head of the Japanese is large, the face is long, and on the average more regular. Finally, the nose is more prominent, better formed, and sometimes even aquiline. According to Dr. Mohnike, the Japanese head is that of the Turanian race.

A JAPANESE LADY AT HER TOILET.

All the Japanese population, without exception, have fine, thick, straight, and lustrous black hair. The women's hair is shorter than in the European and Malay countries. The Japanese have thick beards, but they shave at least every second day. The colour of their skin varies according to the different classes of society, from the copper tints of the interior of Java to the sunburnt white of the natives of southern Europe. The predominant shade is olive-brown, but it never resembles the yellow tint of the Chinese. Unlike those of Europeans, the face and hands of the Japanese are generally less coloured than the body; little children and young persons of both sexes have rosy complexions, red cheeks, and the same indications of robust health which we like to see in persons of our own race.

The women have fairer complexions than the men: we saw several persons of rank, and even in the middle classes, who were perfectly white; the ladies of the aristocracy regard excessive paleness as a mark of distinction. Nevertheless, both one and the other are separated from the European type by those two indelible marks of race—narrow eyes, and the ungraceful depression of the chest which is always evident even in persons in the flower of their youth, and endowed with the greatest natural charms.

Both men and women have black eyes, white and perfect teeth, separated by regular interstices, and slightly projecting. It is the custom for married women to blacken their teeth. In this we trace a tradition of Java, where the women file their teeth down to the gums; or of the Malay country in general, where everyone has black teeth, produced by the use of the betel.

The mobility of expression and the great variety of physiognomy, which we remark amongst the Japanese, seem to me to be the result of an intellectual development more spontaneous, more original, and in short more free, than is to be met with amongst any other people in Asia.

The national garment of the Japanese is the "kirimon." It is a kind of open dressing-gown, made a little longer and more ample for women than for men. It is crossed at the waist by means of a sash, which for men is made of a straight and narrow piece of silk—for women, of a large piece of stuff elegantly tied at the back.

The Japanese wear no linen, but they bathe every day. The women wear a chemise of red silk crape. In summer, the peasants, the fishermen, the artisans, and the coolies do their work in a state of almost complete nudity, and the women merely wear a single petticoat. During the rains they wear large cloaks of straw or oil-paper, and hats of bamboo bark, made like those of Java, in the form of shields.

In winter the working-men wear a jacket and trousers of blue cotton under the kirimon, and the women one or several wadded mantles,[1] but generally there is

THE FINISHING TOUCH.

no difference between their costumes, excepting in the nature of the materials. The nobles alone have a right to wear silk, and only dress richly to go to Court, or to

[1] Persons of the middle class and of the nobility never go out without jacket and trousers.

make visits of ceremony. The officers of the Government, and the Yakounines on duty, wear wide trailing trousers; and replace the kirimon by an overcoat with large sleeves, which however only comes down to the hips, and is rather elegantly cut. Every-one wears the same coverings for the feet, which consist of sandals of plaited straw, or wooden slippers fastened by a cord in which the great toe is caught. When the roads are muddy, the people wear a simple wooden sole, resting upon two smaller pieces placed crosswise. During the greater portion of the year the working people merely use straw sandals. Each, on returning to his own house, or on presenting himself at that of a stranger, removes his socks or his sandals and leaves them at the door.

The floors of the Japanese houses are constantly covered with mats. As they are all of the same size, which is so invariable that the mat is used as a standard measure,—it is never diffi-cult to arrange them in an apartment. They are uniformly six feet three inches long, three feet two inches wide, and four inches thick. They are made of rice-straw, very carefully plaited; by combining them with the grooves made in the floor and with the sliding screens which form the walls of the rooms, the Japanese divides his habitation into small

AN INHABITANT OF THE CITY IN WINTER DRESS.

or large rooms; but the dimensions are always regular, and he modifies this dis-tribution exactly as it pleases him, without trouble, and never departing from the exactly symmetrical lines.

The mat dispenses with all other furniture: it is the mattress on which the Japanese passes the night, wrapped up in an ample dressing-gown, and under a large wadded counterpane, with his head resting on a little bolster made of strips of bamboo; on it he sets out the utensils of lacquer and porcelain used at his meals; on it the bare feet of his children tread: it is the divan where, crouching on his heels, surrounded by his friends and his guests, all crouching like him, he indulges in interminable talk, drinking a decoction of tea unmingled with any other ingredient, and smoking tobacco out of microscopic pipes.

In all the inns of Japan we find what is called the "bali-bali;" a moveable floor like a great table, covered with mats and raised only a foot above the ground. On this the traveller sits or crouches, eats, drinks, takes a siesta, and chats with his neighbours. The Japanese house is nothing more than the "bali-bali" brought to perfection, a *reposoir*, a temporary refuge in which to take shelter when the labours of the street and the country are terminated: but it is not the centre of existence, if we may be permitted to use that expression at all in speaking of a people who live from day to day, forgetful of yesterday, not caring for to-morrow.

One day, when I had been listening to the recitation of half a dozen of the young boys in our neighbourhood, who were squatting in front of their schoolmaster, I asked what was the name of the exercise that they were repeating in chorus. I was told that they were practising to recite the "Iroya," a sort of alphabet in which not the vowels and consonants, but the fundamental signs of the Japanese language, are collected and grouped in four lines. The number of those sounds is fixed at forty-eight, and instead of classifying them in grammatical elements according to the organs of speech, they have been made into a little piece of poetry, whose first word, "Irova," gives its name to the alphabet. As nearly as I can reproduce the sense of the rhyme, this is it :—

> " Colour and odour alike pass away.
> In our world nothing is permanent.
> The present day has disappeared in the profound abyss of nothingness.
> It was but the pale image of a dream ; it causes us not the least regret."

This national alphabet told me more of the character of the Japanese people than I might have found in volumes. For centuries the generations who were departing repeated to the generation who were coming, "There is nothing permanent in this world ; the present passes like a dream, and its flight causes not the slightest trouble." That this popular philosophy of nothingness does not give full satisfaction to the needs of the soul, is quite evident when we consider how largely the manifestations of religious sentiment have developed of late ; nevertheless, it is probable that it acts incessantly as a latent force, and its influence is felt in all the details of life.

The children profit most by the way of life to which this gives rise. In the first place, it is granted by everyone that the child ought to have its own way. Fathers and mothers derive their pleasure from the observance of this natural law. Every means of enjoyment for children, every subject of their amusement, becomes a source of personal satisfaction to the parents ; they give themselves up to it with all their hearts, and it suits the children admirably. Travellers who have said that Japanese children never cry, have stated with very little exaggeration of expression a perfectly real phenomenon. It is explained by circumstances to which I have alluded, as well as by certain external conditions.

The Japanese is husband to only one wife, who passes almost without transition from her doll to her child, and preserves for a long time her natural infantile character. On the other hand, the national custom does not permit her to bring up her baby too carefully. She is obliged to expose it to the atmospheric influences, carrying it into the air every day, even at noon, with its head shaven, and perfectly naked. In order to carry the child about as long as possible without much fatigue, the woman places it upon her back, fastening it like a package between her chemise and the collar of her kirimon. Thus the wives of the peasants may constantly be seen working in the fields with a little head wagging about between their shoulders. In the house the children may be left to themselves without any uneasiness; they can roll about among the mats, crawling on all-fours and trying to stand upright, because there is no furniture against which they can hurt themselves, nor any object which they can knock down or break.

Their companions are the domestic animals—little pug-dogs with short legs and tremendously fat bodies, and a particular species of cat with white fur marked with yellow and black stripes, who are exceedingly bad mousers, very idle, and very affectionate. Like the cats of Java and the Isle of Man, these animals have no tails.

A DOMESTIC SCENE.

Every family in easy circumstances possesses an aquarium, containing fish—red, silver, gold, transparent—some round as a ball, others ornamented with a long wide tail or fin, which performs the office of a rudder, and which floats about like a piece of extremely fine gauze. In all the houses there are cages made of bamboo bark, constructed on the models of the most elegant habitations, and containing large butterflies shut up there on a bed of flowers, or grasshoppers, in whose strident and monotonous cry the natives take great delight.

Such are the surroundings amid which the Japanese child grows up without any restraint in the paternal house, which is merely a sort of shady playground.

G 2

His parents are prodigal of toys, and games, and entertainments, as much for their own enjoyment as in the interest of his education. His lessons, properly speaking, consist in singing in chorus, at the top of his voice, the "Irova," and drawing with his brush and Chinese ink the first letters of the alphabet, then words, then phrases. There is no compulsion and no precipitation about these lessons, because they are certain things of undeniable utility that can only be acquired by long practice. No one ever thinks of depriving his child of the benefits of instruction. There are no scholastic rules, no measures of coercion for recalcitrant parents, and nevertheless the whole adult population can read, write, and calculate. There is something estimable in the pedagogic *régime* of Japan.

BOOK II

KIOTO

A VIEW IN THE INLAND SEA.

CHAPTER I.

THE ORIGIN OF THE JAPANESE PEOPLE.

COMPLICATIONS OF THE SUBJECT.—A SUPPOSED TARTAR IMMIGRATION.—PEACEFUL TRIBES.
—THE JAPANESE LANGUAGE.—PORTUGUESE ADVENTURERS.—COSMOGONY.

IN observing the life of the Japanese, I have frequently asked myself "Whence have come these interesting and original people?" and, like so many other travellers to whom the same problem has presented itself, I have been forced to conclude that science does not afford the means of its solution.

It offers the most curious complications. The first supposition which presents itself to the mind is, that the archipelago must have been peopled by the Tartar immigration; and I would freely admit that there have been very ancient relations between Corea, the north of Japan, the Kouriles, and even Kamschatka; for the chain of islands which extends from the Asiatic continent to the American continent, in the southern regions of the great ocean, appear to us like the dismantled arches of a gigantic bridge, and naturally awaken the idea of a passage from one to the other, established by means of navigation in its most primitive form. But when we go back to the origin of the Japanese people, what we meet is not a nomade and conquering horde, but peaceful tribes of shepherds and hunters, scattered, under the name of Aïnos, a native expression which signifies "Man," along the open coast and in the islands of the southern part of the great ocean. Now, the Aïnos have not

the oblique and shallow eyes, the prominent cheek-bones, nor the thin beard of the Mongols; they are a race of strong men with large round heads, and remarkably hirsute bodies; they might almost be supposed to be contemporaries of the cave bear. The American geologist, Bickmore, who has observed them on the coast of Yeso, includes them in our great Aryan family, regarding them as probably the only branch which was thrust back by foreign immigration, instead of themselves being the invaders.

Just as the Celts have disappeared from certain counties in England in which they seemed to have taken root, the Aïnos have lost, little by little, the territory which they occupied in ancient times in the Kouriles, Saghalien, and Yeso. They are already reduced to a nation of from 10,000 to 12,000 souls. Their memory is held in veneration among the

ANCIENT WARRIOR, WITH THE NECKLACE OF MATAGAMAS.

Japanese people. In the present day it is the custom to serve a very ordinary shell-fish, which was the primeval food of the Aïnos, in the most sumptuous repasts. This is done in commemoration of the ancestors. The name never inspires any idea of contempt; the equivalent to the term "barbarian" used by the Greeks also exists in the Japanese language, but the word is *Yebis*, not Aïnos: only, if the barbarous tribes whom the founders of the Japanese Empire conquered under the name of Yebis were not tribes of the Aïnos, it must be asked in what did they differ from the latter, and what has been the origin of both; and, still more especially, whence came their conquerors and their rulers?

ANCIENT ARCHERS.

So great are the difficulties presented at this point of departure in the ethnography of Japan, that I fear I shall not be able to offer a clear description of the elements which compose the present population of that Empire. In fact, I can say nothing that will not be puzzling. It profits little to lay down as a principle that by the form of their skulls the Japanese evidently belong to the Turanian family, since what we want to find is the link by which the Japanese branch is attached to the Turanian trunk ; and what it will be important to explain is the phenomenon of a common trunk producing branches of the yellow race in China and Corea, and a little further off, in Japan, a branch of the white race.

The results obtained by linguistic research will be the more readily accepted as authoritative by students of ethnography. M. Léon Rosny has established that the Japanese language, with its dialect of the Liou-Kiou Isles, has derived its origin neither from the Chinese nor from any other language. He makes it evident that their autochthonous general roots have nothing in common with any other known idiom, but that their grammar has a certain likeness to the Tartar idioms.

It is not to be supposed that science has yet said its last word upon the classification of languages in this part of the globe. Perhaps it would be interesting to examine into the more or less intimate relations between the idioms of the Islands of the Sound and the dialects of the south of Japan. Whatever may have been its ancient relations with China, and especially with Corea, I am inclined to believe that the southern portion of the Japanese archipelago, comprising the Liou-Kiou Islands, was colonized by emigrants from the south. Maritime currents play a great part in the still mysterious history of emigration. Voyages whose extent astonish the imagination have been accomplished by their means, though often in an involuntary way. All the European residents in Yokohama are acquainted with the Japanese interpreter, Joseph Hico, who was fishing, with the other members of his family, when a sudden gust of wind drove his boat out to sea. The great equatorial current which bathes the southern and eastern sides of Japan and returns to California, describing a curve of several thousands of leagues, swept the unhappy fishermen towards these coasts, where they were taken up by an American vessel which landed them at San Francisco.

Navigation between China and Japan is difficult and dangerous : the cross current of cold water coming from the polar regions sheds itself from north to south through the canal which separates these two countries, while the immense currents of hot water which come from the Indian Ocean, and escape from the Straits of Malacca and the Sound, take the direction of the south-west and the north-east, and pour themselves out, not upon the coast of China, but upon the south-eastern coast of Japan and the north-east coast of America.

The first Europeans who landed in Japan, three Portuguese deserters—Antonio de Mota, Francisco Zimoro, and Antonio Peroto -having embarked in a Siamese port on board a native junk, were carried into the open sea by a tempest, and blown by the eastern current on the southern coast of the island of Kiousiou (1542).

ANCIENT WARRIOR.   ANCIENT ARCHER.

The celebrated Portuguese adventurer, Fernan Mendez Pinto, and his two companions, Diego Ziemoto and Christopher Boralho, met exactly the same fate : having embarked from Macao on board a Chinese junk, they were blown upon the Japanese island of Tanegasima (1545).

In the face of such facts, it is not without interest to recollect that two thousand years ago the great island of Java with its dependencies formed a powerful empire, which maintained commercial relations by its own fleet, on one side with Madagascar and Arabia, and on the other with China and the neighbouring archipelagoes. My thoughts turn in that direction, and to the Malay peninsula in general, whenever I discover any unforeseen analogy between the public customs and the domestic habits of the Javanese and the Japanese.

But I only throw out this observation in passing ; it merely belongs to the domain of conjecture.

If we consult the Japanese themselves, and especially the interpreters, we obtain nothing but evasive replies, which are either the result of their ignorance or of repugnance to unveil the sanctuary of their national traditions before strangers. Not that these traditions are completely unknown to us. They have been, on the contrary, the subject of considerable research and of very patient labour on the part of the Catholic missionaries and the doctors in the service of the Dutch Indian Government. The archives of Niphon, published by F. de Siebold, contain remarkable fragments of Japanese literature with reference to cosmogony and national history. They are translated by the learned Dr. Hoffmann, of Leyden, and accompanied by explanatory notes. Yet these fragmentary studies, however conscientious they may be, cannot give us the key to a civilization so complete in other directions as that of the Japanese people.

In short, certain subjects, which are in their very nature obscure, must be taken as they are. We cannot explain the Japanese system of the formation of the universe otherwise than as it is understood by the Japanese themselves, or rather as they receive it from the hands of their own priests and their own annalists.

In this system we distinguish a philosophical section apparently borrowed from China, and a legendary section which is purely national.

The Chinese system of cosmogony takes as its point of departure the Taï-Khit, or primitive and eternal substance, the absolute and last extreme. It holds that all matter is contained in the Taï-Khit under the two species of Yang and Yin ; that Yang is the active, mobile, male principle, or primitive force ; that Yin is the passive, immobile, female principle, or primitive matter ; and, finally, that the elements of which the universe is formed are the results of the particles Yang and the particles Yin, which have issued from the Taï-Khit and combined together.

In the depths of the chaotic period, a divine trinity brought about the separation of heaven and earth by its creative will.

In the second period, a series of seven celestial dynasties symbolizes the formation of the various elements.

The first three dynasties are regulated by the male principle, created under the action of the Celestial Reason.

During the four later dynasties, there is a passive co-existence of the male with the female principle, formed under the action of the Terrestrial Reason.

Then, all the elements being prepared, the definitive creation was accomplished by the action of the last couple of the celestial gods, and in two successive phases: firstly, by the union, still purely spiritual, of the two co-existent principles, which is manifested by the creation of Japan: and secondly, by a physical union, which gives birth to the dynasty of the terrestrial gods, of whom four generations are reckoned.

The last ends in Zinmou-ten-woo, the founder of the dynasty of the Mikados.

After this brief summary, which contains everything in which we can establish a parallel between the Chinese and Japanese systems, I pass on to the exposition of the latter, under its traditional and popular form.

BENEDICTION OF AMULETS BY THE KAMI PRIESTS.

CHAPTER II.

THE GENESIS OF JAPAN.

THE BEGINNING.—THE PRIMITIVE GODS.—ACTS OF CREATION.—THE SEVEN CELESTIAL GODS.
THE MYTH OF IZANAGI AND IZANAMI.—THE CHILDREN OF THIS PRIMARY COUPLE.—
ZINMON.—THE COMMENCEMENT OF THE HISTORICAL ERA.—KAMI WORSHIP.

IN the beginning, there was neither heaven nor earth.[1]

The elements of all things formed a liquid, troubled mass, like that which is contained in the embryo egg, where the yellow and the white are still mingled.

[1] The female principle (*me*) and the male principle (*wo*) were not divided. (Klaproth's version, revised by M. de Rosny.)

In the infinite space filled by this chaos, a god uprose, a god called the supreme being, whose throne is in the middle of the heavens.

Afterwards came the creator god, raised high above creation ; then the creator god who is the holy spirit

Each of these three primitive gods had his own existence, but they were not yet revealed outside of their spiritual nature.

Then, by degrees, the work of separation was wrought in chaos.

Subtle atoms, rolling away in different directions, formed the heavens.

Solid atoms, attaching and adhering to each other, produced the earth.

The subtle atoms rapidly constituted the rounded celestial vault above our heads.

The solid atoms aggregated themselves more slowly into a compact body; the earth was not made until long after the heavens.

When terrestrial matter was still floating like a fish on the surface of the waters, or like the image of the moon, which trembles in a limpid stream, there appeared between heaven and earth something like a reed, endowed with movement and susceptible of transformation. This was changed into three gods, who are—

Kouni-toko-tatsi, no mikoto, *i.e.* the August, existing perpetually in the empire.

Kouni-satsoutsi, no mikoto, *i.e.* who reigned by the virtue of water (the first of the five elements) ; and

Toyo-koumou-sou, no mikoto, *i.e.* who reigned by the virtue of fire.

All three were of the masculine sex, because they owed their origin to the sole action of the Celestial Reason. After the first three male gods, there were four couples of gods and goddesses, who lived without sexual relations ; namely—

Wou-hitsi-ni, no mikoto, and his companion, who reigned by the virtue of wood (the third element).

Oho-to-tsi, no mikoto, and his companion, who reigned by the virtue of metal.

Omo-tarou, no mikoto, and his companion, who reigned by the virtue of the earth.

Lastly, Izanaghi, no mikoto, and his companion, Izanami.

This second dynasty includes as many goddesses and gods, because Terrestrial as well as Celestial Reason had equally concurred in their formation.

The first of the seven celestial gods just named, Kouni-toko-tatsi, no mikoto, is the initiator of the creation of our universe. The seven gods collectively personify the elements of this creation. The three first generations are purely spiritual.

In the last four, those of the couples of gods and goddesses, there is co-existence of the two principles, male and female; but they only arrive at the consciousness of themselves in Izanaghi and Izanami, in the seventh and last generation.

THE GOD OF LONGEVITY.

The era of the celestial gods, beginning with Kouni-toko-tatsi and ending with Izanaghi and Izanami, comprises an immeasurable duration of millions of years.

I

The myth of Izanaghi and Izanami refers to the creation of the habitable earth, beginning with the creation of the Empire of Japan.

One day, while the god and the goddess were conversing together, leaning upon the bridge of heaven, they began to speak of the possibility of the existence of a lower world.

In order to satisfy themselves, "Let us try," said Izanaghi to his companion, "whether we may not find some submerged world in the waters which are beneath us:" and he plunged into them the diamond point of his celestial javelin, and turned it

KOUNI-TOKO-TATSI, THE FIRST OF THE CELESTIAL GODS.

about in every direction; several drops of salt water fell from it when he withdrew it, which, becoming condensed as they fell, formed the island called Onokoro-sima.

Then the pair came down upon the island, and resolved to make it the centre of a great archipelago, which they should create by common consent.

They proceeded to this first union of their creative power in the following manner.

One went to the right, the other to the left; and so they made the circuit of the island. When they met, the goddess, transported with joy, exclaimed, "Oh, how happy I am to see you, my dear and amiable husband!" But the god, offended at being forestalled, replied : "My position as your husband gives me the right to speak first ; why do you usurp it ? Such precipitation is an ill omen. In order to avert the evil consequences, we must begin again."

On the second occasion the god spoke first, crying out the moment he met the goddess, "Oh, how happy I am to see you, my dear and loving wife ! "

From that moment nothing interrupted their task of creation, which was effected in the following order.

Izanaghi caused the island of terrestrial foam, Awadsi. to emerge from the waters, in the first place ; then the mountainous Oho-Yamato, rich in autumnal fruits and in fine harbours; then Iyo, with its beautiful country ; then Tsikousi, the pentagonal island ; Iki, one of the columns of heaven ; Tsousima, of the excellent harbours; Oki, with its three islets; and the famous Sado, full of gold and copper. These collectively constitute the Empire of the eight great islands. Afterwards arose the inferior islands—Kibi, Adsouki, Oho-sima, Hime-sima, Tsikano-sima, and Foutagono-sima, which were also the creations of Izanaghi.

As for the other small isles, which, in addition to these, are scattered here and there about the ocean, they were formed, much later, by the foam of the sea and the deposit of the rivers.

Now, as the created country was desert and uninhabitable. Izanaghi called into life eight millions of genii, who swooped down all at once upon the archipelago, and instantly produced an abundant vegetation.

Besides this, Izanaghi created the ten thousand things from which the innumerable quantity of existing objects are derived.

On her side, the goddess Izanami created the genii of the mines, of water, of aquatic plants, of the vegetable earth, and of fire.

Until then, divine beings had been produced in the universe by spontaneous creation, and not by generation. Izanaghi and Izanami, having observed the loves of the bird Isi-Tataki (*Motacilla lugubris*), were the first who engendered children. They had a large number : the eldest and the most excellent was the founder of the five dynasties of the terrestrial gods.

From Izanaghi and Izanami the inhabitants of the earth are descended, in a direct line.

Several biographies of the children of this primary couple exist. One of the sons, Hirooko, was exposed in a bamboo basket on the sea. in consequence of his ugliness; another, Sosano, was banished for his cruelty. Izanami disappeared in giving birth to the genius of fire. Izanaghi, inconsolable, descended into the infernal regions, to seek for his beloved companion. He was very ill received, and only escaped by performing various prodigies from the danger of being detained there in perpetual captivity.

Then Izanaghi himself quitted this world, and his departure put an end to the reign of the celestial gods.

The first of the children of Izanaghi and Izanami became the supreme head of all their creative works. This was their eldest daughter, the great divine sun, Oho-Hirou-Mé-Moutsi, also called the great genius who shines in the sky, Ama-térasou-oho-Kami. This divinity is adored through the whole Empire of Japan, and respected even by the rationalist sects, under the popular name Ten-sjoo-daï-zin, the great imperial goddess, heiress of the celestial generation. As she is the only one of the children of Izanaghi and Izanami who left posterity, all the Japanese, and especially their hereditary emperors, the Mikados, do not fail to trace their origin in a direct line to the goddess of the sun.

After a reign of a hundred thousand years, Ten-sjoo-daï-zin was succeeded by her eldest son, and with the great grandson of the latter the generation of the gods of the earth became extinct. The fifth and last of the terrestrial gods had left four sons. The youngest ascended the throne. He bore in his youth the name of Sannoa-no-Mikoto, the lord of a narrow territory. At the age of forty-five years he departed to conquer the countries to the east of his domains. Having subjugated them, he collected into a single empire all the islands of Japan known at that epoch, and founded the dynasty of the Mikados.

After his death he was given the name Zinmou-ten-woo, or the ruler glorified in heaven, and under that description he is paid divine honours.

Zinmou, the first ruler of men, opens the historical era of Japan, which begins with his accession to the throne, B.C. 660.

Such is the Japanese cosmogony, reduced to its simplest expression, stripped of a number of exotic branches imported from India or from China, and yet, under this form, it is far from making a homogeneous whole. Perhaps there is nothing really original in all this crude conception, except the myth of Izanaghi and the heroic episode of Zinmou. On these two points all authorities are concurrent. This is not the case in respect to certain details which might be compared with the Hebrew and Greek traditions. Thus, the sources from which Siebold quotes mention the three primitive gods of creation, in which we might trace the Trinity of the Holy Scriptures, while there is no reference to them in a translation attributed to the Abbé Mermet.

Besides, we are dealing less with a compilation of legends and popular fables than with a work of interested purpose, evidently conceived with the object of glorifying a dynasty by attributing to it a divine character. This work is posterior to the foundation of the Empire of Zinmou. It is remarkable that it should have succeeded in substituting itself so completely for the ancient oral traditions. The latter were, no doubt, less flattering to the national pride, but they would have thrown some light on the origin of the Japanese people.

ZINMOU.

It cannot be said that the Japanese adopt at all points the version held sacred at the Court of the Mikados. I do not think that in these days anyone in Japan seriously claims the title of a descendant of the sun ; but all the Japanese, without distinction, would invoke their national mythology, if required, in order to protest against the attempt to establish an affiliation between them and the Chinese or any other neighbouring people.

Science, confirming the data of tradition, states that at the epoch at which the historical era commences in Japan a religion peculiar to it already existed in that country, which, as Kæmpfer observes, has never been introduced or practised elsewhere, and which has been preserved up to the present time, although under an altered form, and in a condition of inferiority with respect to other sects of later origin. This religion is the worship of the Kamis, which has also received several names borrowed from the Chinese language, and which for that reason I do not enumerate. It must not be regarded as the worship of the spirits of ancestors in general, nor of the ancestors of particular families. The spirits venerated under the title of Kamis belong, it is true, to a mythological or heroic legend, whose glory is reflected upon families still existing ; but they are, above all, national genii, protectors of Japan and of the people who inhabit it. The chapel dedicated to Ten-sjoo-daï-zin, in the Isyé country, is regarded as the most authentic monument of the primitive religion of the Japanese. Kœmpfer asserts that the Sintoïsts (the Chinese appellation for the adherents of the Kami worship) make a pilgrimage to Isyé once a year, or at least once during their lifetime. The period to which the chapel of Isyé belongs is that of the infancy of art, which attained its present form at the dawn of historic time, under the reign of the first Mikados, and whose essential characteristics I am about to trace.

The situation of the building is, in the first place, a capital point. The mias (temples) were always built on the most picturesque and thickly-wooded sites. Sometimes a fine avenue of pines or cedars leads to the holy place. In every instance it is approached through one of those toris or detached portals which I have described in speaking of the temple of Benten. The mias are generally built upon hills, some of them artificial, and supported by walls of Cyclopean massiveness. The temple is reached by a long and well-kept staircase. At the foot of the stair stands the Chapel of Ablutions : it consists of a simple roof sheltering a stone basin, which is always full of water. The temple, properly so called, is raised two or three feet above the ground, supported on four thick pillars, and surrounded, like most Japanese habitations, by a gallery with a short flight of steps. It is built of wood, closed on three sides and open in front, but supplied with sliding panels, which admit of its being shut at need.

The interior of the sanctuary is thus open to view. A certain elegance mingles with the austere simplicity which distinguishes it. The woodwork shines with cleanliness ; the mats which cover the floor are delicately fine ; the metal disc which ornaments the altar produces a good effect in the picture ; and regarded from the symbolical point of view, there is nothing to weaken its mute eloquence, for the eye finds neither statues, images, nor draperies to distract attention and prevent meditation.

The roof of the chapel is remarkable. It may be made of wood, tiles, or thatch, indifferently ; but the form is peculiar to the mias. The roof slopes gradually on either side, and bends towards the base, where it projects so as to jut out over the verandah ; and from this wide base to the summit it presents an elevation which is relatively considerable and disproportionate to the height of the building. The roof ends at the two upper angles in two bare beams, in the form of an X, or of St. Andrew's Cross. The level of the roof does not pass beyond the point of intersection of the two beams, so that of the four arms of the cross, two adhere to the roof and two surmount it, spreading themselves apart in the air; and the latter are scooped out into a deep hollow at the top, probably to give them more lightness. Small beams cut into the form of spindles are placed at equal distances across the span of the roof. The meaning of this singular architecture is not easily understood. Such seems to be the type of the mia in its primitive purity. I assume that the objects which I am about to mention were introduced into the Kami worship at a late period.

These are two statues of mythological animals, in bronze, representing, under fantastic forms—one a sort of dog, the "Koma-Inou;" the other a sort of unicorn, the "Kirin," —both crouching on their hind legs, and intended to symbolize the two purifying elements, water and fire. Also, various other ornaments, coloured lanterns, perfume vases, consecrated urns for the offerings of wine and saki, and flower-pots which contain branches of evergreen shrubs, such as the myrtle, the cypress, and especially the *sakaki*. At the foot of the high altar stands a large wooden coffer, in which the offerings of the faithful are placed. In some of the mias, as also in the Buddhist temples, a metal gong, or a cord with a bunch of pebbles attached to it, hangs in front of the altar, to enable visitors to call the bonzes, or to arouse the attention of the divinity.

Buddhism has borrowed in more than one instance from the national worship of the Kamis. It places the mirror of Izanami on its altars, and sometimes, on the threshold of its bonze-houses right and left of the doorway, we find the mythological dog, carved in granite and mounted on a pedestal ornamented with Chinese characters. A proof that the above-mentioned objects were introduced late into Kami worship is furnished by the remarkable circumstance that that religion had originally no priesthood.

The mias were, in the beginning, no more than commemorative chapels erected in honour of the national heroes, like Tell's Chapel on the shore of the Lake of the Four Cantons. The lord of the favoured country which boasted such a monument watched over its preservation; but no priest served at the altar of the Kami, no privileged caste interposed itself between the worshipper and the object of his pious homage. Besides, the act of adoration accomplished before the mirror of Izanami did not stop at the Kami of the commemorative chapel, but went up to the gods of whom the Kami was the instrument. Thus the chapel was open to everybody, given up freely to the use of the worshippers, and the worship was devoid of all ceremonial.

This state of things is no longer maintained in its integrity. Younger sons of good families were proposed for the guardianship, and then for the service of the holy place. Kami worship, in its turn, had its processions, its litanies, its offerings, and even its miraculous images. Its priests so far preserved the tradition of its origin, that they never formed a clerical caste, properly so called. They wore a surplice while celebrating the offices, but on leaving the sacred precincts they resumed their costumes and arms, as gentlemen. But there was speedily formed below them a real monastic confraternity, that of the Kanousis, which devoted itself especially to the "exploitation" of pilgrims.

Two causes led to the decline of Kami worship from its primitive purity: the foundation of the power of the Mikados, and afterwards the invasion of Japanese society by the religion of Buddha.

THE KIRIN.

JAPANESE EMPEROR IN ANCIENT TIMES.

CHAPTER III.

THE EARLY SOVEREIGNS OF JAPAN.

THE CONQUEROR WHO CAME FROM THE SOUTH.—ORIGIN AND CAREER OF ZINMOU.—
EARLY HISTORY.—FOUNDATION AND CONSOLIDATION OF THE EMPIRE.—THE RACE OF
THE MIKADOS.—ADVANCE OF CIVILIZATION.

THE history of Japan commences with the conqueror who came from the isles of the south. According to the annals of the Empire, he was a native prince and lord of a small territory at the southern extremity of the island of Kiousiou. Obscure tradition attributes to him a distant origin : the birthplace of his ancestors, if not his

K

own, is said to have been the little archipelago of the Liou-Kiou Islands, which forms
the link between Formosa, southern China, and Japan.

Six centuries before his time, an expedition from Formosa and the Asiatic continent, headed by a certain Prince Taïpé or Taïfak, had reached the shores of Kiousiou,
having proceeded from island to island; but it was in the year 660 B.C. that the
first historical personage, Sannoô, whose memory is celebrated under the name of
Zinmou, makes his appearance. Although he was the youngest of four sons, his
father had named him his successor from his fifteenth year. He ascended the
throne at the age of forty-five years, without any opposition on the part of his
brothers. An old retainer, whose adventurous life had led him to the distant isles
behind which the sun rises, loved to describe to him the beauty of their shores, on
which the gods themselves formerly sought refuge. "Now," said he, "they are
inhabited by barbarous tribes, always at war with one another. If the prince desires
to profit by their divisions, their men of arms, however skilful they may be in the
management of the lance, the bow, and the sword, being dressed only in coarse fabrics,
or the skins of savage beasts, cannot resist a disciplined army protected by helmets
and iron cuirasses."

Zinmou lent a willing ear to the suggestions of the old retainer; collected all
his disposable forces, placed them under the orders of his elder brothers and his
sons, embarked them upon a flotilla of war-junks perfectly equipped, and, assuming
command of the expedition, set sail, after taking leave of his home, which neither he
nor his brothers were ever to see again.

After he had doubled the south-east point of Kiousiou, he sailed along the eastern
side of the island, keeping close to the shore after the fashion of the ancient Normans,
making occasional descents, giving battle when he was resisted, and forming alliances
when he found the nobles or chiefs of clans disposed to assist him in his enterprise.

It was evident that all this coast had been the theatre of former invasions.
The population was composed of a ruling class, and serfs attached to the land.

In some of the chapels of the national Kamis, stone arms are exhibited, which
were used by the primitive populations at the epoch when, under certain unknown
circumstances, they came in contact with a superior civilization.

When Zinmou made his appearance, walls and palisades protected the families of
the soldiers and the masters of the country. The latter were armed with bows and

long arrows; a great sword with a carved hilt and a naked blade, worn in the folds of the girdle, completed their equipment.

Their richest adornments consisted of a chain of magatamas, or cut gems, which they wore hanging on the side above the right hip. Among these stones were rock crystal, serpentine, jasper, agates, amethysts, and topazes. Some were in the form of a ball or an egg, others cylindrical; one a crescent, another a broken ring. The women had necklaces of a similar kind. It is said that the use of the magatamas has still some connection with certain religious solemnities in the islands of Liou-Kiou, and at Yeso, in the north of Japan; and it is concluded thence that it must have been common to all the populations of the long chains of islands extending from Formosa to Kamtschatka. If this custom has disappeared from the central region of the Japanese archipelago, the cause of the phenomenon must be sought in the superior culture which characterises the inhabitants of these countries, and which has led them to renounce the display of the family wealth on their persons.

After a difficult voyage of ten months, interrupted by occasional brilliant feats of arms and by profitable negotiations, Zinmou reached the north-eastern extremity of the island of Kiousiou. He was at a loss how to get further, when he discovered a fisherman who was floating upon the waves, squatting upon the shell of a huge turtle. He hailed him immediately, and employed him as a pilot. Thus Zinmou succeeded in crossing the strait which separates Kiousiou from the land of Niphon, and coasted along in the direction of the east, operating with prudent caution, and leaving behind him no important point without having secured its possession. Nevertheless, as the native tribes continually opposed him at sea as well as on land, he disembarked and fortified himself upon the peninsula of Takasima, where he devoted three years to the construction and equipment of an auxiliary fleet.

Then he set out again, and achieved the conquest of the coast and archipelago of the Inland Sea; after which he disembarked the greater part of his army, and penetrating into Niphon, he established his rule over the rich countries, intersected by fertile valleys and wooded mountains, which extend from Osaka to the borders of the Gulf of Yeddo. From that time all the cultivated countries and all the civilized peoples in ancient Japan were under the power of Zinmou.

The conqueror inaugurated and established the preponderance of the south over the destinies of the Japanese people. Whether the race which ruled before him over the native inhabitants had been of Turanian origin or not, it also submitted in its turn to this last and decisive invasion, to which the Empire of the Mikados owes its ancient glory and its actual existence.

It does not follow, however, that Japanese civilization was a simple importation. Zinmou appears to have been in certain respects, especially that of religion, a tributary of the people whom he had conquered. The diverse elements with which he had to deal—the native clans and the Tartar emigrants, with the invaders who had come from the islands of the south, the ancient nobles lately conquered, and their new sovereign, who was won over to their favourite customs—were thus fused into one national body. The tribes which remained aloof from the pacific constitution of the Empire were the Aïnos, who had been driven further and further towards the north, and the Yebis, dispersed during the strife of the invasion, and who lived in the forests on the products of hunting and rapine.

But it would be vain to attempt an analysis of the various elements which have contributed to the formation of the national character of the Japanese. The civilization of the country appears to be the result of a combination of the indigenous and the foreign elements. There has been a mixture of races without an absorption of native qualities, among the islanders of the extreme east, and, as was the case among the islanders of Great Britain, the alliance has produced a new and original type.

When the divine warrior Zinmou had accomplished his ambitious aims, seven years had elapsed since his departure from Kiousiou,—seven years, accompanied with how much fatigue, suffering, and trouble of every kind! His three brothers had perished under his eyes : the first pierced with an arrow at the siege of a fortress ; the two others victims of their own devotion to him, for they had thrown themselves into the sea in order to appease a tempest which threatened the junk of the conqueror.

The sun had always shown itself favourable to his enterprises. To its divine protection it was due that he had not been lost in the dangerous defiles of Yamato. A raven, sent to him by the divinity at a critical moment, had guided him into safety. Thus he had added to his ancestral arms the image of the glittering goddess, such as she appeared to him each day when she arose above the horizon, and had it painted upon his banner, his cuirass, and his war fan. In the fourth year of his reign, when he had attained possession of uncontested power, he instituted a solemn feast of thanksgiving in honour of Ten-sjoo-daï-zin. The national Kamis had also their share in his homage. He ordained sacrifices in honour of the eight immortal spirits, protectors of countries and families, in order to celebrate the inauguration of his royal residence, and to surround his throne with the prestige of that religion which was so dear to the peoples whom he had conquered.

These things happened in the country of Yamato, which occupies the centre of the great peninsula in the south-east of Niphon, whose coasts border the Inland Sea and the ocean. There Zinmou constructed a vast fortress on a great hill. He called this castle his "Miako," or the chief palace of his States, and there he installed his Court, or Daïri. These two names have ever since been retained by the sovereigns of the Japanese Empire to distinguish it from their other residences. The sovereigns themselves bear the honour-giving title of "Mikados," or "august" and "venerable," without prejudice to the glorious surnames under which they figure in the annals of the nation after death. The native historians frequently employ the word "Miako" instead of the proper name of the city in which the Emperor resides, and that of "Daïri" in place of the title of Mikado. They say, for example, such and such a thing has been done "by order of the Daïri," instead of "by order of the Mikado." This custom is, however, common to the language of all Courts.

As Zinmou had been raised to the throne by the free choice of his father, it was enacted that for the future the reigning Mikado should designate one among his sons to succeed him, or, if he had no sons, one among the other princes of the blood, according to his own choice, and without regard to the order of primogeniture. If the throne became vacant during the minority of the elect prince, the widow of the Mikado was to assume the regency of the Empire, and to exercise sovereign rights during the interregnum.

Zinmou terminated his glorious career in the sixty-seventh year of his age, 585 years before the birth of Christ. He has been placed among the number of the Kamis. His chapel, known in Japan by the name of Simoyasiro, is situated upon Mount Kamo, near Kioto, and he is still worshipped there as the founder and the first chief of the Empire. The hereditary right to the crown has subsisted in his family for more than two thousand five hundred years, and is still maintained.

The ancient race of the Mikados was strong and long-lived. Zinmou lived one hundred and twenty years; the fifth Mikado lived one hundred and fourteen years; the sixth, one hundred and thirty-seven years; the seventh, one hundred and twenty-eight years; the eighth, one hundred and six years; the ninth, one hundred and eleven years; the eleventh and twelfth, each one hundred and forty years; the sixteenth, one hundred and eleven years; and the seventeenth, who died in the 388th year of our era, attained the age of three hundred and eight years, or three hundred and thirty years according to the version of some historians.

Seïmou, the thirteenth Mikado, was ten feet high. The wives of the Mikados, who governed the Empire in the capacity of Regent, were equal in point of character to their venerable husbands. One of them, Zingou, A.D. 201, equipped a fleet, and, embarking at the head of a select army, crossed the Sea of Japan and conquered the Corea, from whence she returned only just in time to give birth to a future Mikado.

The progress of civilization kept pace with the aggrandisement of the Empire. From Corea came the camel, the ass, and the horse: the latter animal is the only one which has been naturalized in Japan.

The establishment of tanks and canals for the irrigation of the rice-fields dates back to thirty-six years B.C. The tea-shrub was introduced from China. Tatsima Nori brought the orange from "the country of eternity." The culture of the mulberry and the fabrication of silk date from the fifth century of our era. Two centuries later the Japanese learned to distinguish "the earth which replaces oil and wood for burning," and to extract silver from the mines of Tsousima.

Several important inventions date from the third century: for example, the institution of a horse post; making beer from rice, known under the name of *saki*; and the art of sewing clothes, which was taught to the Japanese housewives by needle-women who came from the kingdom of Petsi, in Corea. The Mikado, enchanted with the first attempt, and wishing to go to the fountain-head, sent an embassy to the chief of the Celestial Empire to ask him for needlewomen. In the fourth century the Daïri built, in various parts of Japan, rice stores, intended to prevent the recurrence of the famines which had more than once ravaged the population. In 543, the Court of Petsi sent a precious instrument to the Mikado—it was "the wheel which indicates the south." The introduction of hydraulic clocks took place in 660, and ten years later that of wheels worked by water-power. At the end of the eighth century a system of writing, proper to Japan, was invented, but from the third century the use of Chinese signs had been introduced at Court.

The obscurity in which ancient national literature is enveloped does not permit us to estimate its influence on civilization. It is all the more interesting to trace the beneficent action which the fine arts exercised upon the people. Human victims were immolated at the funerals of the Mikado, or of his wife, the Kisaki, and these victims were usually servants of the Court. In the year 3 B.C., Nomino Soukouné, a native sculptor, being informed of the death of the Kisaki, had the generous courage to present himself before his sovereign with clay images, which he proposed to him should be thrown into the tomb of his royal wife in place of the servants destined to the sacrifice. The Mikado accepted the offer of the humble modeller, and testified his satisfaction by changing his family name to that of Fasi, or "artist."

ANCIENT SCULPTOR.

The laws remained as they still are, more barbarous and cruel than the customs. For example, the punishment of crucifixion was inflicted on noble women guilty of adultery.

A whole series of measures admirably adapted for the rapid development of the genius of the nation, and for imbuing it with a true sense of its strength and individuality, is due to the political administration. In the year 86 B.C., the sovereign had census tables of the population made, and ship-building yards established. In the second century of our era he divided his States into eight administrative circles, and these circles into sixty-eight provinces. In the fifth century he sent an official into each province, charged with the collection and registration of the popular customs and traditions of every district. Thus the proper names of each family, and the titles and surnames of the provincial dynasties, were fixed. An imperial road was made between the principal cities, five in number, and the Mikado transported his Court successively into each. The most important, in the seventh century, was the city of Osaka, on the eastern coast of the Inland Sea.

In order to confer political union, and also unity of language, letters, and general civilization, upon the country, a capital was indispensable, and this great want was supplied in the eighth century by the foundation of Kioto, which became the favourite city of the Mikado, and was his permanent residence until the twelfth century.

The city of Hiogo, whose secure and spacious harbour has been for years the centre of the maritime commerce of the Japanese Empire, is built on the coast of the basin of Idsoumi, opposite to the north-eastern point of the island of Awadsi. At Hiogo the junks from Simonasaki discharge their cargoes from China, the Liou-Kiou Islands, from Nagasaki, and from the western coast of Niphon, and even of Corea and Yeso, for the supply of the interior and the east of Japan. From these, thousands of other junks transport the agricultural produce and objects of art and industry of the southern provinces of Niphon to the islands of the Inland Sea.

In time, a double line of steamboats, in the great commercial services of England and France, will unite the port of Hiogo to China.

The great and ancient city of Osaka is only eight hours' journey from Hiogo. It is the Venice of Japan. The palaces of the nobility occupy the quays which stretch along the principal arm of the river. All the rest of the town is composed of houses and shops belonging to the trading classes. Only a few old temples, more or less dilapidated, are to be seen. One of them, at the far end of the eastern suburb, has been placed by the Government of the Taïkoun at the disposal of the foreign Embassies. A citadel, a mile in circumference, overlooks the north-eastern portion of the city, and commands the imperial high road to Kioto.

The city of Osaka contains seven hundred thousand inhabitants. From the year 744 to the year 1185 of our era it was the residence of the Mikados. They were well pleased to dwell amid its energetic, laborious, and enterprising population, to whom the Empire chiefly owed the development of its commerce and prosperity. But this was no longer the heroic epoch, when the Mikado, like the Doge of the Venetian Republic, embarked upon his war-junk, and fulfilled in person the functions of High Admiral. He was no longer to be seen inspecting his troops, borne upon a litter upon the shoulders of four brave heralds, or commanding the manœuvres from the summit of a hill, sitting upon a stool, and holding in his right hand his iron fan. At Osaka, the Mikado, who had reached the height of riches, power, and security, built a palace in the midst of a spacious park, which shut him out from the tumult of the city. His courtiers persuaded him that it was requisite for the dignity of the descendant of the sun that he should be invisible to the great body of his subjects, and should leave to princes and favourites the cares of government and the command of the army and the fleet. The life of the Daïri was subject to ceremonial laws which regulated its smallest details and its least movements, and the sovereign dwelt within a circle inviolable by all except his courtiers. Imperial pomp henceforth rarely became visible to the people; who, deceived in their dearest hopes, weary of the arbitrary rule of favourites, ventured at length to raise their voices, and their murmurs reached the ears of their sovereign. He did not convoke an assembly of notables, but he instituted certain bureaus, where the complaints of the people were registered. The courtiers, convinced that the dynasty of the descendants of the sun was in danger, carried away themselves and their Emperor to Kioto, a small town in the interior, on the north of Osaka. They succeeded in making this the permanent residence of the Mikados, and the capital, or miako, of the Empire.

In abandoning the populous city, the great centre of commerce, of industry, and of intellectual activity, independent of the Daïri, they obtained the double advantage of cutting off all communication between the people and the sovereign, and of moulding the new capital to their tastes, and for the convenience of their passions.

Kioto is situated in a fertile plain, open to the south, and bounded to the north-east by a chain of green hills, behind which there is a great lake, called indifferently the lake of Oïtz, or Oumi, the names of the two principal cities on its shores. It is said to offer some of the most beautiful views in Japan. The waters of a dozen rivers flow into it, and give rise to the Yodo-gawa, which runs to the south of Kioto, and into the Inland Sea below Osaka.

Two affluents of the Yodo-gawa rise on the north of the capital, and flow beneath its walls, one to the east and the other to the west. Thus Kioto is completely surrounded by a network of running water, which is utilized in irrigating the rice-fields, in the formation of canals in the streets of the city, and also in the tanks in the imperial parks.

L

In the neighbourhood of Kioto, rice, sarrasin, wheat, tea, the mulberry-tree, the cotton-plant, and an immense variety of fruit-trees and vegetables are cultivated. Groves of bamboos and laurels, chestnuts, pines, and cypress crown the hills. Springs are abundant. Thousands of birds—the falcon, the pheasant, the peewit, ducks, geese, and hawks of all kinds—abound in the country. Kioto is famed for the salubrity of its climate. It is one of those portions of the Empire least exposed to hurricanes and earthquakes.

The successors of Zinmou could not have found a more propitious retreat in which to enjoy the fruits of the labours of their ancestors; to raise themselves to the rank of divinities upon the pedestal of the ancient traditions of their race, and to lose sight of the realities of human life. All these things they did so completely as to allow one of the greatest sceptres in the world to escape from their enervated hands.

The descendant of the Kamis of Japan naturally became the chief of the national religion, which had no clergy. The Mikados created an hierarchy of functionaries, endowed with the sacerdotal character, and charged to preside over all the details of public worship. All the high dignitaries were chosen from the immediate and collateral members of the imperial family.

The same order of proceeding was observed generally in all that concerned the service of the palace and the important functionaries of the Daïri. The chiefs of the civil and military administrations were gradually more and more alienated from the Court properly so called, and the latter took an exclusively clerical stamp. So the capital of the Empire ended by presenting a strange spectacle. Nothing was to be seen there which had reference to the army, the navy, or the government of the country. All these were abandoned to the care of the functionaries employed in the various services, and scattered about in the provinces. On the other hand, all the sects which recognized the supremacy of the Mikado assembled their own dignitaries within his city of residence, and all vied with each other in building temples for their respective religions. Thus, when Buddhism, imported by monks from China, had made sure of the protection of the Mikado by paying him homage under the title of spiritual chief of the Empire, it speedily surpassed all that had been done in the capital to the honour and glory of the Kami worship.

The Japanese Buddhists endowed Kioto with the largest bell in the world, and with a temple no less unique of its kind. It is called the Temple of the Thirty-three Thousand Three Hundred and Thirty-three, which is exactly the number of the idols which it contains. In order to make such a prodigy intelligible, it must be explained that the great statues support a multitude of small ones, placed upon their heads and knees and upon the palms of their hands.

The temples or chapels of Kioto which belong to the ancient national religion still preserve to a certain extent the simplicity which distinguishes them in the provinces. Some are consecrated to the seven celestial dynasties of the native mythology, others to the spirits of the earth, and others to the divinity of the Sun, Ten-sjoo-daï-zin, or to her descendants, the first Mikados.

The Kami worship towards the end of the seventeenth century had two thousand one hundred and twenty-seven mias in Kioto and its suburbs; but the Buddhist religion, in its different sects or ramifications, had no less than three thousand eight hundred and ninety-three temples, pagodas, or chapels.

There are no other monuments worthy of notice in this singular capital.

The palaces of the Daïri are numbered among the sacred edifices, both by reason of the style of their architecture and their purpose. They are enclosed within a circuit of walls occupying the north-eastern portion of the city. Long lines of trees, of great height, which show above the distant roofs, give a vague idea of the extent and tranquillity of the parks, in whose recesses the imperial dwellings hide themselves from profane eyes and the noise of the city.

As it frequently happens that the Mikado abdicates in favour of the hereditary prince, in order to end his days in absolute seclusion, a special palace is reserved for him, under such circumstances, in a solitary enclosure on the south-eastern side of the Daïri.

In the centre of the city there is a strong fort, whose ramparts are surmounted at intervals by square towers two or three storeys high, intended to serve as a refuge for the Mikado in troublous times. The head-quarters of the garrison of the Taïkoun was established there in later days.

The high dignitaries and functionaries, and the persons employed in the various residences of the Emperor and of his numerous family, may be counted by thousands. The number can never be exactly known, because the Court has the privilege of escaping the annual census.

At all times the Japanese Government has occupied itself carefully with national statistics. In the holy city of the Empire, every individual is officially classed in the sect to which he declares himself to belong. In 1693 Krœmpfer reports that the permanent population of Kioto, exclusive of the Court, comprised 52,169 ecclesiastics, and 477,557 lay persons; both one and the other were divided into twenty recognized sects, the most numerous of which included 159,113 adherents, and the least numerous, which was a sort of Buddhist confraternity, 289 members only.

It must not be imagined that this enormous development of sacerdotal life in the capital of Japan renders the city gloomy, or makes the public morals austere. Exactly the contrary is the case; the stories and pictures which exist in Kioto, and record what it was in the days of its prosperity, produce the impression of a never-ending carnival.

Let us suppose that we are reaching the holy city at sundown. Our ears will be assailed by a concert of instruments. On all the hills, which are covered with sacred groves, temples, and convents, the bonzes and the monks are celebrating the evening office to the sound of drums and tambourines, copper gongs, and brass bells. The faubourgs are illuminated with bright-coloured paper lanterns of all dimensions: the largest, of cylindrical form, are suspended from the columns of the temples; the smaller, like globes, hang from the doors of the inns and the galleries of the houses. The sacred edifices and profane establishments, which participate in this illumination, are so considerable in number, and so close together, that the whole quarter seems to be the scene of a Venetian *fête*. In the heart of the city a compact crowd of both sexes throngs the streets, which extend from the north to the south, in the vicinity of the Daïri. The priests are there in great numbers. Those of the Kami worship wear a little hat of black lacquered cardboard, surmounted with a sort of crest of the same colour, and a small white cross. This curious head-dress has an appendage of very stiff ribbon which is tied behind the head and hangs down the back of the neck. It is the ancient national head-dress, which does not belong exclusively to the priests, but may be worn, with certain modifications prescribed by the sumptuary laws, by the nineteen officially titled classes of the population of Kioto. A wide simar, big trousers, and great sword, which is probably only an ornamental weapon, completes the costume of the priests of the Kami temples.

All the members of the Buddhist clergy, regular as well as secular, have the head shaven and completely bare, with the exception of certain orders who wear wide-brimmed hats. The habit is generally grey, but there are some black, brown, yellow, and red, occasionally diversified by a scarf and breastplate, or a surplice.

Kioto boasts of certain hermits, saints who have made choice of the capital to retire from the world. The grateful citizens transform the cells of these monks into little storehouses of abundance. The most mysterious of them is cut out of the front of a rock, and inhabited no one knows by whom or how; but baskets of provisions are lifted up by an ingenious pulley over a great tank, which separates the rock from the public road.

Mendicity is extensively practised.

The annual *fêtes* instituted in honour of the principal Kamis of Japan have no other sacred rites than the ceremonies of purification, and were introduced about the end of the eighth century. On the day before the great solemnity the priests go in procession with lights to the temple, where the arms and other objects which belonged to the divine hero are kept in a precious reliquary called "Mikosi." According to clerical fiction, the Mikosi represents the terrestrial dwelling of the Kami—a kind of throne still preserved to him in his earthly country—and each year it undergoes a radical purification. The reliquary is emptied and brought to the river: while a certain number of priests carefully wash it, others light great fires in order to keep away all evil genii; and the Kagoura, or sacred choir, play softly in order to appease the spirit of the Kami, who is momentarily deprived of his earthly dwelling; nevertheless, they make no delay in restoring it to him, which is done by solemnly reinstating the relics in the reliquary.

As, however, the temple itself equally requires purification, the Mikosi does not re-enter it until this operation has been performed; and during the entire *fête*, which is prolonged during several days, it is sheltered in a *reposoir* specially constructed for the purpose, and duly protected against evil spirits. Should those dread things endeavour to pass through the ropes of rice-straw which bound the sacred enclosure, they would expose themselves to showers of boiling holy water, with which from time to time the dwelling of the Kami is sprinkled; and woe to the evil spirits who should flutter in the air within reach of the Kami's guard of honour, for the priests who compose it are skilful horsemen and accomplished archers. The people applaud their evolutions, and follow with admiring eyes the arrows that they shoot into the clouds, and which fall within the enclosure of the holy place.

Such are the ceremonies which lend a devotional character to the festival. The influence which Kami worship has had upon the development of the dramatic taste of the nation has not been produced, I need hardly say, by these puerile juggleries. The annual festivals have another and worthier side. The historical cortége, a great

A PANTOMIMIC DANCE AT THE COURT OF THE MIKADO.

procession of masked and costumed priests, represents various scenes taken from the lives of their heroes. These theatrical representations in the open air were accompanied by music, songs, and pantomimic dances. Thus the fine arts and poetry are made interpreters of national traditions, and the people flock to receive the patriotic instruction with avidity. Sometimes an exhibition of trophies of arms, or groups of figures in clay, reproducing the features and wearing the traditional costume of the principal Kamis, was added to the entertainment. They were placed on cars or on platforms of pyramidal form, representing the building, the bridge, the junk, or sacred place illustrated by the heroes whose memory was celebrated. Originally these annual festivals, which were called Matsouris, were limited to a small number of the most ancient cities in the Empire. Eight provinces only had the honour of possessing Kamis. But, from the tenth century, every province, every district, every place of any importance wished to have its hero or its celestial patron. Finally, the number of Kamis reached three thousand one hundred and thirty-two, among whom a great difference was made in favour of the most ancient. Four hundred and ninety-two were distinguished under the title of "great Kamis," and the others received the name of "inferior Kamis."

Thenceforth, Matsouris were held in all important places in Japan, and from one end to the other of the Empire a taste for heroic recitals and artistic enjoyments, allied to the love of country and manly qualities, was diffused.

In this respect the national religion of Japan has not been sterile. Something has accrued from it, because it has created a people universally possessed of the sentiment of patriotism, an Empire which has never known the yoke of a foreigner, and a Government which has preserved, in its entire autonomy, even to our time, its relations with the most powerful European States.

CHAPTER IV.

ART AND FASHION IN KIOTO.

IMMOBILITY OF ART AND LITERATURE IN THE ANCIENT CAPITAL.—CONTRAST BETWEEN CHINA AND JAPAN.—DECREPITUDE OF THE ONE; ETERNAL YOUTH OF THE OTHER.— THE FESTIVAL OF THE DEAD.—BURIAL CEREMONIES.—NATIVE DRAWING.—ARCHITEC- TURAL WORKS OF THE JAPANESE.—COURT DRESS AND CUSTOMS.—THE EMPRESS AND HER COURT.— DEVELOPMENT OF CIVIL AND MILITARY INSTITUTIONS.—THE INVISIBLE MIKADO.

NOTWITHSTANDING its bonzes, its astrologers, and its academical poets, the ancient Japanese civilization was not without its popular period, which has left an indelible impression upon taste at Kioto. All works which come out of the workshops of the old capital are distinct from everything that one sees elsewhere. But the admiration which they inspire is mingled with a feeling of regret, for by a singular contradiction they attain an astonishing perfection in the imitation of animal and vegetable nature, whilst on approaching the sphere of human life they present only types without reality, and figures cut on conventional patterns. Evidently the noble faculties revealed in the conceptions and in the handiwork of the national artists were arrested in their development by official rules, and hindered for want of a method superior to that suggested to them by the fashions of the Court.

Thus, art as well as literature became a conventional and hollow routine in its subservience to the Mikados. We may even add, that at the decline of the Mikados it remained exactly the same as it had been in the height of their power ; and it is a remarkable fact that it has not since degenerated or become corrupt.

The working population of the ancient imperial cities has not changed for centuries. Amid institutions which have fallen into decrepitude it does not exhibit the slightest trace of the decadence and debility which are common to every class of Chinese society. China awakes in the mind at every moment the image of a worm-eaten, dusty edifice, inhabited by aged invalids. But in Japan there are really neither ruins nor dust, the fresh vegetation of its always green islands is matched by that appearance of unalterable youth which transmits itself generation after generation among the inhabitants of this happy country, who ornament even their last dwellings with the emblems of eternal spring. Their cemeteries abound with verdure and flowers in all seasons. Their tombs, simple commemorative tablets, preserve the recollection of the dead without any symbol of destruction. Every family has its separate enclosure and every dead person a stone in the common resting-place ; the tradition of those who are no more is carried on from hill to hill among the gardens of the sacred groves, even to the extremities of the suburbs of their cities.

At Nagasaki this picture seems perfect. The city stretches out at the foot of a chain of mountains, of little height, which have been cut out into terraces, forming an amphitheatre of funeral ground in the eastern quarter of the city.

Here, one is in the presence of two cities : in the plain, the city of the living lies in the sun, with its long and wide streets bordered with fragile wooden houses and inhabited by an ephemeral crowd ; on the mountain is the necropolis, with its walls and monuments of granite, its trees hundreds of years old, its solemn calm.

M

The inhabitants of Nagasaki, when they raise their eyes in the direction of the mountain, must think involuntarily of the innumerable generations which have passed away before them from the face of the earth. That multitude of stones raised upon the terrace, standing up clear against the blue haze of the distance, keeps alive among them the idea that the spirits of their ancestors come back from their tombs, and that, mute, but attentive, they contemplate the life of the city.

One day of the year, towards the end of the month of August, the entire population invite these spirits to a solemn festival, which is prolonged during three consecutive nights.

On the first evening the tombs of all persons who have died during the past year are lighted by lanterns, painted in different colours.

On the second and third nights, all the tombs without exception, the old as well as the new, participate in a similar illumination, and all the families of Nagasaki come out and install themselves in the cemeteries, where they give themselves up to drinking abundantly in honour of their ancestors.

But on the third night, about three o'clock in the morning, long processions of lights come down from the heights and group themselves together on the borders of the bay, while the mountain gradually resumes its darkness and its silence. The souls of the dead men have embarked and disappeared before the dawn. Thousands of small straw boats have been fitted up for them, each provided with fruit and small pieces of money. These fragile barks are laden with all the painted paper lamps which had served for the illuminations of the cemeteries, their little sails of mat are spread, and the morning breeze disperses them over the water, where they are soon consumed. Thus the entire flotilla is burnt, and for a long time the traces of fire may be seen dancing over the waves. But the dead go quickly. Finally, the last ship disappears, the last light is extinguished, the last soul has again bidden adieu to the earth.

At the rising of the sun there is no trace of the dead or of the merrymakers.

In ancient times the Japanese had no other religion than that of the Kamis: the honours of a special sepulture were awarded only to persons of a certain importance, who were allowed a resting-place distinct from the cemeteries reserved for the common people.

The ceremonies of the burial of the dead had, in ancient times, a very solemn character, but suggestive to the beholder rather of the triumph of a hero. Beside the dead man, in the tomb, was laid his coat of mail, his arms, all his most precious possessions: even his principal servants followed him to the sepulchre, and his favourite horse was immolated to his manes. These barbarous customs were abolished in the first century of our era. Lay figures replaced human victims, and only the picture of a horse was sacrificed. A few strokes of a brush, boldly dashed upon a plank of wood, represented the image of the four-footed companion of the dead, and this plank was enclosed in the tomb.

The native painters display such skill in the execution of these designs, that these Yemas, or sketches of horses, have become artistic curiosities; and numbers of them exist in various chapels in the towns and country places, and are regarded as votive pictures. Amateurs search eagerly for Yemas upon the screens in the old houses and in the palaces of Yeddo. A few of them may be found among the presents sent by the Taïkoun to foreign Governments.

This kind of drawing was not regarded with favour by the Court of the Mikado, where miniature painting was much in fashion. The works of the miniature painters of Kioto remind us of our mediæval missals: they are painted on vellum, with the same profusion of colour on a golden background; the manuscript is ornamented by plates in the text, and rolled upon an ivory cylinder, or upon a stick of precious wood, with metal ornaments inserted in the ends.

Collections of poetry, almanacks, litanies, prayers, and romances are generally bound up into volumes. Ladies use microscopic prayer-books; and they and the poets of Kioto employ no other almanacks than the calendar of flowers, in which the months and their subdivisions are represented by symbolical bouquets. There is also a calendar of the blind, and collections of prayers exist in characters of unknown origin.

The dress of the women of quality not only indicates their rank and condition, but is always in harmony, as to its colour and the subjects embroidered upon the garments, with the time and the seasons, the flowers, and the productions of the different months of the year. The months themselves are never called by their names, but by their attributes. The month *Amiable* draws the bonds of friendship closer by visits and presents on the new year; the month of "the awakening of nature" is the third month of the year; the month of *Missives*, which is the seventh, has one day assigned to the exchange of letters of congratulation; and the twelfth is that of "the business of the masters," because it obliges them to leave the house in order to attend to the regulation of their affairs.

The architectural works of the Japanese, the products of their industry—everything that comes out of the hands of their corporations of arts and trades—indicate a certain

JAPANESE MOSAIC.

symbolical research mingled with great purity of taste in the imitation of nature. In all the temples and palaces we find ornaments in sculptured wood, which represent a bank of clouds, above which rises the front of the edifice. The grand entrance of the Daïri is decorated with a golden sun surrounded by the signs of the Zodiac; the portals of the temples devoted to Buddhism are surmounted by two elephants' heads, which indicate that this religion came from India; the carpenters' tools all bear symbolical devices.

The favourite designs of their mosaics and their carvings in wood are borrowed from the lines described by the foaming waves of the sea and the basalt rocks cut by the waters; bats and cranes are represented with extended wings; the iris, the water-lily, and the lotus are always in full flower; the bamboo, the cedar, the palm-tree, and the pear-tree, are either isolated or combined with the most graceful climbing plants.

We observed numerous ornaments whose signification we could not discover. Within the precincts of the Daïri there is a bronze vase which coarsely represents a bird of some unknown kind, of the height of a man. This is one of the most ancient monuments of native art. It is called the Tori-Kamé; its origin and use are unknown. Other vases of great antiquity, mounted on pedestals, and which serve as perfume-burners, are carved with designs representing the head and scales of the crocodile, an animal unknown in Japan. The tortoise and the heron, which figure frequently in the composition of perfume-vases and sacred candelabra, are emblems of immortality, or at least of longevity. The Foo, a mythological bird common to both China and Japan, is found upon the lintels of the door of the Daïri, as an emblem of eternal happiness.

These same mythological images, and others which it would take too long to enumerate, are reproduced in the designs of the rich stuffs worked in silk, gold, and silver, which form the glory and the pride of the weavers of Kioto; and also in the carvings and engravings on plates of gold, silver, red copper, and steel, with which the native jewellers decorate the handles and the scabbards of swords, portable inkstands, pipes, tobacco-boxes, and other ornaments; in short, in all the innumerable utensils, pieces of plate, and lacquer and porcelain furniture, which constitute the wealth of Japanese households.

It was pointed out to me one day, amongst a collection of curiosities from the workshops of Kioto, that none of the objects had a perfectly quadrangular form. I verified this in examining a great number of cabinets, screens, covers, paper boxes, and other varnished objects, amongst which, in fact, I did not discover a single acute angle: all were softened and rounded. Supposing that this peculiarity is only one of the caprices of taste, and therefore not to be disputed, there is another fact which may perhaps have a symbolical significance : it is, that all Japanese mirrors, without exception, present the figure of a disc. Such uniformity seems to confirm the opinion of Siebold, that the mirrors of the temples of the Kamis is an emblem of the sun's disc. It would be more embarrassing to divine the reasons of certain fashions among those of Kioto, if indeed fashions ever have a reason.

The Court ladies pull out their eyebrows and replace them by two thick black patches painted half way up the forehead. Is this done because these beauties with prominent cheek-bones are aware that the oval of their faces is not quite so perfect as it might be ; or do they endeavour to lengthen it by this little feminine trick, which tends to place the eyelids, which Nature has put too low, in a more suitable position?

The amplitude of their rich brocade garments leads us to think that at Kioto feminine luxury is measured by the quantity of silk that a Court lady can trail after her. But what can be the meaning of those two long tails which are seen on the right and left below the undulating drapery of the mantle? When the lady is walking, they obey each cadenced movement of her two little invisible feet ; and, looked at from a distance, she seems to be wearing, not a robe, but a pair of long trailing trousers, which oblige her to advance on her knees. Such is in fact the effect which this costume is intended to produce. The ladies of the Court who are admitted to the presence of the Mikado are bound to appear as if they were approaching his Sacred Majesty on their knees.

No noise is ever heard in the interior of the palace except the rustling of silk on the rich carpets with which the mats are covered. Bamboo blinds intercept the light of day. Screens covered with marvellous paintings, damask draperies, velvet hangings, ornamented with knots of plaited silk in which artificial birds are framed, form the panels and the *portières* of the reception rooms. No article of furniture of any kind interferes with the elegant simplicity: in the corners there is, here, an aquarium of porcelain, with shrubs and natural flowers; there, a cabinet encrusted with mother-of-pearl, or an elegant table laden with numerous poetical anthologies of the old Empire, printed upon leaves of gold. The scent of the precious wood, the fine mats, and rich stuffs, mixes with the pure air which comes in on all sides from the open partitions. The young girls on duty in the palace bring tea from Oudsji and sweatmeats from the refectory of the Empress. This personage, called the Kisaki, who proudly rules over twelve other legitimate wives of the Mikado and a crowd of his concubines, squats in proud isolation on the top step of the vast dais which rises above the whole. The ladies of honour and the women in waiting squat or kneel behind her at a respectful distance, composing groups which have the effect of beds of flowers, because each group, according to its hierarchical position, has its especial costume and its colours.

The folds of the garments of the Empress are arranged with such art that they surround her like a dazzling cloud of gauzy crape and brocade; and three vertical rays of gold surmount her diadem like the insignia of a queen of flowers.

The guests are ranged in concentric demi-circles in front of their sovereign. At a gesture from her hand the ladies-in-waiting on duty approach, and, prostrating themselves before her, receive her orders for the commencement of the anecdotical conversations or literary jousts, which form the diversions of her Court.

The Court of the Kisaki is the academy of the floral games of Japan. On the third of the third month, all the wits of the Daïri collect together in the gardens of the citadel, saki circulates, and challenges are exchanged between the gentlemen and the noble ladies, as to who shall find and paint, upon the classic fan of white cedar ornamented with ivy leaves, the most poetic stanzas in celebration of the revival of spring.

The Court of the Empress, however, admitted other amusements than these literary diversions. She had her chapel music, composed of stringed instruments, such as the violin with three strings; the Japanese mandoline, called the samsin; a sort of violon-cello, played without a bow, which is called a biwa; and the gotto, a ten-stringed instrument, measuring, when laid flat, two yards long,—the first was made in the year 300 from the remains of a pirogue belonging to the Mikado. Notwithstanding the difference in dimensions, the gotto reminds us of the Tyrolese zither. Theatrical representations were added to music. A corps of young comedians played little operas or executed character dances, some grave and methodical, in which a long tailed mantle was worn; others lively and playful, full of fancy, and varied with disguises, the dancers coming out occasionally with the wings of birds or butterflies. In addition to this, the ladies of the Daïri had their private boxes, not only at the imperial theatre, but at the circus of the wrestlers and boxers attached to the Court of the Mikado in virtue of privileges dating from the year 24 B.C. They were also permitted to witness cock-fighting in the verandahs of their country-houses, in strict privacy. A certain class of the officers of the Empress's service were especially

detailed to arrange these barbarous and ridiculous representations. They wore helmets
and padded trousers, in which they looked like balls.

The manners and customs of the Court of Kioto are still kept up in our time, with
this exception, that they no longer exhibit the least vestige of artistic or literary
life. They are mechanically preserved in so far as the resources of the treasury permit;
and are the last traces of the civilization of the old Empire. They are concentrated
upon one single point in Japan, where they remain motionless as the old tombs

A YEMA.

themselves. Meanwhile, modern life has invaded the cities and the country all around
the antique miako. The Taïkoun has developed civil and military institutions in
his modern monarchy, and already the smoke of the steamers before the ports of the
Inland Sea announce the approach of the Christian civilization of the West.

These circumstances lend a tragic interest to the actual situation of the ancient
hereditary and theocratic Emperor of Japan, that invisible Mikado of whom one is
not permitted to speak even while describing his Court. But he also must come out
of the mysterious darkness which surrounds him. The force of events will bring him
to light upon the scene of contemporaneous history.

DISTRIBUTION OF MONEY TO THE PEOPLE BY ORDER OF THE SIOGOUN.

CHAPTER V.

THE DECADENCE OF THE MIKADOS.

A CHAPTER IN THE ANCIENT HISTORY OF JAPAN.—ITS DELINEATION BY PICTURES.—THE
SAPPING OF THE IMPERIAL POWER,—THE BEGINNING OF THE END.

MORE than two hundred years ago, under the third Siogoun of the dynasty of Iyéyas,
the successful usurper of the civil and military power of the Mikados, the peace of
the Empire being secure, and the dominion of the Siogoun uncontested, it happened

that the latter made a visit of courtesy to his lord and master, the dispossessed Emperor. This strange event produced a profound sensation; the native artists applied themselves to reproducing the most interesting scenes of the voyage of the Siogoun and of his interview with the Mikado. The zeal with which they endeavoured to satisfy the curiosity of their contemporaries has bequeathed to us documents that throw light upon an entire epoch of the history of Japan, which has been recently presented in a very contradictory fashion. It was a period of absolute calm, without any internal disturbances, without remarkable external facts; and the interest which it presents is entirely concentrated on the relative position and the personal relations of the two sovereigns. The Dutch inhabitants of the settlement of Decima, who were the only witnesses of this state of things, have described it in terms which, however objectionable in certain respects, are admirably adapted to give us the key to the situation—so admirably adapted, in fact, that it is difficult to replace or correct them. They designate the Mikado as Spiritual Emperor, and Kioto as the sacred city, or, the Rome of Japan. They give to the Siogoun the title of Temporal Emperor, and to his residence, Yeddo, the surname of the political capital of the Empire; but, in order to avoid all disputes about words on a subject which has now become ancient history, I shall set aside the Dutch narratives, and in all the details I am about to give, I will be guided by the pencils of the Japanese themselves.

The Mikado occupied the supreme rank in the hierarchical order of the Empire.

The Siogoun was, properly speaking, the first General of the Mikado, and his lieutenant in the administration of public affairs.

Though the Siogoun had abused his position so far as to seize upon the civil and military power, the Mikado, on his side, preserved the advantage of birth as well as the prestige of his sacred character. The descendant of the sun, he carried on the tradition of the Gods, of the demigods, the heroes and hereditary sovereigns, who had reigned over Japan in an uninterrupted succession since the creation of the Empire of the eight great islands.

As the august head of religion, under whatever form it was presented to the people, he officiated as chief pontiff of the ancient national worship of the Kamis. At the summer solstice, he sacrificed to the Earth: at the winter solstice, he sacrificed to Heaven. A god was expressly delegated to take charge of his fate; in the bosom of the Temple built to him on the summit of Mount Kamo, this god watched day and night over the Daïri.

On the death of the Mikados, their names were inscribed in the Temples of their ancestors. They were also simultaneously inscribed at Kioto, in the Temple of Hatchiman, and at Isyé, in the Temple of the Sun itself.

As theocratic Emperor and hereditary sovereign, the Mikado held the power which devolved upon him direct from Heaven.

But it became more and more difficult for him to find an opportunity of exercising it, and also, from time to time, it seemed to him good and necessary to give signs of existence by bestowing pompous titles, which were purely honorary, on some of the old feudal nobles who had deserved well of the Altar. Sometimes he allowed himself the satisfaction of protesting against the acts of his temporal lieutenant, when they were calculated to injure his own prerogatives. Thus, in our own time, the Mikado set his veto upon the treaties concluded between the Taïkoun and certain of the Western nations. Subsequently he sanctioned them, when the allied squadrons presented themselves before the walls of Osaka—a recognition of his supremacy on their part.

The Taïkoun has never been, in the eyes of the Court of Kioto, anything more than the fortunate heir of a vulgar usurper. His ancestors, the Siogouns, were the servants of the Mikado, who had despoiled their master of his army, his navy, his lands, and his treasure, under pretence of relieving him from all earthly anxiety, and the Mikado had lent himself too easily to their designs. They gave him a chariot with two wheels, drawn by a bullock, for his daily excursions in the parks of the citadel ; a considerable privilege, no doubt, in a country where nobody uses a carriage ; but he ought not, therefore, to have relinquished the manly exercises of archery, of falconry, and his brilliant hunting parties in pursuit of deer and wild boar. He acted under the inspiration of an unwise policy which gradually withdrew him from the sight of his subjects ; though, some time after that, they made him take share in a great festival of the Daïri, by exhibiting him on a platform, in a motionless attitude, for the mute adoration of the prostrate Court. But, by degrees, the Mikado ceased to communicate with the external world, except through the medium of the women charged with the care of his person. They dressed him, and fed him, attiring him every day in a new costume, and serving his meals in vessels which each day

N 2

came fresh from the hands of the maker, who had a monopoly of their manufacture. The feet of the sacred personage never touched the ground; his face was never seen by daylight, or by profane eyes; in a word, the Mikado was never subjected to contact with the elements, or to exposure to the light of the sun or moon, to the touch of earth, of men, or of his own hands.

The famous interview took place at Kioto, the holy city, which the Mikado was not permitted to leave. He possessed no other property there, except his palace and the ancient temples of his family. The city was under the rule of the Siogoun, but the latter devoted its revenues to the spiritual sovereign, and maintained a permanent garrison there for the protection of the pontifical throne.

All the preliminaries being arranged on both sides, a proclamation announced the day when the Minamoto Yemitz would leave his capital, the immense and populous city of Yeddo—then a completely modern town, the centre of the political and civil administration of the Empire, the seat of the Naval and Military Colleges, of the College of Interpreters, and of the Academy of Medicine and Philosophy.

He was preceded by a guard of picked troops, who went by land to Kioto, travelling along the imperial high road called the Tokaïdo, and he had ordered his war fleet to sail for the Inland Sea. He himself, the temporal sovereign, embarked on board his great war-junk; and the squadron, leaving the bay of Yeddo, doubled Cape Sagami and the promontory of Idsou, passed through the Straits of Linschoten, and, coasting along the western side of the island of Awadsi, anchored in the harbour of Hiogo, where the Siogoun landed in the midst of the nobility of the seaboard provinces, who knelt to receive him on the beach, which was covered with the richest carpets.

The Siogoun's state entry into Kioto took place later, without any other military demonstration than the parade of his own army, because the Mikado had neither troops nor guns at his disposal, but simply a guard of archers, recruited from families related to himself, or which belonged to the old feudal nobility. It was with difficulty that he provided even for this expense and for the ordinary maintenance of his Court; and he found himself obliged to accept with one hand an annuity which the Siogoun condescended to pay him, and with the other the proceeds of collections made by begging monks of certain monastic orders, who make annual progresses from village to village, even into the most distant provinces of the Empire. Only the heroic disinterestedness of the greater number of his high dignitaries enabled him to sustain his rank; several of them served him without any other remuneration than the gratuitous use of the rich costumes furnished by the old imperial wardrobe.

These circumstances did not deter the Mikado from hastening the day of the interview, when his splendid rival should be invited to witness the grand procession of the Daïri. Attended by his archers, his household, his Court, and all his pontifical suite, he left the palace by the southern gate, which, towards the close of the ninth century, was decorated with historical compositions by the celebrated painter and poet Kosé Kanaoka. He went along the principal streets, to the suburbs on the bank of the Yodo-gawa, and returned towards the citadel, passing through the chief part of the city.

The ancient insignia of his supreme power were carried in great pomp at the head of the procession: the mirror of Izanami, his ancestress, the charming goddess who gave birth to the Sun in the island of Awadsi; the glorious standards whose long paper pennons had waved over the troops of Zinmou the conqueror; the glittering blade of the hero of Yamato, who slew the eight-headed hydra to which virgins of princely blood were sacrificed; the seal which was set to the primitive laws of the Empire; the cedar-wood fan, lath-shaped, used as a sceptre, which, for more than two thousand years, has passed from the hands of each deceased Mikado into those of his successor.

A second display, intended, no doubt, to enhance the effect of the first, was that of the heraldic banners of all the ancient noble families of the Empire who were directly related to the Daïri. Probably the manifestation was to remind the Siogoun that he was only a parvenu in the eyes of the old territorial nobility; but the parvenu could console himself with the reflection that all the Japanese lords, the great as well as the small Daïmios, were none the less obliged to pass six months in each year at his Court of Yeddo, and to do homage to him in the midst of nobles of his creation. The most numerous and picturesque section of the procession consisted of the representatives of all the sects who recognize the spiritual supremacy of the Mikado. The dignitaries of the ancient Kami worship were hardly to be distinguished by their costume from the great officers of the palace; a costume which reminds us that there was no priesthood in the ancient religious system of Japan. Buddhism, on the contrary, which came from China, and spread rapidly throughout the Empire, was represented by an infinite variety of sects, rites, orders, and fraternities. The Buddhist bonzes and monks formed endless files of grave personages with tonsured or completely shaven heads, some bare, some covered with extraordinary caps, mitres, or broad-brimmed hats. A few carried a crozier in the right hand; some, a rosary; others, fly-brushes, sea-shells, or a holy-water brush with paper

ACTORS AND DANCERS AT THE COURT OF THE MIKADO.

streamers. Soutanes, surplices, cloaks of every shape and colour, composed their accoutrement.

They were followed by the household of the Mikado. The pontifical body-guard surpassed all in the elegance of their costume. They left halberts and shirts of mail to the Siogoun's men-at-arms, and each wore a lacquered cap ornamented with an open fan upon each side, and a rich silken pourpoint edged with pink festoons of the same material. Their feet were hidden in the voluminous folds of their trousers, and a large sword, a bow, and a quiver full of arrows, completed their equipment. Some of them, mounted on horseback, flourished a long switch fastened to the wrist by a cord of silk, with large tufts. Under all this external grandeur there lurked great brutality. The turbulence and dissoluteness of the young cavaliers of the sacerdotal Court of Japan have furnished history with pages which recall the time of Cæsar Borgia. Conrad Kramer, the envoy from the Dutch India Company to the Court of Kioto, was admitted to the honour of witnessing the august interview between the two sovereigns. He declares that on the day following this solemnity, the corpses of many women, young girls, and children, victims of nocturnal violence, were picked up in the streets. A still larger number of married women and young girls, from Osaka, Sakai, and other towns in the neighbourhood, who had accompanied their husbands or their parents to Kioto, disappeared in the tumult of the crowded streets, and were not recovered until after a week or a fortnight; and justice on their ravishers was never obtained by their families.

Polygamy exists in Japan as the right of the Mikado only ; or rather it possesses in his case the character of a legal institution. It is not surprising that he should make a great display of the privilege which has cost him so dear ; for this right of polygamy was the flower-bordered gulf which was dug for the successors of Zinmon by the first usurpers of the imperial power. Surely a perfidious smile must have crossed the face of Siogoun when the carriages of the Daïri drew near.

These heavy vehicles, built of precious woods, and varnished in different colours, were each drawn by four black buffaloes, led by pages in white attire. They contained the Empress, and the other twelve legitimate wives of the Mikado, with whom the Empress could not with propriety have refused to share her privilege of using this special kind of conveyance. The favourite concubines of the Mikado, and fifty ladies-in-waiting to the Empress followed, in norimons, or covered palanquins.

Whenever the Mikado came out of the citadel, it was always in his pontifical norimon, a palanquin fastened to long poles, which, carried by fifty bearers in white livery, towered above the crowd. It is constructed in the form of the Mikosis, or reliquaries in which the sacred relics of the Kamis are exhibited ; and it resembles a garden pavilion with a cupola decorated with a fringe of bells. The cupola is surmounted by a ball, on which stands a cock, with outstretched wings and spread tail ; perhaps there exists some symbolical connection between this emblem and the mythological bird known in China and Japan under the name of Foo.

The portable pavilion of the Daïri was built of white wood, and its decoration was all of pure gold. It was so hermetically closed, that it was difficult to believe it could be occupied. The proof that it really did fulfil the lofty purpose assigned to it, is that the women attached to the domestic service of the Mikado walked beside the doors on either side. They only had the privilege of surrounding his sacred person. The Mikado was invisible, mute, unapproachable, for his Court as well as for his people; and this attribute was maintained inviolate, even in his interview with the Siogoun.

Among the buildings in the citadel which gives to Kioto the rank of residence (Miako), there is one which might be called the Temple of the Pontifical Audiences, for it is built in the style of architecture proper to the edifices of the Kami worship, and it bears, like them, the name of Mia. It is attached to the main body of the Mikado's dwelling, in a vast paved court planted with trees, through which the processions defile on occasions of great solemnity.

In this reserved space a detachment of orderly officers and body-guards of the Siogoun took up their position. Then came several groups of dignitaries of the Mikado's suite, escorted by some archers from the Daïri.

The women retired to their apartments. Deputations of bonzes and monastic orders occupied the spaces within the enclosing walls. Soldiers belonging to the garrison of Kioto lined the two sides of the avenue leading to the wide steps of the façade of the building. The courtiers of the Mikado, arrayed in mantles with long trains, majestically ascended the steps, and took their places to the right and left on the verandah, their faces turned towards the closed doors of the vast Throne-room. Before squatting down in their places, they lifted their trains and hung them over the balustrade of the verandah, so as to display the heraldic bearings embroidered upon them to the crowd. The entire length of the gallery was thus brilliantly decorated.

Meantime, from the left wing of the edifice came the sound of flutes, conch-shells, and the gongs of the pontifical chapel, announcing that the Mikado was making his solemn entry into the sanctuary. Profound silence reigned amid the crowd. An hour elapsed in pious expectation before the preparations for the reception were concluded; then, a flourish of trumpets announced the arrival of the Siogoun. He advanced into the arena, on foot, and unescorted; his first minister, the commandants of the army and the fleet, and certain members of the Council of the Court of Yeddo, walked behind him, at a respectful distance. He paused for a moment at the foot of the grand staircase, and immediately the doors of the Temple were slightly opened, and little by little slipped back into their grooves. The Siogoun ascended the steps, and then the spectacle, for which the multitude was silently waiting, was displayed before their eyes.

A DAIMIO IN COURT-DRESS.

A great blind of bamboo-bark, painted green, which hung from the ceiling of the hall, was let down to within two or three feet of the threshold. Through this narrow space a pile of mats and carpet, over which were spread the wide folds of a voluminous white robe, could be discerned.

In this consisted the apparition of the Mikado on his throne. From the other side of the blind he could see everything without being seen, and, as far as his sight could

u

reach, he beheld nothing but heads, prostrate before his invisible Majesty. One head alone lifted itself above the temple stair, but that head wore a high cap of gold, the royal insignia of the temporal chief of the Empire. And even he, that powerful sovereign whose might knew no resistance, when he had reached the last step down, bent and slowly fell upon his knees. Then he stretched his arms out towards the threshold of the Throne-room, and touched the ground with his brow.

From that moment, the ceremony of the interview was accomplished, the end of the solemnity was attained; the Siogoun had ostensibly prostrated himself at the feet of the Mikado.

But, it may be asked, how were the interests of Minamoto Yemitz served by his thus humbling himself in the Temple of the Daïri? Was not this step compromising to that authority which he owed solely to the military and political success of his ancestors?

On the contrary, it appears to me that in this matter the worthy grandson of the astute Iyéyas did exactly the best thing for the consolidation of the still insecure basis of his government. The consequence of the interview of Kioto was the establishment of two facts, one of which might be regarded as a pure formality, but the other had all the weight of the consecration hitherto wanting to the dynasty of the Siogouns. By the first, the act of genuflexion, the temporal sovereign testified that he continued to be, traditionally, the obedient son of the great pontiff of the national religion; but by the second, that is to say, the acceptation of that homage by the Mikado, the theocratic Emperor formally recognized the representative of a dynasty which had been founded alongside of the only legitimate one, and even in opposition to the will of the Daïri. Apparently the two powers merely exchanged courtesies; in reality, the temporal prince did not alienate a particle of his usurped power; while the Mikado publicly abdicated every ulterior pretension to the resumption of secular government.

Such a result was well worth attaining by the Siogoun, at the cost of a political genuflexion.

The great day had a final touch of meaning. Minamoto Yemitz convoked the populace of Kioto to the courtyard of his own citadel. In Japan, as elsewhere, he who pays, rules. The crowd, formed into lines by the troops, knelt down in perfect order. The Siogoun commanded his treasurer to open coffers filled with packets of money, in the presence of the people, and to empty the contents into trays which were placed on the verandah. When all was ready, several officers, each carrying one of these trays, went through the ranks of the people, inviting everyone to help himself, and taking care that no individual was excluded from the largesse of the temporal sovereign.

A POETESS OF KIOTO.

BOOK III

KAMAKOURA

IN THE OFFING.

CHAPTER I.

THE RESIDENCES OF THE SIOGOUNS.

THE RUINS.—THE SIOGOUNS,—YORITOMO,—HIS REFORMS. — A STANDING ARMY.—THE COURT OF KIOTO AND THE SECONDARY SOVEREIGN.

THE environs of Kamakoura are those of a great city; but the great city itself exists no longer. Rich vegetation covers the inequalities of the soil which has evidently accumulated over ruins, overthrown walls, and canals now filled up.

Antique avenues of trees stretch beyond waste groves overgrown with brambles. These avenues formerly led to palaces, of which there is now no trace. In Japan, even palaces, being for the most part built of wood, leave no ruins after their fall.

At Kamakoura the Siogouns had established their residence. Under the name of Siogouns we recall the generals-in-chief, temporal lieutenants of the theocratic Emperor. They governed Japan, under the supremacy of the Mikado, from the end of the twelfth century to the commencement of the seventeenth, from Minamoto Yoritomo, who was the founder of their power, to Iyéyas, surnamed Gonghensama, the thirty-second

THE SIOGOUN AND HIS ESCORT.

Siogoun, who made Yeddo the political capital of Japan, and created a new dynasty, whose last representatives adopted the title of Taïkoun A.D. 1854.

Yoritomo, born of a princely family, was indebted to his education by an ambitious mother for the qualities which made him the ruler and real chief of the Empire. He was brought up at the Court of Kioto, and early appreciated the condition of weakness into which the power of the Daïri had fallen. The Mikado, shut up in his seraglio, occupied himself with nothing but palace intrigues. The courtiers were given up to idleness, or plunged in dissipation. The old families, who were brought into communication with the Emperor either by kinship, alliance, or official rank, thought only of serving the interests of themselves and their children at court. They endeavoured to procure high dignities for their eldest sons, and put the younger into holy orders. As for the girls, rather than send them into convents, they applied for their admission into the ranks of the Empress's fifty ladies of honour, who were all obliged to take vows of chastity. The ambition of the matrons of high degree was perfectly satisfied

AN INVESTITURE.

by the puerile ceremonies which accompanied the birth of the heir-presumptive, and the nomination of its nurse, who was chosen among the eighty ladies of the old feudal nobility best qualified to fulfil this eminent function.

While things were going on thus at Kioto, the Daimios, who lived in retirement in their provinces, became by degrees less and less faithful in the maintenance of the obligations which they had contracted with the Crown. Some arrogated to themselves absolute power in the government of their imperial fiefs; others aggrandized their domains at the expense of their neighbours. Family wars, acts of vengeance and reprisal, stained

A FISHERMAN AND AN EGRET.

the rustic fortresses of the principal dynasties of Japan with blood for many years; anarchy was gaining ground by degrees. Yoritomo, whose family had suffered much from these troubles, obtained a superior command from the Mikado after several vicissitudes, and was invested with extensive power that he might establish order in the Empire. At this epoch the Mikado, as well as the armour-bearing nobles, had no other troops than the territorial militia. At the close of an expedition the men returned to their homes. Yoritomo created a standing army, perfected the art of encampments, utilized them to discipline his soldiers, and neglected nothing to make them discard the habits of domestic life. It is to him, for example, that Japan owes the official organization of the most shameful of occupations, which has been, ever since his time, a social institution regulated by the Government.

Yoritomo succeeded in his designs. He subjugated the Daimios, who had attempted to render themselves independent, and forced them to take an oath of fidelity and homage to him in his quality of lieutenant of the Mikado. Some of them refusing to recognize him under this title, he exterminated them, with their entire families, and confiscated the whole of their property. More than once, when exasperated by the unexpected resistance, he inflicted the most cruel tortures on his enemies.

On the other hand, he incessantly carried on intrigues, by means of agents, in the Daïri. He had commenced his career under the seventy-sixth Mikado—he finished it under the eighty-third. Each emperor who opposed him had been obliged to abdicate: one of them took the tonsure and retired into a cloister.

It was only under the eighty-second Mikado that Yoritomo was officially invested with the title of Siogoun. He had exercised his functions during twenty years. His son succeeded him.

There were thenceforth two distinct Courts in the Empire of Japan; that of the Mikado at Kioto, and that of the Siogoun at Kamakoura.

In the beginning, the new power was not hereditary. It happened sometimes that the sons of the Mikados were invested with it. Far from taking umbrage at what was taking place at Kamakoura, the sacerdotal and literary court of Kioto found a subject of jest in it; now amusing themselves with the airs of the wife of the Siogoun, the bad taste which the Secondary Courts showed in dress, the trivial performances of the actor; the awkwardness of the dancers; and again laughing at the gaudiness of the military uniforms, which Yoritomo had brought into fashion, or at the vulgarity of speech and manners of those new-blown grandees who gave themselves airs as restorers of the pontifical throne and saviours of the Empire.

An unforeseen circumstance arose which gave sudden importance to the Court of Kamakoura, and concentrated upon it the attention and sympathy of the nation.

In the twelfth month of the year 1268, a Mongol embassy landed at Japan. It came in the name of Koublaï-Khan who, worthy descendant of the Tartar conquerors, was destined twelve years later to take possession of China; he fixed his residence at

GYMNASTS AT KIOTO.

Pekin and founded the Yuen dynasty, under which the great canal was constructed. This is the same sovereign who kept at his Court the Venetian Marco Polo, the first traveller who furnished Europe with exact notions respecting China and Japan. His narratives, it is said, exercised so decided an influence upon Christopher Columbus, that the discovery of America is in a sense due to them.

Koublaï-Khan wrote to the Emperor of Niphon :—

"I am the head of a state formerly without importance. Now the cities and countries which recognize my power are numberless. I am endeavouring to establish good relations with the princes my neighbours. I have put an end to the hostilities of which the land of Kaoli was the scene. The chief of that little

A WRESTLING CIRCUS.

kingdom has presented himself at my Court to declare his gratitude. I have treated him as a father treats his child. I will not act otherwise towards the princes of Niphon. No embassy has, as yet, come from your Court to confer with me. I fear that in your country the true state of things is unknown. I therefore send you this letter by delegates, who will inform you of my intentions. The wise man has said that the world should consist only of one family. But if amicable relations be not kept up, how shall that principle be realized? For my part, I have

A CASHIER.

decided upon pursuing its execution, even should I be obliged to resort to arms. Now, it is the duty of the sovereign of Niphon to consider what it will suit him to do."

The Mikado announced his intention of replying favourably to the overtures of Koublaï-Khan.

The Siogoun, on the contrary, declared himself hostile to an alliance with the hordes of the Mongols. He convoked an assembly of the Daimios at Kamakoura, submitted his objections to them, and enrolled them on his side.

The embassy was dismissed with evasive words.

GALLERY IN AN INN.

In the following year the Mongol chief vainly proposed that a meeting of the delegates of the two Empires should take place on the island of Tsousima, in the Straits of Corea. In 1271 a new missive on his part remained unanswered. In 1273 he sent two ambassadors to Kamakoura, and the Siogoun had them sent back.

A short time afterwards he was informed that two generals of Koublaï-Khan were about to attack Japan at the head of an expedition of three hundred large war-junks, three hundred swift sailing-ships, and three hundred transport-barks. The Mikado ordered public prayers and processions to the principal temples of the Kamis. The Siogoun organized the national defence. At every point on the coasts of Isousima and Kiousiou where the Mongols attempted to effect a descent, they were repulsed and beaten.

A WINE-MERCHANT'S SHOP.

Their Khan endeavoured vainly to renew the negotiations. Two ambassadors whom he sent to the Siogoun in 1275, were immediately turned out. The third, having presented himself in 1279, was beheaded.

Then, if we are to believe the annals of Japan, that country was menaced by the most formidable expedition which had ever sailed upon the seas of the far East. The Mongol fleet numbered four thousand sail, and carried an army of two hundred and forty thousand men. It was descending upon Firado towards the entrance of the inland sea when it was dispersed by a typhoon and dashed upon the coast. All who did not perish in the waves fell under the swords of the Japanese, who spared only three prisoners, whom they sent back to the other side of the strait to carry the news.

After the occurrence of these events, it was no longer possible to regard the Siogouns as simple functionaries of the Crown, or even as the official protectors of the Mikado. The entire nation owed its safety to them. From that moment the Court

A STREET SCENE ON NEW YEAR'S DAY.

of Kioto had a rival in that of Kamakoura, which must speedily eclipse it and supplant it in the management of the affairs of the Empire.

At the present time we find at Kamakoura the Pantheon of the glories of Japan. It is composed of a majestic collection of sacred buildings which have always been spared by the fury of civil war. They are placed under the invocation of Hatchiman, one of the great national Kamis. Hatchiman belongs to the heroic period of the Empire of the Mikados. His mother was the Empress Zingou, who effected the conquest of the three kingdoms of Corea, and to whom Divine honours are rendered. Each year, on the ninth day of the ninth month, a solemn procession to the tomb which is consecrated to her at Fousimi, in the country of Yamasiro, commemorates her glorious deeds. Zingou herself surnamed her son Fatsman, "the eight banners," in consequence of a sign which appeared in the heavens at the birth of the child. Thanks to the education which she gave him, she made him the bravest of her soldiers and the most skilful of her generals. When she had attained the age of one hundred years she transmitted the sceptre and crown of the Mikados to her son, in the year 270 of our era. He was then seventy-one years old. Under the name of Woozin he reigned gloriously for forty-three years, and was raised, after

A STAGE NOBLE.

his death, to the rank of a protecting genius of the Empire. He is especially revered as the patron of soldiers. In the annual *fêtes* dedicated to him, Japan celebrates the memory of the heroes who have died for their country. The popular processions which take place on this occasion revive the ancient pomps of Kami worship. Even the horses formerly destined for sacrifice are among the cortége; but instead of being immolated, they are turned loose on the race-course.

Most of the great cities of Japan possess a Temple of Hatchiman. That of Kamakoura is distinguished above all the others by the trophies which it contains. Two vast buildings are required for the display of this national wealth. There, it is said, are preserved the spoils of the Corean and the Mongol invasions, also objects taken from the Portuguese Colonies and the Christian communities of Japan at the epoch when the Portuguese were expelled, and the Japanese Christians were exterminated by order of the Siogouns.

No European has ever yet been permitted to view the trophies of Kamakoura.

While all European states like to display the treasures which they have respectively seized or won in their frontier and dynastic wars, Japan hides all monuments of its military glory from foreigners. They are kept in reserve, like a family treasure, in venerable sanctuaries, to which no profane feet ever find access.

On approaching the Temple of Hatchiman we perceived that our arrival had been announced, and that the bonzes were closing the shutters of their treasure-house.

THE CENTRAL TEMPLE FROM THE TERRACE.

CHAPTER II.

THE TEMPLES OF KAMAKOURA.

THE AVENUES.—THE CHAPELS.—THE TORIS.—THE PAGODA.—IDOLS.—BONZES.—THE
DAÏBOUDHS.

Tʜᴇ Temples of Hatchiman are approached by long lines of those great cedar-trees which form the avenues to all places of worship in Japan. As we advance along the avenue on the Kanasawa side, chapels multiply themselves along the road, and to the left, upon the sacred hills, we also come in sight of the oratories and commemorative

stones which mark the stations of the processions; on the right the horizon is closed
by the mountain, with its grottos, its streams, and its pine groves. After we have
crossed the river by a fine wooden bridge, we find ourselves suddenly at the
entrance of another alley, which leads from the sea-side, and occupies a large street.
This is the principal avenue, intersected by three gigantic toris, and it opens on the

A KAMI TEMPLE.

grand square in front of the chief staircase of the main buildings of the Temple.
The precinct of the sacred place extends into the street, and is surrounded on
three sides by a low wall of solid masonry, surmounted by a barrier of wood painted
red and black. Two steps lead to the first level. There is nothing to be seen there
but the houses of the bonzes, arranged like the side-scenes of a theatre, amid trees
planted along the barrier-wall, with two great oval ponds occupying the centre

of the square. They are connected with each other by a large canal crossed by two parallel bridges, each equally remarkable in its way. That on the right is of white granite, and it describes an almost perfect semicircle, so that when one sees it for the first time one supposes that it is intended for some sort of geometrical exercise; but I suppose that it is in reality a bridge of honour, reserved for the gods and the good genii who come to visit the Temple. The bridge on the left is quite flat, constructed of wood covered with red lacquer, with balusters and other ornaments in old polished copper. The pond crossed by the stone bridge is covered with magnificent white lotus flowers,—the pond crossed by the wooden bridge with red lotus flowers. Among the leaves of the flowers we saw numbers of fish, some red and others like mother of pearl, with glittering fins, swimming about in water of crystal clearness. The black tortoise glides among the great water-plants and clings to their stems.

After having thoroughly enjoyed this most attractive spectacle, we go on towards the second enclosure. It is raised a few steps higher than the first, and, as it is protected by an additional sanctity, it is only to be approached through the gate of the divine guardians of the sanctuary. This building, which stands opposite the bridges, contains two monstrous idols, placed side by side in the centre of the edifice. They are sculptured in wood, and are covered from head to foot with a thick coating of vermilion. Their grinning faces and their enormous busts are spotted all over with innumerable pieces of chewed paper, which the native visitors throw at them when passing, without any more formality than would be used by a number of schoolboys out for a holiday. Nevertheless, it is considered a very serious act on the part of the pilgrims. It is the means by which they make the prayer written on the sheet of chewed paper reach its address, and when they wish to recommend anything to the gods very strongly indeed, they bring as an offering a pair of straw slippers plaited with regard to the size of the feet of the Colossus, and hang them on the iron railings within which the statues are enclosed. Articles of this kind, suspended by thousands to the bars, remain there until they fall away in time, and it may be supposed that this curious ornamentation is anything but beautiful. Here a lay brother of the bonzes approached us, and his interested views were easily enough detected by his bearing. We hastened to assure him that we required nothing from his good offices, except access to an enclosed building. With a shake of his head, so as to make us understand that we were asking for an impossibility, he simply set himself to follow us

THE PAGODA OF HATCHIMAN.

terrace, reached by a long stone staircase, surmounted the second enclosure. It is sustained by a Cyclopean wall, and in its turn supports the principal Temple as well as the habitations of the bonzes. The grey roofs of all these different buildings stand out against the sombre forest of cedars and pines. On our left are the buildings of the Treasury; one of them has a pyramidal roof surmounted by a turret of bronze most elegantly worked. At the foot of the great terrace is the Chapel of the Ablutions. On our right stands a tall pagoda, constructed on the principle of the Chinese pagodas, but in a more sober and severe style. The first stage, of a quadrangular form, is supported by pillars; the second stage consists of a vast circular gallery which, though extremely massive, seems to rest simply upon a pivot. A painted roof, terminated by a tall spire of cast bronze, embellished with pendants of the same metal, completes the effect of this strange but exquisitely proportioned building.

All the doors of the buildings which I have enumerated are in good taste. The fine proportions, the rich brown colouring of the wood, which is almost the only material employed in their construction, is enhanced by a few touches of red and dragon green, and the effect of the whole is perfect;—add to the picture a frame of ancient trees and the extreme brilliancy of the sky, for the atmosphere of Japan is the most transparent in the world.

We went beyond the pagoda to visit a bell-tower, where we were shown a large bell beautifully engraved, and an oratory on each side containing three golden images, a large one in the centre, and two small ones' at either side. Each was surrounded by a nimbus. This beautiful Temple of Hatchiman is consecrated to a Kami; but it is quite evident that the religious customs of India have supplanted the ancient worship:—we had several proofs of this fact. When we were about to turn back we were solicited by the lay brother to go with him a little further. We complied, and he stopped us under a tree laden with *ex-votos*, at the foot of which stands a block of stone, surrounded by a barrier. This stone, which is probably indebted to the chisels of the bonzes for its peculiar form, is venerated by the multitude, and largely endowed with *ex-voto* offerings. Like the peoples of the extreme East the Japanese are very superstitious; a fact of which we had abundant evidence on this and other occasions.

The Temple towards which we directed our steps on leaving the avenue of the Temple of Hatchiman, immediately diverted our thoughts from the grandeur of this picture. It is admirably situated on the summit of a promontory, whence we overlook the whole Bay of Kamakoura; but it is always sad to come, in the midst of beautiful nature, upon a so-called holy place which inspires nothing but disgust. The principal sanctuary, at first sight, did not strike us as remarkable. Insignificant golden idols stand upon the high altar; and in a side chapel there is an image of the God of Wealth, armed with a miner's hammer. But when the bonzes who received us conducted us behind the high altar, and thence into a sort of cage as dark as a prison and as high as a tower, they lighted two lanterns, and stuck them at the end of a long pole. Then, by this glimmering light, which entirely failed to disperse the shades of the roof, we perceived that we were standing in front of an enormous idol of gilt wood, about twelve yards high, holding in its right hand a sceptre, in its left a lotus, and wearing a tiara composed of three rows of heads, representing the inferior divinities. This gigantic idol belongs to the religion of the auxiliary gods of the Buddhist mythology : the Amidas and the Quannons, intercessors who collect the prayers of men and transmit them to heaven. By means of similar religious conceptions, the bonzes strike a superstitious terror into the imaginations of their followers, and succeed in keeping them in a state of perpetual fear and folly.

We then went to see the Daïboudhs, which is the wonder of Kamakoura. This building is dedicated to the Daïboudhs, that is to say, to the great Buddha, and may be regarded as the most finished work of Japanese genius, from the double points of view of art and religious sentiment. The Temple of Hatchiman had already given us a remarkable example of the use which native art makes of nature in producing that impression of religious majesty which in our northern climates is effected by Gothic architecture. The Temple of Daïboudhs differs considerably from the first which we had seen. Instead of the great dimensions, instead of the illimitable space which seemed to stretch from portal to portal down to the sea, a solitary and mysterious retreat prepares the mind for some supernatural revelation. The road leads far away from every habitation ; in the direction of the mountain it winds about between hedges of tall shrubs. Finally, we see nothing before us but the high road, going up and up in the midst of foliage and flowers ; then it turns in a totally different direction, and all of a sudden, at the end of the alley, we perceive a gigantic brazen Divinity, squatting with joined hands, and the head slightly bent forward, in an attitude of contemplative ecstasy. The involuntary amazement produced by the aspect of this great image soon gives place to admiration. There is an irresistible charm in the attitude of the Daïboudhs, as well as in the harmony of its proportions. The noble simplicity of its garments and the calm purity of its features are in perfect accord with the sentiment of serenity inspired by its presence. A grove, consisting of some beautiful groups of trees, forms the enclosure of the sacred place, whose silence and solitude are never disturbed. The small cell of the attendant priest can hardly be discerned amongst the foliage. The altar, on which a little incense is burning at the feet of the Divinity, is composed of a small brass table ornamented by two lotus vases of the same metal, and beautifully wrought. The steps of the altar are composed of large slabs forming regular lines. The blue of the sky, the deep shadow of the statue, the sombre colour of the brass, the brilliancy of the flowers, the varied verdure of the hedges and the groves, fill this solemn retreat with the richest effect of light and colour. The idol of the Daïboudhs, with the platform which supports it, is twenty yards high; it is far from equal in elevation to the statue of St. Charles Borroméo, which may be seen from Arona on the borders of Lake Maggiore, but which affects the spectator no more than a trigonometrical signal-post. The interiors of these two colossal statues have been utilized. The European tourists seat themselves in the nose of the holy cardinal. The Japanese descend by a secret staircase into the foundations of their Daïboudhs, and there they find a peaceful oratory, whose altar is lighted by a ray of sunshine admitted through an opening in the folds of the mantle at the back of the idol's neck. It would be idle to discuss to what extent the Buddha of Kamakoura resembles the Buddha of history, but it is important to remark that he is conformable to the Buddha of tradition.

The Buddhists have made one authentic and sacramental image of the founder of their religion, covered with characters carefully numbered, with thirty-two principal signs, and eighty secondary marks, so that it may be transmitted to future ages in all its integrity. The Japanese idol conforms in all essential respects to this established type of the great Hindoo reformer. It scrupulously reproduces the *pose*, the meditative attitudes; thus it was that the sage joined his hands, the fingers straightened, and thumb resting against thumb; thus he squatted, the legs bent and gathered up one over the other, the right foot lying upon the left knee. The broad, smooth brow is also to be recognized, and the hair forming a multitude of short curls. Even the singular protuberance of the skull, which slightly disfigures the top of the head, exists in the statue, and also a tuft of white hairs between the eyebrows, indicated by a little rounded excrescence in the metal.

All these marks, however, do not constitute the physiognomy, the expression of the personage. In this respect the Daïboudhs of Kamakoura has nothing in common with the fantastic dolls which are worshipped in China under the name of Buddhas, and the fact appears worthy of notice, because Buddhism was introduced into Japan from China.

The first effect of Buddhist preaching in Japan must have been to arouse curiosity among the islanders, who are as inquisitive and restless as the Hindoos are taciturn and contemplative.

What a vast field of exploration for minds which were only making their first voyage of discovery in the regions of metaphysics ! As they did not feel any impatience to plunge into Nirwâna, they were chiefly interested in finding out what was to come to pass between death and final extinction. With the assistance of the bonzes, a certain number of accepted ideas about the soul, death, and the life to come, were put in circulation in the towns and in the villages, without prejudice, it must be understood, to all that had been taught by ancestral wisdom concerning the ancient gods and the venerable national Kamis.

The soul of man, it was said, is like a floating vapour, indissoluble, having the form of a tiny worm, and a thin thread of blood which runs from the top of the head to the extremity of the tail. If it were closely observed it might be seen to escape from the house of death, at the moment when the dying person heaves his last sigh. At all times, the cracking of the panel may be heard as the soul passes through it. Whither does it go ? No one knows ; but it cannot fail to be received by the ministering servants of the great judge of hell. They bring it before his tribunal, and the judge causes it to kneel before a mirror, in which it beholds all the evil of which it has been guilty. This is a phenomenon which is occasionally produced upon the earth : a comedian in Yeddo, who had committed a murder, could not look into his mirror without his gaze being met by the livid face of his victim.

Souls, laden with crime, wander in one or other of the eighteen concentric circles of hell, according to the gravity of their offences.

Souls in process of purification sojourn in a purgatory whose lid they may lift up when they can do so without fear of falling, and resume the progressive course of their pilgrimage.

In the case of a woman who, being deserted, drowned herself with her child, she is popularly believed to present herself before all wayfarers by the side of the marsh, holding up the infant, in protest against her betrayers as the real author of her crime.

Finally, there are souls who return to the places which they have inhabited, or to the resting-place of their mortal remains.

Ghost stories, terrible tales, books illustrated by pictures representing hell or apparitions of demons, have multiplied in Japan with such profusion, that the popular imagination is completely possessed by them. The patron of literature of this kind,

THE APPARITION OF A DROWNED WOMAN.

according to the national mythology, is Tengou, the god of dreams, a burlesque winged genius, whose head-dress is an extinguisher with a golden handle. He leads the nocturnal revelry of all the objects, sacred or profane, which can fill the imagination of man. The refuge of death itself is not closed against him. The candelabra bend their heads, pierced with luminous holes, with a measured motion. The stone tortoises which bear the epitaphs move in a grim, orderly march, and grinning skeletons, clad in their shrouds, join the fantastic measure, waving about them the holy-water brush which drives away evil spirits.

In spite of some difference in style, and of its exceptional dimensions, the noble Japanese statue is the fellow of those of which great numbers are to be seen in the islands of Java and Ceylon ; those sacred refuges which were opened to Buddhism when it was expelled from India. There the type of the hero of Contemplation is preserved most religiously, and appears under its most exquisite form, in marvellous images of basalt, granite, and clay, generally above the human stature. This type, for the most part conventional, although perfectly authentic in the eyes of faith, is, especially for the Cingalese priests, who are devoted to the art of statuary, the unique subject of the indefatigable labour by which they strive to realize ideal perfection. They have in fact produced work of such purity as has hardly been surpassed by the Madonnas of Raphael.

Japan has inherited somewhat of the lofty tradition of the Buddhist Isles. Apostles from those distant shores have probably visited it. On the other hand, it has suffered to an extreme degree, and under the influence of its nearest neighbours, all the fatal consequences of the doctrine of the master himself, and especially the monstrous vagaries of his disciples. M. Martin Arzelier remarks in his *Chrétien Evangélique* (No. 10, eleventh year), that it would be an unprofitable task to undertake to trace the pure and abstract doctrine of the founder of the " Good Tao " in Japanese Buddhism. The Proteus of Greek fable, he adds, is not less intangible than the Good Tao in its metamorphoses among the various peoples of Asia and the Far East.

Every sort of modification and addition is justified beforehand by the following adage, which seems to have been the watchword of the missionaries of Buddhism : " Everything that agrees with good sense and circumstances agrees with truth, and ought to serve as a rule."

The Temples of Kamakoura furnish many examples in support of this observation.

A RESPECTABLE TEA HOUSE.

CHAPTER III.

BUDDHISM IN JAPAN.

INTRODUCTION OF BUDDHISM.—BUDDHIST SYMBOLISM.—THE INFANT BUDDHA.—FESTIVAL
OF HIS BIRTH AND BAPTISM.—THE DOCTRINE OF UNIVERSAL AND INEVITABLE
SUFFERING.—NIRWÂNA.—THE GENERAL INFLUENCE OF BUDDHIST PHILOSOPHY ON
JAPANESE LIFE.—THE LITERATURE OF BUDDHISM.—JAPANESE WRITING.

THE introduction of Buddhism into Japan dates from the year 552 of our era.
At that epoch, Kin-Mei, the thirteenth Mikado, received from King Petsi at Corea,
a statue of Sâkyamouni, together with books, banners, a baldaquin, and other objects
used in the worship of Buddha. With these presents came a letter to the following effect.

" Behold the best of all doctrines ;—coming from distant India, it reveals to us what was a mystery to Confucius himself, and transports us into a final condition whose felicity cannot be surpassed. The King of Petsi communicated it to the Empire of the Mikado so that it may be spread about, and that thus may be accomplished that which is written in the books of Buddha, ' My doctrine shall extend itself towards the East.' " The Mikado immediately consulted his ministers upon the reception which was due to the statue of the great Kami of India. All the nations of the West replied, " Inamé venerate the Buddha, why should Niphon turn its back upon him !"

But, objected Wasoki, " If we render homage to the stranger Kami, is it not to be feared that we shall irritate the national Kamis ?" Thereon the Mikado pronounced authoritatively this conciliatory sentence : " It is just and equitable to accord to man that which his heart desires ; let Inamé revere the image." Inamé accordingly carried away the image, and constructed a chapel for it. Nevertheless, an epidemic having broken out, it was attributed to the new worship, the chapel was burnt and the statue thrown into the river. The family of Inamé remained none the less secretly attached to the strange doctrine. In the reign of Bidas, successor to Kin-Mei, the minister Sogano, son of Inamé, presented to the Mikado a bonze who had come from Siura in Corea. The holy man, warned of the difficulties which must attend the introduction of Buddhism into a country where the national religion united the people and the sovereign so closely, conceived a means of procuring the favour of the Mikado. As soon as he saw the Mikado's grandson at the Court—a little boy of six years old, in whose birth there had been something extraordinary—he prostrated himself at the feet of the miraculous child and worshipped him, announcing that he recognized in him the incarnation of a disciple of Buddha, the new patron of the Empire, the future propagator of religious life. The Mikado allowed himself to be persuaded to dedicate this child to the priesthood and confided his education to the Corean bonze. The rest is easily divined. This boy became the initiator and the first High Priest of Buddhism in the Empire of Japan, where he is now revered under the name of Sjo-Tak-Daisō, the holy, hereditary, and virtuous Prince. Far from denying the foreign origin of their new worship, the Japanese considered it their duty to recall it by various symbols, such as the elephants' heads which I have already described among the architectural ornaments on Buddhist monuments, and, in memory of India, by palm plants of a small species acclimatized in Japan, which are seen in the neighbourhood of the Temples. It was more easy for them to testify their respect for the birthplace of Buddha by certain outward signs, than to preserve the essence of his religion, that is to say, the exact tradition of his life, his personality, and his teaching.

According to the Japanese legend, Buddha came into the world in a miraculous manner. Immediately on his birth he stood upright in the middle of the chamber, made seven steps in the direction of each of the four cardinal points, and, pointing with his right hand towards heaven and his left hand towards the ground, he said, "Above me on high, and below and around me, there is nothing which can compare with me, and no other

A CELESTIAL SENTINEL.   A CELESTIAL SENTINEL.

being more worthy of veneration." In this way is the infant Buddha represented, and when his birthday is celebrated on the eighth day of the fourth month, the people go to his Temple and bathe the statue in a decoction of aromatic herbs, which the bonzes have prepared, and placed at the feet of the image in a sort of holy-water font. The statue then receives the adoration of the faithful, and the more devout sprinkle themselves with this decoction and drink it. From the ninth to the fifteenth day of the second month the remembrance of the meditations of Sâkyamouni in the solitude of the forests is celebrated. This is a week of retreat and of preaching, during which the bonzes teach the people that the awakening of supreme consciousness in the soul of Buddha was in correlation with the apparition of a brilliant star; that the sage, having attained to the full possession of light, proclaimed during thirty-seven days the first book of his Law; during twelve years the second; during thirty years the third; during eight years the fourth, and during one day and one night the last, which treats of the Nirwâna, or final annihilation. They add, that during forty-nine years of his ministry he turned the wheel of the law three hundred and sixty times, an image which signifies the complete exposition of his doctrines.

The seventh and last day of the festival is consecrated to the commemoration of the death of Buddha. In each of the places of worship dedicated to him a cenotaph is erected, and the faithful go from Temple to Temple, vieing with each other in their zeal for the ornamentation of the holy tomb. On this occasion the celebrated picture of Néhanzao, painted by Toödenzou is displayed in the Temple of Toofoukzi at Kioto. In the centre of this great painting Buddha is represented, extended under saras trees, plunged in the repose of eternal nothingness. The solemn calm of his face reveals that the emancipation of his intelligence is consummated; that the sage has irrevocably entered into the Nirwâna. His disciples stand around him, contemplating him with mingled expressions of regret and admiration. The poor and oppressed, the pariahs, weep for the charitable friend who has fed them by his alms, who has begged for them; for the consoler, whose compassionate words open a prospect of deliverance to their souls. The entire creation is moved at beholding him, who constantly respected life under every form which it wears in nature, reduced to the condition of a corpse. The genii of the earth, the waters, and the air approach him with respect, followed by the tenants of their several domains; fish, birds, insects, reptiles, quadrupeds of all sorts, even to the white elephant, the supreme degree of the Brahminical metempsychosis. This composition, extravagant as it is, produces nevertheless a powerful effect. It awakens I know not what mysterious sympathy, and it expresses an idea which is no stranger to Christianity; that is to say, an idea of a certain solidarity established between man and all the beings of the terrestrial creation. As for the principal subject of the picture, I believe that no decision has ever been arrived at as to the meaning to be attributed to it. Does it represent the Nirwâna, the supreme end of all Buddhist aspirations, as the absorption of the soul of the just into the divine essence of the Universal Spirit? or does it actually make it the synonym of annihilation? The doctrine of Buddha is very obscure on this point

A BAMBOO GROVE.

Nevertheless, the best authority pronounces in favour of the latter alternative. The interpretations of M. E. Burnouf and M. Barthélemy Saint-Hilaire are almost precisely as follows :—

The Buddhist takes an incontestable fact as the point of departure of his doctrine; it is the existence of human suffering in some form in all social conditions. Seeking out the causes of this pain, he attributes it to passions, to desire, to faults, to ignorance, even to existence itself. This being so, pain can have no other term than the cessation of existence. But in order that this end should be real, it must be Nothingness, or the Nirwâna. There is no other means by which man can escape from the circle of perpetual re-births, by which he can definitively withdraw himself from the law of transmigration. This compound of body and of soul, which is called man, can be really delivered only by annihilation, because so long as there shall remain the least atom of his soul, the soul may again be born under one of those innumerable appearances assumed by existence, and its pretended liberation would be only an illusion like the others. The only asylum and the only reality is nothingness, because from that one does not return.

If the opinion which I have just quoted really express the thoughts of the Hindoo reformer, we must acknowledge that the Buddhist Nirwâna surpasses in tragical horror every imagination of the ancients concerning the mystery of human destiny. This conception is the last word of despair and the highest exaltation of the Will. In proposing to abolish pain by the suppression of existence, Buddha plainly takes up the ground of atheism, because that end cannot be attained by anything short of the abstraction of the idea of the Supreme Being. At the same time that Buddha welcomes death as the angel of deliverance, he casts at him a sovereign defiance, and places himself for ever out of the reach of his power by destroying, in their last germ, the elements of a new birth. Finally, he finds in this negative victory, in his final annihilation, the means by which he renders himself superior to the gods. This is because the gods remain subject to the law of transmigration.

It is difficult to realize that more than one-third of the entire human race has no other creed than that of Buddhism, that worship without God, that religion of Nothingness invented by despair. We would endeavour to persuade ourselves that the multitudes under this rule do not understand the doctrine which they profess, or that they refuse to admit its consequences. The idolatrous practices which have grown out of the teaching of the book of the Good Law, would seem, indeed, to testify that that book could neither satisfy nor smother the religious sentiments innate in man, and ever living among all peoples.

On the other hand, we must not underrate the influence of the philosophy of final annihilation in a great number of traits of Japanese manners. The Irova, as have seen, teaches the children in the schools that life has no more consistency than dream, and that no trace of it remains. When the Japanese has reached a mature age he will sacrifice his life, or that of his neighbour, with the most disdainful indifference, to the satisfaction of his pride, or to some trifling resentment. Murders and

THE GREAT JUDGE OF HELL.

suicides are so frequent in Japan that there are few gentlemen who do not possess, and make it a point of honour to exhibit, at least one sword belonging to the family that has been steeped in blood.

Buddhism is nevertheless superior, in many respects, to the religion which it has displaced. Its relative superiority is shown in the justness of its point of departure, which is the acknowledgment of a need of deliverance, based upon the double fact of the existence of evil in man, as well as the universal condition of misery and suffering in the world. The promise of the worship of the Kamis has reference to the present life. The rules of the purification were to preserve the faithful from five great evils :—the fire of heaven, sickness, poverty, exile, and premature death. The pomps

BUDDHI-DHARMA.

of its religious festivals had for their sole aim the glorification of the heroes of the Empire. But though patriotism may be idealized to the extent of becoming the national worship, it is no less true that this natural sentiment, precious and praiseworthy in itself, cannot suffice to fill up the mind and satisfy all its needs. The human soul is greater than the world. It requires a religion which detaches it from the earth. Buddhism, in a certain sense, responds to aspirations of this kind previously misunderstood.

This circumstance in itself explains the success with which it is propagated in Japan and elsewhere, by the arms of persuasion alone ; still, nevertheless, we may believe that it is not in this abstract and philosophical form that it has become so popular, and nothing proves that more forcibly than its actual condition.

Japan, like India, has produced ascetics, mortified by abstinence and plunged in abstraction, but their number is very small, and the most illustrious among them was a Hindoo by origin. He is Buddhi-Dharma, the founder of the Sen-sjou sect. He came to Japan in A.D. 613. The legend represents him as traversing the straits of Corea, standing upon one of the large leaves of the tree called "aschi," or upon a simple reed. He had prepared himself for his mission by a retreat of nine consecutive years in the Corean temple of Schao-lin, which he passed in squatting upon a mat with his face invariably turned to the side of the wall.

Buddha had recommended to his disciples the exercise of the Dhyâna—that is to say, Contemplation. The bonzes, desiring to systematize this exercise, made of the Dhyâna a sort of mystic ladder of two stages, each divided into four steps. In order to climb the first ladder, the ascetic must be detached from every other desire than that of the Nirwâna. In this state of soul he still judges and reasons ; but he is sheltered from the seductions of evil, and the feeling that this first step opens to him the perspective of the Nirwâna, places him in an ecstatic disposition which soon permits him to attain to the second degree. At the second step the purity of the ascetic remains the same : but in addition to this purity he has laid aside judgment and reasoning, so that his intelligence, which no longer thinks of things, but fixes itself wholly upon the Nirwâna, experiences only the pleasure of interior satisfaction, without judging it or even understanding it. At the third degree, the pleasure of interior satisfaction has disappeared ; the sage has fallen into indifference with respect even to the happiness which he just now experienced through his intelligence. All the pleasure which remains to him is a vague sentiment of physical well-being diffused through his body. He has, however, not lost his memory of the conditions through which he has passed, and still retains a confused consciousness of himself, notwithstanding the almost absolute detachment which he has reached. Finally, at the fourth degree, the ascetic no longer possesses this sentiment of physical well-being, all obscure as it is ; he has lost all memory. More than this, he has even lost the feeling of indifference, and, henceforth free from all pleasure and all grief, whatever may be their object, whether within or without, he has reached impassibility—he is as near to the Nirwâna as he can be during this life. Then it is that the ascetic is permitted to approach the second stage of the Dhyâna, the four superposed regions of the world without forms. He first enters into the region of the infinite in space. From this he climbs a new step, into the region of the infinite of intelligence. Having attained to this height, he enters upon a third region, that in which nothing exists. But, as in this vacuum and in this darkness an idea might remain, to represent to the ascetic the nothingness into which

A SENNIN, OR BUDDHIST SAINT.

he is plunging, he requires a last and supreme effort to enter the fourth region of the world without forms, where there are no longer ideas, nor even an idea of the absence of ideas.

Such are the mystic exercises of Buddhist contemplation, of which the Buddhi-Dharma was the promoter in Japan. The other apostles, his successors, walk in the footsteps of Buddha in the same manner—that is to say, by substituting, each after his fashion, exterior practices for the spontaneity of piety and the activity of intelligence. The master said to his disciples, "Go, all men of piety, hide your good works, and show your sins." So the bonzes instituted processions of penitents. Gentleness was one of the principal traits of Sâkyamouni's character. His compassion extended itself to all created beings. When his doctrine spread amongst the Japanese, the latter had already made it a law that the flesh of no domestic animal should be eaten. This custom had, among other economical effects, the advantage of preventing a rise in the price of the buffalo, which in a rice country is absolutely indispensable to the poorest cultivators. Certain other Buddhist sects went so far as to proscribe every other nourishment than the vegetable. Sákyamouni recommended abstinence, not only

A SENNIN, OR BUDDHIST SAINT.

from lying and evil-speaking, but also from every idle word. Silence took its place among other monastic vows. In the same way abnegation, purity of morals, patience, and perseverance, were erected into ordinances, regulating, in the most minute detail, the costume, food, and employment of the hours of the day and the night of the various conventual corporations.

Because Buddha had shown himself indefatigable in soliciting the commiseration of the rich on behalf of all who were unfortunate, fraternities of mendicant monks were organized. Because he had declared himself equally well-disposed towards men who were despised by society as towards those who were respected, and that he would expound his law to the ignorant as well as the wise, ignorance was made a cardinal virtue. While knowledge was allied with this faith in the doctrine of the Hindoo reformer, the latter virtue, in the opinion of the bonzes, dispensed with all other virtues. "With the exception of the ' Sen-sjou' sect," writes a Japanese author, "our bonzes tend to maintain the people, and above all, the peasants, in profound ignorance. They say that blind faith is sufficient to lead to perfection."

The High-priest Foudaïsi, who came from China with his two sons Fousjoo and Fouken, invented a mechanical process for the purpose of dispensing the bonzes from turning the wheel of the law according to the sense consecrated among the mystic language of Buddhism, by permitting them to follow this operation to the letter. Then he constructed the Rinzoo, a sort of moveable chorister's desk turning upon a pivot, and spread out upon it the rolls of the sacred books. His adepts received from him, according to the degree of their devotion, authority to make a quarter of a turn, a half turn, or three-quarters of a turn of the Rinzoo; they very rarely obtained the favour of an entire turn, because that was an act as meritorious as if all the books of the law had been recited from end to end. The bonzes Sinran, Nitziten, and thirty others, became famous as the founders of sects, in which each was distinguished by some peculiarity more or less worthy to rival the ingenious invention of Foudaïsi. Thus the monopoly, of the great family rosary is conferred upon a certain confraternity. We must bear in mind that the Buddhist rosary has no virtue unless it be correctly told. Now there is no guarantee that, in a numerous family, some errors may not occur in the use of the rosary; hence it is sometimes reproached with uselessness. Instead of recriminating in the case, true wisdom consists in sending for a bonze of the great rosary to come to the house to put things in good order. He comes there with his bead chaplet, which is something like a good-sized boa, and places it in the hands of the entire family, who are ranged in a circle, while he stands before the altar of the domestic idol, and directs the operations by means of a bell and a little hammer. At a given signal the father, the mother, and the children, shout out their daily prayers at the top of their voices. The small beads, the large beads, and the blows of the hammer succeed each other with cadenced regularity. The exercise of the rosary becomes animated, the cries become passionate, hands and arms obey with the precision of a machine, till the body is worn out with fatigue. Finally, the termination of the ceremony leaves the whole family out of breath, exhausted, but radiant with happiness, because their intercessory gods are now satisfied.

Buddhism is a flexible, insinuating, and conciliatory religion, accommodating itself

RAÏDEN, GOD OF THUNDER.

to the genius and the habits of a widely diverse people. Ever since its commencement in Japan, the bonzes have succeeded in getting hold of the little chapels of the Kamis, and placing them within the precincts of their sanctuaries. They have added to their ceremonies several symbols borrowed from the ancient national worship ; and, in order to mix up the two religions more effectually, they have introduced into their temples the Kamis, to whom they give the title and attributes of the Hindoo divinities, and Hindoo divinities transformed into the Japanese Kamis. There was nothing inadmissible in such exchanges, which naturally explain themselves by the

A BUDDHIST MIRACLE : A BONZE BRAVING DECAPITATION.

dogma of transmigration. Thanks to the combination of the two worships, to which they have given the name of Rioobou-Sintoo, Buddhism has become the ruling religion of Japan.

When we look at it superficially, it seems to do nothing more than add its sanction to the veneration of new objects of worship in addition to those already received by the masses. At first, it was the great Indian Buddha to whom these colossal statues, of which the Daïboudhs of Kamakoura offers the finest type, were erected. The Japanese idea of a supreme Divinity was afterwards personified in the fantastic image of Amida,

THE QUEEN OF HEAVEN.

represented under nine different forms symbolical of its incarnations and essential perfections, one of which is expressed by the emblem of a dog's head.

Buddhism has an image, the Queen of Heaven; the guardians of heaven, of whom some are also the guardians of the temples, the Kings of Earth and the Kings of Hell, beneficent genii, avenging genii; it has placed beside the ancient Japanese divinity of the Sun, the gods of the moon, the planets, the signs of the Zodiac, the genii of the

Rain, Wind, and Thunder. Finally, it has assigned celestial patrons to all classes and all social professions. Among this multitude of images, grave and fantastic, it is not always easy to discern those which properly belong to Buddhism. Several were, no doubt, popular in Japan before its importation. Perhaps we ought to place in this category the god of the thunder, Raïden, and the god of the winds, Fûten.—Raïden, the god of thunder and lightning, is infinitely less majestic than the Olympian Jove.

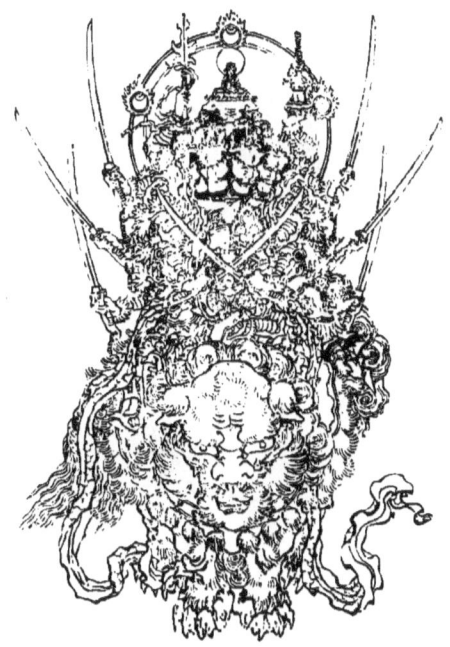

THE PATRON OF ARMS.

It is a grotesque demon, which beats half-a-dozen cymbals, ranged in a circle round its head. There is a great deal of uncertainty about the origin of the numerous grotesque animals of the Japanese mythology. I will only mention those to which some artistic interest attaches.

Two horned quadrupeds, Hino-woo and Midsou-no-woo, genii of fire and water, seem to belong to Kami worship. Foô, a sort of phœnix, must have been introduced into it from China. The Kirin has a woman's head, deer's feet, a horse's body. His apparition, quick as lightning—for his feet hardly touch the ground, and would not even tread upon a worm—is a presage of the birth of a benevolent genius, such as Sâkya, Dharma, Sjôtokdaïsi. The Koma-inou was brought from Corea, it is said, by the

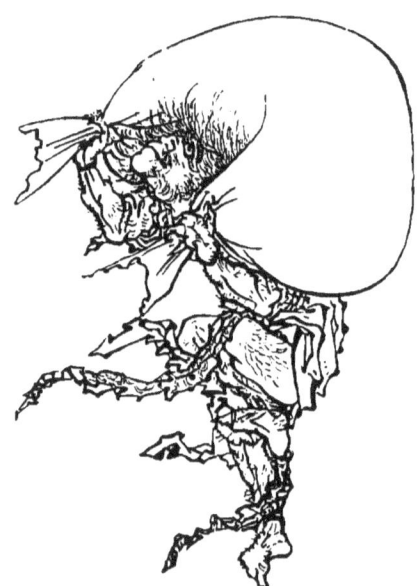

FUTEN, GOD OF THE WINDS.

Empress Zingou. This animal, which is part dog, part lion, may perhaps be a recollection of the cave-lion. Two fine specimens, in cut granite, stand on the esplanade of the Temple of Kami-Hamayou at Simonoséki. The Tats-Maki is the terror of all people. This immense dragon generally haunts the deep sea caverns, but sometimes he comes up to the surface; and springing towards heaven, causes such a perturbation of the atmosphere, that he produces the redoubtable phenomenon known as the typhoon. Mooki is a turtle with a dog's head and a long tail of trailing marine mosses. There are Mookis so old, that the legends tell how trees, rocks, and peaks have grown up on their backs. In the most zealous days of Buddhism, the seventh and eighth centuries, the bonzes themselves lent a hand in the building of the temples and adorning them with pictures and statues.

But though the native arts, especially sculpture and architecture, may be indebted to

THE TATS-MAKI, OR DRAGON OF THE TYPHOONS.

them for some portion of their progress, little good can be said of the bonzes or their literary productions. Let us try to imagine what the monastic lucubrations must be! They consist of thousands of volumes upon the lotus of the Good Law, upon the twenty-eight subdivisions of contemplation, upon the glories of Buddha, and the miraculous lives of the innumerable ascetics, saints, and martyrs of his religion. The true merit of such a literature is that it is absolutely illegible outside that separate world composed by the inhabitants of the bonze-houses and the regular frequenters of those establishments.

At a period in which Chinese characters were still used in writing the Japanese language, a learned man of the sect of Youto, named Kibiko, abridged the complicated forms of those immense large square characters, reducing them to forty-seven

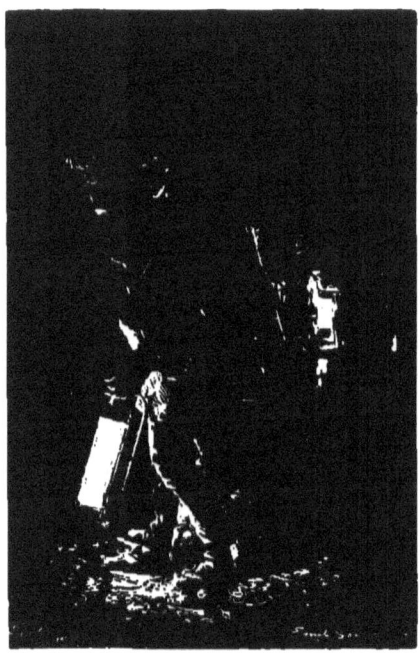

A NIGHT WATCH.

simple elements easily recognized and invariable. This system, which has since been used for notes, glossaries, and interlineary explanations, is named the Katakana. But the bonze Kokai, who was born in the year 755, the founder of the sect of Singous-jou, went still further into the simplification of Chinese signs. He also chose forty-seven proper forms to represent the Japanese syllables; he took away their figurative or metaphorical value, and adapted them to the most cursive form of Chinese writing, and thus composed the system that is called the Hirakana. It is this which is used by women, by the lower orders, and even by the *literati* themselves, in writing ordinary things and composing works of light literature, such as romances, songs, and comedies.

All the Japanese women learn the Hirakana in their childhood, and they are taught no other. The men also learn it; but in addition they are taught the Katakana, and the *literati* add to that the knowledge of a more or less considerable number of Chinese signs. The result of that wise combination is, that the men can always read the writing of the women, but that the women cannot read that of the men unless when they employ the Hirakana system.

A BONZE.

A GUARD HOUSE.

CHAPTER IV.

TAIKOSAMA AND THE TOKAÏDO.

INCREASING ANARCHY FROM FOURTEENTH TO SIXTEENTH CENTURY.—FIDÉ-YOSI.—SPREAD
OF THE BUDDHIST RELIGION.—CONFLICTS.—ORDINANCES OF FIDÉ-YOSI.—THE PRINCE
OF BOUNGO.—FRANCIS XAVIER.—JAPANESE CHRISTIANS.—PERSECUTION.—MARTYRDOM.
IYÉYAS.—THE TOKAÏDO.—SINAGAWA.

THE civil wars which brought about the ruin of Kamakoura had few points of interest
in themselves. From the fourteenth to the sixteenth century, the Empire of Japan
presented a spectacle of increasing anarchy, which threatened the work of political
centralization which had been inaugurated by Yoritomo.

C 2

A domestic quarrel arose within the Daïri itself, which forced the legitimate sovereign to yield Kioto to his competitor ; and, during nearly sixty years, six Mikados successively occupied the pontifical throne, by usurpation, while the real descendants of the Sun had to submit to holding their court at Yosimo, a small borough situated on the south of the capital, in the province of Yomato. At length a family arrangement put an end to this public scandal ; and the hundred and first Mikado, He of the South, resumed possession of his holy city, and solemnly revived the fiction of his theocratic sovereignty.

On the other hand, the power of the Siogouns was the object of strenuous rivalries, which carried fire and sword through Kioto and Kamakoura by turns, and did not shrink even from fratricide. The feudal nobles took advantage of the general confusion to make one more attempt to break through their vassalage to the crown or its lieutenants. When, in the year 1582, the Siogoun Nobounanga was surprised and massacred, with his entire family, in his own palace, the Empire seemed to be on the brink of dissolution. It was saved by an adventurer, the son of a peasant, who had begun life as a groom in the service of the Siogoun. His grave and taciturn demeanour, matured by the vicissitudes of a vagabond youth, attracted the attention of his new master. He was frequently observed squatting in the attitude of persons of his class, near the stalls in which the horses in his charge stood, his arms stretched out on his knees, and his mind plunged in deep reverie. Nobounanga offered him a military career. The ex-groom, become General Faxiba, distinguished himself by brilliant deeds, for which he was raised to the rank of Daïmio. On the death of his benefactor, he undertook to avenge him, and he commanded, under the name of Fidé-Yosi, the troops which were sent into the provinces of the great vassals who had revolted. Two years sufficed for the suppression of the rebellion. His return to Kioto was a genuine triumph. The Mikado solemnly invested him with the chief title of the Daïri—that of Quamboukou, and proclaimed him his lieutenant-general.

Then Fidé-Yosi carried his sword into another scene of strife. Every one of the thousand divinities of the Buddhist mythology had taken his place in Japan. There they had temples, statues, monastic fraternities. Bonzes, monks, nuns, abounded throughout the Empire, and principally in the centre and south of Niphon. Each convent vied with its neighbours for the public favour. By degrees the competition became so vehement, that jealousy, hatred, and envy embittered the mutual relations of certain powerful and ambitious orders. From invective they proceeded to violence. The imperial police interfered in the earlier conflicts of the tonsured foes, but they were soon powerless to oppose the torrent. Bands of furious men in soutanes and habits, armed with sticks, pikes, and flails, came down in the night upon the territory of the fraternity with whom they were at variance; ravaged everything that came in their way; ill-treated, killed, or dispersed the victims of their surprise, and did not retire until they had set fire to the four quarters of the bonze-house. But the aggressors, sooner or later, in their turn assailed unawares, underwent similar treatment. Six times, in the course of the twelfth century, the monks of the convent on the Yeïsan burned the bonze-house of Djensjôsi; twice the monks of Djensjôsi burned the convent of Yeïsan to ashes.

Similar scenes were enacted in various parts of Niphon. In order to protect their convents from a sudden attack, rich priors converted them into fortresses. Their audacity increased with the incapacity of the Government. Inimical fraternities had armed encounters under the very walls of the temples which they possessed in the capital. A portion of the Daïri was sacked, in 1283, after one of these encounters. A temple in Kioto having been fired in 1536, the flames spread to an adjacent quarter, and immense damage was done. The efforts of the Siogoun Nobounanga to reduce the insurgent fraternity to submission were rendered fruitless by the entrenchments from behind which they opposed him.

Fidé-Yosi resolved to make an end, once for all, of the quarrels of the monks. He surprised, captured, and occupied the most militant bonze-houses, demolished their defences, transported all the monks who had broken the public peace to distant islands, and placed the whole of the Japanese clergy, without distinction, under the superintendence of an active, severe, and inexorable police. He enacted that thenceforth the bonzes should enjoy only the usufruct of their lands, the property in them being transferred to the Government, with full and free power of disposal of them.

Then he ordered all the dignitaries among the clergy, both regular and secular, to limit themselves strictly, together with their subordinates, to their religious functions. From this law the Japanese priesthood has never since departed. They officiate at the altar in the interior of their bonze-houses, under the eyes of the people, in a sanctuary which is separated by a *jubé* from the crowd; but they never address the people otherwise than by preaching, and only on the holydays especially set apart for the purpose.

They were forbidden to organize processions except at certain periods of the year, and with the co-operation of the Government officials charged with the ordering of public ceremonies.

Their pastoral duties were restricted to the narrowest limits, and have never been enlarged. The bonzes are charged with the accomplishment of the sacramental ceremonies with which all sects in Japan surround the last moments of the dying. They conduct the funerals, and provide, according to the wishes of the relations of the deceased, for the burial or the burning of the corpse, and for the consecration and preservation of his tomb.

But, in proportion as they reign over the domain of death, they are vigilantly watched and restrained in all their relations with society and the business of life. Most of the secular priests are married, and hold familiar intercourse with a small circle of friends and neighbours ; but they are all the more sternly dealt with if they give any offence in consequence. I saw, in the chief market-place at Yokohama an aged bonze, who had been exposed there for three consecutive days, on his knees, on an old mat, under the burning sun. The poor wretch endeavoured occasionally to wipe the sweat from his bald head with a little crape handkerchief. A placard, stuck in the ground in front of him, apprized the public that this man had practised medicine clandestinely, and had criminally assaulted one of his female patients, and therefore the justice of the Taïkoun had condemned him to transportation for life after public exposure.

In 1586, a short time after Fidé-Yosi had put an end to the monastic troubles of the Empire, strange news caused public attention to fix itself upon the island of Kiousiou. At this time the trade of Japan with the Asiatic continent and archipelagoes was not in any way shackled. The Prince of Boungo, who, forty years previously, had received the Portuguese adventurers flung upon the coasts of his province by a tempest, had hastened to furnish them with the means of returning to Goa, and had begged them to send him every year a ship laden with merchandise suitable for the native markets.

Thus relations between Portugal and Japan were founded and developed. On one of its first voyages, the Portuguese ship, at the moment of setting sail for Goa, secretly gave asylum to a Japanese gentleman named Hansiro, who had committed a homicide. The illustrious Jesuit, Francis Xavier, who had recently disembarked at Goa, undertook the religious instruction of the Japanese fugitive, and administered baptism to him.

In 1549, the first Jesuit mission was established in the island of Kiousiou, under the direction of Saint Francis Xavier himself, and with the assistance of Hansiro.

The missionaries were at first astonished and terrified at finding in Japan so many institutions, ceremonies, and objects of worship closely resembling those which they had come thither to introduce. Taking no heed of the immense antiquity of Buddhism, they declared that that religion could be nothing less than a diabolical counterfeit of the true Church. Nevertheless, they were not slow to perceive that they might turn that circumstance to the advantage of their propaganda. Nothing in the doctrine of Buddhism was opposed to the admission of Jesus among the number of the Buddhas who, in the course of ages, have appeared upon earth. Nor was there any insurmountable difficulty in giving the Virgin pre-eminence over the queens of heaven of the ancient Pantheon. In a word, the ruling creed at least furnished certain useful points of contact, and all sorts of pretexts and good opportunities for introducing the matter. This first mission had a prodigious success, and there is ample room for believing that, thanks to the apostolical zeal and persuasive power of Saint Francis Xavier, numerous and sincere conversions to Christianity took place in all classes of Japanese society.

Several high dignitaries of Buddhism were filled with uneasiness about the future of their religion, and carried their complaints and remonstrances to the foot of the throne.

" How many sects," asked the Mikado, "do you estimate as existing in my dominions ? "

" Thirty-five," was the prompt reply.

" Very well, then, that will make the thirty-sixth," replied the jovial Emperor.

The Siogoun Fidé-Yosi regarded the question from another point of view.

Struck by the fact that the foreign missionaries applied themselves not only to spread their doctrines among the people, but to gain the favour of the great vassals of the Empire, and that the anarchical tendencies of the latter were mysteriously fostered by their relations with these priests, he discovered that they were commissioned by a sovereign pontiff who wore a triple crown, and who could, at his free will and pleasure, dispossess the greatest princes, distribute the kingdoms of Europe among his favourites, and even dispose of newly-discovered continents. He reflected that the emissaries of this redoubtable ruler of the West had already formed a party in the coast of the Mikado, and had founded a house in his capital; that the former Siogoun Nobounanga had openly protected and befriended them; and that there was reason to believe that he, the Siogoun in place and power, was actually surrounded in his own palace by dark intrigues in the household of his young son and heir presumptive.

Fidô-Yosi communicated his observations and his fears to an experienced servant whom he had already charged with several delicate missions. The dark and subtle genius of this confidant, who became so famous in the history of Japan under the name of Iyéyas, applied itself diligently to sounding the depth of the danger. An embassy of Japanese Christians, directed by Father Valignani, the superior of the Order of the Jesuits, had set out for Rome. Iyéyas supplied his master with proofs that the princes of Boungo, Omoura, and Arima, had written, on this occasion, to the Spiritual Emperor of the Christians (Pope Gregory XIII.) letters in which they declared that they threw themselves at his feet, and worshipped him as their supreme Lord, in his quality of sole representative of God on earth. The Siogoun dissembled his wrath, but only in order to render his vengeance more signal. He employed nearly a year in organizing, in concert with his favourite, the blow he meditated. At length, in June 1587, his troops were at their posts, in their suspected provinces of Kiousiou and the southern coast of Niphon, in sufficient force to suppress any attempt at resistance. On one especial day, from one end of the Empire to the other, an edict was published, by order of the Siogoun, by which, in the name and as the lieutenant of the Mikado, he commanded the suppression of Christianity within six months; ordered that the foreign missionaries should be banished in perpetuity, on pain of death; that their schools should be immediately closed, their churches demolished, crosses pulled down wherever they were found; and that the native converts should abjure the new doctrine in the presence of the Government officials. At the same time, in order to make the agreement between the two potentates evident, the Mikado paid a solemn visit to his lieutenant, while the latter, to reward the services of his faithful Iyéyas, raised him to the rank of his prime minister, and made him governor of eight provinces.

All the measures provided by the edict of the Siogoun were punctually accomplished, with the exception of one, which was precisely that which the ex-groom expected to have given him the least trouble. To his profound amazement, the native

Christians of both sexes, of all classes, and of every age absolutely refused to abjure. Those who possessed lands he dispossessed, and enriched his officers with their spoils. Others were imprisoned or exiled. These rigorous examples produced no effect whatever.

The recalcitrants were threatened with capital punishment. They bowed their heads to the sword of the executioner with resignation hitherto unknown; and in many instances the sympathies of the crowd were excited by the testimony which they rendered to their Faith. Then the most ingenious modes of torture were resorted to, and the native Christians were put to death by fire and crucifixion. In a great number of cases the latter mode was selected. The Japanese martyrs rivalled the first confessors of the Church in the constancy of their faith. For three consecutive years the fury of the Siogoun's officers vainly expended itself in the utmost refinements of barbarity and brutality, in ferocious, hideous, unspeakable inventions, practised upon more than 20,500 victims, men and women, young men and maidens, old men and little children. Suddenly, the persecution was relaxed. Fidé-Yosi called the feudal nobles to arms, and threw 160,000 fighting men on the coasts of Corea, with which country Japan was at perfect peace (1592). His general summoned the Coreans to join them in attacking the dynasty of the Mings. The Chinese army marched to meet the invaders, but it suffered so decisive a defeat, that the Emperor of China hastened to offer the Siogoun peace, with the title of King of Niphon and First Vassal of the Celestial Empire.

Fidé-Yosi proudly replied; "I am already King of Niphon; I am so of myself, and I should know how, if I chose to do so, to make the Emperor of China my vassal."

In 1597 he followed up his threat by sending a second army of 130,000 men. But death surprised him, towards the close of the following year, before the issue of the new campaign; and the two Empires, equally weary of an unjustifiable war, hastened to be reconciled, and recalled their armies. During his later years, Fidé-Yosi was honoured by his Court with the surname of the Great (Taïkosama) which history has preserved.

The two Chinese expeditions which ended the career of Taïkosama, and which one might be tempted to regard as foolish adventures, seem to have been, as well as his edict of persecution, acts maturely premeditated with the view to attaining the double

x

end of his ambitious dreams, the crushing of the feudal nobility and the foundation upon its ruins of a monarchical dynasty.

Already the vassals of the Empire were exhausted in sterile internal strife : it was necessary to ruin them by distant and costly wars.

Under the pretext of protecting the wives and children of the Daïmios who were called to military service, Taïkosama obliged the families and the principal servants of the princes to come and live in houses which he had prepared for them within the enclosure of his fortresses. When the nobles themselves returned from China, they could only regain possession of their lands on condition of residing on them henceforth alone, without their families, but with the power of temporarily rejoining the latter at the Court of the Siogoun, where they were still to remain as hostages.

Kæmpfer describes this as a unique and marvellous example of a great number of powerful princes subjugated by a simple soldier of low extraction. But this was not enough to keep the provinces under the domination of the new central power.

Hitherto the cities of residence had been united to one another by a military road. Taïkosama profited by the absence of the nobles to make a road through their lands, extending to the extremities of the Empire, which was to be independent of all other ward, police, or jurisdiction than that of the Siogoun. It was called the Tokaïdo. Posts were established at twenty minutes' distance one from the other—spaces still covered without rest by the Imperial runners who form the postal service at the present time. In each station runners were ready to relieve their comrades ; saddle-horses and pack-horses harnessed ; custom-house officers, police, and a picket of soldiers, who have charge of a rock furnished with guns and lances for arming the reinforcements. Finally, a perfect network of day and night signals covered the heights, in order to spread alarm to the head-quarters of the Government forces at the first indication of danger.

It was in the midst of these works, which by their results were to acquire all the importance of a permanent occupation of the feudal provinces, that Taïkosama was surprised by death in the sixty-third year of his age and the twelfth of his reign. His last wishes were that measures might be taken for the consolidation of his dynasty. Although his son Fidé-Yosi was yet a minor, he married him to the daughter of his first minister Iyéyas, to whom he confided the regency of the Empire.

Iyéyas bound himself by a solemn oath, signed with his blood, to relinquish his powers as soon as the presumptive heir should be old enough to ascend the throne. He closed the eyes of Taïkosama, gave him a magnificent funeral, and governed Japan

A CARRIER OF DESPATCHES.

for five years under the title of Regent, applying himself systematically to keep the young Siogoun out of the management of affairs. But the latter had certain counsellors, who saw through the designs of Iyéyas, and successfully raised all sorts of obstacles to the realization of his ambitious plans. Iyéyas summoned them to give up to him the fortress of Osaka, where they had established the residence of his son-in-law. On their refusal, he invested the place. After several months of heroic resistance, the garrison was obliged to capitulate. Fidé-Yosi set fire with his own hands to his palace, and flung himself, with all his servants, into the flames.

Iyeyas, proclaimed Siogoun, justified his perjury and the tragic end of Fidé-Yosi, by accusing that prince of having secretly conspired with the Christians. The army took the oath of fidelity to him. The Mikado sanctioned his usurpation. The people prostrated themselves before him with the docility of slaves.

To the usurper Iyéyas is due the merit of having made Yeddo the political capital of Japan, and the obligatory residence of the noble families of the Empire. At that epoch, at the commencement of the seventeenth century, Yeddo was not equal in importance to the pontifical Miako, nor to Osaka, the centre of commerce, nor even to Nagasaki. But, like the last city, it has the advantage of a strategical position, easily defended on the land side, and regarded as impregnable on that of the sea. Kæmpfer, who on two occasions went with an embassy of the Dutch India Company to Kioto and to Yeddo, reckons that in the line of the Tokaïdo, or close to it, there are thirty-three great cities with fortresses and fifty-seven small towns unfortified, without mentioning an infinite number of villages and hamlets. It takes no less than from twenty-five to thirty days to go from Nagasaki to Yeddo, by the Tokaïdo, using the means of transport customary among the natives, who know no other than the horse or the palanquin. There are two sorts of palanquin, the norimon and the cango. The former, which requires four bearers for long journeys, is a large, heavy box, in which one may sit with tolerable comfort. The sides are in lacquered wood, and contain two sliding doors. Although this norimon is, *par excellence*, the vehicle of the nobility, it admits of no ornaments, and is used by the ladies of the middle class and by the registered courtesans, because both occupy a certain position of fortune and consideration in society. The cango is a light litter of bamboo, open on both sides; it requires only two bearers, who always walk with a rapid and regular step. They rest for one minute out of twenty. When they go back, each carries in his turn the cango, suspended at the end of a pole, over his shoulder.

The pack-horses intended for the transport of merchandise and of travellers go slowly behind their drivers, the head bent, and attached by a strap which passes under the body to the cord which goes round the animal. The Japanese, instead of shoeing their horses, wrap their hoofs in a little mat, which only lasts one day. According as these mats wear out, they are thrown aside, and immediately replaced, and large provisions of them always make part of the baggage. Foot-passengers do the same with their sandals of plaited straw ; so that all the roads of Japan are covered with these relics.

THE CANGO, OR PEOPLE'S PALANQUIN.

The Tokaïdo is crossed in several places by arms of the sea and by rapid rivers. Large boats do duty as coaches, and cross the strait which separates the island of Kiousiou from Simonoséki, in two hours. Most of the travellers, and even pilgrims, profit by the great merchant-junks of the inland sea to make the journey from Simonoséki to Hiogo. It is only half a day's journey from Hiogo to Osaka, and one day from Osaka to Kioto. Between this city and Yeddo lie the most picturesque portions of the road.

Travellers cross the rivers in flat boats, or on the shoulders of porters. These porters form a corporation, which indemnifies the traveller in case of personal accident

TATTOOED COOLIES.

or loss of baggage. With the exception of a girdle tattooing suffices for their clothing, according to custom among the Coolies of Japan. The subjects of this process are heroic, such as the Strife of Yamato with the Dragon, the Tribunal of Hell, and the image of that incomparable soldier who, when his head was falling under the sword, tore off his enemies' armour with his teeth.

The fare is always extremely moderate, and varies according to whether eight men are employed to carry the norimon, or four men with a litter, two men with a stretcher, or a simple porter. In the latter case, which is the most frequent, the traveller seats himself astride the bearer's neck, and the latter takes him by both legs, and, telling him to sit steadily, steps into the water warily and firmly. Sometimes a sudden rise of the river intercepts the passage, and then the travellers install themselves in the tea-houses on the shore, from whence they watch the water until the porters come to tell them that the ford is practicable.

Three days' journey from Yeddo, the Tokaïdo passes by the foot of Fousi-yama, from which it is only separated by the lake of Akoni. Thousands of pilgrims go annually in procession to the summit of the marvellous mountain, where they are received by the monks of a convent built at the very edge of the crater, which opened for the first time 286 years before the birth of Christ and vomited its last lava in 1707.

The hills of Akoni, covered with forests in which large game abound, give access to no other road than that of the Tokaïdo. All the roads of the provinces to the west and south of Yeddo are connected with this great artery, while this one ends in a narrow defile, provided with heavy barriers and fortified guard-houses. Here all travellers have to exhibit their passports, and submit their effects to the inspection of the Government officers. Neither the rank of the Grand Daïmios, nor their imposing suites, can exempt them from these formalities, whose special object is the prevention of the clandestine conveyance of arms into the provinces, no less than attempts at evasion on the part of the noble ladies whose birth and the laws of Taïkosama condemn them to reside at Yeddo.

Not content with these precautions, which do not extend to the northern provinces, Iyéyas and his successors thought it necessary to protect the approaches to their capital on that side by a long wall, at whose gates an inspection is made by the custom-house and police officers.

Beyond the hills of Akoni, the Tokaïdo overlooks the gulf of Odawara, towards the bay of Yeddo, which it joins at the village of Kanagawa, opposite Yokohama. All these localities have been the scenes of assassinations, committed upon inoffensive foreigners of different nations by men belonging to the class of the Samouraïs, or Japanese nobles having the privilege of carrying two swords.

Major Baldwin and Lieutenant Bird, English officers, were murdered not far from the statue of the Daïboudhs of Kamakoura. The corpse of Lieutenant Camus, a French officer, was found horribly mutilated at the entrance of the village of Odongaïa. An English merchant, Mr. Lenox Richardson, was killed upon the threshold of the tea-house of Manéïa, near Kanagawa. Two Russian officers, and, shortly after, two Captains of the Dutch merchant marine, M. Vos and M. Decker, were cut to pieces in the High Street of the Japanese city of Yokohama. A Japanese interpreter to the English minister, and the Dutch interpreter of the American Legation, Mr. Keusken, perished in the streets of Yeddo. The whole of the British Legation had a narrow escape of falling victims to a night attack, which was repelled with great bloodshed. Two English soldiers were killed at their posts in a second attack on the same legation.

It is difficult to forget these things when one is residing in the country where they have happened, and above all when one has installed one's self at Yeddo.

The Government of the Taïkoun is always disposed to dwell upon the danger presented by a sojourn in the capital. That does not prevent their adding that the Taïkoun is profoundly humiliated that such a state of things should exist in his country. On the other hand, where he finds himself at a loss for expedients to escape the reception of an embassy, or when he has used eloquence in persuading them to retire, he is particularly anxious to prove to his foreign guests that the fears he has thought it his duty to express are well founded.

Thus, when one goes to Yeddo by land, one is obliged to accept the escort of a troop of mounted yakoumines. Ours joined us at the limit assigned to the residents of Yokohama for their exercise towards the north of the bay. We crossed the arm of the sea which separates Benten from Kanagawa in our sampan. Our horses were awaiting us in the latter village, and we enjoyed our last hour of liberty by following the Tokaïdo, with its two interminable files of travellers on foot and on horseback, in norimons and in cangos; those who were going to the capital kept the road to the right ; those who were coming back keeping the left.

We halted at the Manéïa tea-house, which was crowded with picturesque groups of guests. All along the front were stoves, smoking kettles, tables laden with provisions, active waitresses coming and going on the right and left, distributing lacquered trays with cups of tea, bowls of saki, fried fish, cakes, and fruits of the season. Before the threshold, seated on benches, were artizans and coolies fanning themselves, while their wives lit their pipes at the common brasero. Suddenly a movement of horror manifested itself among the guests and the waitresses; a detachment of police officers, escorting a criminal, came to take refreshment. With great haste, boiling tea and saki are offered to the two-sworded men, while the coolies, who carried the prisoner in a bamboo basket, without any opening, deposit their burden on the ground, and rub themselves dry with a long piece of crape. As for the unhappy criminal, who could be seen doubled up in his bamboo prison, a man with haggard eyes, dishevelled hair, and bushy beard, he was going to be tortured in the prisons of Yeddo, as a punishment for the evil deeds set forth upon a placard which hung from his ignominious basket.

The beautiful little town of Kawnsaki boasts of several temples, among which that of the Daïsi-Gnawara-Ileghensi seems to me to be one of the purest monuments of Buddhist architecture in Japan. I had heard different versions of the worship to which it is consecrated; among others, the miraculous legend reputed of the Saint who was the special object of the veneration of the faithful in that place. To so high a degree did he possess the virtue of contemplation, that he did not perceive that a coal fire placed near him in a brazier was consuming his hands, while he was absorbed in meditation.

Although the Tokaïdo is in general as fine a road as any of our great European highways, and has the advantage over them of being bordered over its whole extent by footpaths shaded with fine plantations of trees, it is, in the environs of the capital, strange to say, that it is worst kept. One day of rain turns the streets of the numerous villages beyond Kanagawa into gullies. On this point, as upon many others, the Japanese display, at the same time, a remarkable intelligence in all their works of civilization, and, when they come to the application of them, a carelessness in detail no less extraordinary. At length we reach the populous suburbs of Yeddo. A short halt on the threshold of one of the numerous tea-houses of the village of Omori introduces us to a merry company of citizens, accompanied by their wives and children. Other groups, who were making no less noise, were besieging a great toy-shop; an infinite variety of playthings for children, fancy straw hats, animals

Y

of plaited straw, painted and varnished, were placed in the front. I readily
recognized the bear of Yeso, the monkey of Niphon, the domestic buffalo, the tortoise
a hundred years old, dragging like a long tail great tufts of seaweed growing from
his shell.

But time pressed, and, the sight of the offing covered with white sails exciting
our impatience, we made our way to the sea-board. The road rests on strong
stone foundations, but the waves which formerly came up to it are now lost among
the reeds and sea-plants. On our left is stretched a pine-wood, and some cypress
groves, over which we noticed great flocks of crows were hovering; our guides
informed us that this is the place of capital executions, Dzousoukamori—or at least
that of the southern quarter of the great city, for there is a second in the
northern quarter.

The aspect of the place was exceedingly gloomy. If one is sufficiently fortunate
as to escape the sight of mutilated heads or bodies abandoned to the dogs and the
birds, one cannot behold, without horror, the great extent of earth covering the last
remains of criminals, a granite pillar, bearing I know not what funeral inscription,
a platform appropriated to the use of the officers who have to preside at executions,
and a gigantic statue of Buddha, a gloomy symbol of implacable expiation and
death without consolation.

Immediately after passing the place where the justice of the Taïkoun exhibits
his exemplary vengeance to the people, we enter the most ill-famed faubourg of Yeddo,
Sinagawa, which commences at two miles south of the city, and joins it at the gates
of the Takanawa quarter.

The Government has taken measures to provide foreigners coming to Yeddo, or
residing in that city, with a strong escort in passing through Sinagawa, which they
are only allowed to do by daylight. The regular population of this neighbourhood is
inoffensive, being composed for the most part of boatmen, fishermen, and labourers;
but they inhabit the cabins which throng the beach, while the two sides of the
Tokaïdo are lined almost uninterruptedly with tea-houses of the worst kind, which
harbour the same scum of society as in the great cities in Europe and America, and
in addition a very dangerous class of men proper to the capital of Japan. These
are the lonines; officers without employment, belonging to the caste of the Samourais,
and consequently preserving the right of wearing two swords. Some of them are

men of good family, who have been turned out of their homes in consequence of the debauchery of their lives. Others have lost, through misconduct, their place in the

SINAGAWA: INN GIRLS ASSAILING TRAVELLERS.

service of the Taïkoun, or in the military house of some Daimio. Others have been dismissed by a chief, whom evil times has forced to restrict his expenses by the reduction of his personal following.

Y 2

The lonine, deprived of the pay on which he lived, and knowing no other profession than that of arms, has generally no other resource, while waiting for a new engagement, than to take refuge in these dens of vice, where he repays the hospitality which he receives by the vilest kind of industry. The customers whom he attracts add new elements of wickedness to those with which the faubourg abounds. A kind of organization of discipline even in disorder is established. There are captains of lonines who hold the bands of wretches in blind subjection, and to whom the mysterious agents, who are the instruments of family vengeance or political hatred among the Japanese nobility, address themselves to get their bloody work done.

Sinagawa is abandoned by the police during the greater part of the night. The women come down upon the Tokaïdo, attack belated travellers, and drag them into the inns where they serve. The lonines are so conscious of the state of abjectness in which they live, that, when they come out of their dens, they generally hide their faces under broad-brimmed hats, or wear a piece of crape wrapped round the head, so that the eyes only are visible. It is in this unpleasing neighbourhood on the height of the Takanawa quarter that the Japanese Government has placed the foreign legations.

BOOK IV
Y E D D O

BRIDGE-MAKING EXTRAORDINARY.

CHAPTER I.

THE GREAT CITY.

NATURAL ADVANTAGES OF YEDDO.—THE DISTRICTS.—THE RIVERS.—THE CANALS.—THE
CROWD.—GENERAL FEATURES.—MONOTONY.

ABOVE all other great cities in the world, Yeddo seems to me to be favoured by
nature in situation, climate, vegetable wealth, and abundance of running water. It is
placed at the mouth of two rivers, of which one bathes the Hondjo on the east,
and the other, passing from north to south through the most populous quarters of the
town, separates the Hondjo from the city, and from the two Asaksas.

Two wide streams among seven or eight of less importance flow through the
districts which surround the citadel; they are the Tanoriké, and the Yeddo Gawa.

Basins, tanks, moats, and a whole network of irrigating canals, connect these natural water-courses, and carry commercial circulation, popular animation, and the movement and life of the immense capital, into the heart of the city, as well as to the centre and extremities of the Hondjo.

Among the number of canals on the sea side of the citadel, that of Niphon-bassi holds the first rank; the canal of Kio-bassi holds the second; they are both in the heart of the commercial city.

The most picturesque view of Yeddo is to be had from its Niphon-bassi, the most strongly fortified of the bridges.

On turning towards the north, we have on the horizon the white pyramid of Fousi-yama; on the right, the city, overlooked by terraces, the parks and the square towers of the residence of the Taïkoun. In the same direction, and as far as its junction with the moats of the citadel, the canal of Niphon-bassi is bordered on both banks by innumerable warehouses containing silk, cotton, rice, and saki. On our left, beyond the fish-market, lie canals, and streets which go down to the Ogawa. Hundreds of long boats, laden with wood, coal, bamboo canes, mats, covered baskets, boxes, barrels, and enormous fish, are crossing and recrossing through all the channels of navigation, while the streets seem to be exclusively given up to the people. Occasionally, a string of horses or black buffaloes heavily laden may be distinguished among the crowd of foot passengers, and sometimes we see heavy waggons carrying four or five layers of skilfully packed bales. These two-wheeled vehicles are drawn by coolies. No other kind of carriage is to be seen. The sound of wooden shoes upon the pavements and upon the sonorous bridges, the bells on the harness of the beasts of burden, the gongs of the beggars, the cadenced cries of the coolies, and the confused noises which come up from the canal, form a strange harmony, unlike the sounds of any other cities. All great cities have a voice of their own. In London it is like the surge of the rising tide; at Yeddo, it is like the murmur of a stream. As wave follows wave, so do generations succeed each other. That which I have under my eyes is passing away and disappearing, carrying with it all that its ancestors bequeathed to it; objects of worship, ancient costumes, old arms, laws which dated from centuries; all these will soon be only a tradition to the new Japanese society which is forming itself in the school of the West.

The Ogawa is the principal artery of Yeddo.

The Junk Harbour at the mouth of the great river occupies the entire space between the small island of Iskawa and the large triangular island which makes part of the district of Niphon-bassi. Above the canal of this name the bridge of Yétoi

A DEL ACCIDENT

extends from the regions of the north-east of the triangle to the western bank of the district of Foukagawa.

On both sides the population is essentially plebeian. With the exception of some Yaskis of the second and third class, the houses of fishermen, mariners, and small shopkeepers form these quarters. The bridge, the squares, and the neighbouring streets are constantly crowded with people of the lower classes, who have apparently no other object than recreation. The children play on the bridge and in the streets without any fear of being molested by the passers by.

No less than four gigantic bridges span the banks of the Ogawa, with intervals between them of about twenty minutes' walk; and the squares upon which they debouch, on the Hondjo side as well as on that of Yeddo, are almost all equally spacious.

Ascending the river on the north of Yeddo we come in the first place to the great bridge O-bassi, so named because it is the largest of the four; the third and fourth bridges, Riogokou and Adsouma, are very nearly as spacious; above the Adsouma-bassi the river takes the name of Sumida-gawa. These limpid waters form the extreme limit of the quarters north of the citadel. A single bridge, with sixteen arches, called the Bridge of Oskio-kaido, or Northern Road, places the whole of this

CHILDREN'S GAMES.

portion of the city in communication with the fields, the villages, and the rustic tea-houses of the northern suburb, which abounds in fertile fields and charming views, and is the favourite scene of parties of pleasure. If the inhabitant of Yeddo is proud of his good city, he is additionally proud of the magnificent suburb called Inako, for he is susceptible alike to the charms of nature and the pleasures of society, and loves the cool retreats on the banks of the Oskio-Kaido as well as the crowded quays of the city. There are three things to which the Japanese refuses his sympathy. First, that perfidious element the sea, which he abandons to the fishermen, the boatmen, and the garrison of the six detached forts; secondly, the cold solitude of the bonze-houses; and thirdly, the formidable enclosure of the citadel and the Daimio-Kodzi. He keeps as far away from all these as his business will permit, and such pleasure as he takes in the city itself he seeks for at a respectful distance from the seat of the Government.

The Riogokou, or Liogokou-bassi, may be regarded as the centre of the nocturnal merry-makings of the citizens and the hattamotos. This bridge, which is completely outside the commercial quarter of the city, places the Hondjo in communication with the Asaksas : or two districts on the left bank, which contain the principal places of amusement in Yeddo. The river is not deep enough to float merchant junks at this height, but its surface is covered with hundreds of light boats, which can move about freely in all directions. During the fine nights in summer, rafts, laden with pyrotechnic devices, go up the stream and fling bouquets of stars towards the sky. Gondolas, ornamented with brilliantly-coloured lanterns, cross and recross from one bank to the other, while large barques, all decorated with lamps and banners, are slowly propelled, or lie still upon the water, while their joyous crews are playing the guitar or singing. A crowd of bystanders lines the bridges and the quays, delighting in the animated and picturesque spectacle which the river affords.

Yeddo, at these times, presents an almost identical picture of a Venetian *fête*, without omitting the Syrens, who are not wanting on the waters of the Ogawa any more than on the Lagoons. But, on the other hand, we must be careful not to compare the great family boats of the Riogokou-bassi to the flower-laden barques of China. The former generally belong to respectable tea-houses, and are let out by the hour, the proprietors of the tea-houses furnishing their customers with refreshments and guitar-players. They are only annexes of these tea-houses, and occasionally of the little bamboo establishments which are built on the quays, and used by professional singers and musicians. The neighbourhood of the bridges, far from injuring the effect of the productions of these humble artists, lends them an additional charm.

I have often passed many hours in genuine Japanese *far niente*, listening to the confused sounds of singing and instruments of music rising above the murmur of the crowds of foot passengers from the tea-house of the Riogokou-bassi.

The intervals of silence are broken by the distant noise of comers and goers on the wooden bridge. No roll of carriages, none of the discordant clamour of our European cities breaks the charm of our impressions.

In Venice only, among European cities, can this same movement of the people, this same concert of steps, voices, sounds of music, be heard, without anything to trouble its peaceful cadence and its charming harmony. The Ogawa reminds us of the Grand

Canal, and the neighbourhood of the bridges of Yeddo is, like the public squares of Venice, the rendezvous of the citizen population. The multitudes who meet each other there every evening cause no inconvenience whatever; for though Yeddo is *par excellence* a city of great dimensions, the Japanese people practise spontaneously

A SIGNAL FROM A GONDOLA.

that discipline of circulation which our policemen have so much difficulty in establishing in our capitals.

Musical entertainments in Yeddo are only appreciable by the natives; for the Japanese melodies have something in them strange and incomprehensible to the ear of the European. The musical system upon which they rest is hardly known. Japanese music is very rich in semitones, and even in quarter-tones. M. F. J. Fétis observes that the melodies collected by Siebold seem to destroy the theory of analogy between Japanese and Chinese music ; so that there exists in the musical art, as in the native idiom of that country, the double mystery of a separate system, which has nothing in common with the Western world, or with that of the far East.

THE GREEN ROOM.

Japanese musical instruments are also remarkable for their originality.

Stringed instruments are made of the light and sonorous wood of the *Paulownia imperialis*, and the strings are fine cords of silk thinly coated with lacquer.

The sam-in and the guitar are, above all others, the popular instruments ; they are indispensable articles in the trousseau of a young bride.

The kokiou, a violoncello played with a bow, is frequently used, and also the biwa, a violoncello played with the plectrum of the samsin.

The Japanese clarionet is made of bamboo, like a flute, and they have also a sort of flageolette with eight holes.

The Japanese use the trumpet and the marine conch exclusively in their religious festivals.

They have two kinds of percussion instruments. One is made of copper or composite metal, and includes a great variety of gongs of various shapes : among them shields, bells, fish and tortoise, and the sound they produce varies between

A SAMSIN PLAYER LIGHTING HER PIPE.

the grave and sonorous and the squeaky and shrill. Besides these they have an instrument formed of two rings fastened on a handle, and struck by a light metal rod.

The other instruments of percussion are wooden rattles, stone drums like bowls, which stand on low frames ; a musical drum made of leather ; finally, the tom-tom, or portable tambourine, and the kettle drum.

The tambourines, which invariably accompany the character dances, are sometimes played two at a time, one being held under the arm and the other in the left hand.

The Sibata, or national theatre of the Japanese, occasionally employs the whole of the musical resources of the city, in pieces which bear a distant resemblance to our great operas.

According to a Japanese saying, in order to be happy one must visit Yeddo.

This extraordinary city contained, in 1858, one million eight hundred thousand inhabitants, and notwithstanding the fluctuations to which it is peculiarly subject, I

RIDING-SCHOOL AT YEDDO.

believe the calculation then made of the number of the population, and their division into classes, may be taken to represent its actual condition with tolerable accuracy.

The southern portion of the city, in which the foreign legations are established, includes eight districts, all essentially plebeian. They contain a considerable agricultural population, devoted to the culture of kitchen-gardens, rice-grounds, and all the arable lands not yet invaded by dwellings. These districts are composed of a multitude of mean houses tenanted by fishermen, labourers, small artizans, retail shop-keepers, inferior officers, and low-class eating-house keepers. A few lordly mansions break the uniformity of these wooden buildings by their long whitewashed walls. Bonze-houses and temples are scattered about everywhere, except in the two quarters built on the bay: Takanawa alone contains thirty.

The low streets and quays of Takanawa are filled from morning to night with a great concourse of people. The staple population of this quarter seems to live on taxes levied on all comers. Here tobacco is chopped and sold; there rice is packed and made into cakes; along the whole line dried fish, water melons, and an infinite variety of fruits and other cheap eatables are displayed upon tables in the open air, or in innumerable restaurants. Everywhere there are coolies, porters, and boatmen offering their services. In the small side streets are stalls for the pack-horses and stabling for the buffaloes, who draw in the products of the surrounding country upon the rustic carts which are the only wheeled vehicles in Yeddo.

At the doors of the tea-houses of Takanawa, the singers, dancers, and wandering jugglers, who come to try their luck in the capital, make their first appearance. Among the former there exists a privileged class subject to police discipline. They may be recognized by their large flat hats pulled down on their foreheads; they always go about two by two, or four by four—two dancers accompanying the two musicians who play the samsin and sing romantic songs. The favourite tumblers of the Japanese streets are little boys, who, before they begin their tricks, hide their heads under a hood, surmounted by a tuft of cock's feathers, and wear a little scarlet mask which represents a dog's muzzle. To the monotonous sound of their master's tambourine these poor children play their antics, representing the spectacle of a grotesque and really fantastic struggle between two animals with the heads of monsters and human limbs. The constant sound of gongs, and of the bells of the mendicant monks mingle with the deafening noises of the streets almost as frequently as at Kioto. At Yeddo I perceived for the first time that the monks were not shaven, and I inquired to what order they belonged. Our interpreter told me that they were laymen merely, people of Yeddo who were making a trade or merchandise of devotion. Although they were all dressed in white, the sign of mourning and repentance, those who carried a long stick with a bell, some books in a basket, and a large white hat decorated at one side with a drawing of Fousi-yama, had just returned from accomplishing a pilgrimage to the holy mountain at the expense of public charity; and the others, with a gong at the waist, a great black hat striped with yellow, and a heavy sack upon their backs, were probably ruined shopkeepers, who had nothing better to do than to hawk about idols on commission for a bonze-house.

By following the great street which, beginning at the Tokaïdo, cuts obliquely the chain of hills on which the legations are built, and crossing the southern part of Takanawa in a straight line from north to south, we pass successively through three distinct zones of the social life of Yeddo. First, the southern zone, which I have just described, with its multitudes living in the open air and conducting all their business in the public street. Between the hills we find a sedentary population, devoted to various kinds of manual labour. Even their dwellings and their workshops may be distinguished from afar by their significant signs: here a board cut in the form of sandals or of a kirimon; next an enormous umbrella of wax-paper hanging above the shop; further on a quantity of straw hats of all dimensions suspended from the top of the roof and reaching the shop-door. We look for a moment at the armourers and the burnishers engaged in repairing coats of mail, war fans, and sabres for the Samouraïs; an old artizan perfectly naked squats upon a mat, blowing the bellows of the forge with the great toe of the left foot, and hammering with his right hand an iron bar which he holds in his left. His son, also squatting in a corner, is putting the bars into the fire with a pair of pincers, and passing them to his father when reddened. The chief of our escort bade us continue our march. By degrees the road began to be deserted. We were entering into the vast solitude of an agglomeration of seignorial residences. On our right extended the magnificent shade of the park belonging to Prince Satsouma; on our left the boundary-wall of the palace of the Prince of Arima. When we had turned the north-east corner we found ourselves before the principal front of the building; it stretches out parallel to a plantation of trees forming the bank of a limpid river which divides the Takanawa quarter from that of Atakosta.

One of our party having made preparations to photograph this beautiful scene, two officers belonging to the Prince's household came to him and begged him to dis-

A A

A MÊLÉE IN A DUGGO ON NEW YEAR'S DAY.

continue his operations. Our friend requested them to go and take the orders of their 'master upon the subject; they went, but returned in a very few minutes, saying that the Prince absolutely forbade that any view should be taken of his palace. Béato obeyed respectfully, and ordered the koskeis to take away the machine ; and the officers retired perfectly satisfied, without the slightest suspicion that during their temporary absence the operator had taken two negatives. The yakounines of our escort, who had been witnesses of this scene, unanimously applauded the success of our friend's trick, but when he told them that it was his intention to take a photograph of the cemetery of the Taïkouns, they in their turn opposed him, with a persistency that nothing could shake. We were even obliged to renounce the hope of entering the cemetery. We could perceive very distinctly the lofty red pagoda and the sombre groves of cypress, but we could only obtain leave to pass along the eastern side of the grove of Siba—the name given to the holy place, and which occurs again in the complete designation of our own district Siba-Takanawa.

We pass the river on an arched bridge, not far from the place where Heusken was murdered ; and, leaving on our left a few houses of the Akabane suburb which the fire had spared, we crossed a square, bounded on one side by a matohan or archery garden, and on the other by walls, behind which rise the plantations and roofs of Soïosti—a group of temples belonging to the great bonze-house, which has the honour of receiving the Taïkouns into their last resting-places, there to abide under the combined protection of the two religious of the Empire.

Buddhism, it is true, is supreme in this place, where it possesses seventy sacred buildings, but among this number the ancient gods, Hatchiman, Benten, and Inari, has each his own chapel ; and a temple dedicated to the worship of the Kamis adorns the eastern avenue of Siba on the side of Tokaïdo and the bay. In the same direction is the landing-place of the Taïkoun, on the island of Amagoten at the mouth of the river Tamoriiké, which supplies the moats of the citadel.

Amagoten forms a regular parallelogram, and is united by two bridges, which are closed to the public. I rowed almost all round it in our consular sampan. The walls, the staircases, and the pavilions of the landing-place, and the groves of trees which surround it, are admirable in their grandeur, their simplicity, and their elegance. The river is bordered on both sides with great trees, which droop over its deep, pure waters.

A A 2

We left the enclosure of Siba, after we had reached its north-east limit. On that side is the palace of the High Priest, and beneath it we were shown the avenue and the door exclusively reserved for the use of the Taïkoun; he passes through it but once a year, when he goes to make his obligatory devotions at the tombs of his ancestors. Every courtier, following his example, pays a ceremonious visit on one day of the year to his family burial-ground.

We pursued our route towards the north. The district of Atakosta, which extends on our right as far as Amagoten, is occupied by the residences of the Daïmios and

A VIEW IN THE NEIGHBOURHOOD OF AKABANE.

the great functionaries of the Empire. On our left, fourteen little contiguous temples present themselves; those of Saïsoostji extend to the foot of the hills of Atagosa-yama. A wide stream separates them from the public way; each has its special bridge, door, and wall, surrounded by the chapels and habitations of the bonzes. At the back of the court is the Chapel of the Ablutions, the sacred grove, and the roof of the sanctuary. The sixth bonze-house is the exception. On crossing the threshold we saw a great flagged court, with a majestic tori of granite, and when we passed in at the sacred door we found ourselves in the presence of two candelabra placed at the foot of an esplanade reached by a flight of steps. Then comes a second court, bordered with fine trees, whose interlacing branches form arcades like that of a Gothic cathedral.   Through their foliage we distinguished a wide stone staircase, the summit lost amid verdure.

We ascended the staircase, which consists of one hundred steps very regularly laid, to the top of the hill.   On the right is another road, which crosses the

GREAT TORI OF ATAGOSA-YAMA.

wooded slopes, and is composed of a series of staircases, with flat terraces provided with *reposoirs*.

A dilapidated oratory with two insignificant idols—one standing upon a lotus, the other seated upon a tortoise—with long covered galleries surrounding the tea-houses, occupies the summit of Atagosa-yama.   The young waitresses of the house hasten to

serve us with refreshments, and we take a few minutes' rest before we approach the
pavilions at the two extremities of the terrace.

At length the moment has come when we shall get a complete view of the great
city. We begin at the southern pavilion, and we are at first dazzled by the extent
and brilliancy of the picture. The sun is going down to the horizon in a cloudless

IDOLS AT THE ORATORY OF ATAGOSA-YAMA.

sky; the transparency of the atmosphere permits us to distinguish the forts on the
luminous surface of the bay, but over the whole space which extends from the offing
to the foot of the hill there is nothing to arrest one's gaze. It is an ocean of long
streets, white walls, and grey roofs. The monotony of this picture is unbroken except
by a few groups of trees with dark foliage, or a spire rising above the undulating
lines of the innumerable houses.

In a neighbouring quarter we observe a large hole cut through the streets, as if a bomb-shell had passed ; it is the scene of a recent fire. At a little distance a sombre group of hills, consecrated to the sepulture of the Taïkouns, rises like a solitary island above a tumultuous sea.

THE HERO YASHITZONE.

The panorama seen from the northern pavilion is, if possible, more uniform. It includes the quarters inhabited by the nobility, and its limit on the horizon is the ramparts of the citadel.

The Daïmio-yaski, or seignorial residences to which we improperly gave the name of palace, do not differ except by their dimensions. The most opulent and the simplest present the same type of architecture, the same character of simplicity. They are composed of a first enclosure of buildings reserved for the Prince's servants and men-at-arms. These buildings have only one storey above the ground floor, and form a long square, always surrounded by a ditch; a single roof covers them, a single wall protects them, and most frequently they have no other issue on the public way than this one door. The windows are numerous, low, and wide, regularly placed on two parallel lines, and furnished with wooden shutters. In the interior a more or less considerable number of houses divided into regular compartments, like the barracks of the yakounines at Benten, are placed diagonally all round, or on two sides at least, of the centre

A RECEPTION BY A HIGH FUNCTIONARY.

building. These are the quarters of the Prince's troops. A wide space separates them from a second railed enclosure, which contains the Residence properly so called.

The dependencies of the palace face the military quarter. The principal building is surrounded by a verandah opening upon an interior court, and upon the garden with its tanks and its delicious shades. Such is the inviolable and silent asylum in which the proud Daimio shuts himself up in the bosom of his family, during the six months of each year which the custom of the Empire obliges him to pass in the capital.

We could form an idea of the dwellings of the Japanese nobility only from what might be discerned in a bird's-eye view of this quarter. No European has ever crossed the threshold of a Japanese Yaski. The Taïkoun's ministers, following the example of the nobility, have never permitted the foreign ambassadors to visit their dwellings; their personal relations are restricted to ceremonial audiences, which take place in certain buildings which belong to the administration, and correspond to the ministerial residences in our country. Among this number are the two Marine Schools on the shore of the bay, and the Gokandjo-bounio, the seat of the Finance Department, at the north-west extremity of Atakosta.

THE PATRONS OF SAKI.

Edifices of this kind have in general the same external appearance as the palaces of the Daïmios.

The panorama seen from Atagosa-yama shows us only a fourth part of the great capital. On the north our view was bounded by the walls of the residences of the Taïkoun. We resolved to devote another day to the quarter which, with the citadel, forms the central portion of Yeddo.

The road we were about to follow resembled a mysterious labyrinth of stone, formed of the ramparts, the towers, and the palaces, behind which the power of the Taïkoun has entrenched itself for two centuries and a half.

It is an imposing spectacle, but it creates a painful impression. The political order of things instituted in Japan by the usurper Iyéyas vaguely recalls the *régime* of the Venetian Republic under the rule of the Council of Ten. It has, if not all its grandeur, at least all its terrors—the sombre majesty of the chief of the State, the impenetrable mystery of his government, the latent and continuous action of a system of espionage officially organized through all the branches of the administration, and bringing in its suite proscriptions, assassinations, and secret executions. We must not push the comparison further. We vainly seek at Yeddo, in the vast extent of the citadel,

ROSKIS SEEKING NEW YEAR'S GIFTS.

any monument which deserves mention beside the marvellous edifices of the Piazza of St. Mark; artistic taste is completely wanting in the Court of the Taïkoun. It has been relinquished to the people, with poetry, religion, social life, all those superfluous things which do but clog the wheels of the governmental machine. From end to end of the administrative hierarchy, every functionary is assisted by a controller; the genius of the employés is exercised in doing nothing and saying nothing which can furnish matter for compromising reports. As to their private life, it is hidden, like that of the Japanese nobles in general, behind the walls of their domestic fortresses. While the streets of the town, composed of houses standing wide open on the public way, are constantly enlivened by a crowd of comers and goers of all ages and of both sexes; in the aristocratic quarters neither women nor children are to be seen, except indeed by stealth behind the window bars in the servants' quarters.

There are two societies in Yeddo—one, armed and privileged, lives in a state of

DOMESTIC EXORCISM.

magnificent imprisonment, in the vast citadel; the other, disarmed, and subject to the dominion of the first, seems to enjoy the advantages of liberty; but, in reality, an iron yoke weighs upon the middle classes of the people of Yeddo. For every five heads of families, the Taïkounal administration sets up one as a magistrate over the other four. Iniquitous laws punish a whole family, a whole quarter, for the crime

B B 2

of one of its members. The properties, and even the lives, of the citizens, are secured by no legal guarantee. The extortions and the violence of the two-sworded men remain too frequently unpunished. The citizen finds compensation in the charms of the beautiful city. If the *régime* of the Taïkouns is severe, he remembers that the Mikados were not always amiable, and that one of them delighted in exhibiting his skill as an archer by shooting down peasants who were forced to climb trees within easy reach of his arrows. The peoples of countries accustomed to despotism are puzzled to decide where their patience ought to stop.

A Japanese Emperor, born under the constellation of the Dog, commanded that dogs were to be respected as sacred animals, that they should never be killed, and that at their death they should receive the honours of sepulture. One of his subjects whose dog had died thought it right to inter the animal upon one of the funeral hills. As he was going along, fatigued with the weight of the four-footed corpse, he ventured to remark to a friend who was accompanying him, that the Emperor's decree appeared to him ridiculous. "Take care how you murmur," replied his comrade, "and recollect that our Emperor might just as well have been born under the sign of the Horse."

The Sakourada quarter, which forms the first great line of defence of the citadel on the southern side, is surrounded by water at all parts, except the west, where it communicates with the Bantsiô quarter by the arsenal belonging to the Taïkoun. Ten bridges are thrown over the great ditches. The southern bridges have fortified gates, behind which the road makes a bend, which exposes it to the fire from the ramparts, and from the guns mounted in the interior. A strong detachment of the Taïkoun's troops occupies the guard-house adjoining the gate through which we pass. The common soldiers are men from the mountains of Akoni, who are discharged after two or three years' service. Their uniform is made of blue cotton, and consists of tight trousers, and a shirt like that of the Garibaldian Volunteers, but crossed by white bands on the shoulders. They wear cotton socks, and leather soles fastened by sandals; also a belt, from which hangs a large sabre with a lacquer scabbard. A pointed hat of lacquered cardboard completes their costume, but they only wear it when mounting guard, or on parade. The guns of the Japanese army are all percussion, with varied calibre and construction. I saw four different kinds in the racks of the barracks at Benten, into which a yakounine took me. He first showed me a Dutch model, then an arm of inferior quality, made at Yeddo; then an American gun, and finally the Minié, whose use was being taught by a young officer to a picket of soldiers in the courtyard. I remarked that this officer used the Dutch language. I asked him to come home with me, that I might show him my fowling-piece and a Swiss carbine. Half a dozen of his comrades also accepted my invitation.

A SCULPTOR OF IDOLS.

I have more than once been present at assaults of arms by the yakounines. The champions salute each other before attacking. The one who is on guard frequently kneels on the ground, to parry his adversary's blows more successfully. Each pass is accompanied by theatrical poses and expressive gestures: each blow provokes passionate exclamations on the part of both. Then the judges intervene and deliver their verdict. In the intervals the combatants drink tea, after which they recommence with great spirit. There is even a School of Fence for the use of the Japanese ladies. Their arm is a lance, with a bent blade, which may be compared to a Polish reaping-hook. They carry it with the point towards the ground, and manœuvre regularly in a series of attitudes, poses, and harmonious movements, which would look remarkably well in a ballet. I was not allowed to enjoy this pretty spectacle long. I only caught a glimpse of it in passing before the half-open court. My yakounines immediately shut the door, assuring me that the customs of the country did not permit beholders.

The Japanese nobles display much luxury, and take great pride in their arms, especially in their swords, which are of unrivalled temper, and are generally adorned on the handle and scabbard with ornaments in carved and wrought metal of extra-ordinary richness. But the principal value of these arms consists in their antiquity and their celebrity. Every sabre in the old families of the Daimios has its tradition and its history, whose *éclat* is measured by the blood which it has shed. A new sword must not remain intact in the hands of the man who has bought it; while waiting for an opportunity of dyeing it in human blood, the Samouraï who has become its happy possessor tries it on live animals, or, what is still better, upon the corpses of executed criminals. The executioner gives them up to him upon being authorized so to do by the proper functionary, and he fastens them to a cross in his courtyard, where he practises himself in cutting and hacking until he has acquired sufficient strength and address to cut two corpses, tied together, through the middle.

It is easy to imagine the aversion with which the arms of the West inspire these Japanese gentlemen, for whom the sword is at once an emblem of bravery and a title to nobility. When the son of a Samouraï is too little to carry arms at his belt, he is seen walking, with a koskei, or even an elder sister, following him respectfully, and holding in her right hand, by the middle of the scabbard, a sword suitable to the height of the diminutive personage. In another year or two fencing will become the principal occupation of his life.

The Taïkoun selected a number of his young yakounines, and sent them to Nagasaki, to learn the use of fire-arms, under the tuition of the Dutch officers. They were not very well received when they returned to the capital, and were quartered in the barracks for the purpose of instructing the new Japanese infantry. Their former comrades shouted "Treason!" and threw themselves on them with arms in their hands. There were victims on both sides. Nevertheless the decline of the sword is inevitable. Notwithstanding the traditional prestige with which the privileged

caste still endeavour to surround it, notwithstanding the contempt in which it affects to hold the military innovations of the Government, that democratic arm the musket has been introduced into Japan, and with it an incalculable social revolution has become a fact which the representatives of the feudal *régime* resent bitterly but vainly.

The conduct of their chiefs has precipitated the catastrophe. Conspiracies in the palace and political assassinations multiply themselves at Yeddo with frightful rapidity. It is averred that not only several ministers of state, but two Taïkouns, have successively died violent deaths since the opening up of Japan. The same fate has befallen the Gotairo, or Regent Ikammon-no-Kami, the governor of the young sovereign, who died in 1866. His palace is situated on a hill, in the southern portion of the Sakourada quarter, in front of the wide ditches and the high walls forming the exterior enclosure of the citadel. It overlooks, on the east and the south, the great squares and streets formed by some fifty of the nobles' residences.

It was in this princely neighbourhood that, on the 24th of March, 1860, at eleven o'clock in the morning, the Regent, carried in his norimon, and coming out of the citadel by the Sakourada bridge, with an escort of four or five hundred men, was assailed by a band of seventeen lonines in the spacious public road, parallel with the ditch in the direction of his own palace. On both sides the fighting was severe. Twenty soldiers of the escort fell at their posts; five conspirators perished with arms in their hands, two performed the "happy despatch," four were made prisoners; the others escaped—among them the chief of the expedition, who carried away the Regent's head under his cloak. Public rumour adds that the head was exposed in the chief place of the province. in which the Prince of Mito, the instigator of the conspiracy, resides, and then at Kioto, before the buildings of the Daïri, and finally that the Regent's people found it one day in the garden of the palace, into which it had been thrown, over the wall, in the night.

The portions of Yeddo inhabited by the aristocracy are almost entirely devoid of buildings consecrated to public worship. There is not one in the whole of the Daimio's quarter. Bantsiô and Souronga have each three temples, but they are of little importance. There are half a dozen in Sakourada, amongst which is a celebrated bonze-house under the invocation of Sannô, "the King of the Mountain." Its title is one of the surnames of Zinmou; nevertheless the bonze-house belongs to the Buddhist

religion, and contains an altar consecrated to Quannon. The buildings and the groves of the sacred place occupy a group of hills, which rise above the southern enclosure of Sourouga, with its vast basins of limpid water surrounded by trees and flowers, and its myriads of birds.

COLLECTORS FOR THE KAMI TEMPLES.

The political system of the Taïkouns did not disdain clerical support for their building dynasty. But as Iyéyas and his successors had nothing to hope from the good will of the Mikados, they conciliated the favour of the most influential sects of Buddhism by endowing bonze-houses and temples, which surpass the most sumptuous sacred edifices of Kioto. The munificence of the Taïkouns with regard to Buddhism has, however, added nothing to the reverence professed at Yeddo for the ministers of that religion. It appears to me that, in all the diverse classes of society in the capital, the position of the bonzes is analogous to that of the Popes of the Greek Church

A BONZERY AND BAMBOO GROVE.

when the latter come into contact with the nobles, the traders, or the Moujiks. The priests of the Kami worship are in a still less enviable condition, because their existence

c c 2

is hardly noticed. It is true that the representatives of the Mikado at the Court of the Taïkoun, and some provincial noblemen, honour them by their patronage, but the generality of the feudal nobility in residence at Yeddo stand entirely aloof from what is being done around them, in matters of religion as well as in everything else. They would prefer to pay a chaplain in the house rather than contribute to the support of any public worship whatever. The only thing they will do for the ancient national religion is to authorize the Kami priests to send their collectors once a year to the aristocratic quarters. The priests, on their side, considering that it would be advisable to stimulate the charity of the higher classes by the attraction of some pious jugglery, have created two classes of collectors. The first, who go about in all seasons by order and at a fixed price, is composed of fortune-telling priestesses dressed in white surplices, with a holy-water machine constructed of paper in the left hand, and in the right a bunch of pebbles; they accompany their prophecies with a kind of rhythmical dance, to which a koskei dressed in a Kioto cap marks time by beating a large drum.

The second class of collectors go out only at the new year and pay general visits. The presents made on this occasion are voluntary. The persons charged with this office are the principal koskeis of the Kami temples, each of whom is followed by his own special koskei. The leader is dressed after the fashion of the ancient priests of the Court of the Mikado, with a lacquered cap, a great sword, and padded trousers, and he holds in his right hand a classic fan of cedar-wood. His attendant, who is disguised as a koskei from Kioto, carries a small tambourine, and a bag, destined to receive the gifts. Dances, comic songs, and burlesque pantomimes form the oratorical artifices of the two collectors. The buffooneries of the first are played up to by his attendant. Thus the sacred collection is effected from palace to palace in the midst of the laughter and applause of the noble feudal families, whose political existence rests entirely upon the very religion which they help to bring into contempt.

RESIDENCE OF GOVERNMENT FUNCTIONARIES.

CHAPTER II.

THE TAIKOUNS.

MODERN ASPECT OF YEDDO.—THE RESIDENCE OF THE TAIKOUN.—HIS COURT.—CEREMONIAL OF AUDIENCE.—THE POLICY OF IYÉYAS.—THE LAWS OF GONGHENSAMA.—THE PREROGATIVES OF THE TAIKOUN.—LAW OF SUCCESSION.—THE LAST TAIKOUN.

THE immensity of the Japanese capital is exceedingly striking. Imagination and sight alike become weary of dwelling on this boundless agglomeration of human habitations, all bearing the same stamp of uniformity. Among our old cities in Europe each has a physiognomy proper to itself, though all are united by the charm of ancient memories and artistic achievements. At Yeddo, everything belongs to the same epoch, and is in the same style. Everything rests upon one single fact, upon the same political data—the foundation of the dynasty of the Taikouns. Yeddo is a completely modern city, and seems to be waiting for its history and its monuments.

Even the residence of the Taïkouns, seen from a distance, is remarkable only for its dimensions, its vast extent of terraces separated by enormous granite walls, its parks of magnificent trees, its moats covered with flocks of aquatic birds.

In the interior the vast proportion of everything—walls, avenues of trees, canals, gates, guard and custom houses — is most impressive. The exqu'site cleanliness of the squares and the avenues, the profound silence which reigns around, the noble and simple buildings of cedar with their marble basements, awaken those impressions of majesty, mystery, and fear which despotism demands for the maintenance of its prestige.

Here, as in the Japanese temples, we are forced to admire the sobriety of the means employed by the native architects for the realization of their most daring conceptions. It is always from nature that they borrow their resources and ideas. The audience chamber of the Taïkoun possesses neither columns, statues, nor any kind of furniture. It is composed of a long line of saloons of great extent and height, separated from each other by moveable partitions which reach the ceiling. They are ranged in perspective, like the wings of a theatre, and the back of the scene opens on the lawns and avenues of the immense parks.

The throne of the Taïkoun is a sort of divan raised on a few steps, and placed in front of a screen which faces the principal entrance. On his right and left sit the residents delegated from the Court of Kioto, the ministers of state, and the members of the representative council of the Daimios. Throughout the whole extent of the hall, as far as the eye can reach, the high functionaries of the Court, the princes of the feudal provinces, the nobles of the cities, the castles, and the country districts, the Hattamotos or military nobles, are ranged by hundreds, and at the great receptions by thousands, in the places assigned to them by their hierarchical positions. No sound is heard throughout this vast crowd. Everyone is unarmed, unshod, his feet hidden in the folds of his great trailing trousers. The Daimios may be recognized by their high pointed caps and long mantles of brocade, embroidered on both sleeves with their family escutcheon. The functionaries of the Taïkoun wear a surcoat of silken gauze, spread out over the shoulders like two stiff wings.

The assembly, divided into two distinct groups, squat in silence, before the arrival of the Taïkoun, on the thick bamboo mats which cover the floor; they prostrate themselves before their sovereign as soon as he appears, and they remain in that attitude until, having taken his seat upon his throne, he has ordered his ministers to receive the communications on the orders of the day. Each speaker or petitioner prostrates himself when he approaches the throne.

The costume of the Taïkoun is composed of a wide-sleeved robe, drawn in at the waist by silken cords, and of wide trousers, which fall over his velvet boots. On his head he wears a golden toque, resembling the cap of the Doges of Venice.

What more splendid and more majestic decoration could his throne have, than this living gallery of the glories of Japan, this august assembly of the princes, nobles, and high functionaries, who personify the wealth, power, and dignity of the Empire?

This picture, which the Taïkoun views with pride, is the characteristic work of Iyéyas. It belonged to him alone, and is not a continuation of the work of Taïkosama. Iyéyas is the real founder of the dynasty of the Taïkouns, though he never actually received recognition as such. His honorary name in the annals of Japan is Gonghensama. The title of Taïkoun dates only from 1858.

During the conferences between Commodore Perry and the delegates of the Japanese Government at Yokohama, the American negotiator requiring to designate the political head of the Empire, and finding himself greatly embarrassed how to choose among the titles of Siogoun, Koubasama, and others which had been conferred by the Mikados on their temporal lieutenants, the interpreter Hyashi proposed that a uniform denomination should be agreed upon, to be expressed by the two Chinese signs, Taï-Koun, which signifies a great chief; and this was assented to. Since then, although the Government of Japan has shown itself on several occasions little satisfied with the innovation, the title of Taïkoun has passed officially into all conventions concluded with other Governments, and it has become easily and completely popular. This circumstance alone proves that, in the mind of the Japanese people, the notion of the Taïkounate was entirely distinct from that of the power of the Siogouns, long before it had received its proper denomination.

A few words respecting the career of Gonghensama will explain how the political *régime* which he inaugurated is distinguished from that of the Siogouns.

The conflict with the territorial nobility commenced in the first place by Yoritomo, and carried on valiantly by Taïkosama, could not fail to result in the annihilation of the feudality and of the Daïri, and in the transformation of the Empire of the Mikados into an absolute monarchy, whose sceptre should remain hereditary in the family of Faxiba, the ex-groom.

Since Iyéyas had rid himself of the last scion of that family, he had only to consolidate his own dynasty. Far from becoming intoxicated by the success of his arms, he profited by the moment of his greatest good fortune to make terms with the heads of the feudal nobility who still held the country. Iyéyas offered them peace, which they gladly accepted; and he laid down, in concert with them, the conventions which have formed, up to our time, the constitutional basis of the Empire, under the title of the Laws of Gonghensama.

It is important to observe that the minister of Taïkosama was not simply a *parrenu*, or a vulgar usurper.

Tokoungawa Inimnato-no-Iyéyasu was descended from the ancient race of Ghendjis, who go back to the 56th Mikado, who died A.D. 880. This is one of the line dynastic stems from which the great Daimios, or Kokoushis (or Gok'chis) of Japan, spring.

The latter are nineteen in number, comprising the head of the Tokoungawa family. He has the title of Prince of Kwanto.

In treating with the heads of the territorial nobility, Iyéyas was entering into negotiations with his peers, who might without any derogation recognize him as their legislator. On the other hand, this explains the concessions which he was about to make to them in the interests of the public peace and the future of his dynasty.

According to the compact of Gonghensama, the prerogatives of the Taïkoun were singularly limited. He disposed, it is true, of the sea and land forces, and concentrated in his own hands the legislative authority as well as the administrative power. He nominated the five ministers who composed his Cabinet, or Council of State, "the Gorogio," and from him all the civil functionaries and all the military officers in the various services of the Government received their commissions. On the other hand, his edicts were submitted to the control and placed under the guarantee of the Mikado, and the eighteen Kokoushis who formed the representative council at Yeddo, and who, without playing an active part in the administrative questions of their fortunate colleague, could oppose him with the Mikado, and interfere, in certain doubtful cases, in the election of a new Taïkoun.

The law of succession, which makes part of the compact of Gonghensama, ordains that the Siogounal power shall be maintained in the direct descent of the heir chosen by Iyéyas in the person of his eldest son; but it adds that, in default of direct descent, this power shall pass to one of the collateral branches.

There is, therefore, a competition on the part of the collaterals, who appeal to the intervention of the Council of Kokoushis, whose decision is submitted, in the final instance, to the sanction of the Mikado.

The chief object of Iyéyas was to place the power of his family upon an imposing and permanent footing.

In proportion as he made himself agreeable to the eighteen Kokoushis, whose neutrality it was necessary to secure, he was inexorable with respect to the nobles of secondary rank who had attached themselves to the fortunes of the unhappy Fidé-Yozi. Not content with having beaten and dispersed them in the battle of Sekigahara, in the year 1600, he despoiled them of their domains, which he distributed among his children and his partisans.

To his eight sons he gave eight great fiefs, known as Gokamongkés, and whose chief bore the title of Kami.

In addition, Iyéyas created three hundred and forty-four Kofdais, or noble vassals, whom he also provided with hereditary fiefs. To this category of Daimios belong several remarkable personages, who have figured in the history of the modern relations between Japan and the West.

The political achievements of Gonghensama were consummated by an audacious act, which rapidly developed his residential city, and opposed to the old feudal nobility —who were subject to the Mikado only—an entirely new privileged caste, a military nobility without land, and who, being dependent upon the favour of the sovereign, were exclusively devoted to the service of the new-born' dynasty.

By one single act he ennobled and endowed eighty thousand of his partisans. Such was the origin of the numerous classes of petty officers or functionaries of Yeddo, who are called Hattamotos.

The founder of the Taïkounal power took care to display the national standard of the Empire of the Rising Sun upon his residence. But in his quality as head of the clan of Tokoungawa, he caused all the branches of his family to adopt arms, and thus commemorated the most glorious reminiscences of his ambitious career. The bodies of troops which he commanded in the battle of Sekigahara having been ordered to affix to their banners a common sign of recognition—three marshmallow leaves, so arranged as to meet at their points, was the design agreed upon. This humble emblem led them to victory. We see it at present, not only in the liveries of Kokoushi Kwanto, but among the arms of numerous princes of the same blood.

Fidé-Tada, the son and successor of Gonghensama, wishing to retain the power which he had inherited as much as possible among his direct descendants, instituted three special fiefs, the investiture with which could alone give access to the throne, for his three sons. They are called fiefs of the Gosankés, and each is known by the name of one of the rich provinces with which they are endowed—Owari, Ksiou, and Mito ; their owners bear the title of Dono, Owari-dono, Gosanké d'Owari ; Kii or Ksiou-dono, Gosanké de Ksiou : Mito-dono, Gosanké de Mito.

The third successor of Iyéyas, desiring to secure possession of the throne to his descendants, in case the Gosanké families should become extinct, founded for his three sons the three Gosankios or fiefs, which were endowed in the second degree with the same titles and the same rights as the preceding.

The Gosankios are : Stotsbashi-dono, Taiusou-dono, and Shimidsou-dono. The latter fief is retained by extinction in the immediate domain of the Princes of Kwanto.

The family of Stotsbashi is also extinct, but the fief was conferred upon a cadet of Mito. In 1853, the family and the princes of Ksiou having given an uninterrupted series of Taïkouns to the Empire, the fifth—he who admitted the squadron of Commodore Perry into the waters of the Gulf of Yeddo—did not survive until the return of the American mission. There is reason to believe that in 1858 the Taïkoun, with whom Lord Elgin was supposed to be in negotiation, no longer existed when these delegates affixed his seal and their signatures to the British Treaty. I have heard several Japanese express great uneasiness on the subject of the young Prince who was occupying the throne during my sojourn in Japan. "For a long time there has not been any Taïkoun except those of the dynasty of Ksiou, and it is very much to be regretted that there should be none of the family of Mito." I asked whether the family possessed a presumptive heir since the last Lord of Mito, to whom the assassination of the Regent was attributed. "We do not know," was the reply; "he has left an adopted son, who is universally respected—he is the Stotsbashi; he is invested with the dignity of Vice-Taïkoun."

Towards the end of 1866, correspondence from Japan brought intelligence of the death of the Taïkonn at Osaka on the 28th of August, in consequence of the fatigue of his campaign against the Prince of Nagato: and that his lieutenant, Gosankios Stotsbashi, who had become the head of the chief Tokonngawa family, had been raised by the Mikado to the dignity of Daï-Seï-Siogoun of the Empire. He was, since Yoritomo, the forty-sixth Siogoun, and since Iyéyas, the fifteenth and last Taïkoun of Japan.

A PHYSICIAN'S VISIT.

CHAPTER III.

THE POLITICAL SYSTEM OF THE TAÏKOUNS.

FAMILY FEUDS.—GOSANKÉS AND GOSANKIOS.—THE DEVELOPMENT OF THE TAÏKOUNATE INTO
A DESPOTIC SYSTEM.—POLITICAL ASSASSINATION.—THE SPY SYSTEM.

AN inherent permanent cause of dissolution existed in the Taïkounate. The
law of succession devised by Gonghensama, and perfected by his son and his great-
grandson, could not fail to retain the power in the family of Tokonngawa; but by

guaranteeing to the three Gosankés an equal right to competition in case of a failure in the direct descent, it provoked dangerous rivalry, and authorized candidatures which were afterwards disallowed by the Council of Daimios.

Brothers were then seen arrayed against brothers, soliciting favour and begging for support from the feudal dynasties. As soon as the choice of the council was made, the discarded pretenders gave free course to their discontent, or secretly conspired against the rival who had been preferred to them. Analogous intrigues took place among the Gosankios, when the chance arose for them to take precedence over the Gosankés.

Thus, the Taïkounate, that is to say the ancient office of the Siogoun, was changed into a dynastic institution, presenting the combined inconvenience of despotic government and elective monarchy—insecurity, internal jealousy, family hatred, palace intrigues, and political assassination.

The Taïkoun, surrounded snares, by the exercise of his power checked by the coalition of an aristocracy, at first silent, and then audacious, was still more sorely threatened in his family interests by the ambitious designs of his favourites and those who surrounded him.

Such a state of things necessarily led to an extraordinary political system. The Court of Yeddo raised the necessity of espionage to a high art, and made it its principal means of government. Capital punishment and transportation became the necessary complement. By way of corrective, voluntary suicide, or suicide officially prescribed, were admitted.

The spy system in Japan comprehended, in the first place, the organization of a secret police, analogous to that of the states which are at the head of European civilization; but, it had a complete hierarchy of public functionaries, known under the general title of Ometskés, or Inspectors. From the sergeants of police up to the ministers of state there was not an employé, not a high dignitary of the Taïkounal administration, who was not controlled in the exercise of his functions by his official inspector. I have been present at negotiations in which the Japanese minister presented his Ometské to me, and discussed with him what response was to be made to my questions. The scribe of the minister and the scribe of the Ometské compared notes respectively of all that was said. Consequently every matter became the object of two parallel reports; the superior functionary to whom it was addressed had in his turn to submit his report to the control of his acolyte, and so on until the record of the whole affair should have reached the supreme authority, who picked it to pieces and pronounced upon it.

Suicide—here I speak only of the noble suicide—consists, as its name of hara-kiri indicates, of cutting open the stomach. It is said sometimes to replace the

A NOBLE SENTENCED TO THE HARA KIRI.

duel, but I doubt the accuracy of the assertion. The Japanese do not understand duelling, but they supply that defect in their social organization by assassination. There are circumstances, however, in which honour can be satisfied only by the hara-kiri, or by the immolation of a voluntary victim, which serves as a pretext for the vengeance of the outraged family. An example will serve to illustrate this case.

The Governor of Kanagawa, Hori-Oribé-no-Kami, exchanges with M. Heusken, the Dutch Secretary and Interpreter of the American Legation, an official correspondence which seems to him to be derogatory to his dignity. He complains to his chief, Ando-no-Kami, Minister of Foreign Affairs, and requests him to procure M. Heusken's expulsion from Japan. This being refused by the minister, he consults the members of his family and his friends. They all agree that his birth and his title do not permit him to survive such an affront, and the proud Governor performs the hara-kiri in their presence. The witnesses are prepared to do their duty. The careless Heusken fell under the swords of a band of conspirators, who put his escort of yakonnines to flight, as he passed along the street of Akabané. The minister Ando never went out except by daylight, strongly escorted, his hand on the pommel of his sword, which lay beside him in his norimon, and his eyes always on the watch. Thus the moment the conspirators appeared he was up and ready, encouraging his men and setting them an example by his own bravery. The assassins dispersed, leaving their dead and wounded on the ground. From that moment the quarrel was over; public opinion was satisfied, and the family of Oribé had only to keep themselves quiet, which they were quite ready to do.

Suicide, officially prescribed, replaces capital punishment in the case of a Japanese noble, where the sentence has been pronounced by his peers on account of forfeiture of the honour of his caste, or by order of the Taïkoun, when it is the crime of high treason. The trial, the judgment, and the execution of the sentence are conducted with great solemnity. A vast wooden hall, with a roof supported by four pillars, is erected in the interior of the citadel. It is surrounded by a paling of bamboo, hung on the inside with white silk. Men-at-arms are posted around the enclosure. At each of the extremities there is a door, one for the use of the accused, accompanied by two friends or witnesses chosen by himself, and by his legal defenders; the other for the use of his accusers and his judges. The accused, dressed in white, as are also his witnesses, squats in front of his accusers, who sit on folding stools, upon a white carpet, bordered with red. The judges are placed on their left, and on their right the counsel for the defence stand, at a respectful distance. All are in full dress. A person who stands behind the accused wears a military uniform, and has a large sword passed through his belt. His orders are to strike off the head of the accused, should he, so soon as the sentence has been pronounced, refuse to put an end to his own existence.

The instrument of punishment is, till the last moment, hidden behind a screen. It is a long knife, with a very strong blade, and a thick large handle. Every Samouraï is taught in his youth what is the exact spot into which the entire blade is to be plunged, in order to make the blow mortal, and destroy consciousness immediately. Beside the little table, on which the instrument lies, are placed a bowl of saki, a canful of water, and a large empty tub, which is slipped under the victim as he falls with his face towards the ground. When the case has to be legally debated, the jury retire behind the screen to consider their verdict ; and on their return into court, the accused prostrates himself while the sentence is read.

I am assured that it is extremely rare for a Samouraï, condemned to suicide, to exhibit the slightest hesitation in the accomplishment of the hara-kiri.

It sometimes happens that capital punishment is commuted to banishment. The condemned man is then sent to one of the convict islands, Sado, Oki, Ison, or Fatsisio. The chief among them is Fatsisio, the most distant of the Japanese possessions on the south.

We are far from understanding the political mysteries of the Venice of the Far East, and it is difficult even for the Japanese to arrive at a just knowledge of them. But everybody at Yeddo knows that the prisons of the Daimiô-Kodzi have their torture chambers, their dungeons, and places for secret executions.

In Japan, the simple repression of common offences is marked from beginning to end by ferocity.

The police fall upon suspected persons like a vulture on its prey.

All investigations are accompanied by the bamboo ; the act of accusation is unrolled before the eyes of the prisoner, and if he does not reply according to the pleasure of the prosecutor, blows rain upon his shoulders. Woe to him if he is suspected of lying, or of entrenching himself within a system of denial ; he is then forced to kneel upon a framework of hard wood, and in that position great slabs of stone are placed upon his bended legs, until they are reddened with his blood, and the pain extracts from him an acknowledgment, either real or fictitious, of the guilt of which he is accused.

In the eyes of a Japanese judge every accused man is guilty. The tribunals thirst for victims, which are supplied by the agents of the police. In the depôt there are always twenty or thirty prisoners in each hall. They wear the same dress,

composed of only one garment, a coarse kirimon of blue cotton. As they are not permitted either to comb their hair or to shave, in the course of a few days the beard and hair suffice to place them in the category of the impure, and inspire the beholder with contempt and disgust. They sleep upon bare planks on the prison pavement.

Those who can pay for it may sometimes obtain a mat or a wadded quilt from the gaoler. Rice is their only food. Absolute silence is imposed upon them, and to this rule there is but a single exception; it is when one of the prisoners has been condemned to death. When the officers of the prison take him away from his companions in captivity, the latter are permitted to utter together, and with all their strength, a long cry of despair, after which the silence is more impressive than before.

The laws of Gonghensama do not admit of imprisonment, except accompanied by corporal punishment or death. Grandees of the Empire and bonzes may be banished. They are sent according to their rank to one or other of the convict islands, and permitted to occupy themselves during their exile in weaving silk stuffs. Imprisonment is never of long duration, except as a preliminary to trial. The sentence may add a few weeks, or some months, as I have seen at Yokohama, where the koskei of a resident European was condemned for theft to three months' imprisonment at the residence of the Governors of Kanagawa. He was shut up, with other malefactors, in a lofty cell composed of four whitewashed walls, surmounted by a thick railing, and he daily received for his food a bowl of rice and a tempo, or small piece of money, worth about a halfpenny (English), for which sum the gaoler gave him a piece of fruit or some vegetable. But, generally speaking, imprisonment is only an accessory to corporal punishment, such as flogging or branding.

For small thefts, branding is inflicted. It is not done with a hot iron, but a kind of lancet is used, with which an incision is made in the left arm, and the scar is rendered indelible by tattooing powder.

Every malefactor who falls into the hands of justice, after having been marked twenty-four times, or who commits a theft of the value of forty *itsibous*, is condemned to capital punishment. The ordinary plan is to wait until three or four executions are to take place, and then they are carried out in the yard of the prison with only the Governors and their officers for witnesses. The condemned are brought one by one into their presence, their eyes are bandaged, and the kirimon thrown back over their shoulders; one of them is then made to kneel; four assistants, who squat beside him, hold his feet and arms, and his head falls under the practised sword of the chief executioner. They throw the head into a tub, and wash it; and it is afterwards exhibited with the others for twenty-four hours in one of the marketplaces of the city. The body, which is immediately stripped and washed, is placed in a straw sack; when the first sack has been tied up, they bring out the second criminal, and the same operation is repeated, until the task of the executioner is completed. Then nothing remains except to hand over the corpses to the claimants for them, to be used for the noble purposes of their sword exercise.

Only great criminals, such as incendiaries and assassins, are put to death at the public place of execution. The former are given over to the flames. When they are attached to the fatal pile, their hands are covered with a layer of earth; for the Japanese do not yet understand the use of chains—and their straw ropes, however well plaited, would not long resist the action of fire. Former residents in Japan have described to me, as eye-witnesses, the execution of an incendiary, who had attempted to burn the "Frank Quarter." He was taken in the act at his second or third attempt. Had I felt so disposed, I might have witnessed the crucifixion of two parricides; for I received one morning an illustrated broadsheet, detailing their crime, and announcing their approaching execution; it had been bought from a newsman who was crying it publicly, after a fashion not altogether unknown to Christian civilization.

Assassination without aggravating circumstances is punished by decapitation, as was formerly the case in Europe. Public executions are justified under the pretext that they produce a salutary impression on the crowd. The criminal is placed on horseback upon a high wooden saddle, and a rosary is hung round his neck. The cortége is headed by certain officials, who direct the attention of the people to a large inscription, borne by coolies, and detailing in emphatic terms the lugubrious drama whose final act is about to be accomplished.

In Japan, as in all despotic states, it is principally upon the middle classes that the yoke of power weighs most heavily.

The middle class has been formed, and exists in reality, only in the Taïkounal towns, Kioto, Yeddo, Hiogo, Osaka, Sakai, Nagasaki, and Hakodate, to which were added the new ports of Yokohama and Nigata.

This recent class of Japanese society bears within it the germ of the great future to which contemporary Japan seems to be called. Nevertheless, it enjoys no civil rights, and the meanest of the Hattamotos would disdain an alliance with the best of the city families.

The territorial nobility and the governmental caste affect to regard indifferently the artizan and the shopkeeper; even the great merchant is inferior to the agriculturist, as occupying the lowest scale of social liberty; beneath whom are only Yetas, persons who live by impure trades, butchers, leather-sellers, and beggars.

Should a Daimio and his suite, or some great functionary of the Taïkoun, be passing by in state, it is the business of the citizen to pay attention to the

THE COMMUTATION OF A CAPITAL SENTENCE UPON A NOBLE INTO ONE OF BANISHMENT.

announcements of the heralds-at-arms and the runners, and to withdraw immediately to the edge of the road with uncovered head, and motionless, crouching body, if he would not receive a blow with a sword, or be crushed under the feet of the horses. It is, however, just to add, that most frequently the nobles and the functionaries from the citadel traverse the streets of the city in a sort of incognito, without insisting upon the honours due to their high position. When they do think proper to exact them, they take care to have their approach announced from a distance, not only by their advanced guard, but by means of ensigns, which are hoisted upon the end of long pikes which are borne at the head of their cortége, and easily recognized by the people.

Whenever any matter of business brings an akindo, or tradesman, into the presence of a Samouraï, the former is bound to salute his superior by prostrating

A NEWSMAN.

himself several times. On approaching the threshold of the dwelling of a noble, he kneels, and, touching the ground with his forehead, waits in that position until the master of the house gives him leave to rise, and then he must never speak without a bowed head, his body leaning forward and his two hands hanging upon his knees.

A fire having ravaged an entire quarter of the citadel, an officer from Yeddo went to seek some Japanese carpenters who were employed in the European buildings at Yokohama. One of the overseers of the works having made some observation to him respecting the vexatious consequences which might arise from the unauthorized departure of so many men who were working by contract, the impatient officer instantly cut down the unfortunate remonstrant.

This same intolerance, fatal to progress and to true civilization, and utterly hostile to humanity, extends throughout everything connected with the nobility and the Government.

The Taïkouns have never been able to understand that the only real basis of their power, and the certain source of prosperity in their Empire, is precisely that middle class which they keep in iron subjection. The victims of this system occasionally contrive to escape from the meshes of the net, and to forget the official world which rules them. If we would observe the bright side of a Japanese citizen's life, we must follow him to his family meals, to his country excursions, to the scenes of dissipation in the capital and in the society of his numerous friends; *literati* and poets, physicians and students, painters and comedians.

SEA FISH.

CHAPTER IV.

THE HONDJO.

THE COMMERCIAL CITY.—ITS EXTENT AND FEATURES.

THE City, properly so-called, extends to the east of the castle, from the bridge named Sen-bassi, which unites it to the Atakosta quarter towards the south, to that named O-bassi at the limit of the northern quarter.

It is composed of three districts, which lie exclusively in the direction of the south-west to the north-east—Kio-bassi, Nihon- or Niphon-bassi, and Niphon-kito.

In the latter district, the city stretches down to the Ogawa ; while, in the two preceding, the banks and islands of the great river are for the most part occupied by public buildings or the residences of the nobles. Among them are a dozen palaces of the Daimios, and some small yaskis belonging to the Hattamotos. In the vicinity of the race-course is the great Temple of Nisihongandji, a few light batteries, and a Government naval school.

The whole of the remaining space comprised between the citadel and the Ogawa resembles an immense draught-board, so completely symmetrical are all its sections ; with their longitudinal streets regularly intersected by cross roads.

The district of Niphon-bassi, which is in the heart of the city, contains five longitudinal and twenty-two transverse streets, cutting each other at right angles, and forming seventy-eight squares of houses almost identical with each other. It presents the figure of a long parallelogram : navigable canals surround it on the four sides. Fifteen bridges communicate with the adjacent quarters—two on the west, which span the great moat of the citadel, five on the east, five on the south, and three on the north.

The Bridge of Niphon, on the north, which gives its name to the quarter is held to be the geometrical centre of Japan : from which all the geographical distances of the Empire are measured. It is also at the Bridge of Niphon that the Tokaïdo commences. Starting from the faubourg of Sinagawa, it crosses, under the name of the Street of Ottari, the quarters of Takanawa, Atakosta, Kio-bassi, and Niphon-bassi ; and, at the extremity of the latter, a central bridge forms the limit between this great political, military, and commercial artery of the southern Empire, and another, no less important, which stretches to the north. It is also called Ottari within the precincts of Yeddo ; and beyond them the Oskio-kaïdo. It ends at the northern point of Niphon, from whence we cross the strait of La Perouse in order to reach Hakodate, on the island of Yeso.

Although they have a completely homogeneous character, the city quarters do not convey such an impression of pompous monotony as the yaskis of the Court and the feudal nobility. The citizens' houses, like the palaces, preserve the type of architecture proper to them ; they are simply wooden constructions, having but one storey above the basement, generally enclosed within an open gallery ; their low roofs are made of slate-coloured tiles, and ornamented with mouldings in gypsum at

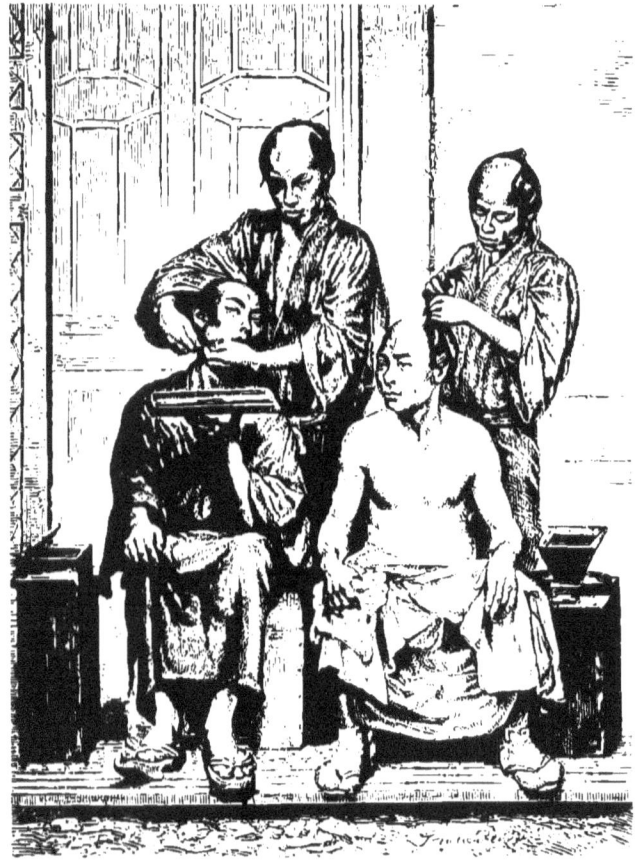

JAPANESE BARBERS.

the two ends. But, if the frame be uniform, the pictures which it displays are of charming variety, oddity, and ingenuity.

F F

At the upper end of the street of Niphon-bassi we come upon a barber's shop, in which two or three citizens, in the simplest apparel, are making their morning toilet. Seated upon a stool, they gravely hold in the left hand a lacquered tray, destined to receive the soapsuds. The barbers, free from all clothing which could trammel the freedom of their movements, lean sometimes to the right and sometimes to the left of their customers' heads, over which they pass both the hand and the razor, like antique sculptors modelling cariatides. I need hardly add that the illusion ceases when, holding between their teeth a long silken cord, they roll it round and tie it at each end, leaving the pudding-like ball which forms the Japanese head-dress.

At a little distance we find a shoemaker's shop. It is adorned with innumerable wooden soles and numberless wooden sandals, which hang from the roof by long ropes of the same material. The shoemaker, squatting on his shelf, reminds me of the native idol to whom the beggars make presents of sandals. Many persons of both sexes stop before the shop-front, examining or trying on the merchandise, exchanging some amicable phrase with the shoemaker, and, without disturbing him from his quietude, lay the price at his feet. The accounts, so far as I could see, were kept in *szénis*—little pieces of iron, of which twenty make up a *tempo*, or bit of copper money, worth fifteen centimes. The szénis, like Chinese *cash*, have a small square hole in the centre ; they are strung on a cord and hang from the girdle.

Next to the shoemaker's came the shop of a dealer in edible seaweed, which forms one of the principal articles of export trade between Japan and China. This seaweed is called *tang*, and is found in great floating masses in all the bays of the insular Empire. When the sea is calm, its rich golden purple and olive tints are distinctly seen through the still surface of the blue water. By means of a boatman's hook the fishermen draw it through the sea like an immense net, load their boats with it, and clean it carefully, collecting the little shells which cling to it in immense numbers. When the cargo has been landed, it is dried in the sun, and then formed into bundles tied with bands of straw, or in small parcels wrapped up in paper ; the former are for exportation, and are sold by weight to the junks ; the others are sold by the packet for a few szénis, and are to be bought either in the market or the eating-houses.

At Yeddo there is an immense consumption of shell-fish : the dealer fills his tubs, in which he shakes and turns them about with long bamboo sticks, after which he sets forth, crying his wares. Sea-leeches, and all sorts of little molluscs, the trepang, and the whole class of radiates are sold in a dry state. They are eaten fried, and most frequently cut into pieces mingled with rice. One sort of fish, very thin, long, and narrow, is simply dried in the sun, and eaten without any

SPARROW-HAWK FISHING.

further cooking. Oysters are abundant, but coarse. The Japanese have no method of opening them except by breaking the upper valve with a stone.

Uraga supports the whole Empire with dried oysters, belonging to the large kind called awabis : the Taïkoun is said to have the monopoly of this trade.

Although the Japanese profess, from an æsthetic point of view, a profound disgust for shell-fish, they do not seem to disdain them when they are fried and laid out on herbs and coloured paper. I have remarked that delicacies of this sort have a great sale in the public markets.

The shops of the grain-dealers at Yeddo are very interesting, from the immense quantity and the infinite variety of the products, the diversity of their forms and colours, and the art with which they are ranged upon the shelves. But surprise and admiration succeed to curiosity when we perceive that on each of the parcels already done up in paper, on each of the bags ready to be delivered, is a coloured drawing

A TORTOISE-CHARMER.

of the plants themselves, together with the name of the grain. This drawing is often a little masterpiece, which might figure in an album of the flora of Japan. Presently we see the painter and the workshop. The painter is a young girl, who lies at full length on mats covered with flowers and sheets of paper, and works incessantly in this singular attitude.

As we approach the central bridge of the commercial city the crowd increases, and on both sides of the street shops give place to popular restaurants, and confectioners, where cakes, rice, and millet are sold, and where hot tea and saki may be purchased.

We are close to the great fish-market. The canal is covered with fishing-boats, either discharging their cargo of both sea and river fish—great fish of the ocean currents which come down from the Pole, and those of the equatorial stream, tortoises and mussels from the gulfs of Niphon, hideous jelly-fish and fantastic crustaceæ. In this place Siebold reckoned seventy different kinds of fish, crabs, and mollusca, and twenty-six sorts of mussels and other shell-fish.

Fish-sheds, roughly put up near the landing-place, are besieged by buyers. In the middle of the tumultuous crowd we see strong arms lifting full baskets and emptying

FIESTA.

them into the lacquered cases of the coolies. From time to time the crowd has to open, to give passage to two coolies laden with a dolphin, a shark, or a porpoise, suspended by ropes on a bamboo pole, which they carry on their shoulders. The Japanese boil the flesh of all these animals, and salt the whole blubber.

One of the strangest pictures in the environs of Niphon-bassi is a group of shark and whale sellers, wholesale and retail. The stature, the dress, and the gestures of these personages, their fantastic equipment, the dimensions of the huge knives which they plunge into the sides of the sea monsters, suggest the prodigious exercise of human strength and employment of the resources of nature, which can alone suffice for the supply of the great city.

At the southern extremity of Niphon-bassi, a barrier encloses several pillars covered with notices painted on white wood; and, a little further on, we find a pavilion raised upon a granite platform, and containing a quantity of printed notices. This is the Kokôsatsou of Yeddo, from whence the ancient laws which are still in use are explained, and the daily ordinances of the Taïkounal police are announced.

Close by is a yakounine guard-house and a post of the flying brigade. Wooden tubs and jars, filled with water and ranged in pyramids, are placed at intervals on the thresholds of the warehouses, and on the edge of the public pathways. These precautionary measures are taken in all the populous streets of Yeddo, and generally in all Japanese cities. Reservoirs of water occupy the upper galleries and roofs of the houses. Long and strong ladders are planted against the great wooden buildings, such as temples and pagodas. Stores, known in the commercial language of the Far East under the name of *godowns*, are said to be fireproof. They are multiplied as much as possible in the wooden quarters, so as to present numerous obstacles to the spread of fire. These square, high buildings are constructed of stone, and covered outside with a thick layer of whitewash. Their doors and shutters are of iron, and from the four walls great hooks stick out, from which wet mats and mattresses may be hung when there is imminent danger.

The godowns, the ladders, and the tubs do not contribute to the embellishment of the capital. In this, as in other details of Japanese life, the beautiful is sacrificed to the useful, and visitors must just make the best of the charming accidental views which occur in the city. Its religious buildings would render it exceedingly beautiful, were not its chief sites occupied by the endless lines of warehouses.

Pursuing our route from street to street, we look into the interior of the houses, with hardly any interruption from the sliding panels, and see the picturesque groups of men, women, and children squatting round their humble dinners. The straw table-cloth is laid on the mats which cover the floor; in the centre is a large wooden bowl containing rice, which forms the principal food of every class of Japanese society. Each guest attacks the common dish, and takes out enough to pile up a great china cup, from which he eats without the aid of the little stick which serves him for a fork, except just for the last few mouthfuls, to which he adds a scrap of fish, crab, or fowl, taken from the numerous plates which surround the centre bowl.

These viands are seasoned with sea-salt, pepper, and soy—a very strong sauce made from black beans by a process of fermentation ; eggs, soft and hard, fresh or preserved ; boiled vegetables, such as turnips, carrots, and sweet potatoes, slices of young twigs of bamboo, or a salad of lotus bulbs, complete the bill of fare of a Japanese citizen's dinner.

The meal is invariably accompanied by tea and saki, and these two beverages are ordinarily drank hot, without any other liquid, and without sugar. The teapots which contain them stand upon a brasier shaped like a casket ; it is a little larger than another corresponding article of furniture called a tobacco-bon, on which coal, a pipe-rack, and a supply of tobacco are placed.

TEA AND SAKI.

I have never examined the pretty utensils used at a Japanese table —the bowls, cups, saucers, boxes, lacquered trays, vases of porcelain, jugs and teapots in glazed earthenware—nor have I ever contemplated the people while eating, seen the grace of their movements, and watched the dexterity of their delicate little hands, without fancying I was looking on at a number of grown-up children playing at housekeeping, and eating rather for their amusement than because they were hungry.

Maladies resulting from excess or from unwholesome diet are generally unknown, but the immoderate use of their national beverage sometimes produces grave results. I have seen more than one case of delirium tremens.

The ravages caused by dysentery and cholera in certain parts of Japan, especially at Yeddo, will cause no surprise to the European resident, who has seen how greedily children and the lower classes of the people devour water-melons, limes, Siam oranges, and all sorts of fruits at the beginning of the autumn, before they are fully ripe.

Japanese houses are rarely supplied with really wholesome water, because, even at Yeddo, where springs are abundant, they use only cisterns, though it would be easy

SKETCH OF A MONKEY.

to establish fountains in every quarter in the town. The inconvenience and danger of this state of things are, however, reduced by the fact that the Japanese are in the habit of using hot drinks in all seasons.

Their popular hygiene demands hot baths, which they take every day. This extreme cleanliness, the salubrity of their climate, and the excellent qualities of their diet, aid in making the Japanese one of the healthiest and one of the most robust of peoples. There are, however, very few of them who do not suffer from diseases of the skin, and from chronic and incurable maladies, which are not to be traced to their natural conditions. This great misfortune dates from the epoch at which the government of the Siogouns authorized the foundation and officially protected the development of a disgraceful institution, whose fatal consequences sap the entire edifice of society.

There are a great number of physicians in Japan, principally at Yeddo. Those who are attached to the Court of the Taïkoun belong to the Hattamoto class, carry two swords, shave the head, and occupy a more or less elevated rank according as they belong to either category of functionaries. The first, which is necessarily very limited, comprises the physicians of the Taïkoun's household; they do not practise outside the palace. The second category are the officers of health who accompany the army in time of war, and who, when they are not on service, practise among the families of their own relations. Both one and the other are nominated by the Taïkoun or his Government.

The members of the medical body who are neither functionaries nor officers, that is to say, who practise as physicians of the third class, belong to the bourgeoisie. They have generally been educated at the University of Kioto or that of Yeddo; but some of them, who belong to families where the medical profession has been followed from father to son, have received an education under the paternal roof.

As no examinations are required for the practice of medicine, each man enters the profession when he pleases, and practises according to his own fancy; some healing by the routine of the native empirics, others treating their patients according to the rules of Chinese science, a third claiming to be adepts in Dutch medicine; but in reality they have actually neither method nor system. University studies in Japan are exceedingly superficial. It cannot be otherwise in a country where no one possesses the preparatory knowledge, which is taken for granted on entering upon a University course. This state of things can only be reformed by frequent contact with Europeans. The people, however, do not care about it. All they want is to have a number of doctors at their disposal; to be treated and physicked rather upon these conjoint methods than upon the best, supposing it to exist; in fact, to find in their physicians pleasant servants, who will not contradict the notions of their patients, and who scrupulously justify the confidence with which their profession is honoured. This obliges them to adopt a certain demeanour which impresses the public, and sets them apart from the rest of society.

Japanese medical practitioners may be easily recognized by their dress, by their methodical demeanour, and some other peculiarities, which vary according to the fancy of these grave personages. I have seen one whose head was shaved like that of a bonze, or of an Imperial doctor, though he certainly belonged to a physician of the third class. I have seen others wearing their hair long and plaited, the ends coiled upon their neck, and others with a profuse beard. Their middle class extraction not permitting them to wear two swords, they wear one, passed through the folds of their girdle; but it is always a very small one, and generally carefully wrapped up in crape or velvet.

Certain members of the faculty take care never to show themselves in public unattended by a koskei carrying their instrument case and medicines.

The third class command public esteem and enjoy uncontested respect. I have heard it said, that when they are sent for to aristocratic houses they are paid by those sentiments rather than in itzibous. It is well known that the greater number—even those who possess an extensive connection—can hardly live; for the citizens' families generally find at the end of the year, when they have met their indispensable expenses—housekeeping, annual fêtes, the theatre, the baths, the bonzes, and the parties of pleasure—that they have very little left to give to the doctor.

The latter, on his side, accepts the situation with philosophy, and it must be added to his credit, that he is generally a truly disinterested person. Many possess real scientific zeal, and a taste for the observation of nature which might produce remarkable results if these qualities rested upon a solid basis or sufficient preparatory instruction. There is no doubt that the medical fraternity is one of the most energetic agents of progress and civilization in Japan.

This fraternity is one of a Corporation of arts and professions which enjoys an official constitution and certain privileges. It was placed by the Mikado under the invocation of a holy patron called Yakousi, and is evidently of great antiquity. We learn from the Imperial annals of Kioto that the first Japanese pharmacy was founded in 730, that in the year 808 medical science was enriched by a collection of recipes published in one hundred volumes by Doctor Firo-Sada, and that the year 825 endowed the Empire with its first hospital.

For a long time Japan was tributary to China in all that concerns medical science, as well as in the other branches of human knowledge. The Celestial Empire supplied it with works on anatomy and botanical treatises, books and recipes, as well as professors,

SKETCH OF A WEASEL.

medical practitioners, and ready-made medicines for curing an infinity of ailments. In the second half of the eleventh century, the Chinese merchant Wangman made a fortune by selling medicines and parrots in Japan.

At that time the resources of art were added to the secrets of magic. In the present day the successors of the early practitioners in this line carry about kirimons covered with cabalistic signs through the towns and villages. These kirimons, placed at an opportune moment upon the body of a patient, have the power of recalling a dead man to life. The monks, on their side, know prayers of a sacramental kind which stop bleeding, heal wounds, exorcise insects, cure burns, and counteract the evil eye, in the case of men and animals.

Two great events, of which one occurred at the beginning and the other at the end of the seventeenth century, prevented the scientific labours of the medical fraternity from being shrouded by degrees in the great darkness of Buddhist superstition. The first was the arrival of the Dutch, who received their letters of franchise and inaugurated their factory at Firado under the direction of the superintendent, Van Speex, in the year 1609 ; and the second was the foundation of the University of Yeddo, which took place in the reign of the thirty-sixth Siogoun, Tsouna-Yosi, the fourth successor to Iyéyas, in 1690.

Thunberg recounts that, towards the middle of the following century, he, being at Yeddo as attaché to the biennial embassy from the Dutch superintendent of Decima, obtained permission from the Siogoun to receive a visit from five physicians and two astronomers attached to the Court ; he had long conversations with them, and convinced himself from the observations of the former that they had derived their knowledge of natural history, physics, medicine and surgery, not only from the traditional Chinese sources, but from Dutch works.

At a later date, the physicians of the factory, having been authorized to take pupils, strove, with great zeal and devotion, to impart to them the medical science of the West.

If the judgment of civilized peoples were not distorted by the manner in which they are taught history—if they had learned that science has its honours as well as war—they would look with admiration upon the peaceful conquests which have been made in the Empire of Japan, to the advantage of the whole world, by the physicians of the factory at Decima since the time of Kœmpfer to the present day.

Hondjo, properly so called, answers in some respects to the industrial quarters of our great cities. It contains manufactories of tiles and of coarse pottery, kitchen utensils in iron, paper factories, and workshops for the cleaning and preparation of cotton, for the weaving of cotton and silk fabrics, dyeing vats, weavers' shops, basket makers, and mat plaiters.

Japanese industry has not yet utilized machinery. There are, indeed, iron foundries, in which the bellows are moved by an hydraulic wheel, over which the water is directed by tubes of bamboo. The combustible material is composed of charcoal and coal, the former of excellent quality. Women have their share in every kind of industry. No great manufactories exist in Japan; neither the occupation nor the population of our factories is represented there. The working classes labour in their own houses, interrupting their toil by eating when they are hungry, and resting when it pleases them. In a group of six artizans of both sexes, we always find one or two smoking their pipes and enlivening their comrades by their gay

A FUNERAL PROCESSION LEAVING THE HOUSE.

talk. Thus from generation to generation an instinct of sociability is transmitted, and good humour and repartee generally characterize the lower classes of the capital. At Yeddo, as in all other capitals through which a river runs, the population of the lower bank and that of the centre of the city present entirely different features. Hondjo has not the continual movement, the imposing mass of the residences within the citadel, nor the animation of the places reserved for the pleasures of the crowd in the northern quarter. Nevertheless, we find in it commerce, industry, temples, palaces, and places of public amusement, but under quite special conditions. Some of the great merchants of Japan live in Hondjo, while their counting-houses are in the quarters of Kio-bassi, or Niphon-bassi, after the fashion of the great merchants of Rotterdam, who have their houses at Vercade, and their counting-houses among the stores of Wijnstraat.

The relative tranquillity of the left bank, and the facility with which ground can be obtained there, have been favourable to the establishment of numerous bonze-houses. Some of them possess very large temples. Among the twenty or thirty temples of the Foukagawa quarter, the ancient national worship is principally represented by the two celebrated Mias of Temmangô and Hatchiman ; and the Buddhist worship by the Tera of Sandjiou-san-Ghendhô. In Hondjo, where there are forty temples of different denominations, that of the five hundred genii, the Goïaka-Lakan or Goïakoura-Kaudji, consecrated to the memory of Racans and other illustrious Buddhist saints, are chiefly distinguished. Formerly this venerable army, entirely composed of wooden statues, larger than life and faded in colour, was displayed upon the galleries of the nave, the choir and the side chapels of the holy place, or the right and left of a colossal idol of Buddha, revered under the name of Tô-Schabori. An earthquake flung its ranks into confusion. The mutilated victims were collected in the barns in the neighbourhood, and the devastated temple has not yet been repaired and restored for the purpose of worship. At a little distance, another bonze-house has founded its reputation upon a less fragile basis than the images of the defunct heroes of asceticism and contemplation. Twice a year it engages the services of the chief wrestlers of Yeddo for a series of public representations, and this pious speculation never fails to attract an immense crowd belonging to all classes of society. Every monastery has its peculiarity, for instance, the avenue of the bonze-house of Hondjo is guarded by half a dozen statues of pigs, mounted on granite pedestals. Public opinion admits, without difficulty and by silent consent, anything which the bonzes please to imagine may lend a novel attraction to the exercise of devotion.

A certain number of families of the old nobility have made of Hondjo a sort of Faubourg St. Germain, where they live in profound seclusion, far from the noise of the city, and from all contact with the Court and the Government functionaries. In addition to the larger industries which I have enumerated, we find in Hondjo important manufactories of silk, stuffs, and porcelain utensils, household furniture, and toilet ornaments of lacquered wood, as well as great workshops of sculpture, cabinet-making, and wood-inlaying. I never saw marble works anywhere, though there are quarries in the mountains of the interior. All the candelabra and the pillars of the toris are granite, as are also the candelabra of the holy places, the tombs, statuettes, and funeral stones, as well as the Buddha; the sacred tortoises, and foxes, are made of a very

STATUE FROM THE TEMPLE OF THE FIVE HUNDRED GENII.

fine kind of earthenware. Sculptors in wood make domestic altars with very rich panels, elegant reliquaries and coffins in the form of mikosis, elephants' heads, monstrous chimeras for the adornment of the temple roofs, wood carvings and mosaics, representing cranes, geese, bats, and mythological animals; the moon half-veiled by a cloud, branches of cedars, pines, bamboos, and palms. The idols, which are generally gigantic, come from the workshops of Yeddo, and are frequently surrounded by a golden nimbus, and painted in very bright colours ;—the guardians of heaven, for example, in vermilion : Tengou in indigo ; the foxes are white, brown, or gilded, and generally have a golden key in their mouths. Several interesting branches of industry are connected with the work of the sculptors. The panels of the moveable partitions are ornamented with drawings in Chinese ink, traced by a few strokes of the brush, or with groups of trees and flowers, brilliantly coloured with paintings of birds famous for the richness

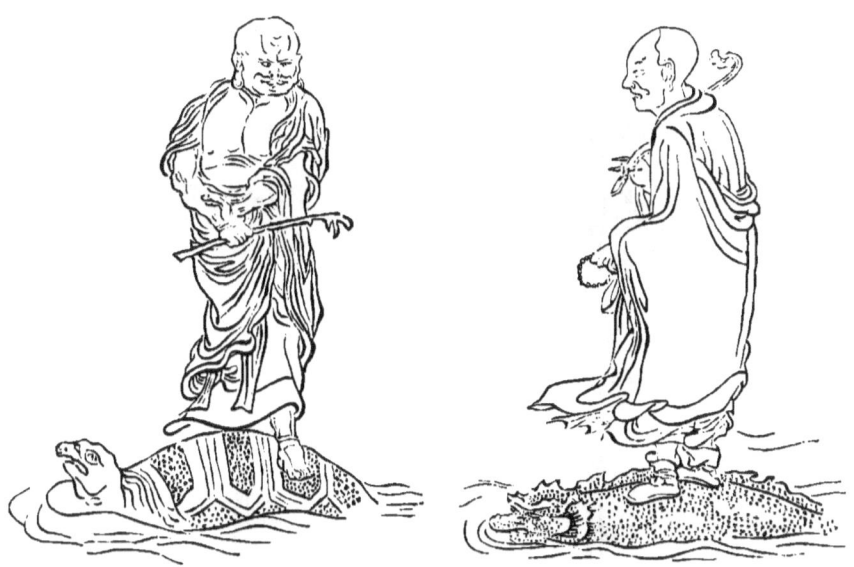

STATUES FROM THE TEMPLE OF THE FIVE HUNDRED GENII.

of their plumage. All this is done in the manufactory, but by the hand. Nothing is printed except the papers for wall-hangings or the woodwork. The embroideresses, who make the screens which serve for blinds and shutters, work beautifully ; they employ silk, and reproduce, according to the subjects, either the lustrous tissue of leaves, the velvet down of birds, the thick fur of quadrupeds, or the brilliant scales of fish. The silk plaiters add to the woodwork and the hangings of rooms a beautiful ornament composed of garlands and knots of various colours, headed by groups of flowers and birds. These delicate arts of embroidery and braiding are also applicable to the heavy stuffs brocaded in gold and silver, of which the Court mantles and long trailing dresses are made. We also find crape and gauze of extreme fineness, adorned with needlework of the purest taste. The Obi, or girdle worn by all Japanese women, married and unmarried, with the exception of the ladies of the princely families, is that portion of female dress which presents the greatest variety according to the taste and

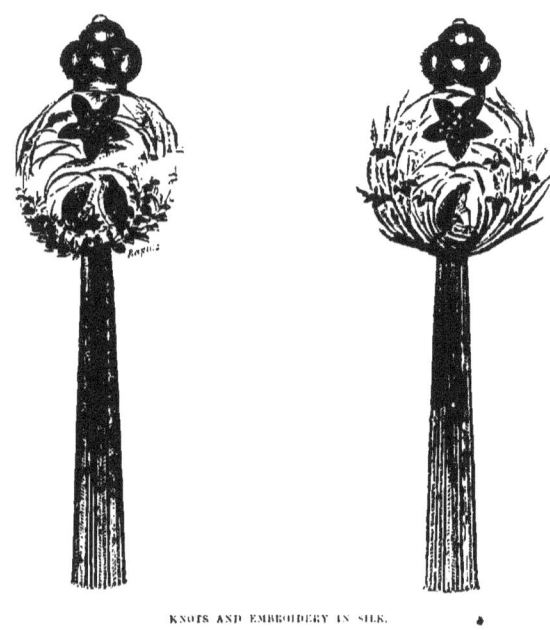

KNOTS AND EMBROIDERY IN SILK.

fancy of the wearers. Sometimes the Obi affects great simplicity—sometimes it is distinguished for richness of material and profusion of embroidery; it is generally wide enough to suffice at the same time for girdle and corset; it is rolled round the body and tied behind the back in an elegant bow, in which the end is caught up. The result is a sort of wide floating knot, which falls squarely down upon the hips, or a large loop, which hangs from the girdle with much elegance. A widow who has made up

H H

her mind not to marry again ties her Obi in the front of her dress. Every woman, after her death is clad in her best costume; the Obi is arranged after the fashion of a widow's; it is then tied as tight as possible in two knots.

It is not an easy thing to get admission to Japanese workshops, especially when one's escort is formed of the yakounines. Notwithstanding the promises of their masters, I was not permitted to witness the process of dyeing, to see the manufacture of rich silk stuffs, or any paper factory. On the other hand, I found the wholesale and retail shops quite accessible, and was even allowed to go into the back shops, which are by no means unworthy of a visit, because the Japanese merchant does not care about show; far from putting his most valuable objects for sale in the front, he keeps them in reserve—a fact well known to amateurs; so that, in order to have an idea of the wealth, variety, and artistic merit of Japanese fabrics, it is necessary, not only to visit the trading streets of the natives, but to make friends with the shopkeepers, and come back again and again to the shops, until one has explored all their corners and recesses. This is the more indispensable as there is no bazaar in Japan, and every shop and workshop has its speciality. There is, indeed, a small native bazaar, established under the name of "stores," in the ports open to Europeans; but these are only permanent exhibitions of samples, and offer no real opportunity for studying Japanese industry, which in some branches is but little developed—for instance, that of saddlery, which must necessarily remain so while religious prejudices shackle the trades of the tanner and the leather-worker. This circumstance obliges Japan to lie under obligations to foreign countries, especially since the Taïkoun and the Daimios have carried on a jealous rivalry in the reform of their artillery and cavalry. Germany supplies them with leather, Holland and France with saddles and horse-trappings, gloves, and belts. Trade in skins, which is so widely extended in China, has scarcely any existence in Japan.

The Mongols delight in wrapping themselves in furs, while the children of the great Niphon regard fur with repugnance. Neither the Chinese nor the Japanese preserve or prepare the skins of beasts for stuffing. The Chinese make artificial birds, whose bodies are modelled in wax, with real feathers gummed on one after the other with the most minute care. The Japanese employ nothing but silk in making images of their favourite animals. They excel in reproducing, in miniature, cocks, hens, pheasants, ducks, cats, and little spaniels. They employ hair and natural feathers only in making dust-brushes, fly-brushes, and fans. These objects are sometimes very elegant, especially the fly-brushes and the fans of white feathers spotted in the middle with two or three little feathers of bright colours. The making of paint-brushes is carried to extreme perfection and cheapness, which is to be expected in a country in which this one kind of instrument is used for writing, drawing, and painting. The Japanese brushes are made of the hair of otters, weasels, and foxes. Those which are got from the principality of Satsouma are considered to be the best.

Silken cord plays a great part not only in the fabrication of horse-trappings, but for the fastenings of casques and cuirasses, in all military equipments, and civil costumes, for men as well as women, because our buttons, hooks, clasps, and aiguilettes are perfectly unknown in native toilets. Coarse ropes and cables are made of Manilla cotton, and vegetable paper. The silken cords do great honour to the art of those who make them; those used for flying kites and for use in falconry are very elegant. The strings of musical instruments are made of silk covered with varnish.

Window blinds are generally ornamented by drawings of flowers and birds very skilfully done. The fishermen's cloaks, and brooms, are made of fine strips of palm bark. Bird-catchers and sellers of poultry use bamboo cages, whose forms vary from the common type of the beehive and the covered basket, to beautiful models of country pavilions and garden-houses. We also noticed tall turrets made of bamboo trellis, in which the restaurateurs hang their finest specimens of game, such as the wild boar, the deer, and the black bear of Yeso. Animals famed for their malignity are not shown so much honour; the fox, extended upon the stall, holds the knife with which he is about to be cut up in his mouth; and the monkey, suspended by his four paws to the lintel of the door, is exposed to the ridicule of the street children, who laugh at his grinning red face.

The artizan of Yeddo is a true artist. If we except the conventional style which he retains in his reproductions of the human figure, and excuse the insufficiency of his studies in perspective, we shall have nothing but praise to bestow on him. His works are distinguished from those of Kioto by simplicity of form, severity of line, sobriety of ornament, and exquisite feeling for nature in all the subjects of decoration which he borrows from the vegetable or animal kingdom. In such subjects he delights. Flowers and birds inspire him with compositions full of truth, grace, and harmony; while the execution is equally admirable in the works of the artists of both capitals.

The Japanese do not understand the fabrication of panes of glass and of bottles; but they delight in making all sorts of little objects in glass—pipes, and water-bowls, and long blue stems, little white cups at the bottom of which we see a tiny

red crab, which rises to the surface according as the cup becomes full of liquid; and little balls half filled with coloured water, ornaments much used by the women in their head-dresses.

At Yeddo I was shown some attempts at painting on glass, and at enamel-work which denoted more goodwill than science. But among a number of native curiosities which are really original, are little balls of stone pierced and cut in facets and enriched with enamel arabesques. These are extensively bought by foreigners for necklaces, and used in Yeddo itself for making rosaries. For the latter purpose they are strung on silk.

Mother-of-pearl competes with enamel in certain miniatures which are applied on metal. The gilders' art consists entirely in the application of their leaves of gold

JAPANESE ARTIST PAINTING A YEMA.

to such things as are thought worthy of this decoration; for instance, the nimbus round the heads of saints in the Buddhist temples, the frames of theatre scenes, the sculptures of altar-pieces, the lances from which the military standards are displayed, and the leaves of screens of the very first style. Among the latter we find exquisite specimens of drawings in Chinese ink representing hunting scenes, and horses, all done with two brushes and a single line on a gold background.

The stories which come to us from former embassies singularly exaggerate the decorative richness of the palaces of the Mikados and the Siogouns. The truth is that there is no royal residence in Europe which does not represent a greater intrinsic value than the imperial palaces of Kioto and Yeddo. Strictly speaking there are neither goldsmiths nor jewellers in Japan. The serpentine, the malachite, the amethyst, the topaz, are all found in the country, but no one, not even the most elegant among the women, wears jewelled ornaments. Their only luxury after that of material consists in loading the heavy edifice of their head-dress with large pins of

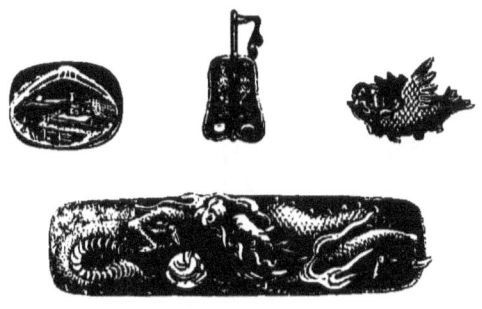

ORNAMENTS.

shell or metal, ornamented with small pictures on emblematic subjects. The lapidaries of Yeddo have nothing to do except to cut rock crystal, of which very fine specimens are brought to Europe. These are exquisitely polished, and cut either round or in facets, but they cost an exorbitant price.

The closest approach to goldsmith's work is found in the ornamentation of the arms of the yakounines, which are sometimes marvels of carving, and of the mingling of metals. Gold, silver, steel, copper, brass, and a composition known as *Sawa metal*, are used for this purpose, and also for paper weights, clasps, locks, portfolios, and rulers. Of all the cities of Japan, Yeddo can boast of the most skilful workers in metals. Numbers of depôts in the city are among the most interesting of the native curiosities.

I need not dwell upon the perfection of their porcelain, second only to which are their master-pieces in brass and their works in lacquered wood. Such is the talent with which the native workman utilizes the incomparable varnish of Japan, such is their skill in combining its effects with the processes of their decorative art, that articles of furniture whose material is held of no value at all rival in brilliancy, and we might almost say substance, those which in our country are made of marble and precious metals.

In the interior decoration of cabinets, boxes, and coffers, brown lacquer spangled with gold is extensively used; but for the exterior the lacquer is generally of one clear

A DAIMIO AND HIS SUITE. (CARICATURE.)

red, brown, or black, adorned with drawings of two or three colours, or with gold-leaf, with or without relief. There is seldom anything in the form, in the drawing, or in the ornamentation which cannot sustain criticism by the most cultivated taste. If, however, the kotans, which we call cabinets, are sometimes too heavily laden with incrustations of porcelain and mother-of-pearl, silver, and even gold, we may be quite sure that the native workmen have been obliged to study the caprices of foreign purchasers, who want to find in the Niphon market something of the heavy splendour of the Chinese shops.

An indispensable ceremonial in all Japanese banquets is the service of *Saki.* This beverage is brought in solemnly in large lacquered jars or in cans of metal. The large or small cups from which it is to be drunk are made of fine red lacquer, and ornamented with fantastic designs, with gold-leaf or rich paintings, covered with a transparent glaze. Some of these beautiful cups represent the most celebrated landscapes in Japan, or the most remarkable towns situated between the two capitals. There are even some of a still more sumptuous order formed of the nautilus in mother-of-pearl, the heliotis, and other beautiful shells ornamented with silver filigree.

OGAWA-BATA DOCKS AND WAREHOUSES.

CHAPTER V.

ASAKSA-TERA.

BONZE-HOUSES. — QUANNON. — A DISTRIBUTION OF TALISMANS. — BRAZEN STATUES. — AGGLOMERA-
TION OF BUILDINGS. — FOX-WORSHIP. — PORTRAITS OF COURTEZANS. — BUDDHIST WORSHIP.
— MODERN CORRUPTION OF THE OLD DOCTRINES AND PRACTICES.

OVER one hundred bonze-houses, each composed of a more or less considerable number
of buildings, such as monasteries, temples, pagodas, chapels, tea-houses, and shops, form
the central division of the quarter of Asaksa-Imato. The greatest and most famous
is that of Quannon, a Buddhist divinity, to whom is attributed the magical power of
intercession between heaven and earth. The celebrity of this bonze-house completely eclipses
all the other holy places of the neighbourhood, so that in the language of the people
the word Asaksa-Tera is never used to designate any other temple than that of Quannon
in the quarter of Asaksa.

At the southern extremity of the square, in which there is a permanent market of shrubs and flowers, stands a heavy portal adorned with colossal lanterns. Two of the guardians of heaven, wooden giants painted in vermilion, are posted on the right hand and on the left of the principal entrance, defending the passage, and levying upon each pilgrim the traditional tribute of a pair of enormous straw sandals. Under their eyes,

on the eve of each new year, a gratuitous distribution of paper amulets is made to the populace. The bonzes for the most part visit their clients on this day, and for a small consideration bring to their houses bits of the brush with which they distribute holy water. These scraps are fastened to the lintels of the door, and are believed to preserve the house from evil spirits. The coolies, and labourers of all kinds, flock to

Asaksa to have their share in the same privilege, because there they can obtain it without expense, though not without trouble. Two bonzes, perched at the risk of their lives upon a platform composed of planks suspended by hooks half way up the high columns of the doorway, are distributing an abundant provision of blessed papers. They take handfuls of them at intervals, and throw them into the air. The koskeis

standing on either side, provided with large palm-leaf fans, make the amulets fly about and fall upon the people like snow-flakes. Let him catch them who can. Soon the entire space presents a spectacle of extraordinary confusion; people pushing, elbowing, pursuing each other—some stretching out their arms in order to catch the morsels of paper in their flight, others bending, and even rolling themselves on the ground, in order to pick them up. Nevertheless, as the most fortunate and the most skilful retire when they have obtained their share, success becomes for their rivals a mere matter of patience, and no one is compelled to return home empty-handed. Beyond this great gateway is a long, wide, paved street, which is called Kindjousan-Asaksa-Tera. It is intersected by cross-lanes, and occupied from one end to the other by booths for the sale of sacred objects, such as rosaries, wax candles, statues, perfumed vases, and domestic altars. Above and beyond the middle-class houses are oratories, small temples, and various curiosities, which warmly interest the pilgrims from the town and the country. Here is a mia, or chapel, consecrated to the Kami worship. There, surrounded by a bamboo railing, stands the venerable trunk of a cedar of unknown age. Further on, in an oratory hung with ex-votos, is a miraculous image; beyond that comes a small aristocratic temple approached by an avenue of banners planted in the ground, each bearing the arms and the family names of some one of the illustrious personages who have honoured this place by their visits. At the eastern extremity of the street, a hill surmounted by a temple rises above a little lake covered with water-lilies. The tea-houses stretch out their long wooden galleries amid the leaves and flowers of the splendid aquatic plants. On the other side of the public road, a small bonze-house is half hidden by a cedar grove.

At length we reach the second gateway, which stands in the great square, almost surrounded by shops and by the booths of strolling actors. On the right, two huge sitting statues of brass, the heads crowned by the Buddhist nimbus, overlook the crowds from the height of the granite terrace. Two enormous guardians of heaven defend the second doorway, as their colleagues defend the first. From the galleries which surround the upper storey of this building we can see the whole square, the high road, and, on the north, the first enclosure of the principal temple, which has numerous dependencies. Under the name of Asaksa-Tera is in reality comprehended an agglomeration of from forty to fifty sacred buildings, including the sanctuary of Quannon-sama, the chief divinity and patron of the place, whose power of intercession is signified by an enormous statue, with thirty-six arms and one hundred hands, placed at the entrance of the temple. Under its protection are grouped the chapels of Sannoô, the ruler of men; Daïkok, the god of riches; Benten, the goddess of harmony; Hatchiman, the patron of warriors: in a word, the entire national mythology, not excepting the worship of the fox. This diabolical animal is worshipped, as well as his companion

Inari, the patron of cereals, on the summit of a wooded hill, within the enclosure of the bonze-house. His little chapel, thickly hung with ex-votos, is reached by an avenue in which we pass innumerable toris painted vermilion. From the one to the other the distance is only that of a fox's jump, and they are hardly as tall as a man. The road is steep, winding, and impeded by the roots of the pines of the sacred grove. It is impossible to climb it, except with great care and by bending the head.

In that humble attitude we reach the esplanade of the holy place. There we must pass between two granite images representing the malicious divinity in a sitting posture, his tail turned up, his muzzle in the air, but his oblique eye watching every person who approaches the sanctuary. The faithful bow respectfully, make their ablutions, cast their pieces of money into the box, and kneel in prayer on the steps of the chapel.

Among the numerous buildings placed in the enclosure of Asaksa-Tera, a pagoda of five storeys symbolizes the supremacy of Buddhism over other religions. The central building is an enormous quadrangular edifice,—the body painted red, and the colossal roof covered with grey tiles. The basement only is in stone, and supports a spacious gallery raised some yards above the ground. In the interior of the temple, the ceiling rests upon colonnades of red pillars; the walls of the nave are adorned with pictures on a golden ground. Framed images, statuettes, ex-votos, lacquered boards, with inscriptions in gold letters, are to be seen on all sides—on the columns, and on the panels of the side chapels. One of the latter contains a gallery of portraits of the most celebrated courtezans in Yeddo, as well as other pictures of a similar nature. Not only do the bonzes of Miôdjin and the priests of Sannoô invite courtezans to take a share in the periodical religious processions; but every year, in the enclosure of Sin-Yosiwara, a fair takes place, accompanied by a grand parade, which is simply a public exhibition of the five thousand registered courtezans who inhabit this quarter; and the bonzes of Asaksa-Tera have portraits of the queens of the festival taken on these occasions, and suspended in their sanctuary as if in a pantheon. The choir of the temple, dark and smoked from the vapour of the incense, does not present any remarkable peculiarity, except that on the high altar, is the idol Quannon, symbolizing the mother of Buddha, behind a trellis of wirework, wearing a nimbus and seated upon the sacred lotus. This mysterious combination excites little notice from the crowds of people who pass to and fro, and keep up a perpetual tumult in the nave, which is not spacious, and is separated from the choir by a lofty barrier of carved wood like a Gothic jubé. In the choir

A SCENE IN ASAKUSA PARK.

the bonzes, laden with their heavy sacerdotal vestments, officiate to an accompaniment of gongs and tambourines. Some of the faithful merely throw iron money

INTERIOR OF THE TEMPLE OF QUANNON.

wrapped in a white paper at their feet from behind the barrier; others buy the candles which the sacristan offers them. Before and after the hours of worship, a large covered box which, in front of the railing, communicates with the underground portion of the temple, receives the gifts of the visitors.

The solemn entry of the High Priest into the choir makes an immediate diversion in the monotony of the service. This majestic personage wears a red cloak, with a pointed hood and a green silk stole over his white robe. He is followed by a young novice, who might be taken at first sight for a young girl, so effeminate are his face, complexion, and dress. His head-dress is an elegant edifice of plaited hair, he wears loose white trousers, a white sash tied in wide bows, a short vest of green silk, with long hanging sleeves lined with white satin ; he accompanies his master, step by step, to offer him, at the first sign he makes, a cup of tea contained in a portable vessel, the handle of which he holds in both hands.

On beholding the present ministers of the religion of Buddha, we cannot refrain from thinking rather sadly of the pious reformer whose disciples they claim to be.

The Buddhist pentalogue is conceived in these terms :—

    1. Thou shalt not kill.

    2. Thou shalt not steal.

    3. Thou shalt not commit fornication.

    4. Thou shalt not lie.

    5. Thou shalt abstain from all intoxicating liquor.

What has become of the ascetic purity of the "Good Law" in the hands of men who are plunged, for the most part, in the lowest degradation ? What ironical destiny pursues the precepts of the great Sâkya-Mouni in the midst of this temple, where art glorifies the corruption of morals, where incense burns before an idol who gives indulgences for every crime, where the industry of the monks is exercised in making money of the vices, as well as of the sanguinary passions, of the nobility, in imposing upon the credulity of the people and fostering their profligacy ?

The bonze-house of Asaksa is distinguished for the luxury and variety of the costumes of its priests, and for its immense personal staff; also for the theatrical pomp of its ceremonies. The most imposing is the general procession of the Annual Dedication which follows the feasts of the purification of the temple and its dependencies. The superiors of the convent have the head shaved, and conform in all its details to the rule of Buddhist sacerdotalism ; but their authority extends over several fraternities attached to the ancient national worship ; and each of these wears the hair according to the ordinances of the Daïri to which they belong. There is no less variety in the costumes and liveries of the masters of ceremonies, heralds-of-arms, cooks, grooms, porters, and valets attached to the different sects of the bonze-house.

The grooms of Quannon-sama have the care of a couple of Albinos horses, called "the horses of the goddess." These sacred horses are fed with consecrated beans, and enjoy

DANCE OF THE PRIESTS OF FOUNABAS.

the privilege of sleeping upright, sustained by a sort of hammock made of strong suspending bands. At morning, the priests lead them forth before the statue of Quannon, and ask her if she does not wish to go out riding. The heralds-at-arms have charge of a whole arsenal of casques and steel armour, and figure in the *fêtes* and in the processions. The bonzes often give spectacles in which artists play their parts either as dancers or as comedians. On these occasions there may be seen, on the fifteenth day of the sixth month, a very curious piece,—a sword-dance, or

K K

great military pantomime exclusively executed by the priests. But the triumph of
Asaksa-Tera is its Kermesse at the end of the year. Although there is a permanent
fair which is frequented by crowds every day, and is the habitual resort or playground of its great bonze-house, it is from the eighteenth to the last day of the twelfth
month that the sacred residence of Quannon-sama displays all its prestige and
becomes the centre of circulation, not only for several hundreds of thousands, but
for three or four millions of inhabitants of the city and surrounding provinces. The
entire precinct is invaded by the multitude, whose waves form regular currents which
pass backward and forward under the skilful and silent direction of the police. Such
perfect order in the midst of such a multitude is only possible in a city like Yeddo,
where not only there are no vehicles, but where one word from a magistrate suffices to
prohibit the use of horses and palanquins for a fortnight throughout the vast space.
Thus there is no crush at any point. Cords made of straw limit the space reserved
to each industry. At certain specified places there are *reposoirs*, and the exits and
entrances are skilfully arranged. No fixed hour is named for closing ; the tide of humanity
rises all day, attains its height at sunset, and ebbs rapidly from midnight until dawn.

BEGGING FOR THE KAMI TEMPLES.

CHAPTER VI.

EDUCATION AND LITERATURE AT YEDDO.

SEPARATION OF RANKS.—CONFUCIUS AT THE UNIVERSITY.—ECLIPSE OF FAITH.—THE DOCTRINES OF CONFUCIUS.—DIFFICULTIES IN THE STUDY OF CHINESE LITERATURE.—PRIMITIVE WRITING.—THE FORMER LITERARY CENTRE OF JAPAN.—BOOKS.—POEMS.—LEGENDS. —ANCIENT ENCYCLOPÆDIAS.—STORY-TELLERS AND SINGERS.—WORSHIP OF OLD TREES.— FANTASTIC STORIES OF ANIMALS.—DEMONS.—GHOSTS.

THE high class schools which compose the University of Yeddo are perhaps the only neutral ground on which the sons of the Japanese nobility meet daily and live in common with the young people of the middle classes. The separation of ranks exists between them nevertheless in all its severity; their studies also differ in essential points. The young gentlemen receive only a certain classical culture based upon the books of the Chinese philosophers, while to the middle class populace the career of liberal professions is open, such as the teaching of languages, and the practice of medicine ; they are also prepared to become interpreters and engineers in the service of the Government.

The University of Yeddo is not only placed under the invocation of Confucius, but it patronizes the doctrines of the Chinese philosopher, and spreads them over all the educated classes of Japanese society. This is done in the form of an aggressive propaganda openly hostile to the established worships. The University tolerates existing institutions, but it destroys the creeds which form their soul. I have heard it said by an interpreter at Yeddo, "The pupils in our University no longer believe in anything ;" and I know a functionary of the citadel who stated at a diplomatic dinner that all the people of cultivation in his country were quite on a level with those of our own, from the point of view of religion. The clergy, whose temporal position is not threatened, preserve a modest and prudent attitude towards the literates. The bonzes are not inclined to attack the popularity with which the memory of Confucius is regarded in Japan, where he is universally venerated under the name of Koò-ci, a corruption of the Chinese name Khoung-Tseu. Nevertheless, he was never known there until the year 255 of our era. At that epoch Ozin, the sixteenth Mikado, enraged at seeing the paternal intentions of his Government paralyzed by the ignorance of his subjects, begged the King of Petsi in Corea to teach him what he should do to instruct the people. The King sent him the learned Wang-Jin, who made known to the Daïri the books of the great teacher to whom China was indebted for more than six centuries for its wisdom and its prosperity. The services rendered by the learned Corean to the Empire of the Mikados had been so highly appreciated, that Wang-Jin, foreigner though he was, was admitted among the number of the national Kamis, together with the founders of the monarchy and the heroes or benefactors of Japan.

When we endeavour to account for the influence which the writings of Confucius have exercised upon Japanese society, we must acknowledge at the same time that they have contributed more than anything else to endow it, not indeed with civilization, but with the civilism in which it takes such pride. It is very difficult to reduce the general principles from which he deducts his moral sentences to a scientific form.

Men, according to Confucius, are by nature the friends of each other ; it is only habit and education which separates them.

To perfect oneself is the basis of all moral development.

The means of obtaining this development consists in pursuing the enlightening principle of reason which we receive from Heaven.

This reason teaches us perseverance of conduct in a right line equally divided from extremes.

Invariability in the *juste milieu*, such is the rule or formula of wisdom.

The perfecting of oneself is, however, only the first part of virtue ; the second and most important part consists of the perfecting of others.

The supreme doctrine of humanity is that we should act towards others as we wish that they should act towards ourselves.

All social conditions are not equally proper to the development of good natural dispositions.

He who has the power or faculty of pursuing his moral development, and he who attains to it, is distinguished from the crowd, and to him Heaven gives a mandate to govern and to instruct the peoples.

Nevertheless, although the sovereign holds his power from Heaven, the sole guarantee whereby he preserves that power resides in the support which he derives from the affection of his people. Finally, men who are supremely perfect have the faculty, not only of governing peoples, but of contributing to the development of beings, and of identifying themselves by their works with heaven and earth.

This is, so far as I can discern, the substance of the doctrine of Khoung-Tseu ; and no doubt it leaves little to desire, if we regard man merely as a reasonable being ; but if the human organization includes love, the life of the heart with its infinite aspirations and its mysterious intuitions of eternal things, the sage of the Celestial Empire deceived himself, his doctrine is insufficient : it has only the appearance of life, it encloses men and states in a circle within which humanity becomes atrophied. Great thoughts come from the heart and enthusiasm makes a great people.

China, disciplined by Confucius, has become the type of stagnant nations. The Japanese people have escaped from the fate of their neighbours, but the Government of Japan, formed in the school of Chinese philosophy, has been unable to assimilate Christian civilization and has merely let its power slip into the hands of the old national Theocracy.

It is a fact worthy of remark, that Khoung-Tseu has never been the apostle of any of the aristocratic classes of society. His real moral grandeur consists in having isolated himself, while in the midst of paganism, in the domain of reason, as it were in a fortress, and of never having pretended to elevate himself into the founder of a new religion. He expressly forbids innovations in anything whatsoever. All

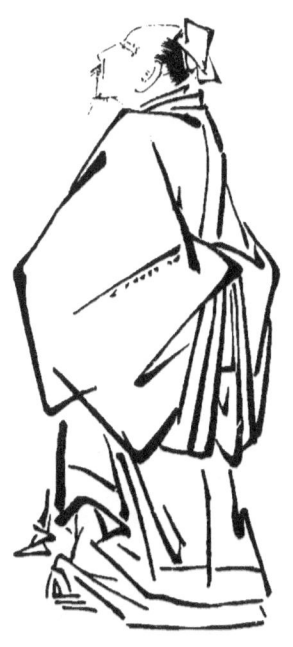

ALLEGORICAL PICTURE IN THE NOBLE STYLE.   ALLEGORICAL PICTURE IN THE POPULAR STYLE.

his instructions are limited to recommending the study and the example of the old customs. The worship which is paid to him in China and Yeddo in the temple of the University does not constitute, properly speaking, an act of adoration, but merely one of pious commemoration. It is unhappily true that this homage degenerates into a superstitious respect for the words of the master, strengthened by the difficulties presented by the dry study of his works.

In China, and in all countries subject to the preponderance of the classical Chinese literature, the attachment of the *litterati* to the texts of their favourite author, is strong in proportion to the trouble which it gives them to fix them in their memory. The study of a Chinese book is a most arduous task, even for a Japanese; because the national idiom of the latter has neither analogy nor any point of contact with the language of the Celestial Empire.

The primitive writing of the Japanese exists no longer, except as an archæological curiosity; it has given place to Chinese writing, which on its side has undergone the most extraordinary transformation under the reed of the Japanese.

Kioto was formerly the literary centre of Japan. At present the ancient pontifical city possesses a speciality in albums containing miniatures; almanacs of the Daïri; religious books; romances and poems inscribed upon vellum-paper spangled with gold stars. But the presses of Yeddo are far more important in the number, variety, popularity, and immense sale of their publications. The greater part of the literary novelties of the capital are produced by the Professors of the University or the principal pupils of the Interpreter's College. They are almost all didactic, of a practical tendency, with an utilitarian aim. There are among them certain works which we may entitle the Scientific Year, the Review of Inventions and Discoveries, Statistics of Europe and of North America, the Manual of Modern History, the Précis of Contemporary Geography, the Annals of Physical and Natural Sciences, of Medicine, of Navigation, of Mechanics and of Military and Naval Engineering. The ancient Encyclopædias, which consist of more than two hundred volumes, are replaced by a sort of Dictionary of Conversation published annually in a single volume adorned with a quantity of wood engravings. The ethnographical portion of this work is the most interesting. All that which relates to the clerical and political institutions of the Empire reduces itself to a dry nomenclature. The chapters devoted to the description of foreign nations are extremely tame and meritical. One of the most categorical deals with the Spaniards and Portuguese, of whom it says, in so many words, that they have an extremely bad religion.

I do not believe that there exists in Japan any treatise upon religious or philosophical controversy. The doctrine of Confucius excludes every kind of polemics, because if men are beings naturally good, if several of them have during distant centuries attained perfection, then there is really nothing more to dispute about;

perfectibility becomes a non-sense, and progress consists in retrogression, as far as those Emperors of the ancient ages, who, according to Chinese philosophy, furnished

A JAPANESE WRITER.

humanity with its supreme and definitive type. We must, however, acknowledge, that the time has not yet come for us to judge of Japanese literature. Those learned

Europeans who are by degrees making it known to us have only translated in the first place useful books; treatises whose study may be of immediate service to one or other of our great industries. Such are the important works on the art of sericulture, and the manufacture of porcelain in China and Japan, which have been published since 1848. As for the purely literary productions of Japanese writers, we have very few of them, and the selections made by the translators have not been judicious. No doubt deeper research will give us more valuable results, but they will only be really profitable when we shall have penetrated into the private life of the middle classes, and shall have succeeded in getting hold of the repertory of their plays, their legends, their stories, and their festival songs.

The lower classes are passionately fond of listening to story-tellers and singers. Every day, at the cessation of labour and of traffic, groups of persons of both sexes may be seen about the workshops, or at an angle of the cross roads, ranged in a semicircle around the professional *raconteur*. National romances and legends are abandoned, by the common consent, to the women who live by the trade of singers and musicians. They form a very numerous class of the Japanese proletariat, but some of them are much less nomadic than the others, and of an evidently superior class. The most distinguished among the public singers go about accompanied by three or four musicians, and do not themselves play on any instrument. The artistic productions of these feminine associations are at once dramatic and musical, and the effect is very charming when they play in the open air, on a fine summer evening, within a frame-work lightly constructed of bamboo, ornamented with climbing plants and with garlands of coloured-paper lanterns. This is one of the popular spectacles which delights strangers.

One evening when we had been present at a concert by these musicians, I said to our yakounines on our way home, that I regretted very much that I could not understand the words of their national romances. They assured me, laughing and shrugging their shoulders, that I lost nothing by my ignorance. One of them, however, had the politeness to add, that books containing the legends recited by the professional singers were to be bought of the booksellers in the city. I afterwards asked a carrier in Yokohama to purchase for me all the best productions of the kind; and I am sure he executed my commission very faithfully, for he brought me a complete library of moral tales, historical anecdotes, and heroic or marvellous legends. As the greater

L L

number of this collection was illustrated. I had no difficulty in recognizing the most popular of their subjects, and, dipping by chance into the warlike series, I found poetical and artistic illustrations of exploits which would put Ariosto's heroes to shame.

Asahina-Sabro charges a troop of enemies and passes through them, lifting up with his right hand a soldier wearing a casque and cuirass, and spinning him round

A BONZE HOUSE.

in the air, while with the left hand he kills two equally redoubtable warriors with one blow of his mace.

Nitan-Nosiro, the dauntless hunter, astride on the back of a gigantic wild boar,— which has flung down and trodden under its hoofs all the companions of the hero,— holds the furious monster between his knees, and plunges his cutlass into its shoulder.

Sousigé, one of the horsemen of the Mikado, finds his comrades squatting round a draught-board; he spurs his horse, and with one bound it stands in the centre of the board motionless, on its hind feet, while its master, who has not lost his stirrups for a moment, sits as firmly in this difficult position as the equestrian statue of Peter the Great on its granite pedestal on the banks of the Neva.

The bow of Ulysses, king of Ithaca, has for a long time enjoyed unrivalled reputation, but I fear it is about to be eclipsed by the bow of Tamétomo; with which that warrior conquered the Island of Fatsisio. He desired to avoid bloodshed, and to convince the islanders that all resistance on their part was useless: he therefore summoned

A MAGICIAN.

the two strongest men of the race of Aïnos, and, seated calmly upon a mass of rock, he presented his bow to them, holding it by the wood, and ordered them to try and bend it. Each seized it by both hands, and, setting their heels against the wood of the bow, they leaned back with all their weight and pulled the string with all their strength. Every effort was in vain; the bow yielded only when Tamétomo took it delicately between the finger and thumb of his right hand and shot an arrow, which was immediately lost in the clouds.

Such is the nature of the heroic literature of Japan. It would be much more difficult to give an idea of their marvellous or fantastic legends. The merit of these productions, which are generally short poems, appears to me to consist essentially in the choice of expressions, in the structure of the verses; in fact, in the elegance of the style without any reference to the subject, because most frequently we find, on translating them, that they have only a childish meaning, with no moral signification or any value in point of intelligence. What, for instance, can be the point of the following anecdote? "The soul of a thieving weasel having hidden itself in a bonze's kettle, the bonze saw it come out one day when he set the kettle on an unusually hot fire." This is all: and this absurdity is the subject of an exceedingly popular picture. There are, however, among these legends a few which, notwithstanding that good sense and good taste protest against them, to a certain extent captivate the imagination, excite curiosity, and provoke reflection.

THE OLD WOMAN AND THE SPARROW.

Several times I have asked myself what can possibly be the origin and the traditional cause of the almost religious importance attached by all the middle-class families to a picture which represents an old man armed with a bamboo rake, of the sort which is used for raking the ears of rice or small shell-fish; and an old woman holding a broom, with which she seems to be about to sweep up dead leaves. They stand together side by side, or they sit at the foot of an ancient cedar, whose cavernous trunk seems to be their abode. Whenever I saw this picture, I thought of the fable of Baucis and Philemon; but the legend never speaks of the end of the venerable Japanese couple. An interpreter told me that the people of his province regard these two personages as the Adam and Eve of their country. We often find the tortoise and the crane, two animals endowed with eternal peace and a very long life, frequently associated with them, and the good old man and old woman are exhibited at all wedding feasts, either in the form of a picture or as a table ornament. No doubt they symbolize to the young married couple domestic happiness, lasting to the extreme limit of old age, as the reward of a simple life and a faithful affection.

On the other hand, there is a tree called the Enoki, dedicated to unhappy households. It is said to have sprung up on the tomb of the first Japanese woman who was divorced. If a married couple no longer suit one another, they have only to go secretly, each without the knowledge of the other, to the foot of the Enoki, and there form the intention of separating. In a short time the separation is accomplished without any difficulty, and the grateful husband suspends a votive tablet on the trunk of the tree representing a man and a woman crouching upon the ground, and turning their backs on one another.

Tree-worship, which has existed among all ancient races, is limited by the Japanese to very old trees. When the lord of Yamato wished to furnish his house completely

PHILEMON AND BAUCIS.

from the trunk of the finest cedar in his park, the axes of the woodman bounded from the bark, and large drops of blood flowed from every stroke. This, says the legend, is because ancient trees have a soul, like men and gods, granted to them on account of their great age. They are also capable of sympathy with the misfortunes of fugitives who place themselves under their protection. More than one unfortunate warrior on the point of falling into the hands of implacable enemies has found a retreat in their branches, or in some old trunk.

Japanese legend has its Geneviève de Brabant. A noble lady driven forth into the woods, gave birth to a son, whom she nursed at her breast while she laboured for their common support. When her innocence had been recognized she was brought back with great pomp to the Court of the Mikado, and her kirimon of leaves was exposed in a temple for public veneration. To the end of his life her son retained the weather-beaten complexion and the crisp hair, which he owed to his early mode of life. He was accustomed to combat with wild beasts, to tame bears, and to resist the attacks of brigands ; he possessed prodigious strength and skill, and he has become one of the principal heroes of the Empire under the name of Rouïko.

The forests, and the pine and bamboo groves shelter great numbers of wild beasts, among which the monkey, the polecat, the badger, and especially the fox, furnish inexhaustible subjects for fantastic stories and drawings. Animals who attain to a great age end, like trees, in becoming endowed with a human soul and supernatural virtues. The polecat, when it is old, calls the wind and the clouds from the mountain-tops. The hail and rain obey him. He allows himself to be carried away upon the wings of the hurricane. The traveller caught in the open country may courageously brave the tempest, but he cannot protect his face from being cut as if by a knife. This is the effect of the claws of the polecat, who passes him in the storm. Old frogs upon the borders of the tanks bring down a damp fog into the eyes of the belated passenger, who believes that he sees the roofs of his hamlet upon the horizon, but this is only an illusion which lures him still farther into the vast swamp.

The Yama tori, or silver pheasant, makes a mirror of his plumage. He is an invulnerable being. He does not fly from the sight of the sportsman ; but woe to the latter if he attempt to harm him, or to pursue him into the defiles of the mountains, for he will never return.

Old wolves have the gift of metamorphosis. One especially large wolf suddenly disappeared from the country, in which he had long been the terror of travellers, but when they thought they might henceforth go their ways in safety, they met at nightfall, just at the corner of the wood, a beautiful girl who carried a lantern, painted like a bouquet of roses, in her hand. She is well known through all the country-side under the name of "the Beauty with the Rose-lantern." Alas ! every traveller who has followed

THE SOUL OF THE OLD CEDARS.

her has fallen into the jaws of the wolf. There was another girl, who, as seen from afar, had all the graces of her sex, but a man who saw her face to face beheld a demon.

Tadé-yama is a very high mountain, with a deep crater in its summit. On looking into the gulf, the horrified traveller beholds a basin filled with human blood, and this blood boils, heated by the volcano; such a place, says the bonze, can only be one of the departments of hell.

All maladies which break out for the first time among the people have a diabolical origin. The demon of small-pox came to Japan by sea. He was dressed in a red tunic, and he bore a letter addressed, no one knows by whom, to the Divine patron of the Empire. In the sanctuary of some of the old bonze houses, barbed arrow-heads of flint and jasper, lance-heads in the form of spits, knives and axes of basalt and of jade, are exhibited. These instruments, according to the bonzes, are for the most part relics which have come down from the time of the ancient dynasties of the Gods of Heaven and Earth. In the southern part of Niphon there exists a kind of axe formed of thunderbolts; and stone arrows, which bear witness to the strife reigning among the spirits of the tempest, still fall in showers when the unchained elements menace the habitations of men.

Great respect is due to printed books, respect in fact equal to that claimed for ancestral monuments. The bonze Raïgo, having in a moment of anger destroyed the library of his convent, was after his death changed into a rat, and condemned to gnaw scraps of paper and old fragments of parchment as his only food.

The evil spirits of the air haunt during the night all places where crimes, either detected or secret, have been committed.

The souls of misers return to the earth, while their treasures, however skilfully they may have been concealed, are carried away, no one knows how or where. A woman who had great revenues refused to marry; her motive was pure avarice. When she was dead her sisters inherited her property. One of them, who loved to adorn herself with a dress which had belonged to the dead woman, and who hung it up every night on a nail at the back of her bedroom door, saw a long lank arm protruding from the dress and shaking it violently.

The souls of women who have been unhappy wander about the scene of their misfortunes.

The souls of women who have committed suicide by drowning float in the air as if they were about to fall head foremost.

Women who have died in childbed appear to the passers-by carrying the infant in their arms, and crying, in a supplicating voice,—"Have mercy, and receive my child' that it may not remain in the tomb."

A woman having died in consequence of the ill-treatment of her husband, the latter sent for a bonze immediately after her interment, and directed him to place a blessed paper, which has the property of dispelling evil spirits, upon the lintels of his doorway. When the soul of the dead woman came back from the cemetery, it could not pass the sacred barrier, and thenceforth she cries incessantly to all persons who approach the house : " All you who pass by take away that paper."

The historical anecdotes present a totally different character from the heroic and marvellous legends. They bear the modern impress of the critical studies of the University of Yeddo, and are marked by the cold reasoning which distinguishes the philosophical school of Confucius.

The American Missionary, Verbeck, has made us acquainted with one of the most remarkable specimens: " The Collection of Virtuous Actions accomplished in Japan and China," the work of a Japanese, a native of Yeddo, and a pupil in the University. A short quotation will enable my readers to appreciate the book, and the school to which it belongs : " All men," says the author, "invoke some deity to preserve them and their families from ill-fortune. Some address their prayers to the moon : others watch all night, in order that they may salute the rising sun by their homage ; others invoke the gods of Heaven and Earth, and also Buddha. But to adore the sun, the moon, the gods, or Buddha, without doing that which is good, is to ask that rice-stems should come out of the earth before the grain has been planted. Learn, then, that in that case, the moon, the sun, the gods, and Buddha may perhaps have a great deal of compassion for you, but they will never cause the rice to grow until you have sown the seed."

Confucius has said : "He who offends heaven has nobody whom he can invoke with profit ;" and the Japanese sage, Kitamo-no-Kami, has written : " If thou turn not away thine heart from truth and goodness, the gods will take care of thee without thine invocation. . . . . .

" To be virtuous is to adore."

Under the reign of one of the ancient Mikados, an unknown star appeared in the sky. A celebrated astronomer having observed it, declared that it was the presage of a great calamity about to fall upon the family of one of the generals-in-chief of the

M M

Empire.   At this epoch Nakahira was the general-in-chief of the left, and Sanégori was general-in-chief of the right.   On learning the prediction of the astrologer, Sanégori and his family fled to the temples of Buddha and of Sintô, in the neighbourhood, and there worshipped without cessation, while the family of Nakahira took no precaution of the kind.   A priest, remarking this, went to Nakahira and expressed his surprise. " Sanégori," said he, " visits all the holy places, and offers up prayers in order that he may escape from the misfortune presaged by the unknown star; why do not you do the same ? "   Nakahira, who had attentively listened to the priest, replied : " You have seen what is going on, and you will know how to understand my justification.   When I am told that the unknown star presages a misfortune to one of the generals-in-chief, it stands to reason that the predicted calamity must fall upon either Sanégori or upon me.   Now when I come to reflect, I know that I am of very advanced age, and that I have no military talent : Sanégori, on the contrary, is in the prime of life, and perfectly suited for the post he holds.   Consequently, if I were to pray and were to be heard, so as to turn away from myself the calamity which threatens us both equally, it could only take place to the greater peril of Sanégori, and to the detriment of the Empire.   I abstain therefore from prayer, in order to aid as far as I can in saving the precious life of this man."

On hearing these words the priest could not restrain his emotion, and he exclaimed : " Certainly so noble a thought is the best act of worship you could make, and most undoubtedly, if there be gods, and if there be a Buddha, it is neither upon you nor your family that the calamity will fall."

ENTRANCE TO THE GARDENS OF MYASKI, YEDDO.

CHAPTER VII.

DOMESTIC SOLEMNITIES.

GARDENS. —BATHS.—POPULAR MEDICINE.—THE SHAMPOOERS.—WEDDINGS.—A SOCIAL COMEDY.
— A JAPANESE BABY. — DEATH.— BURIAL. —INCINERATION. — YÉDAS. — CHRISTANS. —
FURTHER CUSTOMS.

CHINESE civilization possesses nothing which resembles the beneficent institution of a
day of rest recurring regularly after a certain series of working days. There are
monthly festivals, by which the working classes commonly profit very little, and an

entire week, the first of the year, during which all labour is suspended, and the
population of the cities and the countries give themselves up to the amusements within
their reach, each person choosing them according to his social position and the resources
at his disposal.

The citizens of Yeddo, the artizans, the manufacturers, the Japanese tradesmen in
general, lived, until the arrival of the Europeans, under the most exceptional economic
conditions in the world. They worked only for the internal supply of a country highly
favoured by nature, sufficiently large and sufficiently cultivated to supply all its own
needs; for centuries they had enjoyed the pleasures of an easy and simple life. This
is no longer the case. I witnessed the last days of the age of innocence, in which,
with the exception of some great merchants whom fortune had obstinately pursued
with its favours, no one worked except to live, and no one lived except to enjoy
existence. Work itself had a place in the category of the purest and deepest enjoyments.
The artizan had a passion for his work, and, far from counting the hours, the days,
the weeks, which he gave to it, it was with reluctance that he drew himself away from
it till he had at length brought it—not to a certain saleable value, which was less
the object of his care—but to that state of perfection which satisfied him. If he were
tired, he left his workshop and rested himself for as long or as short a time as he
pleased, either in his house, or in company with his friends at some place of amusement.

There was not a Japanese dwelling of the middle classes without its little garden,
a sacred asylum for solitude, for the siesta, for amusing reading, for line fishing, or
for long libations of tea and saki.

The hills on the south, west, and north of the citadel, are rich in pretty valleys
and grottoes, springs and ponds, all utilized in the most ingenious manner by the
small proprietors. If nature has not isolated the demesne by means of hedges or
natural palisades of bamboo covered with climbing plants, industry supplies the
deficiency. When the garden is approached from the street, a rustic bridge is thrown
across the canal before the door, and hidden with tufts of trees and thick-leaved shrubs.
On crossing the threshold, the visitor might believe himself to be in a virgin forest
far from all human habitations. Blocks of stone, negligently arranged as steps, help
him to mount the hill, and suddenly, when he has reached the summit, a delightful
spectacle lies at his feet. Below the flower-covered rocks is a gracefully-formed pond,
its banks adorned with lotus, iris, and water-lilies; a little wooden bridge crosses it.

The path descends through groves of tufted bamboos, azaleas, dwarf palms. and camellias ; then through beautiful groups of tiny pines which hide the ivy-covered rocks, and along hill-sides enamelled with flowers, amid which the lily lifts its white crown above the dwarf shrubs, which are cut into fantastic forms.

This scene, when beheld from the bottom of the valley, offers an equally harmonious combination of form and colour. There is nothing to excite particular attention, but the whole landscape and all its details wrap the mind in calm, and leave it no other impression than the vague pleasure of perfect rest.

Although the Japanese delight on occasion to plunge themselves into a condition which closely approaches the physical insensibility and ideal annihilation recommended by Buddhism, they do not systematically indulge in it. The spirit of order presides over their daily conduct, and regulates their hygienic practices.

Among the latter the bath holds the first place. In addition to their morning ablutions, the Japanese, of every age and of both sexes. take a hot bath every day, at a temperature rather above that of fifty degrees centigrade. They remain from five to thirty minutes in

A GOD OF HAPPINESS.

the water, sometimes plunged up to the shoulders, sometimes only up to the waist, according as they lie down or squat ; and during all the time they take the greatest care to avoid wetting the head. It not unfrequently happens that congestion of the brain, and even apoplexy, is the result of this unreasonable habit.

A custom which has become a daily need, and is practised by all classes of an enormous population, could not be in any sense private. A tacit agreement has therefore been established at Japan, which places the bath, from the point of view of public morals, in the category of indifferent actions, neither more nor less than sleeping, walking out, and drinking. As the superior classes of society have dormitories and dining-rooms, so each house belonging to the nobility or the upper ranks of the citizens

has one or two bath-rooms reserved for domestic use; and there is no small citizen's
dwelling without some little room where a bath, with its heating apparatus, may be
found.   When the bath is ready, the entire family profit by it in succession; first the
father, then the mother, then the children and all the household servants included.

THE PALACE OF PRINCE SATSOUMA AT YEDDO.

Nevertheless, the common bath is rarely used, because the expense of the fuel which
it would involve would be much greater than the expense of a family subscription
to the public baths. Accordingly the majority of the population regularly use the
latter.   They are to be found in every street of a certain importance, and everywhere
they are so crowded, especially during the two last hours of the day, that it has become
absolutely necessary to allow the bathers to bathe in community. There are generally two

reservoirs, separated by a low iron or wooden bridge, and sufficiently spacious to receive from twelve to twenty bathers at a time. The women and children collect on one side, and the men on the other; but without prejudice to the leading principle that every new comer shall install himself where he finds a place, no matter who may be the previous occupant. The proprietor squats upon a platform, from which he can observe the persons who come in, and who pay in passing. Sometimes the proprietor smokes, and sometimes he reads romances to amuse himself.

The national law which regulates the public baths extends beyond the threshold of these establishments,—that is to say, if the bathers of either sex wish to take the air on the pavement outside, they are respectively regarded as partaking of the benefit of the accepted fiction; and more than that, it shelters them to their own dwelling, when it is their pleasure to proceed thither with the fine lobster-colour which they have brought out of the hot water intact.

However strange this custom may appear to us, no Japanese, before the arrival of the Europeans, supposed that it could have a reprehensible side. On the contrary, it was in perfect harmony with the rules of domestic life, and irreproachable from the moral point of view.

Many singularities find explanation in the fact that the Japanese have decidedly no pretension to plastic beauty. Nothing is more characteristic in this respect than the manner in which the native painters draw the heroes and heroines of their stories of love and war. In a little while, however, Japan will be under the influence of the Japanese who have visited Europe, and especially those who have made a prolonged sojourn here. If the comparison which they institute between the two civilizations does not induce them to recommend the adoption of ours in its lesser details, we may be quite sure that they will reform all such national customs as have provoked the ridicule of foreigners.

Several of the great public baths of Yeddo have added modern therapeutic inventions, such as douches of hot and cold water, to the ordinary resources of these establishments.

The physicians of the opulent classes of society are always certain to win the good graces of their patients by recommending them to try a cure in one of the mountain districts famous for the efficacy of their waters. There are some particularly celebrated in the island of Kiousiou, at the foot of the volcanoes of Aso and Wounsentake. The thermal springs which are found there are, generally speaking, sulphurous and very hot. They are used in rheumatic affections and skin diseases.

It has not yet occurred to the mind of the Japanese to enhance the charms of the bathing season by the attraction of *roulette* and *trente et quarante*. Games of chance

A SURGICAL OPERATION.

are disdained by everyone in good society. Cards are left to servants and coolies, and these are not permitted to play for money.

The small tradesman does not trouble himself to go to the thermal baths; when doctors do not seem to be doing him any good, he prefers to undertake a pilgrimage. He is not, however, without his own notions about medicine. According to him the latent cause of all the disturbance of the human machine resides in the more or less ill-regulated action of the internal vapours; apparently those of which Sganarelle speaks, "the vapours formed of the exhalations of the influences which arise from the region of the malady." The daily baths, no doubt, contribute to disengage and to dissolve them. If, however, some unexpected indisposition arises during the hours of work or of recreation, it is good to have a little medicine case at hand, and, therefore, he wears it hanging from his girdle, on the same bunch of strings with his pipe and his tobacco bag. But if the morbific gas resists the powders and the pills in his little box, he must have recourse to cautery. The former does not absolutely demand the intervention of the surgeon. Every well-arranged household has its supply of the little cones of mugwort with which moxas are applied, and every good housewife ought to know what are the portions of the body to burn according to the symptoms of the malady : as, for example, the shoulders in indigestion, stomach complaints, and loss of appetite; the vertebræ in attacks of pleurisy, the muscles of the thumb in a case of toothache, and so on. Such is the reputation of the moxa among the Japanese people, that it is frequently used as a preventive, and even at fixed times once or twice a year.

YEDIS.

A sovereign remedy against cholic consists in making six or nine deep incisions, by means of fine needles of gold or silver, in the abdominal region.

As in certain countries in Europe, there exists a class of quacks who add teeth-drawing to the barber's profession, and who put on leeches and blisters, so Japan possesses a whole host of subaltern surgeons specially devoted to the practice of cautery and other empirical remedies. They are called Tensasi, or "men who punish," in reference to their preliminary operations. Whatever talent they may display in their various functions, they are never permitted to add shampooing—a kind of treatment much resorted to in Japan in cases of nervous irritation or rheumatic affections—to them.

The reason for this exclusion was told me by a shopkeeper, at whose house I witnessed a spectacle which at first sight I could not understand. A woman, lying on her left side at full length upon the mats in the back shop, was patiently bearing the weight

N N

of a big fellow, who was kneading her shoulders with both hands. "Is that your wife?" said I to the shopkeeper. He made an affirmative sign, and then placing his thumb and middle finger of his left hand upon his two eyelids, showed me that the operator was blind, and went on to inform me that the laws of society among the Japanese limited the office of shampooers to men deprived of sight. I remembered to have met

THE PROCESSION OF THE BLIND. CARICATURE.

blind men in the street carefully feeling for the footway, a rough staff in their right hand, and in the left a reed cut into a whistle, from whence they extracted a plaintive and prolonged sound at intervals. Thus they announce to the citizens that they are passing by, in case any one wants to be shampooed. The shampooers have the head shaven, and wear one garment, of grey or blue stuff.

I was told that they form a large fraternity, which is divided into two orders. The most ancient, that of Bou-Setzous, has a religious character and belongs to the Daïri. It was instituted and endowed by the son of a Mikado, Prince Sen-Mimar, who became blind by dint of weeping for the death of his Empress.

The rival order of more recent origin, but not less chivalrous, is that of the Fékis. In the great battle which the Taïgoun Yoritomo won at Simonoséki, having put an end to the civil wars which rent the Empire, Féki, the chief of the rebel party, was slain. His brave general, named Kakékigo, soon fell into the power of the conqueror, who treated his prisoner with great consideration. When he imagined he had gained him over by his attentions, he called him into his presence and proposed to him to ally himself to the Imperial cause. "I have been the faithful servant of a good master," replied the general, "and I have lost him; no other in the world shall succeed to him in my esteem. As for you, the author of his death, I could never look on you without longing to strike your head off at my feet, but you confound me by your magnanimity, therefore, accept the only sacrifice by which I can render homage to it." So saying, the unfortunate man tore out his two eyes and offered them to his new master.

Yoritomo set him at liberty, and gave him an estate in the province of Fiougo. The general founded the order for the blind under the authorization of the Mikado, and the Fékis soon exceeded the Bou-Setzous in numbers and in wealth. All the members of this society must exercise a profession. There are some who become musicians, special players on the biwà, but the greater number practise shampooing. All the money which they collect from city to city is deposited in a central treasury, from which the associates receive a fixed sum, sufficient for their subsistence to the end of their lives.

The governor of the order resides at Kioto. I am told that he exercises the right of life and death over the members, subject only to the Imperial supremacy.

It is not difficult for a foreigner sojourning in Japan to mix with the people, and even to penetrate into the intimacy of the middle classes; but I doubt whether he would ever succeed in gaining admission to family festivals in any rank whatever of native society.

In all the countries of the far East, the marriage of a daughter is always celebrated with more or less prolonged rejoicings in the house of the husband. But, while the

Chinese is proud to invite foreign guests to the wedding of his son, in order that he may make a pompous parade before them, the Japanese, on the contrary, surrounds the ceremonies which belong to this solemn act with the discreetest reserve. He regards it as much too serious an affair to be interfered with by the presence of any but the nearest relatives and the confidential friends of the two principals.

Most Japanese marriages are the result of family arrangement made long beforehand, under the inspiration of the practical good sense which is one of the national characteristics.

The bride brings no dowry, but she is given a *trousseau* which many a lady of higher rank might be proud of. She is required to have an unsullied reputation, a gentle and yielding disposition, the amount of education fitted for her sex, and the acquirements of a good housekeeper.

Considerations of pecuniary interest hold only a secondary place, and they generally lead rather to business combinations than to mere money bargains. Thus, when a good citizen who has no son, gives his only, or his eldest daughter in marriage, her husband receives the title of his father-in-law's adopted son, takes the name of his father-in-law, and succeeds him in the exercise of his industry, or the transaction of his commercial affairs. Japanese weddings are preceded by a betrothal ceremony, at which the principal members of both families are present; and it not unfrequently happens that it is on this occasion the young people discover for the first time the projects which their respective parents have formed for them. From that day forth they are given opportunities of meeting, and of appreciating the wisdom of the choice which has been made on their behalf. Visits, invitations, presents, preparations for their installation in their new home succeed each other so rapidly and so pleasantly, that the young people are rarely otherwise than delighted with their prospects.

The marriage generally takes place when the bride-elect has attained her sixteenth, and the bridegroom-elect his twentieth year. Early in the morning the young girl's *trousseau* is brought to the bridegroom's dwelling, and laid out very tastefully in the apartments in which the wedding feast is to be held. In the chief room a domestic altar is erected, adorned with flowers and laden with offerings; and in front of this altar, images of the gods and patron saints of the two families are hung. The aquariums are supplied with various plants, grouped picturesquely, and with symbolical significance. On the lacquer-work tables are placed dwarf cedars and small figures representing the first couple, accompanied by their venerable attributes, the hundred-years-old crane and tortoise. To complete the picture by a lesson in morals and patriotism, some packets of edible seaweed, of mussels and dried fish, are placed among the wedding presents, to remind the young couple of the primitive food, and the simple customs of the ancient inhabitants of Japan.

About noon a splendid procession enters the rooms thus prepared ; the young bride, veiled and arrayed in white, advances, led by two female friends, and followed by a crowd of relatives, friends, and neighbours, in robes of ceremony composed of splendid scarlet brocade, gauze, and embroideries. The two friends do the honours, distribute the guests, see to the arrangements for the repast, and flit about from one group to another. They are called the male and female butterfly. They must personify, in the cut and decoration of their crape and gauze robes, the charming couple who, in popular story, set an example of conjugal felicity. May you, too, they seem to say to the betrothed pair, taste the flowers of life, hover in aërial flight over the earth, during your terrestrial career, always joyous, always united, until your happy existence exhales in common in a final embrace.

With the exception of certain Buddhist sects, whose rites include a nuptial bene-diction, the priest has no place in the celebration of marriage in Japan. The decisive ceremony by which the Japanese replace our sacramental ordinance possesses an affecting symbolism. Amongst the objects displayed in the midst of the circle of the guests is a metal vase, in the form of a pitcher with two mouths. This vase is beautifully ornamented. At an appointed signal one of the bride's ladies fills it with saki ; the other takes it by the handle, raises it to the height of the mouths of the kneeling bride and bridegroom, and makes them drink alternately, each from the pitcher mouth placed opposite to their lips, until the vase is emptied. It is thus that, husband and wife, they must drink from the cup of conjugal life ; he on his side, she on hers, but they must both taste the same ambrosia, or the same gall ; they must share equally the pains and sorrows as well as the joys of this new existence.

If the poetical charm of the symbolism of the natural affections sufficed to render people moral, the Japanese should be the best husbands in the world. Unhappily, the same man who has the right to kill his wife on the simplest suspicion—if, for example, he should see her in conversation with a stranger—no relation of the family—has no scruple about introducing a first concubine, and soon a second, then a third, and it may be even a fourth, under the conjugal roof.

It is said that, in order to spare the dignity of the legitimate wife, and in deference to her rank as a mother and the mistress of the house, the husband deigns to consult her upon the choice of each of the pearls of beauty he thinks fit to add to the treasures of his domestic felicity. It is said that the proudest dame, the most tenacious of her rights and of her prerogatives, feels no jealousy, and sees with no displeasure an augmentation of her household which permits her to rule over a numerous suite of women, her humble servants, and little pages, slaves to the caprices of her own children. But this picture is not true to life. There is, no doubt, a class in Japanese society in which the marriage tie is much relaxed; that of the Daïmios, formerly condemned by the inhuman policy of the Siogouns to leave their wives and children as hostages at Yeddo, during the prolonged absences rendered imperative by their feudal position and its administrative duties. But the licentious habits of the nobility never propagate themselves among the middle classes with impunity. When the mother of the family forces herself to suffer humiliation in silence, thenceforward peace and domestic happiness are at an end. When the relaxation of the ties of esteem and mutual confidence leads to a breach of the community of interests, disorder creeps into household affairs, the husband neglects the exercise of his profession, and endeavours to blind himself to his true moral condition, by an ever increasing consumption of saki. Finally, poverty, sickness, and frequently even some violent catastrophe, bring about the dissolution or the ruin of the household, which had been founded under such fair auspices.

The middle classes, and the masses in general, are saved by their narrow means from the scourge I have just indicated. The great majority of households, those of shopkeepers, artizans, workmen, and cultivators, require the common toil of both father and mother for their maintenance; the constant combination of their efforts, not to secure ease, but merely to supply the commonest necessaries of life.

The introduction of one single vice into such a state of things would bring about its immediate ruin. Many a young couple have to struggle bravely for years, in order to defray the expenses of their marriage. Others have had sufficient courage and good sense to resist the temptation of the national custom. The proceedings in the latter instances testify to the national talent for acting. An honest couple have a marriageable daughter, and the latter is acquainted with a fine young fellow, who would be a capital match, if only he possessed the necessary means of making his lady-love and her parents the indispensable wedding presents, and of keeping open house for a week. One fine evening, the father and mother, returning from the bath, find the house empty,—the daughter is gone. They make inquiries in the neighbourhood ; no one has seen her ; but the neighbours hasten to offer their services in seeking her, together with her distracted parents. They accept the offer, and head a solemn procession, which goes from street to street, to the lover's door. In vain does he, hidden behind his panels, turn a deaf ear ; he is at length obliged to yield to the importunities of the besieging crowd ; he opens the door, and the young girl, drowned in tears, throws herself at the feet of her parents, who threaten to curse her. Then comes the intervention of charitable friends, deeply moved by this spectacle ; the softening of the mother, the proud and inexorable attitude of the father, the combined eloquence of the multitude, employed to soften his heart ; the lover's endless protestations of his resolution to become the best of sons-in-law. At length the father yields, his resistance is overcome ; he raises his kneeling daughter, pardons her lover, and calls him his son-in-law. Then, almost as if by enchantment, cups of saki circulate through the assembly ; everybody sits down upon the mats ; the two culprits are placed in the centre of the circle, large bowls of saki are handed to them ; and when they are emptied, the marriage is recognized, and declared to be validly contracted in the presence of a sufficient number of witnesses, and it is registered next day by the proper officer, without any difficulty.

The fashion of wedding-trips is unknown in Japan. Far from leaving the young people to enjoy their happiness in peace, their friends resort to every sort of pretext for overwhelming them with invitations and visits, which are always accompanied by prolonged bouts of eating and drinking.

As soon as the young wife has the hope of becoming a mother, all her relatives, near and distant, assemble at her house, and the announcement of the good news is welcomed by a concert of coarse congratulations, indiscreet questions, and hygienic confidences absolutely untranslatable. The young wife is, from this moment, placed under the direction of an experienced matron, called the okassan, whose sole real service consists in making herself an indispensable fixture in the house for the rest of her days. At the third month a fresh solemnity takes place, no less difficult to describe than the first. On this occasion the obassan unfolds, exhibits to the company, and finally invests her charge with the girdle of red cords, which is only to be laid aside on the completion of the sixth month. When the time of delivery approaches, the poor patient is surrounded by a crowd of friends, relations, and neighbours, and is

A WEDDING.

obliged to submit with humble resignation to the suffering imposed by the orders of the obassan, and the contradictory advice of her innumerable counsellors. The birth of the child does but redouble their officiousness. An incomprehensible prejudice deprives the young mother of the necessary sleep which her whole being craves, and she is not allowed a moment's repose until her child, having been washed and dressed, is placed in her arms.

Here commences the second phase of her conjugal career. For two years at least she will nurse the child, and according to the rules of politeness which regulate the visits of Japanese ladies, she must extend her lacteal gifts to the children of her friends. Another demonstration of courtesy is made by the young girls of the neighbourhood. They dispute for the privilege of carrying the new-born infant out for its air and exercise, not only as an act of neighbourly kindness, but in order that they may, quite seriously, serve an apprenticeship to the main duties of their future vocation.

On the thirtieth day after his birth, the new citizen of Niphon receives his first name. He will take a second on attaining his majority, a third at his marriage, a fourth when he shall be appointed to any public function, a fifth when he shall ascend in rank or in dignity, and so on until the last, the name which shall be given him after his death, and inscribed upon his tomb; that by which his memory shall be held sacred from generation to generation.

The ceremony, which corresponds to baptism among us, is a simple presentation of the newly-born child in the temple of his parents' gods. Except in certain sects, it is not accompanied by sprinkling with water, or any of the formalities of purification. The father hands a memorandum containing three names, to the officiating bonze, who copies them on three separate sheets of paper, which he mixes together and shakes up at random, pronouncing a sacramental invocation in a loud voice. Then he throws them into the air, and the first which, in falling, touches the floor of the holy place, indicates the name most agreeable to the presiding divinity. The bonze immediately inscribes it upon a sheet of blessed paper, and gives it as a talisman to the child's father. Then, the religious act being complete, it remains only to celebrate the event by visits and banquets proportionate to the social condition of the infant hero of the festival, who receives a number of presents on this occasion, among which two fans figure, in the case of a male, and a pot of pommade in that of a female child. The fans are precursors of swords, and the pommade is the presage of feminine charms. In both cases, a packet of flax thread is added, signifying good wishes for a long life.

The baptism of a child is always an occasion for generosity on the part of the parent towards the priests of their religion. It is understood that the priests shall not fail to inscribe the child's name on the list of their pupils, and shall follow all the phases of his life with solicitude. The registers in the bonze-houses are said to be most accurately kept; they must always be at the disposal of the police authorities.

At three years old, the boy begins to wear a sword belt, and at seven, if he be a Samouraï, the two swords, which form the insignia of his rank. These weapons are, of course, provisional, and adapted to his size. At fifteen, he exchanges them for the proven swords confided to him, as a glorious trust, by his family, during his lifetime.

In the middle class, the chivalrous ceremonies have no place, but the three before-mentioned dates, and chiefly the last, are kept with rejoicings which yield in importance only to marriage festivities. On the day which completes the boy's fifteenth year, he attains his majority, adopts the headdress of grown men, and takes a part in the business of the paternal house. The day before he is addressed as a child ; all of a sudden everything around him is changed ; the ceremonious forms of national civility increase his importance in his own eyes, and he hastens, on his side, to respond to the congratulations which he receives, so as to prove that while he is proud of his new position, he is also awake to its responsibility. This noble testimony does not, indeed, limit itself to vain declarations, and I do not hesitate to assert, that among the most interesting traits of Japanese society are the zeal, perseverance, and seriousness with which young people of fifteen forsake the pleasures of childhood, and enter the severe school of practical life, each preparing himself to make his way honourably in the world.

Apprenticeship to any manual profession is equivalent to ten years' service. During this time the master feeds, clothes, and lodges the apprentice, but he never gives him any salary, until quite near the end of the term, when the apprentice having become a workman, receives sufficient pocket-money to buy tobacco. Professional instruction, nevertheless, does not suffer from this state of things. The master is interested in teaching his apprentice as thoroughly as possible, because it is he who presents the workman, in his turn aspiring to the rank of master, to the "tribe" or trade. This rank cannot be attained under the age of twenty-five years. As soon as the workman has reached that time of life, his master gives him his liberty, and presents him with the tools necessary for the setting up of a modest workshop. Then comes marriage to consecrate the new establishment.

It frequently happens that the workman marries before he is set up in a workshop of his own : but this takes place only when his parents' circumstances admit of his bringing his wife to live under their roof until he can make a home for her.

In all Japanese families death gives rise to a series of domestic solemnities, more or less sumptuous, according to the rank of the deceased, but in every case in a proportion very expensive to his nearest relatives. They have to bear the cost of the religions ceremonies which are in the province of the bonzes: they have to pay for the last sacraments; the watching and the praying, which is kept up without intermission in the house of the deceased until the funeral, the service which precedes the departure of the funeral procession, the funeral mass celebrated in the temple, and all the requisites for the burial or the burning of the corpse; such as the coffin, draperies, torches, flowers,

A VISIT OF CONDOLENCE.

combustibles, urn, tomb, collections and offerings given to the bonzes. Then comes the turn of the coolies who have washed the body, of those who have carried the coffin, and the convent servants whose duties lie within the enclosure of the cemetery. But this is not all; a pious custom ordains that all persons of a certain station shall install a servant at the house door charged with the distribution of alms, in small coins, to all the poor, indiscriminately, who come to seek them. And also, on the **return** of the funeral procession, all the party are expected to take leave of the head of the afflicted family, who testifies his gratitude by giving them a handsome repast.

It is not, however, in these harassing expenses only that we must seek for the source of the hardly disguised impatience with which the Japanese discharge the last offices towards their neighbours. The truth is, that though they are hardened to the sight of blood, and to scenes of homicide, they cannot overcome, even in the case of members

FUNERAL SERVICE IN THE HOUSE OF THE DECEASED.

of their own family, the instinctive repugnance, the profound horror which the presence or even the vicinity of a corpse causes them, when the death has been a natural one. There are, however, noble exceptions. Among the Japanese women, we find wives and mothers, who, overcoming every superstitious fear, know how to prove that love is stronger than death; while the men of the household consider themselves acquitted of their task when they have sent for the bonzes to recite prayers, and for a barber and his coolie assistants, who lay out the corpse, and retire to smoke and drink at the greatest possible distance from the chamber of death, the mother of the family remains to the last beside the corpse of the husband or the son. During the first hours of mourning, it is she who receives the condolences of the friends and neighbours. Humbly prostrated on the reversed mat, at the foot of a screen, also reversed, which hides the corpse from view, she mingles her sobs with the sighs and consoling words of her visitors. But as soon as the undertakers (as we should call them), arrive, she rises and assists in all the preparations they have to make. The head of the deceased must be completely shaven, and his body carefully washed, which is done by plentiful douches of tepid water, showered into the bath-room in which he is placed sitting on a turned up tub. When the coolies have dried the corpse, they lift it up respectfully, in order to place it in the coffin. The operation is not always an easy one. The rich Japanese who favour inhumation, like to rest in the earth, doubled up into enormous jars, which are masterpieces of native pottery. It requires a certain amount of energy and very strong wrists to squeeze a corpse who is at all broad-shouldered into the narrow neck of one of these jars.

The lower middle class and common people use, for coffins, simply barrels made of fir planks, with bands of bamboo bark. Whether the corpse is going to be buried or burned, it is squeezed into the same narrow compass. The head is bent, the legs are doubled up under the body, and the arms are crossed on the breast. It is not accidentally that the Japanese bury their dead in the attitude in which a child rests in the mother's womb. The practice enforces the dogma of a future life under an eloquent symbolism, of which the concluding action of the final parting is a most significant feature. At the moment when the coolies are about to place the cover on the jar, or the lid on the barrel, the mourning woman who has previously assisted in all the melancholy preliminaries, bends for the last time over the corpse, and places between its hands a viaticum, no doubt the strangest, but also the most remarkable in all the mythologies of antiquity. It is a little sheet of paper, folded in four, containing a small shred of the umbilical cord which united the dead person with his mother at the moment of his birth. When maternal love, or that of his successor has confided this strange emblem of a future birth to the mysteries of the tomb, and made, under this curious form, its humble protest against the seeming triumph of death, the coffin is closed ; and the most important of the national funeral ceremonies, the "domestic solemnity" is accomplished.

The rest consists merely of superstitious practices, vain pomp, and pure formalities, in which exorcism alternates with the glorification of family pride. It does not suffice that the Mikosi should protect the coffin, at its exit from the house of death, it passes under an arch of blessed bamboo, which prevents evil influences from following it. The bonzes, carrying their rosaries, open the procession. The nearest

INCINERATION.

relatives are dressed in white, or they wear common straw hats, which they do not remove until after the completion of the ceremonies of purification. An inscription, carried before the Mikosi, proclaims the name which the deceased is to receive in his epitaph. The horses of a military chief figure in his funeral procession, caparisoned in white, and led by grooms in mourning. His swords, his armorial bearings, his banner, various precious things which recall the rank that he held in the world, are exhibited among the groups of his relations and followers.

The funeral procession of the poor man consists of a small number of friends and neighbours, who hurry, at sunset, to the sombre valley where the vulgar rite of incineration takes place under the auspices of some bonze of low station, sent from a neighbouring convent.

COLLECTING THE REMAINS.

The Yédas, who are the pariahs of Japanese society, and deprived of the aids of religion, disdain every kind of ceremony. They simply lay the corpses of their brethren in abjectness on rude stretchers, and carry them away to a desert place. There, they pile up a heap of dead wood on which they stretch the bodies, covered with straw mats; and kindle with their own hands the fire that is to restore these miserable remains of humanity to the elements.

There is a class still lower than that of the Yédas, properly so called, that is to say the artisans who practise unclean arts, such as skinners, tanners, leather dressers; and one lower still, public executioners, purveyors of vice, lepers, cripples, registered beggars; then comes a final category of individuals held in the extreme degree of legal infamy, it is the class of "Christaus," the tolerated descendants of such of the native Christian families as were not entirely destroyed in the great

THE END OF THE PARIA.

persecution of the 17th century.   Their condition is worse than that of the mere Yédas, who live among themselves in freedom, outside the city boundaries; so utterly ignored by the law, that the space of ground occupied by their camp of thatched huts does not count in the measurement plans.   The Christaus, on the contrary, are assigned a miserable crowded quarter in the city, like the ghetto of the

Jews in the Middle Ages, which is virtually a prison. The police keep watch over them until they have drawn their last breath, and it is their business to remove the corpses, and dispose of them somehow,—no one knows where or how ; but so that the name of the crucified one shall not be pronounced over their ashes.

A TOMB IN WHICH THE URN IS PLACED.

Respect for the dead, and tomb-worship, which is one of the seemingly estimable features of the Buddhist religion, does not exist, properly speaking, except among the privileged classes, and in proportion to the profit which the bonzes extract from it. The method of inhumation, the form of the coffin, and especially the practice of incineration, introduced, in the year 700, by the priest Josco, have enabled the

P P

bonzes to make an immense trade out of the lots of ground of which they dispose. A small enclosure is sufficient for a whole family through a great number of generations. The commemorative table, which stands over the spot in which the cinerary urn has been buried, occupies no greater space than the urn itself. The badly-kept condition of the burial-places of the common people contrasts strongly with the orderliness of the fine terraces and great funereal monuments in their neighbourhood. Both are entrusted to the care of the same bonze-house; but it is the same with tombs as with indulgences, the bonzes have made each a question of tariff.

SHAMPOOING.

A FRIED-FISH SHOP, STREET JUGGLERS.

CHAPTER VIII.

SOCIAL INSTITUTIONS IN YEDDO.

JUGGLERS AND ACROBATS. — TEMPLES. — TEA-HOUSES. — THE LIVERY OF VICE. — SIGNALS. — SOCIAL DEMORALIZATION. — FISH-CURING. — IMITATION OF EDIBLE NESTS. — STREET AMUSEMENTS. — THE LION OF THE COREA. — TRADES.

THE public performers in the service of the Sibaïa, or National Dramatic Institution, form a corporation independent of the fraternity of Comedians. They are, properly speaking, jugglers, equilibrists, and acrobats, of whom it is easy to form an idea, since several of them have been for years exhibiting in Europe. Another corporation, infinitely more interesting, is that of the conjuring jugglers, the most skilful among whom perform principally at the fair of Yamasta, and in all the dependencies of the Grand Temple of Quannon at Asaksa. They also make provincial tours, although we have not heard of their having quitted Japan. But we may leave them aside, and even their superiors, and pass on to the bonze-houses on the great Tera of Quannon, in the district of Asaksa-Imato, which combine within their vast space all the seductions and all the juggleries, every industry and every artifice, by which it is possible to contribute to human superstitions and human passions.

The great river which divides Yeddo into two distinct cities, encloses in one vast circuit the districts to the north of the citadel. Two portions of the town of Yeddo are known by the name of Asaksa-Okouramaya, the region of tea-houses; and Asaksa-Imato, the region of bonze-houses. Now the two Asaksas, as well as Neghis and Staïa (smaller districts), are specially consecrated to the pleasures of the inhabitants of the capital. In those pleasures centres the industry of the district, and it excludes no class of society. It accommodates itself, on the contrary, to all tastes, responds to all caprices, and satisfies all exigencies.

Hundreds of temples rival the tea-houses; the circuses compete with the theatres; the fairs with the groves, the lakes, and the canals—those refuges of tranquil joy; while towards the north, in the solitude of the rice-fields of Asaksa-Imato, the great square, which we may almost call the City of Sin-Yosiwara, harbours, with the full sanction of the Government, countless dens of vice and debauchery.

The northern road beyond Ogawa-Bata is divided into two branches; one branch leads directly to the great Tera of Asaksa; the other borders the river as far as the quarter of the theatres, which is north-east of the bonzeries; thence it enters the rice-fields and takes the direction of Sendjoô-bassi. On the right and left of the high road, and all along the avenues of Asaksa-tera, on the bank of the Ogawa, and in the side streets which diverge from the high road, there are temples, tea-houses, public gardens, eating-houses, oratories, shops, and reposoirs, booths in which consecrated rosaries and profane curiosities are exhibited—in a word, everything that the most ingenious speculation can offer to the travellers, the pilgrims, the frequenters of theatres, and the idlers of all ages, who are coming and going by thousands, by night as well as by day, through these distant quarters of the capital. There are, however, almost within the same district, and generally throughout the meridional zone of the triangle formed by the Ogawa, two kinds of establishments which only prosper at a certain distance from the great arteries of circulation, because their speciality consists in keeping themselves apart from the floating population, while permitting their frequenters to mingle for a

IN THE PURLIEUS OF THE THEATRES.

few minutes, when they please, with the movements of the crowd. The first are the aristocratic tea-houses. They can hardly be distinguished externally from those of the middle classes. Their entire superiority consists in the arrangement of the halls and of the furniture, of the garden, and above all in the ceremony of the entertainments. When the haughty Samouraï enters one of these establishments, the mistress of the house, and the young waitresses who accompany her, prostrate themselves at his feet. The youngest of the girls rises, and begs the favour of carrying the sword of the noble person, who presents it to her. She hastens to unfold a silken handkerchief, with which she covers her right hand, in order to take hold of the

IN THE STREETS.

sabre by the end of the scabbard, and she holds it in front of her breast until the Samouraï has gone into the vestiary, when she places it upon a lacquered rack. The gentleman then proceeds, with the aid of his female suite, to make the most luxurious and minute nocturnal toilet. The one lock of hair which constitutes his head-dress is twisted by means of a knot of crape into a sort of nightcap. On his neck and shoulders is laid a thick silken handkerchief, which serves him for a shawl. His cloak is replaced by a sumptuous dressing-gown, fastened by silken cords most gracefully disposed; a pair of white socks, which serve as slippers, completes his costume, and after having washed his hands and face in perfumed water, he majestically takes his way to the salon, where a collation is prepared. It is a rule for houses of this rank to maintain a very numerous staff, so that it would be considered beneath their dignity to have recourse to the services of professional singers, guitar-players, and dancers. It is only in the inferior restaurants and other public places that such persons may be engaged either by the night or by the hour. These women, on their side, never set their feet in such establishments, unless they are expressly sent for. In this respect, as well as by the correctness of their behaviour, they are distinguished from the street musicians and the dancers at fairs. The law does not permit them to come into private houses; they can only be asked for in places subject to police regulation. Theatres are comprised in this category; they appear there at the request of the performers in the plays in order to figure in the ballet. The other tea-houses which I have indicated are also reckoned highly distinguished. They are patronized by retired functionaries, officers without ambition, or merchants who have made their fortunes, peaceful people and very exclusive, who during the day require nothing but shade, freshness, retirement, and silence, and in the evening hours the quiet chat in the verandah in front of the groves and the garden tank. Sometimes the hostess or one of her young attendants is invited to take part in the conversation. Women of this class are renowned for their wit and freedom of speech. They conduct themselves with graceful modesty towards men in good society, but they encounter with perfect ease the barrack talk of the yakounines. This is not a symptom of effrontery on their part; we must recognize it merely as the effect of national education, which permits both sexes indifferently to speak of everything without the slightest periphrasis, or any respect for persons, even for children. This excessive liberty of speech is common to the Japanese of every rank, but it must not be confounded with laxity in morals, which, even among unmarried women, is much less general than we might be tempted to suppose. Women of the class to which I am alluding are not supposed to advertise themselves so shamelessly in Japan as they are in Europe; it is only by a certain exceptional head-dress and luxurious costume that the livery of vice can be recognized. Outside the enclosure of Sin-Yosiwara, and especially in the northern quarters, it may be perceived under various forms, but none of them are indecent. Among the crowd of boats upon the Ogawa we may perhaps notice an elegant gondola, in which a young girl, negligently leaning

ON THE NORTHERN ROAD.

against the roof of the cabin, attracts attention by her tasteful attire. Her long robe, in particular, will be distinguished by some strange embroidery which facilitates the recognition of her person. For example, it may be a double wreath of bats, one black and the other white. Suddenly the girl will draw out of her girdle a roll of tissue-paper, which forms the Japanese handkerchief, and shaking it with the right hand, will give a discreet signal, which no doubt has been understood, for she immediately changes the course of the gondola, which is speedily propelled towards the shore in the direction of the tea-house, the number on whose lantern corresponds with that upon the prow of her boat.

NEAR THE BRIDGES.

Again, on the footpaths of the northern road, another girl, not less strangely attired, seems to have set herself the task of guiding benighted travellers, who have not yet made choice of a place of abode, to a neighbouring hotel, by the seductive play of her rich fan. Two hundred thousand travellers on the average are lodged every night in this City of Vice and its suburbs. They are of all orders, and of all conditions; but no class escapes the vigilance of the female hotel-keepers. Those who are posted in the proximity of the theatres belong to establishments of a very inferior rank ; thus their toilet displays neither silk nor velvet—the only thing they can allow themselves is a little prodigality in the stuff of their girdle and in the sleeves of their kirimon. They add a few mock

TAVERN SERVANTS.

tortoiseshell pins to their head-dress, and they carry a little paper lantern painted in the most brilliant colours. All who succeed to this third category hide themselves from the light. Sometimes under the spacious roof of a tea-house we may see the servants watching from an angle of the gallery, and clapping their hands to attract the attention of the passers-by.

Other servants, of a still lower condition, the poor little slaves of the pot-house keepers, wander in the darkness of the fœtid alleys. But where must we look for the lowest degree of abject misery? Are we to find its type in the poor girl who lingers about the bridges shuddering with cold, and hardly decently covered by her single garment of thin cotton? Or must we look for her in the depths of the abyss of Sin-Yosiwara? The police of Yeddo can tell us this with hideous precision; for there it levies its infamous tribute, and enforces the code of female slavery, not only for that portion of the city which knows no other rule, but in all the hotels and among all the lodging-house keepers, whose privilege is sanctioned alike by law and custom.

Not one of these unfortunates is permitted to free herself from her owners; neither is there one who escapes the vigilance of the authorities, which, however, does not extend beyond purely police and fiscal action. Nothing whatever is done in the interest of the public health. All attempts in that direction made by Europeans, in the ports open to them, are frustrated by the insurmountable repugnance of the natives. From year to year this horrible evil extends in every grade of society, and assumes more and more strongly the characteristics of a national scourge, and an immense public calamity.

We made frequent morning excursions to the Foukagawa quarter, which forms the southern faubourg of Hondjo.

On reaching the shore we could see the quays of Takanawa, Amagoten, Tetpozoo, and the block of the city over which the enormous roof of the temple of Monzeki towers. We have frequently ascended the coast of the isle of Iskawa at the mouth of the great river, and, turning to the left, disembarked behind the fortifications and the Government docks on the southern extremity of Hondjo.

The streets in the vicinity of the harbour are the centre of innumerable industries, whose raw materials are furnished by the ocean. There we saw vast drying-houses for the fish, the molluscs, and the seaweed destined for exportation, and also the great stages on which the preparations of the aboura-kami, or oil-paper stuff used by the Japanese instead of our waterproof materials, are stretched.

The native artizans excel in the fabrication and imitation of the edible birds' nests of Java. They produce these forgeries by means of a glutinous exudation of certain marine herbs, and they are then exported to China, with every trick in their packing and labelling which can possibly deceive the experts of the Celestial Empire; and I am by no means sure that Europe has not also been extensively taken in.

Fish sausages are extensively made in this quarter. They are of various kinds, each having a special colour. A great whitewashed oven is set up in the centre of a spacious kitchen; it contains bowls of iron, and a jar in which a certain class of fish is cooking. Others are chopped up very small; and as soon as they are sufficiently dried and reduced to a powder in mortars of hard wood, they are sorted, seasoned, and rolled into paste, pressed, and tied up in their envelopes, of which each receives its dip of colour. They are then packed in bales. Half a dozen persons generally work together on all these operations, which are performed to a monotonous song. The

A DEALER IN OLD CROCKERYWARE.

knives and the pestles are used in time to the rhyme. But when any noise comes from the street the men throw them down and go out and swell the gaping crowd.

Perhaps nothing more serious is going on than the dance of the Lion of Corea. How often everyone there has seen it! And nevertheless the discordant appeal of the fife and the tambourine which announce its approach is never resisted.

Four actors come out of a neighbouring street; three form the orchestra, and the fourth gives the representation. He is wrapped in a very large striped cloak surmounted by an enormous lion's head. The monster can make himself longer or shorter at will, and suddenly raise himself up two yards above the people who are with him. The children utter cries of mingled admiration and fear. Some, bolder than the rest, venture to lift up the skirts of his cloak, and even to pinch the legs of the mysterious tumbler. He sometimes frightens them, by turning his head towards them, opening his mouth, and shaking the thick mane of scraps of white paper which surrounds his scarlet face ; then he will begin to dance to the sound of the instruments of his companions. He carries his tambourine himself, but as soon as he leaves off dancing he sets it down, and, suddenly stooping, transforms himself into a quadruped, executes

PUPPET EXHIBITORS.

some grotesque gambols, and finishes by stripping off his accoutrements. Then the monster vanishes, but the juggler remains. He seizes a drumstick and balances it on the thumb of the left hand ; he puts a second stick on the end of the first, and a third crosswise above the other two ; finally, he throws them into the air, catches them in his hands, and spins them about more and more rapidly and uninterruptedly, adding one, two, or three balls, which come from no one knows where.

The admiration of the spectators is at its height. One of the musicians passes round a plate—that is to say, a fan. The representation is finished, and the juggler lights his pipe from that of some benevolent neighbour. It is not uncommon to see him negligently putting on his costume again, and sitting calmly smoking, with his head covered down to his nose with the enormous and grotesque mask of the monster. The latter is the most picturesque part of the spectacle.

By degrees, as we penetrate into the streets and populous places of the faubourg, we discover a whole world of small trades and small pleasures.

Here and there we see the humble dwellings of various classes of wandering workmen who start for the city before the sun rises, and who will only return late at night. These are cobblers, who go about mending wooden sandals; tinkers, coopers, traffickers in broken porcelain, vendors of old clothes and remnants of stuff for girdles and women's kirimons; all these people are trained to the exercise of great patience, and also to the calculation of fractions of fractions. It is a very curious sight to watch them counting on their frames of beads strung on wires.

But we must not forget the rag-picker of Yeddo, who unconsciously contributed for many years to the maintenance of the paper factories in England. In the morning and the evening he goes ferreting about in the public places, and in the populous streets of Hondjo and the merchant city, laden, not with a hod, but with a sort of paper basket which he carries in his left hand; in his right hand is a pair of long canes, by means of which he picks up everything that appears worth the trouble, and throws it into the basket.

The professional tramps pay no attention to the curiosities they meet in their path. Nevertheless, at Yeddo I have seen them exchange some amicable phrases, accompanied by two or three puffs of tobacco, with their natural friends the tumblers, with whom the good city abounds. These performers go about with what we should call a Punch and Judy Show, but it is really a doll with joints, arrayed in the costume of the sect of jumping priests. They exhibit, on a table, a model of the temple of Amida, a white mouse runs up the steps, rings a bell at the door, and performs its devotions at the altar. A third exhibitor goes about with birds trained to fire a bow, to pick rice, to draw water out of a well; and to pull a little car laden with balls of cotton. A street juggler balances himself upon two high planks, and turns somersaults, or spins over his head three or four porcelain jugs or cups; he breaks an egg, and pulls twenty yards of string out of it. He crumples a bit of paper in his hand, and immediately a cloud of artificial flies fills the air.

The greater number of these schemers speculate less on the receipts of their representation than on the sale of certain small wares which the city shopkeepers let them sell on commission. Marionettes and mice exhibitors bring crowds of children round the box which they use as a stage, and these children know well that the box is full of sweetmeats. The mender of fans has a store of new ones. Other street actors bring specimens of the industry of the faubourgs into the

A PIPE CARVER.

aristocratic quarters, and get a small commission on all orders which they succeed in obtaining.

They also sell packets of the hard wood or bamboo canes which they use for forks; also toothpicks of scented and savory wood, tooth-brushes made of white wood, with one of the ends beaten out into a little fringe.

The Japanese have a peculiar tooth-powder; one of its ingredients is, I am told, ivory-dust. It is sold in small boxes, with variously coloured and decorated lids, which vary according to the quality of the merchandise. The powder with which married women dye their teeth black is sold in metal caskets.

Workmen of the most humble appearance, cabinet-makers, joiners, turners, and wood-carvers, fabricate a multitude of pretty things, in elm-wood bark, bamboo, bone, ivory, deer-horn, yellow-amber, sea-shells, tortoiseshell, and cocoa-nut.

The Chinese workmen who carve ivory excel in the execution of masterpieces of patience, such as little empty balls, three or four in number, which turn one within the other. The Japanese artists do not build their fame on conquering difficulties; a more noble ambition animates them; they aim above all at the perfection of the imitation of nature, and when they yield to the caprice of their imagination, it takes ordinarily

A MAKER OF LANTERNS.

a humorous direction, full of genuine mirth, and not the taste for burlesque and eccentricity which characterises the Chinese workman. The most exquisite things among the small figures in ivory to be found in Yeddo are incontestably those representing animals, and more particularly the tiger, the buffalo, the bear, the monkey, and the mouse. These little art objects, which for us are only *curious*, are an integral part of the outfit of the native smokers of both sexes. In order to carry their pipe in its case and their tobacco-box, they fasten them to the end of a silken cord, whose either extremity is ornamented with one or two of these dainty little trifles, which keep down the cord and prevent it slipping when it has been passed through the girdle. They do the same with their medicine-box.

I remarked at Foukagawa a very curious assemblage of large and small trades, the greater part very vulgar, but all, without exception, worthy of observation.

The weavers' trade is not only applied to silk and cotton, but to canvas, which the Japanese painters use very largely; and to flax cloth, which cannot be of an inferior

A COOPER.

quality in a country like Japan, where the most precious of our European textiles grows to two yards in height.

The workshops of the hosiers, mat-borderers, binders, and box-makers present a picturesque assemblage of workpeople of all ages and of both sexes. The coopers work in spacious enclosures behind bamboo palings.

The shops of the box-makers contain an immense collection of coffers and caskets in wood of every kind, among which the camphor-wood of Kiousiou, which never loses its aromatic perfume, is particularly remarkable. An assortment of these boxes means half a dozen, which can be placed one within the other so as to be packed in a single parcel.

There is also an immense quantity of very strong boxes in lacquered paper; an infinite variety of household utensils, and small articles of furniture, some lacquered, such as rice bowls, others in white wood or in bamboo.

The extreme scarcity of mechanical appliances at the disposal of the Japanese artizans strikes the European visitor forcibly.

A BOWYER.

Near the shops or warehouses of which I am speaking were four or five booths, which were assigned to as many different trades. I am convinced that all the tools of the five workshops put together were not worth five pounds.

In the first booth a man was making dolls of papier-mâché, which are especial favourites in Japanese houses. They consist of the head and the face only, wrapped in a scarlet mantle; and it is said that in this form they perpetuate from generation to generation the memory of a high priest of Buddha who had used up his legs completely in the practice of his devotions. These dolls can be turned inside out, and are of all dimensions.

Further on were two workmen, each using a little hammer and chisel in carving

A DOLL-MAKER.

metal pipes, and a third was preparing wooden stems; here a lounger was holding wood

A VENDOR OF SECOND-HAND CLOTHES.

before the flames of a fire of shavings, in order to give it the necessary bend, while his companion was putting together with a little cement and string the tufts of silk, horse-

R R 2

hair or paper, which are hoisted at the ends of long pikes in order to indicate the rank or functions of a civil or military chief.

In a neighbouring workshop an old man was adjusting the hoops and hooks of a number of paper lanterns with a pair of pincers.

At the entrance of a side street we see half a dozen workmen making wooden sandals. Here the work is divided; everyone has his speciality. One cuts a piece of wood into equal lengths with a saw, and then splits them into soles or cross planks.

A CLOCKMAKER.

A third rounds the edges of the heavy sandals, and a fourth makes holes in them, through which the straw cords are passed. Other workmen are employed in finishing sandals of a more luxurious kind, and packing them by dozens of pairs into the bales which are to be carried to the retail warehouse.

I had yet to see the most peculiar of the shops in this quarter, that of the clockmaker. He was making small dials and clocks, rivalling the "Cuckoos" of the Black Forest, but with this difference, that they are on the system of moveable hours, which increase or decrease according to the seasons.

The artist, squatting before a little anvil fixed in the ground, is busy with the mechanism of his chronometer, with the exception of the gong which strikes the hours. His tools, scattered round him on mats, consist of a hammer, two or three files, a couple of pincers, and some gimlets.

With the exterior of the small dials, which are portable instruments of the form and size of a big chestnut, he has nothing to do ; the cases are made by the copper-workers.

SIN-YOSIWARA. RECEPTION HALL.

CHAPTER IX.

SIN-YOSIWARA.

A MOTHER'S SACRIFICE.---DEALING IN VICE.—BUDDHISM AND INFANTICIDE.

Whither goes that poorly-dressed woman, holding by the hand a young girl seven years of age, decked out in her best clothes? After having laid her offering before the altar of Quannon, she slowly traverses the road across the rice-fields, which turns to the east, and goes to Sin-Yosiwara. After an hour's walking, she reaches the external wall of the City of Vice, accessible only on one side—that of the north. She has met no woman upon her way. The elegant norimons of the ladies, whose coolies are carrying them in that direction, are closely shut. Individuals of every rank meet in the city, but without saluting each other, without exchanging the smallest politeness. Those who belong to the class of Samouraïs hide themselves in a complete disguise. The houses on both sides of the public way appear to be dependencies of the privileged quarter. The most miserable are tenanted by an immense population of coolies and norimon-bearers, bric-à-brac sellers, and mat-plaiters. The larger houses contain bathing establishments, provision sheds, stores of bad books, restaurants, lottery offices, and taverns, in which the apparent toleration of the police adroitly conceals the control which is in reality exercised over the dangerous classes of the capital. A bridge crosses the canal through the rice-fields. Nothing which takes place in this neighbourhood escapes the notice of a double post of yakounines installed before the gates in two guard-rooms opposite one another. The gatekeeper on duty conducts the poor traveller with her child into the presence of his chief. After a few minutes, the mother and the daughter come out of the guard-room, accompanied by a police agent, who leads them to one of the chief buildings in the street. This is the residence of the functionary known as the chief of the great Gankiro. The mother returns alone, carrying in the sleeve of her kirimon a sum of money, amounting to about the value of 100 francs (£4 sterling). The bargain she has made is duly signed and sealed. She has sold her child, body and soul, for a term of seventeen years.

The countries of the far East which suffer from an excess of population are those in which the inhuman, fundamentally anti-social, unnatural character of Buddhist paganism is revealed in all its horrors. Its every form of pagan worship finds an accomplice in the measures which the Governments of China and Japan have taken to preserve their cities from the invasion of Christian civilization. The opposition put in the way of native intercourse with foreigners, the absolute prohibition imposed upon their desire to leave their native country, have been the true causes of the overcrowding of maritime cities. In order to remedy this evil, Buddhism, which is its real origin, palliates and absolves everything which has been resorted to by perversity, in order to stop the progress of population. Thus Buddhism tolerates, in China, polygamy and infanticide; in Japan, concubinage; in both countries, prostitution organized under every form, brought within the reach of all classes of society, and fed without scruple by all the resources of speculation, not excepting traffic in children under age, or, indeed, in children of every age, because majority is only an illusory right when brought into conflict with the will of parents.

In the greater number of cases these poor creatures are the victims of the ill-conduct of the father, who has fallen into dissolute habits, and who, in order that he may be perfectly without restraint, has turned his wife and children out of their home. Japanese wives have no security against a rupture of the conjugal bond, which may be broken by the husband with no greater formality than the procuring of a letter of divorce. The forsaken wife will never have an opportunity of contracting a second

BIN ZAI-TEN-TJO.

marriage. Society condemns her. If she has no relations who will receive her, she is left to utter solitude, and her only prospect is poverty. Under such conditions, to give up a child under age to the Gankiro is to save her from destitution, and to defer, at least for a time, her own penury. If the girl be grown up, the bargain is still more advantageous, because the mother will derive from it an annual income of 100 or 200 francs (£4 or £8 sterling) during four or five years.

But what becomes of the girl when the contract has expired? She does not retain a farthing of the money which her wretched profession has brought her. She has generally been allowed to get into debt, for dresses and for food, to the chief of the Gankiro, and in order to discharge her obligations she is obliged to form a new engagement; so that she generally ends her life as a servant, or an overlooker, or a housekeeper, in the house where her career began. If it sometimes happen that a man forms an attachment to a courtezan, purchases her, and even marries her—that is a

DAIKOKOU.

very exceptional case, and might happen in any country, but which we cannot regard as general in Japan.

Within the quadrangular enclosure of Sin-Yosiwara nine distinct quarters exist, each in the form of a parallelogram stretching from east to west. On the left of the great gate there are five; on the right there are four. The former are separated from the latter by a long and spacious avenue of trees, which forms a beautiful promenade. At one end is a watch-tower; and where three angles of the city meet is a chapel, built out from the wall of the enclosure. A wide cross avenue in the centre of the quarter on the right also looks like a public promenade; but it is reserved for the inhabitants and visitors of the first-class houses by which it is surrounded. There, either· by day or by night, according to the seasons, the feminine notabilities of the Gankiro are to be found walking up and down, all dressed in the invariable kirimon, loaded with embroidery, and in a marvellous head attire of tortoise-shell combs and pins. Each of these women is accompanied by two or three pupils attached to her personal service.

DISJAMON.

These young followers wear the colours of their mistress, and an elegant head-dress of artificial flowers.

The great ladies of Sin-Yosiwara have their apartments and their reception-rooms furnished with extreme elegance. Some of them are "under the protection" of young men of high family, who pay a stated sum to the chief of the Gankiro. The secrecy of such relations, more easily hidden than others from parental vigilance, gives them a peculiarly dangerous character. The women take advantage of this secrecy to gratify to the full extent their taste for luxury and ornament. More than one patrimony is swallowed up in the satisfaction of their caprices and the ridiculous vanity of their adorers. The Gankiro properly so called is the casino of the fashionables of Sin-Yosiwara; payment is made to the door-keeper on entering, and the visitor is introduced to the conversation room. Admirable order is preserved. Pipes and refreshments, such as are ordinarily given at all Japanese entertainments, are to be had in profusion to season the witty conversation of the ladies, one of whom undertakes to guide the visitor through the gardens and the various rooms. Every amusement has its tariff. In one of these rooms a vocal and instrumental concert will be going on; in another, character dances, both executed by women, professional artists residing at Yeddo and who have nothing in common with the inhabitants of Sin-Yosiwara. These performances, even from our point of view, would be by no means unworthy of the best company.

A banqueting hall in the Gankiro is very curiously decorated; the walls are hung with beautiful sketches, either in "genre" or in landscape, some in Chinese ink, others coloured, but all painted on pieces of cardboard cut after the pattern of the different sorts of fans used in the far East. But the greatest curiosity of the Gankiro is its children's theatre. All the actors are young girls from seven to thirteen years of age, whose education is confided to the retired courtezans of Sin-Yosiwara. The latter teach their pupils reading, writing, arithmetic, singing, music, dancing, acting and declamation. Operettas, little fairy pieces, and costume ballets, are executed by these children with infinite grace and dexterity. It is doubtful whether these pieces are not superior in literary value to the vaudevilles, the comedies, and the dramatic proverbs which are played in schools in Europe; but the little theatre is certainly superior to such things among ourselves in talent, vivacity, and charming childish poetry. The spectacle is very pretty and very interesting, and yet, at the same time, what can be more sad than to see the young girls of the Gankiro so carefully educated? The sight only supplies an additional protest against these horrible institutions.

From time to time in the midst of the nocturnal rejoicings, a terrible rumour of a bloody catastrophe is spread around, and suddenly reveals the real horrors of these hideous places. Sometimes an unfortunate woman has completed with her own hand the work of destruction which disease had commenced. Sometimes a young man, having reached the end of his expedients, fearing rejection by his mistress because he has no more money, kills her, and himself, in the apartment which he has taken for her.

Generally, however, the courtezans of high rank in this place know how to avoid the double scandal. There are many whose pride consists in the number of their victims. Several of the most celebrated openly avow their contempt for men and for human life, their love of gain and taste for expenditure. The dread Gigokoô

GIGOKOÔ.

attributed to herself a Satanic power over the human race; the embroideries of her kirimon representing scenes of hell, the great judge summoning before his tribunal souls laden with guilt, and the damned expiating their sins in cauldrons of boiling water, or clothed with the bodies of monstrous beasts.

Of a lower grade in the social hell of Sin-Yosiwara are the regions frequented by the small traders and the hattamotos. Suicide through love is frequently committed. The lover kills himself because he is not rich enough to purchase his mistress, and she kills herself because she has sworn to be faithful to him.

I have seen on the stage at Yokohama a play representing the tragical end of a courtezan, whose tender declarations had been interpreted by a young Samouraï in another sense than that known in Yosiwara. Deceived in his love, outraged in his honour, the furious lover strikes off the head of the faithless woman with one blow of his

HOTEI.

sword. The Japanese Sibaïa represents this scene, with full detail. The bloody sword flashes, and the victim falls under the eyes of the spectators; the orchestra breaks out into an expression of horror by the combined effect of all its instruments. Suddenly silence ensues, and the hero of the piece turns toward the public to give a pathetic explanation of his reasons. At the same moment the machinist moves a trap in the front of the stage, and the bloody head appears within two paces of the murderer, as if it had rolled to his feet.

Sin-Yosiwara is closed against Europeans; but, in the ports which have been opened by treaty, the Japanese Government has instituted, and provided with every possible facility, a Gankiro accessible to natives and foreigners alike.   Feminine servitude seems to me to present itself under the hardest conditions known to humanity in this wretched place.   Imagination which may conceive the hell of Dante, might fail before the horror of the reality of such lives.

THE DANCE OF THE PRIESTS.

CHAPTER X.

RELIGIOUS FESTIVALS.

ANNUAL PURIFICATION.—THE PROCESSION OF SANNOÔ.—THE PROCESSION OF COURTEZANS.—
THE GO-SÉKIS.—FESTIVAL OF MATRONS.

Each of the bonze-houses in the city of Yeddo has its Matsouri, or annual patronal *fête*; but among them there are several which celebrate this festival only once in two years. The solemnities are generally interesting only to the quarter, the street, or the small group of faithful who contribute to the maintenance of the bonze-house. To this rule, there are, however, remarkable exceptions. Certain matsouris are in favour with one entire section of the city, such as Hondjo ; and others seem to enjoy an unlimited popularity with the whole of Yeddo.

These matsouris, as we may easily conceive, are far from having preserved patriotic elevation and the noble simplicity which distinguished them in the splendid days of the national Kami worship. The mythical sense of the solemnity is lost, its moral signification has fallen into oblivion. The fairs and rejoicings which in earlier times were only the accessories of the festival have now become its principal object, or rather its only interest. Thus in our own countries we see how the religious festivals of the Middle Ages have disappeared, leaving behind their kermesse, or popular fair, which was developed year after year under their protection. So at Yeddo certain feasts recall the names of the ancient national divinities ; the goddess of the sun ; the god of the moon ; the god of water ; the patron of rice ; the god of the sea ; the god of war, whose anniversary is celebrated on the first day of the Hare, which signifies the second month, corresponding to our March. But the chief characteristic of these solemnities is the theatrical pomp displayed in them, in the processions and the choirs of music,—the dances and the pantomimes of the priests on the one hand, and the masquerades and scenic representations in the open air on the other. In addition to these attractions, there are illuminations, public games, archery, horse-racing, wrestling, public lotteries, and everywhere a market of fruit and fish according to the season, pastry, sweetmeats, flowers, articles in common use—such as fans, umbrellas, paper lanterns, and children's toys.

The subject of the matsouris in a city like Yeddo, where the temples are counted by hundreds, is one which it is impossible to treat in minute detail. I can only give a few rapid sketches of those festivals which excite general attention, and attract the entire population of the city to their scenes.

On the fifth day of the fifth month (June and July) the crowd repairs in the early morning to the woods of the suburb of Foutchiou, to gather herbs whose virtue is held to be sovereign in cases of contagious maladies. An improvised fair on the border of the forest enables the pilgrims to provide themselves with everything which they will require during the day. In the evening the priests of the Roksa-mia in the neighbourhood proceed to the annual purification of the holy place. While the temple is being cleaned, a solemn procession marches through the woods during the greater part of the night, carrying relics belonging to the sanctuary. Piles of resinous wood are prepared in the court of the sacred enclosure, at the foot of the tori in the avenue, and at the openings of the forest paths at their diverging points, and all along the road which the cortége is to take. At a given signal, all these are lighted at

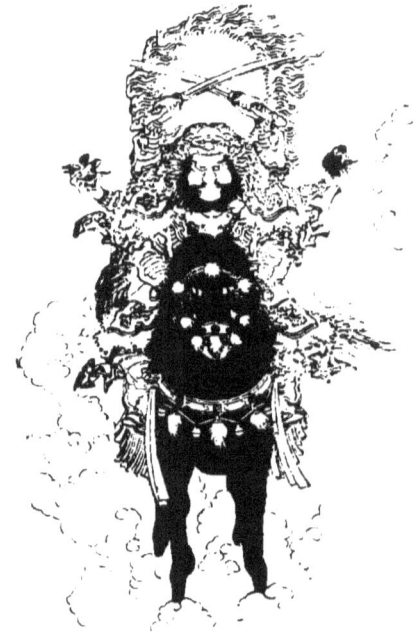

THE PATRON OF HORSEMANSHIP.

once, and the procession sets out, having been provided with abundant paper lanterns of various colours and accompanied by the music of fifes, gongs, and the big drums of the bonzerie. From every side a crowd accumulates upon the route of the procession, uttering cries, which are echoed by thousands of startled birds disturbed from their sleep by the strange light and clamour.

T T

At the head of the procession, immediately after the band, march the horses of the Kami, led by the bridle by grooms attired in an antique national costume. They are followed by the High Priests and their acolytes and servants, carrying the sacred arms, trophies of the ancient heroes. Then, preceded by the gohei, or antique holy-water brush, come two personages, who wear masks representing heads of Corean dogs. They are followed by the entire body of priests and their servants, the employés charged with the care of mikosis, the furniture and utensils of the temple and its dependencies. When the cortége has passed through all the exterior stations, it returns to the sacred place, and the flames are extinguished; the crowd disperses to the restaurants in the fair and on the road side, darkness and silence take possession of the forest.

On the twenty-fourth day of the eighth month (September and October), the fraternity of the temple of the Temmangò, in Hondjo, which is purified on the twenty-fifth day of the second month, exhibits the image of its god, which is drawn through the principal streets of Yeddo on a buffalo cart. The chief officers of the families who patronize this bonze house, and the priests who serve in the temple, precede and follow the car, accompanied by coolies carrying coffers and baskets, which contain the utensils and sacred objects belonging to the temple.

The Tohicïsan celebrates its annual procession on the second day of the tenth month (December and January). The bonzes, on their return, read aloud to the people certain passages from the holy books; they also give them tea prepared and consecrated by them, and permit them free entrance into the gardens and the sacred wood attached to the convent. The seventh day is consecrated to pantomimes, with subjects taken from the ancient history of Niphon. In the great biennial procession of the temple of Kanda-Miòdjin, which is placed under the invocation of Kanda the patron of Yeddo, there is a whole cavalcade of historical personages, among whom Taïkosama is especially distinguished. In order to add to the effect of this procession, the bonzes invite a certain number of courtezans, who are carried in elegant palanquins. The car of the saint of Miòdjin is drawn by two buffaloes, and by an unlimited number of the faithful, voluntarily harnessed to the sacred vehicle by straw ropes. A few feet behind it a hideous colossal head of the demon over whom the saint triumphed is carried on a platform. The people contemplate with horror the gigantic horns and erect crest of this monster; they point out to one another its bloody eyes, its scarlet skin and horrible jaws. To add to the effect of this spectacle, the bonzes blow through their conch shells, producing a terrible noise. A little further on an enormous axe, with which the victorious hero cut off the monster's head, is exhibited.

But all the united wonders of the procession of Miôdjin fade before the splendour of the festival given annually by the priests of the temple of Sannoó, which is sacred to the memory of Zinmou, the founder of the Empire of the great Niphon. This is the most imposing of the matsouris of Yeddo. It takes place on the fifteenth day of the sixth month. Tengou, the faithful porter and messenger of the gods, heads the procession, adorned in his brilliant costume as the celestial herald. He half unfolds a pair of iris coloured wings. His smiling air, his cunning eyes, his crimson colour, his nose of preposterous length, excite merriment in the people, and secure the warmest welcome for the cortége. When the evil spirits find the image of Tengou at the door of the temples of the national religion, they hasten on. The procession has therefore nothing to dread from them.

The municipal police is charged with the maintenance of public order. More than a million of spectators preserve perfect discipline during the whole of this great day. In all the streets and all the squares through which the procession is to pass, platforms are erected for the women, old men, and children. Places are reserved for those who choose to pay for them ; free space is assigned to the workmen, but everybody is bound to remain quietly in his place during the entire festival. Only the sellers of fruit, cakes, and saki, have permission to go beyond the boundary-rope which separates the crowd from the road kept for the procession.

The procession of Sannoó is a kind of national encyclopædia in action, in which we find all sorts of historical lessons, mythological symbols, traditions, and popular actions mixed up together, just as we see Bacchus, Silenus, Noah's Ark, Ceres, and Pomona, introduced indiscriminately in the old *fête* of the vine dressers at Vevy. When art attains this democratic breadth, criticism must merely bow and be silent. I pass on to the most picturesque details of the ceremony. Here comes the patron of the sacred dance of the Daïri. The image, dressed in the old theatrical garments of Kioto, is raised upon a huge drum, supported by figurantes in costumes of festive form and crowns of flowers. This is followed by the procession of the white elephant. The animal is made of cardboard, and its bearers are skilfully hidden in its capacious body ; their feet are hardly seen moving under the legs of the colossus, which is preceded by a band of music, composed of flutes, trumpets, big drums, cymbals, gongs, and tambourines. The men of this group wear beards, a painted hat with an aigrette, boots, a long robe with a wide girdle, and some of them carry Chinese banners covered with images of dragons. A little further on a gigantic lobster is carried by a priest of the Kami worship, and surrounded by a troop of negroes. Then

PROCESSION OF COURTEZANS AT THE FÊTE OF THE TEMPLE OF SANNOÖ.

come a hundred cultivators who are harnessed to the chariot of the buffalo; this king of domestic animals is placed upon the vehicle under the shade of a flowering peach-tree, and is accompanied by the demi-god who introduced him into Japan. Six other chariots are laden with picturesque trophies formed of the implements and products of rice culture. A cortége of the priests of the Kami religion generally forms a guard of honour to a carriage made in the likeness of that of the Mikado, a splendid chariot, surmounted by the sacred gong and the cock of the Daïri. Antique banners, some ornamented by sketches of horses, precede a cavalcade of superior officers costumed according to the Court fashions of Kioto. Suddenly two terrible monsters appear ; they have the face of the tiger with the horns of a bull. Their great tails are elevated high above the helmets of the men-at-arms who surround them. Perhaps they recall under a fantastic form the memory of those tigers who gave so much trouble to the soldiers of the heroic mother of Hatchiman in the Corean fields. To this group belongs the exhibition of the antique arms of the arsenal of the Sannoô ; lances and halberds, two-handed swords, bows, arrows, war-fans and insignia of command. By degrees the exhibition loses its warlike character ; in their turn appear priests and koskeis, carrying the mikosis, the vases of the sanctuary, and all the furniture of the temple and its dependencies under banners covered with hieroglyphic signs. Another troop of koskeis carries paper lanterns at the end of long poles. Among the banners we recognize that of the quarter of Sin-Yosiwara. This very effective group terminates the procession.

Then come seven of the handsomest women in this reserved portion of the capital, majestically attired in state costume ; each is accompanied by her waiting-woman and by a koskei who carries a wide and lofty parasol, which shades her from the rays of the sun. Her head-dress is two or three storeys high, and the edifice is supported by large pins of red tortoise-shell. Her face shines with cosmetics carefully applied. We may count the number of her robes - thanks to five or six collars which hang over her shoulders. A wide kirimon envelops her and sweeps the ground ; its folds are slightly raised by means of an enormous girdle composed of an entire piece of silk or velvet ; and some inches are added to her already noble stature by the curious manner in which she is shod with little planks of wood. These seven figurantes are well known to all the people. As they pass, their names are mentioned on all sides, and indeed these names are embroidered on their rich costume. The first is the lady of the War-fan, which she displays upon her wide velvet sash ; her robe is embroidered with four cocks of various plumage, two of which are white, worked upon the ample sleeves of her kirimon : the silken feathers of their tails wave gracefully in the air with each of her movements. The second is the lady of the Golden Fish. She wears one on each side of her robe on a background of waves and foam in silver thread. The accessory embroideries represent little children playing with ribbons of all sorts of colours, who sport on her kirimon. Need I speak of the lady of the Death's head; the lady of the Candelabra, the lady of the Slaves, the lady of the Chrysanthemums? No! For where should I stop if I were to describe in all its details the public homage paid

A CHILD WITH A FOX MASK.

to the courtezans by the priests, and by the people of Yeddo? In the presence of such customs we can only admire the appropriateness with which the great Sannoò admits to the rank of its idols and solemnly exhibits in the streets of the city, a monkey, with a red face, wearing a sacerdotal mitre, and carrying a holy-water brush.

That mocking image mounted on a drum, with the rich drapery, is lifted high above the crowd, an ironical caricature of the religious exhibition which the crowd just witness.

The matsouris or kermesses of the temples of Japan do the Government of that country a service which will be strongly appreciated in Europe, by absolving it from the charge of amusing its subjects, who supply all funds needful for the purpose out of their own pockets. There are Japanese festivals which do not consist of representations and amusements given by the bonzes to the people but of real public rejoicings, in which the people themselves are the only actors and the real heroes of the day.

These are the Go-Sékis, or five great annual festivals. They had originally a religious stamp, which did not actually militate against the gaiety of their exterior manifestations, because the moral of the Kami worship is, that a joyous heart is integrally in a state of purity. The Séki of the first day of the first month is naturally the chief festival of the new year. It is that of visits, of congratulations and presents, the latter consisting of at least two or three fans, which the visitor brings, according to custom, in a box of lacquer tied with silken cords; but, no matter what the nature or the value of the principal gift, it is always accompanied by a screw of paper containing a dried morsel of the flesh of the shell-fish named awabi, or of the siebi, an exceedingly common fish; and this manifestation is a piece of homage paid to the frugality of the antique national customs. The family receiving the visit gives a little collation composed of saki, rice-bread, and mandarin oranges. The lobster plays an important part in the exchange of presents. Every house religiously preserves one until the following year, unless it should be required as a remedy against certain maladies, in which case it is ground to powder and eaten.

The second of the Go-Sékis, the Feast of Dolls, takes place on the third day of the third month. I witnessed it at Nagasaki on the 20th of April, 1863. It is consecrated to feminine youth. The mother of the family adorns the guest chamber with branches of the flowering peach, and there lays out an exhibition of the dolls which her children received at their birth. These are very pretty and elegantly dressed, representing the Mikado, the Kisaki, and other personages of the Imperial Court. The offering is made complete by a feast, which is prepared by the young girls who are old enough to do so, and towards evening the viands are eaten by the company.

On the fifth day of the fifth month (June) a festival of a less domestic character, called that of the Banners, is celebrated in honour of the boys. Yeddo is on this day a charming spectacle, especially when contemplated from a gallery looking upon one of the wide streets of the city, which is decked out from early morning with tall bamboos surmounted with plumes, or waving horse-tails, or balls of gilded paper, and with long floating banners of painted paper, fish made of lacquer or of plaited straw, and above all, with great banners stretched on reed-frames, and adorned with armorial bearings, family names, patriotic sentences or heroic figures. The bronze workshops exhibit casques, sets of complete armour, and gigantic halberds of fantastic forms. Groups of boys in full dress occupy the public roads, some wearing two small swords, similar to those of the yakounines, at their girdle; others with fine paper ribbons on their shoulders carry an immense wooden sabre ornamented with various colours, and others bear small flags, which reproduce the favourite subjects of the street banners. The people of Yeddo take special delight in the picturesque figure of the brave Shyoki, the hero without fear and without reproach of the first Corean war. The crowd delights in contemplating the austere face, always immoveable in the midst of danger. The wind blows about his beard and his long hair; over his head float the two classic feathers of the old helmet of the Daïri; his calm, large, and vigilant eyes, his right hand armed with the sword, and the firmness of his attitude make him a finished type of bravery and prudence.

When the Mongols attempted to invade the island of Kiousiou, the Siogoun not only opposed them with his best troops, but displayed before them a great number of banners bearing the image of Shyoki, and this spectacle alone petrified them with terror.

The fourth great annual feast, that of the seventh day of the seventh month, is known under the name of the Feast of Lamps or Lanterns. Little girls parade the illuminated streets of the city of Yeddo in great numbers, singing with all their heart, and swinging paper lanterns. In certain cities of the south the population visit the hill cemeteries and pass the night amid the tombs.

The thirteenth, fourteenth, and fifteenth are the days on which every one goes to the temples to pray for the dead and to burn candles for them; the fifteenth being the day fixed for the regulation of accounts for the first half of the year. The public rejoicings which succeed the fulfilment of this troublesome duty are particularly varied and brilliant. Masquerades, accompanied by national dances, take a high place among the popular pleasures. All the masks have their signification and traditional character. There are the noble types: first the placid faces of the gentlemen and ladies of the Daïri; then the fierce physiognomies of the heroes of the civil wars. There are also masks with moveable jaws, in imitation of those worn by the Mikado's actors. Others represent the grotesque and divine Tengou, the good Okamé, the jolliest of the Japanese women mentioned in history, or the unhappy Hiyotoko, the ideal of ugliness. These masks reproduce all the varieties of the race of demons—those with one eye, with two eyes, with three and four eyes, with horns and without horns, with two or even three horns, from the sprites to the giants, and even to the odious Hanggia, the feminine devil. The final category includes masks made in the likeness of Kisné the fox, and Sarou the monkey, or the lion of Corea, or of Kappa, the man-frog who haunts the shores of Nippon. The dances are of every conceivable description; the rice-dance alone numbers thirty figures, executed by men whose entire clothing consists of a girdle of rice-straw, a round hat of the same material brought down over their eyes, and a small cloak with large sleeves imitating the wings of nocturnal moths.

The fifth of the Go-Sékis falls on the ninth day of the ninth month. This is the Feast of Chrysanthemums. In all family repasts leaves of these beautiful flowers are scattered on cups of tea or the bowls of saki. Libations prepared in this fashion are supposed to prolong life. The citizen of Yeddo would believe that he had failed in his duty as a husband and father if he drank only moderately of this precious specific.

Among the festivals of the fourth month, the eighth day is sacred to the baptism of Buddha as he is represented at his birth, standing, pointing one hand to heaven and the other hand to the earth. Not only do his devotees bathe with consecrated tea the bronze image of the holy child in the places which serve for fonts in the Buddhist temples, but the koskeis of the bonze-houses go through the streets carrying his statuette fixed in the centre of a tub, so that the same ceremony may take place in private houses; such solicitude brings them in a considerable reward.

On the twenty-eighth day the people are invited to plunge themselves in the contemplation of Fousi-mi, the *Dolichos polystachios*, and to make libations to the gods under bowers of the plant, which is very common in the public gardens.

The festivals of the sixth month are in honour of the cereal harvest—rice, millet, wheat, and paddy. The priests bless little squares of white paper fastened to sticks,

U U

which the cultivators buy and plant at the four corners of their fields, under the persuasion that these rustic amulets are indispensable to the fruitfulness of the soil. This season of the year is a time of rejoicing for the citizens of Yeddo, who assemble in the shady groves on the shores of the Sumida-gawa, or in the gardens of Odji, under green arbours moistened with the foam of the cascades, or crowd the boats on the great river, until the last day of the month convokes them to solemn expiation and general purification.

The god of the water, an ancient divinity of the Kami worship, is fêted from one end to the other of the Empire during the whole of the seventh month, which represents the entire term of the rainy season. Bamboos, from whose upper branches glass bells and strips of blessed paper are suspended, are planted beside the springs, the wells and the irrigating channels; and every morning and evening banners are waved inscribed with this sentence, " *Respect and homage to the God of the Water.*" In the houses of the country people offerings, consisting of rice, fish, and small money, are made on the domestic altar of the Kami.

The eighth month commences by a ceremonious exchange of civilities between clients and their patrons, employés and their chiefs, subalterns and their superiors.

The fifteenth day is dedicated to the god of the moon. It is said to be the moment of the year in which the orb of night emits its utmost brilliancy. The rivers and canals are crowded with gondolas, from which the citizens contemplate the full moon. The stillness of the air and the warmth of the temperature during the evenings of the months of September and October are favourable to these nocturnal parties of pleasure, also to those which take place in the public gardens of the city and its suburbs.

The tenth month is placed under the invocation of Yébis, who is at once the god of fishing and one of the favourite patrons of the shopkeepers, who make each other presents on this occasion, among which are millet-cakes and a large red fish named Taï, much admired for its beauty and the delicacy of its flavour.

The ladies of Yeddo are not less diligent in the performance of the duties imposed upon them by their social position. They pay each other neighbourly visits, and do not neglect to burn candles before the image of Yébis for the prosperity of their husbands' commercial enterprises. Early in the morning they may be seen going in groups to certain bonze-houses, in whose sanctuaries there are altars privileged to receive the homage of the citizenesses. To perform this ceremony the pilgrim is attired in a head-dress, consisting of a cotton handkerchief of dazzling whiteness, artistically wound through the thick hair.

Towards the middle of the month everyone is bound to notice and to communicate to his friends the fact that the leaves of the maple-palm are beginning to change colour. At the commencement of the eleventh month the maple is in all the magnificence of its autumn dress. Crowds assemble in the gardens of the bonze-houses and

NEW YEAR'S VISITS.

the tea-houses. With the winter solstice come general congratulations. This is the Festival of Matrons. No pressure of business, no journey to the city, no cause or pretext whatever, can on this occasion excuse the absence of the husbands from their homes. They come from all parts of the country, and in the evening the city is illuminated on all sides. The sounds of guitars and joyous voices fill the air on this universal festival.

The fifteenth day is called the passing of the river, by reason of a religious domestic solemnity ; it symbolizes the flight of time, and the transition to the new year.

The twelfth month is devoted to the settlement of affairs, the renewal of furniture, and the re-arrangement of the household ; operations which involve such a succession of ceremonies, formalities, festivals, and rejoicings, that a whole volume might be written upon the four or five weeks at the end of January and the commencement of February in the cities and the villages of Niphon.

ACROBATS

CHAPTER XI.

THE SIBAIA OR NATIONAL DRAMA OF JAPAN.

HUMAN INTEREST OF THE DRAMA IN JAPAN.—THE SIBAÏA.—MALE COMEDIANS.—FEMALE
DANCERS. — HARANGUES BY THE ACTORS. — RESTAURANTS. — CONSTRUCTION OF THE
THEATRE.—SCENES ON AND OFF THE STAGE.—THE GREEN-ROOM.

ALTHOUGH the great dramatic system of modern Japan, the Sibaïa, is far from being
an aristocratic institution, it is one of the most curious in the world. If it does

not attain to the distinguished literary merit of the Chinese drama, or to the perfection of acting, it far exceeds both in poetic value, because it has more simplicity,
more passion, more individuality and a more purely human character. In China, the public
look on at the piece and criticise the actors; in Japan, the public take part in the piece
in concert with the actors, exchange sentiments with them, and, in fact, are part of the
spectacle. In this respect the Sibaïa reminds us of the little day-theatres of Italy,
but with all the difference which exists between an amusing and easy recreation and a
great popular subject, confused, often unintelligible, and whose gaiety is strange and
fantastic. Although the Sibaïa is implanted in all the cities of Japan, it is at Yeddo,
and especially in the city and the northern departments, that it is most active and
important. The theatres are exceedingly numerous, one group occupying three longitudinal and four cross streets.

The dramatic authors of Yeddo write principally for these theatres. From thence,
new pieces are distributed throughout the Empire, and companies of comedians from
the capital take, like the wrestlers, their holidays in the provinces. The actors are
all male. Only female dancers appear upon the boards, and then in the ballet of
the Grand Opera only. Comedians form a separate class, who are regarded by the
higher orders with contempt. The Sibaïa is, properly speaking, the theatre of the
middle classes of the Japanese population. It attracts great numbers of coolies and
labourers, when they can afford to go there, but all classes above the traders abstain
from dramatic representations, or, if they go, take care to sit in latticed boxes. Among
the crowds which frequent the theatrical district it is extremely rare to meet two-
sworded men, not but that the Samouraïs are sometimes mixed up with the
people, but they take good care to disguise themselves on this and other compromising
occasions. Just before sunset certain delegates from the company of actors appear on
platforms raised on the right and left of the doors of the theatres; they are in ordinary
dress, and harangue the multitude, explaining the subject of the pieces about to be
performed, and the merit of the principal actors who perform in them. After this
exordium come familiar jokes, pleasant talking, the eloquence of mimicry, and the high
art of managing the fan. Presently the lanterns are lit. "Come in, gentlemen! come
in, ladies!" they cry; "take your places! now's the time! the piece is about to begin."
Nevertheless, nobody is in a hurry, for the spectacle in the street captivates general
attention. The illuminations afford great pleasure to the people. The first row of red

lanterns hangs all along the whole length of the roof. A little lower is a second range under the roof. Between the two hang balls of transparent paper, each containing a painted candle. Near the doors enormous oblong lanterns light up the pictures and the inscriptions, illustrating the principal subjects and scenes of the pieces. Every theatre has its own arms and its own colours painted upon banners and lanterns, along three sides of a sort of belvedere or square tower which springs from the roof.

The buildings which adjoin those of the Sibaïa are occupied by restaurants, and are as gaily decorated as the exterior of the theatre, with designs and carvings which have some relation to the name of each of these establishments. One is the restaurant of Fousi-yama, and another of the Rising Sun; farther off we see those of the Tori, the Taï Fish, the Merchant Junk, the Stork, the Two Lovers, &c. &c. But it is time to go into the theatre, and we ascend a wooden staircase leading to the second gallery. A functionary opens a spacious box, and a servant brings saki, tea, cakes, sweetmeats, and pipes and tobacco.

The interior of the theatre forms a long square. There are two ranges of galleries, the upper containing the best places in the theatre. Numbers of ladies are to be seen there in full dress,—ladies, that is to say, covered up to their eyes in crape dresses and silk mantles. The whole of the remainder of the house is occupied exclusively by men. There is no orchestra. The floor of the house, as seen from a distance, resembles a draughtboard. It is divided into compartments, containing from eight to twelve places each, most of which are hired by the year by the citizens, who take their children regularly to the play. There are no lobbies. Everyone walks to his place on the planks which enclose the compartments at the height of the spectators' shoulders, who squat on their heels or crouch on little stools. There is neither a ladder nor a staircase by which to get down into the midst of them. The men hold out their arms to the women and children. The settling of the audience in its place forms a very picturesque part in the preliminaries of the representation. Tobacco and refreshments are served during the whole evening by koskeis and servants, by the same means of communication. On two sides of the pit are two bridges of planks, which also communicate with the boards of the stage; the first is nearest to one of the doors; the second, which is four planks wide, forms an angle with the extremity of the boxes. On this bridge certain heroic or tragi-comic personages perform their parts, and the ballet is danced. The house is lit by paper lanterns tied to the galleries; there is no chandelier from the roof, which is perfectly flat, the cupola being unknown in Japanese architecture. I have, however, seen large lanterns held up to the roof of a theatre at Yokohama in order to light up the performance of the acrobats, especially that of the flying men, who cross the theatre by means of cleverly contrived mechanism.

The curtain which hangs before the stage is ornamented by a gigantic inscription in Chinese characters, and surmounted by a target with an arrow in the centre. This symbolical sign is supposed to be a prognostic of the talent about to be displayed by the actors, and which will hit the bull's-eye in the hearts of their audience. The performance generally lasts until one o'clock in the morning. It consists of a comedy, a tragedy, an opera with a ballet, and two or three interludes of acrobats, wrestlers, and jugglers. The principal parts are announced by a clicking noise, produced by striking a small piece of wood against the floor of the stage. The appearance of infernal personages is always preceded by lightning. The actors worthy of particular notice are escorted by one or two koskeis, who carry a long stick, at the end of which is a little candlestick with a lighted candle. The spectators have only to follow the combined movement of the two lights to know exactly what they ought to admire; sometimes it is the expression of the actor's face, sometimes his attitude and gesture, and sometimes the details of his costume and head-dress.

The same custom prevails with regard to the dancers. The koskeis may be seen during the ballet squatting upon the bridge which I have described, and profiting by the immediate neighbourhood of the spectators to get them to snuff the candles with their fingers, an office which they always perform with pleasure; it would indeed be impossible to find anywhere a more good-humoured audience. In homely comedies the spectators frequently interrupt the actors, and answer them. Thus audience and actors contribute alike to the success of the evening and the satisfaction of all concerned. The zeal and contentment of the public are manifested by their gifts, in addition to the price paid for admission.

Almost every theatre displays innumerable scraps of paper fastened to the walls by which artists relate acts of generosity, and record the name and address of their benefactors.

We cannot yet form an appreciation of Japanese drama from a literary point of view. No piece has been translated into any European language. Sir Rutherford

Alcock gives a detailed analysis of a performance which he witnessed at Osaka. In comparing my own observations with his and those of M. Layrle, I have come to the conclusion that dramatic art is still in its infancy in modern Japan. The political circumstances of the country render historical drama impossible. The nearest approach to it in the repertory of the Sibaïa is an incongruous mixture of history, mythology, and burlesque. Opera, less advanced even than drama, is very much inferior to that of the Celestial Empire, and imitates it only on its most fanciful side, the marvels of the Buddhist demonology. Comedy seems to me to promise well, because it observes the conditions of the natural and the real. It admits, no doubt, like opera, of scenes of incredible coarseness. Nevertheless, nothing appears more immoral to the Japanese than our drama. This apparent contradiction is easily explained. Japanese realism admits on the stage, as in romance, types and situations of which *La Dame aux Camélias*, *Les Filles de Marbre*, and all our licentious literature, gives only a feeble idea. On the other hand, it absolutely excludes every intrigue by which the character of a married woman is compromised. Neither Phædra, nor Hamlet's mother, the husbands depicted by Molière, nor Werther, nor Charlotte, nor the infamous Madame Bovary, could have offered the slightest attraction for the imagination of the Japanese. The green-rooms and the side-scenes of the theatres of the far East are no less interesting to the foreign observer than the theatre, properly so called, and the audience which crowds it. In these places none but men are to be seen, excepting from time to time some servants, or the artists' wives who bring refreshments to their husbands, or come to give the last touch to their toilet before they go on the stage in the costume of either sex. In the midst of the general disorder we find some very characteristic groups. Here are musicians occupied in refreshing themselves, and indifferent to everything else until the signal to return to their posts shall reach them; there two actors are rehearsing together the attitude and gesture which in a few minutes are to delight the spectators; and another, sitting on his heels before a looking-glass placed on the floor, is painting his face and adjusting his feminine head-dress. A young devil beside him has thrown back his mask, with its horns and its mane, over his shoulders, and is fanning himself, while the chief of the wrestlers is tranquilly smoking his pipe in the midst of the acrobats. Among the crowd, carpenters are coming and going, carrying the screens and the partitions destined for the change of scene; the machinist is working a trap through which a whirlwind of flame is about to escape;

x x

and the piece is going on outside to the accompaniment of drum beating, amid the conversation of the public in the house and that of the disengaged actors.

In the restaurant there is apparent inextricable confusion. Everyone crouches on his mat, except the servants. All sorts of games are in progress, and saki is circulating freely. Sometimes a group of dancers install themselves round the domestic altar under the image of the god of contentment, and seldom fail by their guitars and their voices to arouse the enthusiasm of some young dandy, who will forsake his party, advance towards the performers, and execute under their fair eyes a very elegant dance to the accompaniment of the solemn motion of his fan. The restaurant supplies all the deficiencies of the theatre in point of refreshment, and is frequently crowded during the greater part of the piece. Everybody knows all about it, and does not mind sacrificing a few scenes to the pleasures of the table. The so-called spectators will eat and drink at the restaurant until the gong gives the signal for the great interlude of the jugglers. Then the restaurant changes its aspect completely : everyone hastens to his place in the theatre.

RESTAURANT, WITH A VIEW OF FOUSI-YAMA.

CHAPTER XII.

INAKA.

THE BELOVED SUBURB.—BEAUTIFUL SCENERY.—PLEASURE PARTIES—CARICATURE.—MIXTURE OF CHILDISH AND HEROIC ART.—GOOD NATURE.—POLITICAL SATIRES.—CHIMERAS.—THE HORRIBLE AND THE FANTASTIC.—ODJI-INARI.—KITSNÉ.—FOX WORSHIP AND ITS ORGIES.

THE northern portion of Asaksa-Imato, which is bounded by the curve formed by the great river, belongs, with the three neighbouring districts, to the zone of Inaka.

Nothing gives such an idea of the immense circumference of Yeddo than following the outer zone of the quarters situated on the south, the west, and north of the citadel, for it extends from the faubourg of Sinagawa, opposite the six forts of the bay,

and the country traversed by the northern road beyond Senjou-Obassi ; and embraces
on the north of Hondja those fertile fields which are watered on one side by the
Sumidagawa, and on the other by the small river which forms the eastern boundary
of the three districts on the right bank. But a description of the quarters comprised
in this suburb would be tiresome, because they have all a uniform agglomerate character,
and the curiosities which they contain are all of the same kind : sometimes rustic temples built upon the funeral hills, sometimes granite statues or commemorative tables
raised upon the tomb of some celebrated personage, and destined to perpetuate the
remembrance of a remarkable event in the history of the ancient Siogouns. Here
are tea-houses, great orchards, horticultural establishments ; there, are sacred trees,
reposoirs set up at the best points of view, and sometimes an isolated hill, cut in the
shape of Fousi-yama.

Inaka, in a word, seen from a birdseye view, looks like a park, or a continuous
garden dotted with rural habitations ; or it resembles a garland of verdure and flowers,
cast round the faubourgs of the south and the districts of the west, and uniting them
to the artizan's quarters, in the heart of the city and to the villages which extend to
the rice-fields.

When the orchards are in flower, the citizen, the painter, and the student, are seized
with rural fancies: they fly from the labours and the pleasures of the capital, and hide
themselves for a day, or for many days, if it be possible, among the rustic roofs of the
tea-houses. These charming retreats, rich with the beauties of nature, are innumerable.
Most of them can hardly be distinguished from the country houses in their neighbourhood. Their vast roofs come down to the ground floor. Domestic birds flutter,
or plume themselves in the sun, on the moss with which the roof is covered, and
which rises to the summit, where we see long lines of iris in full flower. When
there is no gallery, arbours of vines, or other climbing plants, shelter the guests
grouped negligently upon the threshold. A limpid spring murmurs and flows along
the path, which descends towards the plain across the gardens and vineyards, the
poppy and bean-fields, or the great expanse of cereal and textile plants.

In February, in June, and in October, three times a year, certain societies
accomplish a rural pilgrimage into the villages at three or four miles distant from
Yeddo, merely to behold with their own eyes the vicissitudes of the seasons and the
transformations of nature.

In winter, if the snow should fall, it is considered a duty as well as a pleasure that whole families should go and contemplate the strange aspect of the statues in the enclosure of Kanda-Miôdzin, in the high pagoda of Asaksa; but above all, no one must fail to retire to certain tea-houses in the faubourgs, such as those of Niken-Tschaïa, in the neighbourhood of Foukagawa, to admire the spectacle of the bay and the country under the novel decoration. In summer, it is agreed that the concert of grasshoppers must be listened to upon the heights of Dökwan-yama, and a good family man would never fail to take his children thither, plentifully supplied with little wicker cages, in order to bring back some of these sweet songsters.

Poets of the spring, choristers of the summer, painters and artists who seek for new inspirations, delight to abandon themselves from morning to evening to charming study and reverie among the orchards of cherry, plum, pear, and peach trees, among the groves of bamboo, citrons, oranges, pines, and cypress, which surround the temples, the gardens of the tea-houses of Okaubo, Songamou, Itabasi, To-neghis, Haghitera, Mimegori, and a multitude of other classic retreats of the Muses of Niphon. When night has come they meet in excellent inns, and combine with the pleasures of the table the enjoyment of society, where conversation alternates with songs and music, and drawings are exhibited in exchange for pages of poetry which have been written during the day.

The pencil often intervenes in the capricious conversation, and the subject of a tale or a discussion is illustrated or travestied by the imagination of the painter amid the applause of the company.

Japanese caricatures generally bear the impress of good nature. They are, for the most part, taken from middle-class life. A grave physician is studying the state of his patient's tongue, or examining with a vain expenditure of spectacles the ailing eyes—he is lifting up the corner of the eyelid with great care; quacks are engaged in the operation of shampooing or in the application of moxas; a band of blind shampooers on their travels have gone astray at a ford, and are disputing in the midst of the water as to the direction which they should take on reaching the opposite bank. Then we have types of the begging friars; of fishing misadventures; scenes of feminine jealousy and household quarrels pushed to violent measures. There are also very complete series of caricatures, such as the small troubles of life in the great world; the household of the fat man, and the household of the thin man; and the different grimaces which can be formed by the human face. And the artists do not spare themselves; for rapid painting, which is held in such esteem in Japan, is symbolized under the figure of an artist who is working with six brushes at once, two in each hand and one between each great toe.

The method which rendered Grandville so popular in his illustration of the fables of La Fontaine is not unknown to Japanese caricaturists. But their pencil is less

CARICATURE OF A BONZE.

sparing; they only exceptionally reach to the dramatic energy of the human passions. Most frequently they limit themselves to giving animals a costume, or an attitude which invests them with a certain symbolic character. This is the lower degree of anthropomorphism. Such for example is the personification of the twelve signs of the Zodiac—the mouse, the bear, the tiger, the hare, the dragon, the serpent, the horse, the ram, the monkey, the cock, the dog, and the wild boar—each adorned with vestments and attributes relating to their astronomical functions, or to the parts which they play in astrology.

A sketch by Hokusaï, no less harmless, but more amusing, represents a rice-warehouse in which rats, the most dreaded enemies of that precious cereal, form the warehousemen. Nothing is missing in this pretty scene, from the cashier making his calculations with his bead frame, to the salesman turning over his books in

THE RAT RICE MERCHANTS.

order to demonstrate to a purchaser that he cannot abate a farthing in the price. The shopmen are carrying the bales, of which the purchaser is taking an invoice, on their shoulders. The money is in little straw bags, which the coolies carry at the ends of their bamboos. Everything is conducted with the order and regularity

becoming to a great house. The smallest details are drawn with the care which would
be bestowed upon a serious composition. It is in this kind of comic art, childish or
heroic by turns, that the Japanese display most ease and originality.

I frequently noticed a dash of satire of a political kind in the numerous and
varied sketches whose subject is furnished by the "trains" of the Daimios. For
instance, I have seen many in which the personages of the cortége, beginning with the
prince himself, are represented as foxes or monkeys.

The satirical intention is not less manifest in those pictures in which we see the
superior of a bonze-house with a wolf's head, and a group of nuns under the image of

THE HARE AND THE WILD BOAR.

weasels. The most expressive picture I have seen of this kind represents an audience
in which a hare has prostrated himself, trembling, at the feet of a wild boar. The
hare is a little hattamoto out of employment, and the wild boar is a high-class
functionary in Court dress, who wears the toque of Kioto.

The taste for the fantastic goes along with that for caricature. In Japan, political
institutions, religion, and nature, all concur to excite the imagination and to set it
wandering to the region of chimeras. On the sea-shore, the basaltic rocks take forms
now grotesque and now frightful. The ocean itself is a world of mysteries.
Sometimes, when it is very dark, a light may be seen under the water which resembles

a dragon. Sailors have seen shells darting along among the waves. Under the waters of the Strait of Simonoséki is a grotto, or rather a temple, encrusted with pearls and mother-of-pearl. It is called the Riogoun. It is situated in the place where the young Mikado Antok was submerged with his suite, as he fled from the field of battle where his partisans, the Fékis, were defeated by Yoritomo (1185). In this temple he reigns and holds his Court. His men-at-arms carry long rods

A DAIMIO'S "TRAIN." (CARICATURE).

surmounted by sharks' fins; these are his banners. All the sea-gods, wearing diadems representing the heads of seals, little fishes, medusas, crabs, and dragon's jaws, come to pay him homage. This Court of marine monsters and drowned men-at-arms has inspired the strangest artistic compositions; equalled only by the revolting scenes in which we see the bloody and slaughtered victims aiding demons in the punishment of their murderers in the infernal regions. The pencil of Callot has produced nothing so completely horrible.

Y Y

The Japanese delight in the imitation of hideous realities. The wax-work museum at Asaksa-téra possesses figures of executed criminals, and corpses in a state of decomposition, which form a collection very superior to the celebrated "Chamber of Horrors" at Madame Tussaud's.

PROCESSION OF TALISMANIC RAKES.

They can also, like Callot, ally the burlesque to the horrible, but they do so only in subjects which are not tragical. For instance, they will change the vessels used in religious ceremonies, gongs, holy-water brushes, candelabra, perfume vases,

altars, images, and statuettes, into so many animated monsters, jumping or crawling
in an infernal dance led by evil spirits.

The fantastic has its part in the fascinations of the tea-houses in the suburbs of
Yeddo. Some are erected in places propitious to the contemplation of Fousi-yama,
and the sight of that extraordinary mountain, as it appears at sunrise or at sunset
under the clear sky, or when swept by storms, is such as to satisfy the most
exacting imagination. The charm of the landscape and mysterious cataracts forming
cascades, is enhanced in other places by mineral springs and basins of thermal water,
like certain watering-places in the Swiss mountains. People do not go there for the
purpose of cure, properly so-called, but they go to pass a few days with their families
in elegant cedar chalets shaded with magnificent trees, on the banks of the water-course,
which may be compared to the finest Alpine rivers. The most frequented are those
of Ottona-Sigawa, one of the principal affluents of the great river.

Other places of pleasure are specially devoted to one or other of the popular superstitions. The people go from the temples to the tea-houses with the satisfaction which
accompanies the accomplishment of a pious task. During the first days of the eleventh
month the hotel-keepers and the bonzes of Yousima-Tendjin receive thousands of pilgrims
of both sexes, small traders, and agriculturists, in the faubourgs or the country immediately around the city ; they come to buy rakes at an isolated temple in a marsh
on the north of the capital. These rakes are of good augury for harvest, and are
simply pious playthings, which are held as talismans in the dwellings of the faithful.
They suit all purses and the most varied tastes ; some, of colossal size, are decorated
with a picture, representing the junk of happiness ; others, of smaller dimensions, are
ornamented with the sign of the god of riches ; the simplest have only pictures on paper
or on papier-mâché, such as the head of the god of rice, the mask of Okamé, and all
sorts of mythological emblems.

As fortune does not confer its favours among men in proportion to their stature, it
frequently happens that, on their return from Yousima, the poorest pilgrims carry
away the thinnest loads, while their companions, rich but feeble, stagger under the
weight of the enormous instruments which their social position has obliged them to
purchase.

The comic effect of the procession is increased by the peculiarities of the costumes
of the season. The men wear tight trousers of blue cotton and a wide mantle with

large sleeves; they are mostly bareheaded, but their noses are protected by crape handkerchiefs tied at the back of the neck; others cover the head with an ample hood, which hides the whole face with the exception of the eyes. The women generally adopt this ugly hood, and, stuff their arms into the thick sleeves of their winter kirimon, so that they look like as if they had none. Amulets to be placed at the edges of the fields, in the form of squares of paper fixed on a wooden peg, are sold at the temple of Yousima; and the bareheaded pilgrims stick them behind the one plait of hair which forms their head-dress, like hair-pins, so that they look as if they had come from an agricultural exhibition with the number under which they were exhibited stuck on their head.

On the other side of the Sumidagawa the cultivation of trees used in manufactures occupies a no less important place among the labours of the country-people than the culture of the rice-fields and their kitchen garden. Among others we may see great plantations of *Rhus vernix* and *Broussonetia papyrifera*, which supply the lacquer and paper fabrics of the capital. The former of these shrubs acquires in about thirteen years an annual value of from £3 to £4; the sap is taken away twice, by means of incisions made in January and renewed in September. The varnish produced in the latter month is of inferior quality.

In order to avoid the contact of the skin with the native lacquer, which possesses venomous properties, the workpeople cover their hands and face with a thick coating of oil.

On the right bank of the river, and on the shores of its principal affluents, the builders and master-carpenters of Yeddo have their timber-yards, where the trunks of trees brought from the forests of the interior are cut into beams, laths, and planks. These forests are inexhaustibly rich in woods fit for building purposes, such as the oak, which attains an immense height in Japan; the pine, of which some forty species exist; the cedar, *Cryptomeria*, of a native species; the fir-tree, also remarkable for its variety; and the brown woods, and black employed in cabinet making or in small ornaments.

The Gardens of Odji-Inari, which stand high in the estimate of the city population, are situate at the opening of a mountain gorge on the northern side of Yeddo. A small river forming several cascades winds gracefully through the valley. On the bank above its limpid waters, rises the long galleries and pavilions of the tea-house, which enjoys the coolness of the water and the shade of the great trees. The guest chambers, the verandahs, the partitions, and the mats, are kept in a state of dazzling cleanliness. The whole establishment is distinguished by elegance and simplicity. Historical remembrances attach to many places in the neighbourhood.

THE GAME OF THE FOX.

A hunting-lodge of the Siogouns formerly occupied the summit of one of the hills, which commands an extensive view of the plains watered by the Sumidagawa. In a narrow valley, at some distance, is pointed out a temple consecrated to Iyéyas, who was its founder, also a miraculous spring which falls from an elevated wall of rocks. This spring is placed under the invocation of a stone idol, to which the frequenters of the gardens address their prayers. When heated by the fumes of saki, they place themselves under the falling water and enjoy the natural bath. In the little hamlets of the plain a quantity of shops or booths offer all sorts of curiosities and trinkets to the choice of the visitors and their children. A lively

KIESNE.

trade is done by these traders, for no family ever returns from a party in the country without bringing home some remembrance of the village markets.

The real secret of the celebrity of the gardens of Odji is, that they were placed in very ancient times under the patronage of Inari, the tutelary god of the rice-fields, and conjointly under the protection of the sacred animal which is his "attribute," that is to say, Kitsné, the fox, who deigns to honour the country with his particular favour. He is worshipped on the hill which bears the name of Odji-Inari. On the seventeenth day of the first month an innumerable crowd of citizens and country people flock to his temple. They hang up ex-votos, and deposit their new year's tribute in the money-box. Then the crowd disperses, wandering in groups through the groves, and contemplate from afar a great tree in the marsh, around which an annual *sabbat* of the foxes has been held on the previous night. Persons who pretend to have seen the assembly of the foxes preceded by a Will-o'-the-wisp and followed by the Spirits of the rice-fields, are eagerly interrogated, and bear their testimony gravely to the character of the festival, the number of the foxes, and the greater or less gaiety manifested on the occasion. These particulars having been ascertained, inferences are drawn from them respecting the year which is commencing, and the abundance and the quality of the harvest are prognosticated. Then the visitors, seat themselves around the "brasero" in the guest chambers of the tea-house, and talk in a low voice of the mysterious influence of Kitsné in the affairs of this world. What is chance? what is hazard? good or bad fortune?—words devoid of sense. And, nevertheless, there is something behind these words, because every time that one uses them one is forced to it by circumstances. The fox has come that way. "I," says one of the guests, "have had the misfortune to lose a child; the doctor could not even tell me the seat of his malady." While the mother was grieving, the lamps, which were placed beside the corpse, threw the shadow of the poor woman upon the opposite wall; everyone in the chamber of mourning perceived at once that the shadow had taken the form of a fox. "And travellers," continues a neighbour, "when they see their road prolonging itself indefinitely, although they have calculated the distance, is it not because they have omitted to count with the tail of the fox? How many times have they not wandered about the rice-fields, misguided by the Will-o'-the-wisp, which Kitsné can make to flicker where he chooses. And the hunters, how many tricks has he not played upon them? If a good sportsman was to dare to attempt to revenge himself, he would only have the mortification of seeing the fox bounding and jumping before him, and carrying away in his mouth the arrow which had been let fly at him."

The annals of Japan state that Kitsné is capable of metamorphosis. When the Mikado, who reigned in 1150, found himself under the painful necessity of dismissing

FESTIVAL OF THE FOXES.

his favourite in order to save the finances of the Empire from complete ruin, the fair one escaped from her apartments in the farm of a white fox adorned with six fan-shaped tails. On the other hand, cases no less extraordinary are quoted of the abduction of young girls, some of whom have never returned, while others on their return have closed their parents' mouths by the word Kitsné! Kitsné!

When it pleases the latter to disguise himself as an old bonze, he is most dangerous. There is always one means of defeating him. Kitsné, whatever may be his disguise, never resists the suggestions of his nose. Let anyone place a rat newly roasted in the path of the false priest, and he will not fail to forget his personation, and fall upon the prey, forgetful of everything else.

The yamabos or bonzes of the mountains generally succeed in keeping Kitsné at a distance, because they know how to practise upon his weakness; but they also must be particularly on their guard to avoid a surprise. If the fox succeeds in discovering their

A SCENE OF SORCERY.

barrel of saki, woe to them who shall taste it afterwards! It is thus that some very respectable yamabos have become objects of popular derision. A few cups suffice to turn their heads: they throw off their clothing, utter cries, gesticulate like madmen, and execute the most eccentric dances; also danced by two foxes in the same step, and who mark the time, one by blowing a sacred conch, the other by flourishing about the holy-water brush of the poor bewitched bonzes. It is also said that the peasants, whenever they have slept in the rice-fields, are liable to be caught in the nooses of Kitsné, who deprives them, according to his fancy, of the use of their limbs or of freedom of movement.

The Japanese people have also their romance of the fox. They amuse themselves with their hero, though they are afraid of him.

z z

Kitsné becomes in turn a sacred, amusing, perfidious, and diabolical personage. In the morning they pay him homage, in the evening they turn him into ridicule. But if he lends himself to jesting, it is only to take a more signal revenge. Let anyone try, for example, in family festivals or in social banquets, to amuse himself at the expense of Kitsné and to try his patience ; when he shall have joined the party in earnest, he will then soon turn all their heads the wrong way, and the night will not pass without his strewing the ground with those who have given him provocation. The game of the fox begins, very innocently in appearance, with a kind of song and clapping of hands. Three attitudes are taken alternately. The first consists in raising the hands, and holding them half shut behind the ears ; the second, in doubling the fist and stretching out the fore-arm : the third, of opening both hands and spreading them on the knees. This is called the game of the fox, the gun, and the yakounine. The fox loses against the gun, because the gun kills ; the gun loses against the yakounine, because the yakounine can defend himself : finally, the yakounine loses against the fox, because Kitsné is the most cunning animal in creation. The losing party is compelled to drink a cup of saki.

It is easy to conceive that under the influence of such a penalty the game becomes more and more animated. Some of the players find it too sedentary ; one of them rises, and, amid the acclamations of the company, procures a long rope, makes a running knot, holds it by one end, and throws the other to a companion, who stretches the rope as tight as he can without spoiling the running knot. Behind the latter is placed a little stand, on which lies what is called the rat—it is a cap or cup, or any other object—which the fox must take away quickly, without letting himself be caught in the noose. If the guardians of the rat pull the cord between their hands too quickly or too slowly, they pay the penalty. If the fox be caught, were it only by the end of the finger, he has to defray the expense of any amount of drinks so long as it pleases the guests of both sexes who enjoy the spectacle of his captivity. In such cases, the ordinary resources of the orchestra fail to express the delight of the company. The guests knock their glasses or porcelain cups together like bells ; the singers imitate the cries of all sorts of animals ; the more active hop round the unfortunate fox, and mock him with every kind of grimace. Kitsné of the mountains, from his hiding place, contemplates all the details of this Bacchic scene, and thrills with pleasure when it attains its height.

Better than this foolish amusement are the quiet picnics which take place in the suburbs during the fine season. Two or three families arrange to pass an evening together in the country, either on the shady hills which overlook the bay, or in the great orchards on the north side, whence a full view of Fousi-yama may be had. They are preceded by

A RURAL TEA-HOUSE.

koskeis, who, on reaching the place agreed upon, trace out a reserved space by means of long pieces of stuff stretched on poles. Within this they lay down mats. Stoves are prepared, with kettles for making tea, and pans for frying fish. The company arrive and install themselves, the ladies unpacking the provisions, and the festival begins. It lasts until sunset; games, singing, and music, animate the scene. Sometimes professional singers are summoned to the festival, and occasionally even a couple of wandering dancers, whose speciality consists of pantomime, posturing, and character figures. One of their prettiest performances is called the fan-dance; it is a kind of pantomime, generally executed by a young girl in the costume of a page. There are also some national dances kept up in the society of the town, and these naturally have a place among the diversions of the country parties. Generally, ladies dance alone; they form a quadrille, and the dance consists principally of gestures, without any change

THE FAN-DANCE.

of position, except in passing from one attitude to another. They stretch out their hands and arms; sometimes the right, and sometimes the left, not without grace or elegance, but the movement is exceedingly monotonous. A man never dances, except when, inspired by the fumes of saki, he imitates some choreographic feat which he has witnessed upon the stage.

But, as I have already said, it is not only pleasure which attracts the citizen to the groves of Inaka; he loves the place for its own sake; he knows it under all aspects and in all seasons; he knows its curiosities and peculiarities, its local kermesses, its annual markets, at which he purchases a part of his household provisions. He goes to the public auctions of rice, vegetables, fruits, and coal, which take place at fixed periods in certain rural districts; he also goes to see the antique cedar on which he has painted the initials of his name and the date of his first visit; and he knows one still more ancient which contains a natural reservoir of water celebrated for its efficacy against certain diseases. This tree was planted by a Kami.

For a few centimes he is permitted to fish in the tanks of the bonze-house, and to carry home the results of his sport. There is not a convent, or temple, or chapel in the neighbourhood which is not distinguished by some more or less interesting peculiarity. Here a group of palm-trees, there bananas and bamboos, or evergreen oaks, or maples, or

gigantic azaleas; and the monastic orders to which the convents belong devote themselves to the education of tortoises and mandarin ducks, or to making sweetmeats.

Many of the hills have a special reputation; this one because it affords the best open-air view of the princely spectacle of hawking; that one because it overlooks a famous battle-field. Several are covered with tombs, ranged in terraces like little gardens. The monuments present an infinite variety of style of ornamentation according to the social condition and sect of the deceased; most frequently a tablet bearing an epitaph rests on the shell of a large stone tortoise, the symbol of Eternity. A great number of tombs are formed of a socket surmounted by a statue of Buddha, or some auxiliary divinity of Buddhism, such as Quannon or Amida, standing on a lotus flower. These images are cut in the granite, or the basalt, in extremely fine workmanship. The most ancient are moss-grown, or smothered in branches of ivy and other climbing plants. Gigantic pines, cypress-trees, and laurels, lend a charm by their picturesque grouping to the burial places.

One of the most interesting cemeteries in the neighbourhood of Yeddo is that of the Schorin ; it is specially reserved for men illustrious in letters or sciences.

At the entrance of the villages, and sometimes in the open country, we find stones erected to commemorate some historical event; and frequently little chapels built in honour of some hero who fought in the wars which founded the dynasty of Iyéyas. Buddhism has affixed its stamp to every place worthy of exciting the attention of travellers. There is no grotto without its idol and its story ; there is no lake which does not contain a little islet with its temple dedicated to Benten.

It is fortunate for the Japanese that their popular superstitions have developed in them a love of country life, and a proper regard for the vegetable wealth in which their country abounds.

THE GANKIRO.

CHAPTER XIII.

THE NEW ORDER OF THINGS IN JAPAN.

INTERNAL POLITICS AT THE EPOCH OF THE TREATIES.—WISDOM OF THE LINE TAKEN BY ENG-
LAND.—STOTSBASHL—THE ASSEMBLY OF PRINCES.—THE FALL OF THE TAÏKOUNAT.—
THE MIKADO.—GENERAL INFORMATION POSSESSED BY THE JAPANESE.—PROSPECTS OF
COMMERCE.—SANITARY FACTS,—PRODUCTS AND EXPORTS.—IMPORTS.

THE bombardment of Kagosima, and the destruction of the batteries at Simono-séki,
were, in reality, only incidents in the question of the external relations inaugurated by

the treaties. It was, however, difficult to avoid connecting them with the internal political question which was agitating the privileged classes of the Empire. These events, in fact, were apparently of a nature to confirm the previsions respecting the future of Japan which had long been cherished in secret. The country, hitherto so deeply divided, was about to reconstitute itself upon a fresh basis. It aspired to order, to unity, to political centralization. What was there to prevent its attainment of them? Just two things, which the Government might easily realize with the moral support of the Powers interested in its preservation. The first was the definitive subjection of the feudal nobility to the civil and political power concentrated in the Taïkoun; the second was the complete emancipation of the Taïkounat from the supremacy of the Mikado in everything concerning temporal affairs. The successors of Iyéyas regarded the latter point as settled, as an acquired right, so decidedly, that the Court of Yeddo considered it highly improper and unconstitutional that the legations should have demanded from the Mikado the ratification of the treaties concluded by the Taïkoun in all the plenitude of his legal competence. At the rate at which events were succeeding each other in Japan, the double solution, which was to secure the unification and the peace of the Empire and to consolidate its commercial relations with the West, was advancing with rapid strides. The rising of the Daimios of the south against the Taïkoun, and the succession to the throne of a man of the capacity of Stotsbashi, would no doubt precipitate the *dénouement*, the issue could not be doubtful.

Europeans inevitably commit the error of transacting their affairs in the Eastern world in too systematic a spirit. In this particular case, England, happily guided by the instinct of commercial interests, made an exception to this rule. She became the friend and confidant of the prince whose capital she had, shortly before, burned to ashes. The insurrection of the Daimios of the south speedily assumed threatening proportions. In place of opposing to it the resistance which had been expected from his energy, and from the considerable military preparations which he had made with the assistance of France, Stotsbashi suddenly abdicated, "through patriotism," according to the version of the Tokoungawa;[1] and begged the Mikado to convoke all the great men of the Empire, in order to establish the government upon a solid basis, to revise the constitution, and thus to open up for the country a path of progress which should lead it to power and prosperity.

[1] Notified by the Japanese embassy at Paris, in February, 1868.

The Mikado complied with the request of Stotsbashi; but the assembly of princes was tumultuous, and ended by a sort of *coup d'état* on the part of the confederates of the south, who carried the Emperor and his Court forcibly into their camp, dispersed the friends of the Taïkoun, and promulgated decrees abolishing the Taïkounat and placing the executive power in the hands of the Mikado. But then Stotsbashi made up his mind to open the campaign. The four palaces which Satsouma possessed at Yeddo, and which served as a centre of operations for the conspirators in that capital, were attacked and destroyed by cannon. The preceding Taïkoun had previously demolished the residence of Nagato, in order to disprove his connivance in the aggressions of that prince on the Europeans. The army of Stotsbashi formed in line at Fousimi, on the north-west of Osaka. The troops of Satsouma, of Chosiou (Nagato), of Tosa, of Awa, of Aki, and others, occupied Kioto. The first engagement took place January 28th, 1868. Stotsbashi remained in observation at Osaka. His forces, ill-directed, fell back on the fortress of Yeddo. On the following days they lost it, retook it, and were finally beaten in a pitched battle, when a great number of his men passed over to the enemy, on the pretext that the latter, having hoisted the standard of the Mikado, any further struggle would have been sacrilege. The citadel of Osaka fell, without the firing of a shot, into the hands of the conquerors of Yeddo, who burned it to ashes. Stotsbashi fled by sea.

The troops of the confederates pushed their advantage boldly, and marched on Yeddo; but, after the Prince of Aïdzen had obtained some successes over them, an arrangement was come to between the moderates of both camps. Aïdzen, Shendaï, Nambou, and Yonesawa, made submission. Stotsbashi, who was invited to resume his functions, refused; and a child of six years old, the son of Taïasou, a member of the clan of the Tokoungawa, was elected in his stead. But, as the child's father did not give his assent to this transaction, the Mikado pronounced the definitive suppression of the office. He made a solemn entry into Yeddo on the 25th November, 1868. The citadel was delivered up to him by Prince Owari, who belonged to the camp of the confederates. The branch of the princes of Ksiou played no ostensible part in these troubles.

The Taïkounat went down before the first onslaught, under the reign of a prince of the branch of Mito, and we must seek the cause of this defeat in the bloody rivalry among families which has exhausted the dynasty of the Tokoungawa.

It cannot be said that the pacification of Japan is complete. The last partisans of
the north have succumbed after heroic struggles in the island of Yéso, of which they
had taken possession under the leadership of the gallant young Enomoto Idsoumi-no-
Kami, admiral of the Taïkounal fleet.   Nevertheless the two parties are still in an

A MOUSMÉE.

attitude of mutual observation, and their forces remain almost equal. The traditional
antipathy which reigns between the Daimios of the south and those of the north is
an obstacle to the complete centralization of the administration. A proposal made by
Satsouma, that all the Daimios of Japan should make a return of their fiefs to the

Mikado, served only to compromise that prince in the eyes of his own allies. The Mikado's Government has recognized the necessity of raising Yeddo officially to the rank of a second capital of the Empire. In that capacity, it is called To-Keï.

The Mikado himself cannot do otherwise, in the interest of his relations with the representatives of foreign powers, than reside there for at least a portion of the year. But, in addition to this, there is already a question of the nomination of a Viceroy, in order that each of the two capitals may have its Court as well as its share of influence in the affairs of the State. This would be the re-establishment of the Taïkounat under another name, and probably the restoration of the Tokoungawa dynasty.

In any case, the fair days of Aranjuez are past, in the realm of the Daimios, and for the gentlemen of Kioto in general. They must resign themselves to exchange cock-fighting and tennis-playing for the burden of public business, and to a daily contact with the Western World. The civil war produced extreme perturbation in the finances of the princes and the Government. The Mikado was constrained to create paper money (kinsatz), and to give it a forced currency, while refusing to accept it at the public treasury. Commerce complains, according to its right and its duty; but I presume its lamentations are accompanied by a slight smile, and a tolerably clear notion that, in a very short time, dating from the day on which this economic measure shall have fallen into complete discredit, the Japanese will have begun to open the almost virgin mines in which the country abounds, and to hand over the concession and the working of them to the industry of Europeans. Thus, everything is coming to the assistance of the latter, even including those events which are apparently most injurious to the interests of commerce; and in fact it is very natural that as breach after breach is made in the old walls of the Japanese edifice, the place should speedily fall into the power of the invaders.

But we must not indulge in illusions with respect to our advantages. It is not our political prestige, it is not the splendour of our embassies, which constitute the strongest argument with the Japanese; it is simply the superiority of our civilization from the point of view of the ceramic and industrial arts.

The Japanese are much better informed than we suppose upon the general situation in Europe, and the resources of the various States. Their embassies to Europe, between 1860 and 1868; to England, Holland, France, Belgium, Prussia, Russia,

Switzerland, and Italy; the share in the Paris Universal Exhibition taken by the Taïkoun, the Prince of Satsouma, the Prince of Fizen, and the commerce of Yeddo; and the studies made in Europe by a relatively considerable number of young Japanese, a contingent which is renewed year after year; have all tended to consolidate the work of the treaties, and secure our improved relations from all the vicissitudes of politics.

Japan has fallen to the West. Since the expeditions of Taïkosama in Corea, when the troops beat the Chinese auxiliaries despatched to the aid of that kingdom, the Government of the Celestial Empire has been estranged from Niphon. It seems that it has even forbidden its subjects to entertain commercial relations with that country, for the junks which visit Nagasaki and the ports of the inland sea come exclusively from Niphon, and belong to a trading corporation which is barely tolerated by the Governors of Chékiang. Of all the countries of the far East, Japan, that is to say, the South of Niphon, Schoff, and Kiousiou, is the country which is most convenient and agreeable to Europeans.

The four seasons are very distinctly marked there: from March to the latter half of May, a splendid spring; from June to September, summer, commencing with a brief rainy season, followed by heat, during which the thermometer marks from 63° to 70° Fahr.; from September to the end of November is autumn, without great heat, and free from rain, storm, and mosquitoes; finally, three months of winter usually free from tempests, and under a perfectly serene sky; with a temperature which sometimes falls at Yohokama as low as 43° Fahr.

From September to April the predominant winds are north and east, and the rest of the year south and west.

Earthquakes, though frequent, are rarely disastrous, and are generally less dreaded than fires. The latter scourge furnishes one of the most picturesque spectacles of Japanese life. I have frequently been struck, during the conflagrations which I have witnessed, by the attitude of the squadrons in the offing, in which the glare of the flames is reflected; the vessels answering, one after another, by luminous signals, to the orders of the admiral; and the men lending their perfectly disciplined aid, in total silence, in the midst of the confusion of the natives. In a short time, the advance of civilization will have considerably reduced danger from fire in Japan. Excellent health may be maintained by combining certain European improvements with the ordinary diet of the Japanese. Tropical fevers are unknown in Niphon; and there is less danger to foreigners from cholera, dysentery, and small-pox, all much dreaded by natives, than in Europe.

But the great attraction of Japan is that the commercial preponderance is not so crushing there as in China and the East Indies. On this subject I can amply confirm the judicious and practically interesting observations of M. Jaques Siegfried of Mulhause, who says, in his work entitled *Seize Mois au Tour du Monde* (Paris, Hetzel) :—

"The commerce of the East is becoming more and more democratic; each one may take his little share in it; and the door is now open to all the world. The Germans and the Swiss have profited largely by this state of things. They are not content to occupy themselves with the affairs, relatively small, but of still increasing importance, of their own respective countries, but they have mixed themselves up more and more in the commerce of the English, and have succeeded in establishing a formidable competition with them on their own ground, and one which increases daily. The commercial relations of Europe with Japan are doubtless very far from having such importance as those with China and the Indies. The Chinese, Indian, and Japanese trade with Europe and its colonies amounted in 1867, including both exports and imports, to three and a half milliards of francs, which was more than double the amount of ten years before.

"The private business done at the principal Japanese port, Yokohama, has also doubled in less than ten years. It may be estimated at 100 millions of francs. This is little; but it is also much, if we take an account of the abnormal and unfavourable circumstances of our early relations with Japan. When we look at the proportions between the 30 or 34 millions of Japanese, the 200 millions of Hindoos, and the 300 or 400 millions of Chinese, there is room, not only for satisfaction with, but also for astonishment at, the considerable progress which we have made in the brief space of ten years. Of all Oriental races, the Japanese accustom themselves most rapidly to our civilization and its necessities; and most readily acquire a taste for the products of our industry. In Japan, therefore, European commerce finds most encouraging elements."

Two principal articles form the basis of the normal commerce of Japan, as regards exportation. They are raw silk and tea; and notwithstanding inevitable fluctuations, the importance of these products cannot do otherwise than augment year by year.

The export of silk from Japan to Europe is estimated at 15,000 bales per annum, and it sends to America alone from 10 to 11 millions of pounds of tea. Japanese tea has not yet found favour in Europe, but I am convinced that, sooner or later, it will be highly appreciated there for its hygienic qualities. The exports of secondary value, but which are in the category of regular commerce, are vegetable wax, camphor, nutgalls, and the juice of fermented beans known under the name of soïa (soy). Raw cotton, destined for the Chinese market, copper, highly esteemed in European indus-

A MOUSMÉE AND HER CHILD.

tries, and coal, which is still very imperfectly worked, are only occasionally objects of any considerable operations.

The trade in silkworms' eggs, being due to accidental causes, cannot be included in the number of the permanent commercial resources of Japan. It has given rise during the last seven years to some considerable transactions; but it is becoming more and more spoiled in the hands of speculators. So long as Japan does not employ machinery in weaving her silks, Europe will be able to utilize her waste as she does at present.

The other Japanese products available for occasional transactions of a very limited kind, are tobacco, flax, ginseng root, fish oil, turnip oil and seed, colza, linseed, twine, brocades, crapes, pierced cocoons, mushrooms, mats, deerhorns, paper—of which there are seventy kinds, ranging from the finest tissue paper to wrappers as thick and as strong as our waxed canvas,—lacquer, and other art-objects; vitriol, alum, saltpetre, and sulphur. The latter article may sooner or later rival Sicilian sulphur in the American market. To complete this enumeration I must mention the trade solely intended for the Chinese market. The Japanese export to China iron bars of native manufacture; algæ—which are much prized for their saline properties in those Chinese provinces in which salt is scarce—chestnuts, potatoes, the pulp of fruits, dried oysters, shrimps, sharks' fins, and timber for building.

The import trade rests, like the export trade, on two capital articles alone: cotton—spun, woven, and printed; and certain woollen stuffs, or woollen and cotton mixed, which it would be wearisome to enumerate.

The sums which the annual export of these manufactures bring to us are far from replacing those which are expended in our purchases of Japanese rice and teas. Up to the present, however, exceptional circumstances have enabled us to strike the balance between the exportations and the importations, and we may hope that this unforeseen advantage will not fail us for a long time to come.

After the negotiations concerning exchange had been effected, we received commissions for ships of war, armed steamers, batteries of rifled cannon, breech loaders, and ammunition of all kinds, which the Japanese needed for the prosecution of their civil war. We even built a military port for them with docks and a marine arsenal, at Yokoske, south of Yokohama. They will soon be asking us to work their mines, to establish their telegraphic communication, and to make their railroads. Afterwards the time will come when their windows will be made of glass, instead of slides of transparent paper; when they must have curtains to their windows and mirrors in their drawing rooms; when they will burn gas instead of smoky candles; and when Parisian millinery will have its establishments at Niphon; for the Japanese men are already adopting European attire, and we cannot suppose that the women will not follow the fashion.

In the meantime, imports of the second class are limited to the following articles, and in small numbers: lead, tin, tin and zinc in sheets, wire and pewter, watches, *articles de Paris*, counterpanes, leather, hides, ivory, rhinoceros horns, and sugar.

Besides these, there is a special import trade in supplies for the strangers' quarter: window-glass, furniture, pottery, glass, clothes, wine, spirits, and preserved

SLEEPING MOUSMÈS.

meats. Far from having exaggerated the commercial importance of Japan, I may add, that from this point of view Japan will not for a long time yet give us as much as we might expect. The country is only emerging from a state of things under which it had no consumers outside its own population. The northern portions of the Archipelago are generally untilled, and even in the south of Niphon there are thousands of uncleared acres, covered with bush and scrub, or turned into parks and unproductive gardens, the mortmain properties of feudal lords and monastic confraternities. Nevertheless, though all this should be utilized, planted with mulberry and camphor, with tea- and cotton-trees, the smallness of its territory must always prevent Japan from competing in commercial value with countries of such colossal dimensions as China and Hindostan.

We must also bear in mind that, in our day, neither the exploitation of textile fabrics, nor that of alimentary products, is the monopoly of any people in particular. Competition in this kind of supply makes giant strides, for the greater good of humanity. Cotton from India has made a place for itself in our markets beside cotton from America, and the Suez Canal will soon be bringing us cotton from

BLACK SQUIRREL AND MARTEN FERRET.

the newly-explored regions of Africa. Ten years ago, Europe depended wholly on the Chinese market for tea and for silk. She now has two rival markets at her disposition —China and Japan. Soon perhaps there will exist a third—the Californian ; for European speculators are already planting the mulberry, and introducing the culture of silkworms into California, with the assistance of Japanese colonists.

Agriculture is at the basis of all societies, but they grow great only by the arts, or by commerce ; and, better still, by the constant simultaneous development of those three branches of human activity.

The foundation of social order among the Japanese, as among the Chinese, is agriculture, which both have pushed to the highest point of perfection. It may be said, generally, that the Japanese possess the mercantile faculty in only a slight degree, and that they show a great natural disposition for the arts and for industry. The Chinese, on the contrary, satisfied with their traditional technical processes, and indifferent to all progress, excel in banking as in usury, in high commerce as in the smallest traffic. Let us then leave trade to the Chinese, and give to the Japanese industry.

M. Siegfried has called them, not without reason, "The French of the East." It behoves them, henceforth, to develop, side by side with their amiable qualities, those of which manufacturers, mechanicians, and magistrates are made. The introduction of the mechanical arts within the tropical zone is, if not impossible, at least devoid of any chance of being made remunerative. China, in so far as she is concerned, rejects every innovation of this kind. Japan, by its geographical position, by the wealth of its soil in coal and metals, by the conditions of its climate and the genius of its inhabitants, seems destined to become the central seat of the manufactures, the works, the industry, and the navigation of the whole western basin of the great Ocean.

WATER FOWL.

RETURN OF THE SIOGOUN.

CHAPTER XIV.

PATRIOTIC ACT OF THE DAIMIOS.—SWEEPING REFORMS.— THE CALENDAR OF THE CHRISTIAN NATIVES ADOPTED.—THE MIKADO VISIBLE.—RAILWAY OPENED.—REACTIONARY MOVEMENT.—FIDELITY OF THE SAMOURÏ.—COMMERCE AND COMMUNICATION INCREASING.

A BRIEF account of the latest events in Japan is necessary to the completeness of the record contained in the preceding pages.

The patriotic act of the Daimios after the downfall of the Taïkoun, and the recovery of the executive power by the lawful Emperor, formed a striking conclusion to the revolutionary drama. These powerful and semi-independent feudal nobles agreed voluntarily to resign their heritages into the hands of the Mikado, and to receive about one-tenth of their former incomes as sufficient to keep up their diminished status. This

3 B 2

extraordinary movement was started by Prince Akidzuki in a memorial addressed to his fellow nobles, which ran as follows :—

"Let those who wish to show their faith and loyalty act in the following manner, so that they may firmly establish the foundations of the Imperial Government :—

"1. Let them restore the territories which they have received [in times past] from the Emperor, and return to a constitutional and undivided country.

"2. Let them abandon their titles, and under the name of kazoku (noblemen) receive such small properties as may suffice for their wants.

"3. Let the officers of the clans, abandoning that title, call themselves officers of the Emperor, receiving property equal to that which they have hitherto held.

"Let these three important measures be adopted forthwith, in order that the Empire may be built up on an imperishable basis."

The whole body of Daimios, two hundred and sixty-four in number, gradually gave in their adhesion to this scheme of patriotic sacrifice ; their fiefs were given up to the Emperor, and their extensive domains became henceforward subject to taxation by the Imperial Government. As the right to maintain large bodies of armed retainers was also relinquished, the vast revenues they formerly drew from their territories were no longer necessary.

The revolution being so far accomplished, and political unity and administrational centralization attained, the Mikado and his advisers proceeded with rapid strides to the completion of the work of reform. Edict after edict issued from the Imperial palace. Yeddo was to be styled henceforward *Tokei*, "the eastern capital," and to become the seat of Government, with the *shiro*, or citadel, as the place of the Imperial Court. Contracts were entered into for constructing a Grand Trunk Railway to connect Yeddo and Yokohama with Kioto, Osaka, and Hiago, and for laying a line of telegraph from one end to the other of the Empire—between Nagasaki and the Eastern capital. Promising Japanese youths were sent forth by hundreds to Europe and the United States to study the language, laws, literature, and science of those natives of the West who had produced the mental ferment which had led to such great changes. Among the students were many belonging to the highest families, such as Prince Higashi Fushimi, who came to England, and Prince Fushimi Yoshi-Hisa, who went to Prussia, both uncles of the present Mikado. His Majesty also applied himself diligently to the study of English. Colleges and schools for acquiring all branches of Western knowledge were established in various cities of Japan, and professors invited from Europe and America to fill the posts of instructors. Schools for popular education were formed throughout the Empire. The Christian religion was officially tolerated ; and further, the Calendar of the Christian nations (new style) adopted. To effect this change, "the third of the twelfth month of the fifth year of Meiji" was made to correspond with the 1st of January 1873. The year was to consist of three hundred and sixty-five days, which were to be divided into twelve months. The 25th of December was to be celebrated as a holiday, not for the same reasons as the Christmas Day of the Christian world, but in honour of the founder of the dynasty of the Mikado, the Emperor Jimmu. Each day was to be divided into twenty-four hours, and not into twelve watches, as heretofore ; and every seventh day was to be kept as a holiday. Other edicts were directed against ancient customs and habits, ordering this and forbidding that, all with a view to assimilating the life and habits of the people to those of the nations of the Western world.

Amongst the important reforms are those connected with Religion. Buddhism has been discouraged ; the revenues of many of the temples have been appropriated to Imperial purposes, and the priests are being compelled to realize as much of their moveable property as possible, selling their bells and bronze images and ornaments to so great an extent, that the metal has been lately one of the most considerable articles of export from the Japanese ports. Houses for the poor have been established, with the aim of doing away with the numerous beggars in the streets and roads. The great popular festivals and fairs—*the matsouris*—in which this excitable and joyous people took so much delight, have been forbidden, or at least greatly reduced in number. The two-sworded gentry have been abolished, and measures adopted to induce the dangerous *Samourai*, or military class, to adopt the safer pursuits of commerce or the civil professions. One of the few changes which are regretted by those who watch the astonishing transformations that are so rapidly taking place, is that of the easy and graceful native costumes, which are giving way in most of the chief centres of population, but chiefly in the male sex, to the conventional dress of London and Paris.

In 1872 the first railway in Japan was opened, with imposing ceremony and amid cheering prognostications. It was the first completed section of the Trunk line which is to connect the great cities, and extends from Yokohama to Yeddo, but at present consisting only of a single line of rails. The Mikado, throwing aside the traditional mystery which for ages had surrounded the sacred person of the monarch, resolved to open the railway in person, and show himself publicly to the people. A vast concourse of people assembled on the 14th of October at the Yeddo terminus, and the day was observed as a national holiday. Accommodation was provided for 10,000 persons on the platform, and the Mikado desired that all who wished to see the procession that was announced in the programme for the day should find admittance. The Imperial

JAPANESE IDEA OF A RAILWAY TRAIN.

pleasure gardens, formerly the private grounds of the Taïkoun, were thrown open to the public. All the foreign ministers from Yokohama were present, and the representatives of the press invited to attend, in accordance with the most advanced views of modern enlightenment. At nine in the morning the Mikado left the castle, in a state carriage of European construction, and attended by a prince of the Imperial family, the prime minister, and a squadron of cavalry; followed by the other members of the Japanese Government and by some of the chief nobles then resident in the capital.

Arriving at the station, where he was received by the Minister of Public Works, the chief Commissioners of Railways, the Foreign Ministers and other officials, he inspected a plan of the railway; and a procession was then formed to the platform, from which he entered the train, followed by the rest of his suite and the privileged few who were invited to make the journey. On arriving at Yokohama he was received by the Governor of Kanagawa, the railway officials, and the Consuls of the Treaty Powers; and, in reply to addresses presented on the part of the foreign residents, delivered the following speech through his Minister for Foreign Affairs:—

"I am profoundly pleased to hear the congratulatory words which have been addressed to me by the foreign guests residing at Yokohama. Of the people who live in this country, whether born on the soil or merely temporarily residing here—whether here by chance or voyaging of their own accord—none are deprived of protection or lose their rights. This work will be still further extended, with the object of increasing our prosperity and of advancing my country in the path of civilization; and, as long as the harmonious relations now existing between this and foreign countries continue to prevail, I shall have both foreign and native people close to my heart."

The strong feeling of loyalty and veneration entertained by the Japanese for the representative of their ancient line of monarchs, a sentiment which has contributed so much to the success of the late revolution and the overthrow of the usurping Taïkounat, was strikingly shown on the departure of the Mikado from Yokohama. Immediately he left the pavilion the crowd rushed forward, and, seizing the chair of state and the carpet on which the sacred foot had trod, tore them both to shreds, each possessor of a scrap glorying in his prize. The police were powerless; the crowd was so immense, and their eagerness so uncontrollable, although full of good-humour, that it was quite impossible to check them. On the return to Yeddo the Mikado thanked the railway officials, and in another brief speech repeated his intention to develop still further the railway system, until it extended throughout the country. The remainder of the day was spent in joyous festivities, and at night Yeddo and Yokohama were illuminated.

The spectacle of a great and gifted nation, so long kept in jealous exclusion from the rest of the world, thus emancipating itself from the trammels of a narrow Eastern policy and entering into sympathy with Western Christian civilization, excites the deep interest of moralists and statesmen. It is naturally asked, Will the change be lasting? Is not the pace too fast, and will not the conservative principle in princes and people, at present stunned by the suddenness of the movement, re-assert itself in a disastrous reaction? Some of the reforms suggested by the more excited partisans of change fairly take away one's breath; but they have not at present been adopted. One was a proposition made by Arinori Mori, recently Japanese Minister at Washington, for the transfer bodily of the English language into Japan. This would be a clenching method of solving the enormous difficulties in the way of free intercourse presented by the Japanese language. The difficulties lie, however, chiefly in the abstruseness and complication of the written and printed characters, and is partly met by the adoption of the Roman letters and syllabic forms, which are being tried by native scholars and printers.

The fears of a reaction, entertained in Europe and by the foreign mercantile community in Japan, have been to some degree stimulated by the most recent occurrences. During the summer of the present year, serious riots broke out at several places in the interior; the most important of which was at Fukuoka and the adjoining districts, about 150 miles from Nagasaki. Alarming rumours reached the foreign residents, and were transmitted to Europe and America. It was said that the discontented peasantry and farmers had risen to the number of 80,000 men; that the regular army had been defeated and the Government stations pillaged and burnt. Subsequent and more reliable accounts show that the number of the rebels had been exaggerated, although they do not diminish the importance of the revolt, which was a reactionary movement against the reforms of Government, which so many observers had expected. The exciting cause was the excessive taxes and imposts levied in consequence of the greatly increased public expenditure. All taxes and official salaries, under the old system, were paid in kind—in rice; and one of the greatest economical difficulties of the new order of things has been connected with the substitution of money payments for the old, no longer practicable, system. The introduction of a uniform scale in a country where a system of land taxation in kind had grown up full of complication, of local diversities of measure, allowances, compensations and so forth, was sure to be productive of local discontent. The attempted enforcement of the new taxation laws appears to have been the sole cause of many of the riots which have taken place; but the Fukuoka rebellion, after it had made some progress, revealed a deeper discontent, as shown by the following six concessions demanded by the rebels as a condition of laying down their arms:—

1.   A return to old *han*, restoring to the Daimios their lands and incomes.

2.   That the officers of the district shall be appointed from among the inhabitants of the district, and not from a distant *ken*.

3.   That the incomes and all property of the *Samouraï* shall be returned.

4.   That the taxes shall be reduced by one-half for the space of three years.

5.   That the Government shall cease cutting down the trees in the surrounding district.

6.   That the old Japanese Calendar be returned to.

According to the latest news this serious outbreak, like many other minor ones, has been overcome; partly by concessions with regard to taxes and small matters involving no sacrifice of new principles, and partly by the valour and constancy of the native troops.   A most encouraging feature of the Fukuoka revolt was the fidelity of the *Samourai* to the Government, and the aid they lent, as a volunteer force, in the defeat of the rebels.

The present attitude of outside observers with regard to Japan is one of expectancy. The effects of the great political and social changes that have taken place have not yet had time to develop themselves, and it is hoped, by all who take an affectionate interest in this singular people, that those effects will not involve the decay of the better traits in their national character. In some respects the recent news from Japan is encouraging, as showing the vigour of the executive and some progress among the people in the assimilation of the new ideas. Evidences of greater caution in the Government than was first observed are not wanting, though perhaps the caution may be displaced; thus whilst foreigners are clamouring for the right of free access to all parts of the Empire, the Mikado and his ministers withhold the privilege, or make it known that they will not grant it, except on the condition of the submission of foreign residents to Japanese jurisdiction. It is the same with regard to the great mineral resources of the country: no facilities are given by law to the working of coal and other mines by foreigners, or to the formation of equitable contracts with foreigners; so strong, in fact, is still the jealousy of foreign participation in the benefits of their country, that it is delaying, by the preference given to inefficient native contractors, the completion of great public works, such as the telegraph line from Nagasaki to Yeddo. Commerce, however, is steadily increasing, and a whole fleet of passenger steamers keeps up continual communication between their ports and the great marts of Europe and America. The Japanese have become great travellers and accomplished linguists. To this extent at least the change is beneficent and irrevocable.

THE STORK OF THE RICE-FIELDS.

RICHARD BENTLEY & SON'S
ANNOUNCEMENTS.

THE LIFE OF LORD PALMERSTON.—THE THIRD VOLUME.
By the late Lord Dalling and Bulwer. 8vo. 15s.

HISTORY OF THE INDIAN ADMINISTRATION OF LORD ELLENBOROUGH,
in his Correspondence with the Duke of Wellington. To which is prefixed, by permission of Her Majesty, Lord Ellenborough's Letters to the Queen during the Affghan War. Edited by Lord Colchester. 1 vol. 8vo.

SIR ROBERT PEEL AND LORD MELBOURNE.
By the late Lord Dalling and Bulwer. 8vo.

JAPAN AND THE JAPANESE.
By Aimé Humbert, Envoy Extraordinary of the Swiss Confederation. From the French by Mrs. Cashel Hoey, and Edited by W. H. Bates, Assistant-Secretary to the Royal Geographical Society. Illustrated by 207 Drawings by Italian and French Artists, and Sketches from Photographs. Royal 4to. 42s.

NANCY.
By Rhoda Broughton, Author of "Cometh up as a Flower," "Red as a Rose is She," "Goodbye, Sweetheart." 3 vols.

MASTERPIECES OF SIR ROBERT STRANGE.
A Selection of Twenty of his most important Engravings reproduced in Permanent Photography. With a Memoir of Sir Robert Strange, including portions of his Autobiography, by Francis Woodward. Folio. 42s.

THE LIFE AND WORKS OF THORVALDSEN.
By Eugène Plon. From the French by Mrs. Cashel Hoey. Imperial 8vo. Numerous Illustrations.

THE LIFE OF GREGORY THE SEVENTH.
By M. Villemain, of the French Academy. Translated by James Baker Brockley. In 2 vols. 8vo. 26s.

M. Villemain's Life of Gregory VII. occupied the learned Author's thoughts and leisure in my years of his life, and was left complete at his death. During the disastrous days of the first siege of Paris, the MS. of Gregory VII. was removed for safe keeping to Angers. At the capitulation of Paris, it was brought back to the capital, and housed in the Rue de Lille, where it narrowly escaped the flames kindled by the Commune, the next house being burnt to the ground.

THE LIFE AND LABOURS OF ALBANY FONBLANQUE.
Including his Contributions to "The Examiner." Edited by E. B. De Fonblanque. In 8vo.

FRENCH SOCIETY FROM THE FRONDE TO THE GREAT REVOLUTION.
By Henry Barton Baker. 2 vols. crown 8vo. 21s.

A SALON IN THE LAST DAYS OF THE EMPIRE, AND OTHER SKETCHES.
By Grace Ramsey. In Crown 8vo.

TERESINA PEREGRINA; OR, FIFTY THOUSAND MILES OF TRAVEL
ROUND THE WORLD. By THERESA YELVERTON, LADY AVONMORE. 2 vols. Crown 8vo. 24s.

ANECDOTE LIVES OF THE LATER WITS AND HUMOURISTS:—
Canning, Captain Morris, Curran, Coleridge, Lamb, Charles Matthews, Talleyrand, Jerrold, Albert Smith, Rogers, Hood, Thackeray, Dickens, Poole, Leigh Hunt, &c. By JOHN TIMBS, F.S.A., Author of " A Century of Anecdote." 2 vols. Crown 8vo.

THWARTED; OR DUCK'S EGGS IN A HEN'S NEST. A CHRISTMAS
STORY. By FLORENCE MONTGOMERY, Author of " Misunderstood," " Thrown Together," &c. 6s.

MISUNDERSTOOD.
By FLORENCE MONTGOMERY. An Illustrated Edition of this popular story. With Eight full-page Illustrations by GEORGE DU MAURIER. Foolscap 4to. 10s. 6d.

BYE-GONE DAYS IN DEVONSHIRE AND CORNWALL.
By Mrs. H. PENNELL WHITCOMBE. Crown 8vo. 7s. 6d.

SERMONS IN STONES.
A new and revised Edition, in Roxburgh Binding. With a Memoir of the Author. Crown 8vo. 6s.

THE NEW MAGDALEN.
By WILKIE COLLINS, Author of " The Woman in White." A new and popular Edition, in crown 8vo. 6s.

WORD-SKETCHES IN THE SWEET SOUTH. *6L 186- C*
By MARY CATHERINE JACKSON. In Demy 8vo. 10s. 6d.

FRENCH HUMOURISTS FROM THE TWELFTH TO THE NINETEENTH
CENTURY. By WALTER BESANT, M.A., Christ's Coll., Cam., Author of " Studies in Early French Poetry," &c. 8vo. 15s.

HENRY FOTHERGILL CHORLEY:
Autobiography, Memoir and Letters. Edited by HENRY G. HEWLETT. 2 vols. Crown 8vo., with Portrait. 21s. With Letters and Reminiscences of Dickens, Carlyle, Thackeray, Lord Lytton, Mrs. Hemans, Barry Cornwall, Lady Blessington, G. P. R. James, Count d'Orsay, Miss Mitford, Sydney Smith, Isaac Disraeli, Talfourd, Grote, Samuel Rogers, Moscheles, Mendelssohn, Lady Morgan, Southey, Grisi, Paul de Kock, Alfred de Vigny, Douglas Jerrold, Mr. Browning, Mrs. Barrett Browning, Sir William Molesworth, Harriet Martineau, Thomas Campbell, Meyerbeer, Jenny Lind, Hawthorne, &c.

DR. CURTIUS' HISTORY OF GREECE.
Translated by A. W. WARD, M.A. The Fifth and Concluding Volume, with a Copious Index, in demy 8vo, 18s. Vols. I. and II. separately, price 15s. each. Vols. III. and IV. separately, price 18s. each.

RICHARD BENTLEY & SON, NEW BURLINGTON STREET,
Publishers in Ordinary to Her Majesty.

LONDON : R. CLAY, SONS, AND TAYLOR, PRINTERS.